"A superbly stylish author whose
books deserve the widest audience."

—*New Yorker*

"Malone combines humor, compassion
and literate writing with a storytelling
ability that is rare in contemporary fiction."

—*Houston Chronicle*

"Michael Malone is one of those rare writers
who can slowly uncover the heart of an entire
town....A wonderful storyteller."

—*Alice Hoffman*

"One remembers Mr. Malone's creations the
way one remembers those of another brilliant
social caricaturist, Charles Dickens."

—*New York Times Book Review*

by Michael Malone

THE LAST NOEL

THE LAST NOEL

a novel by Michael Malone

SOURCEBOOKS LANDMARK™
AN IMPRINT OF SOURCEBOOKS, INC.®
NAPERVILLE, ILLINOIS

Published by Sourcebooks, Inc.
P.O. Box 4410, Naperville, Illinois 60567-4410

ISBN 1-4022-0012-9

Printed and bound in the United States of America

For Dr. Virginia Hill
…Always there

Acknowledgments

My thanks to Jennifer Fusco and Hillel Black for wise editorial counsel, to Judith Kelly for her indefatigable, invaluable support, and to Megan Dempster for her elegant designs. Thanks as well to Peter Matson and to Todd Stocke, Alex Lubertozzi, Peter Lynch, Bill Osterman, Chris Pierik, Heidi Kent, Maggy Tinucci, Sean Murray, Jeff Tegge, Tom Murphy, Wayne Donnell, and George Carroll. For musical advice, my thanks for Nancy Goodwin and Kelsey Weir.

As ever, my gratitude to Dominique Raccah for her remarkable vision as a publisher. And to Maureen, always my first and fiercest and favorite reader, thank you.

The First Day of Christmas

❋

December 25, 1963
The Sled

"Come on," a voice said. "Come look at this snow."

From the foot of her four-poster bed she peered into the night. Then with a yawn, she asked the strange dark-skinned boy across the room in her window, "How did you get all the way up here?"

"Climbed," he said, pulling himself over the ledge to lean into her bedroom. "Wake up and come on outside with me."

For more than thirty years they were to quarrel about who had said what when they met, and whether she'd been frightened when he scrambled through her second-floor bedroom window, whether taking the sled from under the Christmas tree had been her idea or his, whether she had kissed him when they fell into the snow bank at the bottom of Heaven's Hill, or he had kissed her, or the kiss had never happened.

He always claimed that when she first heard her window open, she cried out, "What do you want?" and hid under the coverlet on her high tulipwood bed, the white blankets like the great drifts of snow falling on all the holly and boxwood outside.

But she said he had not scared her at all. She had just turned seven that day, and it wasn't until long afterwards, not until her teens, that somehow her courage began to fail her. Besides, she insisted, she'd known from the first glance that this late-night intruder was only, like herself, a child, and would do her no harm. What had awakened her was not the rasp of the window rising, but rather the cold sharp air and the fresh wet unfamiliar smell of snow blowing into her room. At the smell of the snow, she had come fully awake, shaking off her dream with a shiver. She saw at once that this night was different, filled with soft whirling light. It was the unexpected snow that first drew her attention, not the strange child who'd come so surprisingly to tell her about it.

They were the same age, born within hours of one another, but because she had arrived first, late on Christmas Eve, and his birth was not until the early dawn of Christmas Day, she would sometimes fight against his dominance with claims of her own seniority. It was a battle waged for years and never won.

Their names were Noni and Kaye.

Before her birth her parents had already named her Noelle, because she was expected at Christmas. Noelle Katherine Tilden. Her godfather, head of obstetrics at the southern university where her father had once played basketball, the university whose library bore her mother's family name, had delivered the baby girl without complication at nine in the evening on the 24th of December. He gave her to some nurses and went home. Her mother was unconscious at the time, designedly so. Several hours afterwards, slightly intoxicated, her father drove to the hospital from a holiday party, late to his daughter's birth. The party had been at the bank where he held with a lovely indifference a position as his father-in-law's loan manager. When Bud Tilden first held his daughter, so pink and gold, so solemn and poised and earnest in his arms, he christened her "Princess." And Princess he always called her until his death years later, when, again slightly intoxicated, he died with the same careless nonchalance that in his youth had been so charming.

That first night as he kissed the infant girl, her perfect nose wrinkled in displeasure and she turned away from the woody smell of his cigarettes and bourbon. Her father laughed in his sweet easy way. "The princess doesn't like it, do you, honey?" And he tapped her nose with a tan finger.

The following dawn, in Montgomery, Alabama, the boy John Montgomery King was born prematurely in an emergency room. His mother gave him her family name, which was King, and the middle name Montgomery, because of the bus boycott in that city, led by a young Baptist minister not much older than she was, and with the same last name. Martin Luther King Jr. wasn't Deborah King's kin—her people lived in North Carolina, his in Atlanta—but whenever she saw Dr. King she felt so proudly related to him that her heart beat like a great drum against her breast, and a wordless shout rushed uncontrollably out of her, so loudly that it frightened people.

Before Deborah King's son was taken off to the ICU, a nurse let her hold him. As the infant stared up at his mother, his cloudy eyes almost crossed in their fierce fight against confusion, she told him in an angry whisper, "Fight for me," and she pressed her lips over his tiny lips and blew air hard into his tiny mouth. Then she kissed his hands, which were so diminutive they could not reach around the thin finger they clung to. So small was he that more than a month would pass before his aunt was allowed to bring him home. By then his mother had been transferred to a different ward in the hospital, where, fed Thorazine and Milltown, she sat listlessly in a chair by the window, unless the pills wore off, when she'd shout and flail at anyone who came near her.

The boy's aunt made an effort to call him Montgomery, but the syllables came out stiffly, like a reprimand, so in the end, by the time they moved to Philadelphia, everyone was calling him Kaye.

Everyone in Noelle's hometown of Moors, North Carolina, except the girl's father, called her Noni.

"Come on," the stranger said from across the room. "Come look at this snow."

Leaning out from the foot of her bed, she stared across at the boy who crouched in her opened window, snow flying in around him, the shiny bill of his red plaid cap turning from side to side as he looked into the large gabled bedroom, his arms braced over the sill.

"How did you get all the way up here?" she demanded. Not—she would point out over the years—not "Who are you?" or "What do you want?" Just a practical question, "How did you get up on the second floor?" That's how unafraid she was.

"Climbed," he said, thrusting head and snowy shoulders into her room. "Come on outside with me. It's Christmas."

"Climbed what?" For Heaven's Hill was a large house, both tall and wide, with a Palladian center and two gabled wings. And while there was a full balcony with white columns running along the second floor to match the porch with white columns below, there were no outside stairs leading from one to the other. "You couldn't climb those columns."

"Climbed your tree," he said. "I can climb anything."

Annoyed by his vaunt (as, all of their lives, she would be exasperated by his impenetrable confidence), the girl slid off the side of the high antique bed, and in her long nightgown hurried, chilled, across the cold pine floor. She could see that, inside his shambly brown wool car coat, the boy was even smaller than she was. And she could see that he was, as she'd been carefully taught to say rather than "colored," a Negro. That realization immediately identified him for her, placed him in the world the way she knew it to be, a world in which there was only one possibility whereby a Negro child could be inside the gates of Heaven's Hill in the middle of the night. He'd come across from "Clayhome," the white-frame house across the lawn where her mother's maid lived with her invalid husband. The maid's family had lived there for generations, and their name was Clay, so at some point during the last hundred years their home had come to be called Clays' Home and then, as if it were one word, "Clayhome."

"You live at Clayhome," she told him. "You belong to Aunt Ma and Uncle Tatlock."

Flinging himself over the sill and hopping down into her room, the boy threw back his thin chest and comically placed both red-mittened fists at his sides. "You know what? I belong to me, myself, and I." He said it loudly, his grin so wide and infectious that she giggled herself, then quickly hid her face behind her hands because her mother had often told her that laughing with her mouth open was unbecoming and gave a poor impression of the laugher's background.

Pleased with her response, the boy strode into the room with long exaggerated steps and repeated in an even louder voice, "I belong to me, myself, and I."

Alarmed at his noise, she shushed him with a finger to her lips, pointing at her open bedroom door. But the truth was, it was unlikely anyone would hear him: her parents' room was in the other large gable, too far to be bothered. Their old dog, an English setter called Royal Charlie, slept in that room with them, and was practically deaf anyhow. Her brother Gordon, a sophomore at the nearby university, had driven off to Chicago with his friends to hear Bob Dylan, upsetting their mother who thought it was wrong for children to abandon their families at Christmas. Her brother Wade was home from his military academy, but he was sleeping out in the brick guest cottage, and Wade wouldn't awaken if she jumped up and down on his back, banging pans. But "Be quiet!" she told the boy anyhow, to assert her authority in her own home.

"Aunt Ma's my grandmama, don't you know that?" replied her strange guest.

"Why should I know it?" she countered.

He tapped the shiny brim of his red plaid cap and held out his mittens to her. "I got these for my birthday. And this." He tugged a huge shiny metal flashlight from his pocket, then shoved it back inside.

"Are you visiting Aunt Ma for Christmas?"

He didn't answer her but wandered over to her small pink sofa stacked neatly with unopened toys and white tissuey boxes of new clothes, presents from her birthday, which had been celebrated that morning at breakfast, in order to put as much distance as possible between the day of her birth and, as her mother said, the more important birth of Christ. The boy looked at the gifts without touching them and without much enthusiasm for the large stuffed animals and small adult dolls behind cellophane, the pink vinyl record player, the Puff the Magic Dragon schoolbag, the silver brush, and all the rest.

He pulled back his sleeve to show her a huge flat watch on a black plastic band that swung loosely on his small wrist. "My mama gave me this. You and me were born the exact same time. My birthday's Christmas, too," he informed her. "And that's what it is, Christmas, 'cause it's on the one and that's after midnight."

"My birthday's Christmas Eve," she said. "That's sooner than yours."

He ignored this. "You got a brother out in that little brick house." He pointed at the window. "He's smoking like a chimney and drinking from a whiskey bottle."

"Wade?" She was astonished. "How do you know?"

"'Cause he went to sleep and left the door open. All the heat just flying out. I shut it. He's dead to the world. So's your daddy and mama. Bud and Judy Tilden." He took out the flashlight again, aimed it right at her face, and clicked it on and off as he added, "My grandmama was baby-sitting you 'til they got home from their party up the street. I don't need a baby-sitter."

This amazing recital of facts put her at a terrible disadvantage. He seemed to know everything about her when she knew nothing at all about him, not even—until he had appeared in her window—that he existed. She'd never seen him before, and yet, no older than she, here he was strolling around Heaven's Hill just as he pleased, in the middle of the night, in the middle of a snowstorm, opening and closing doors and windows as if he owned the place and were checking it over to be sure that all was well.

She struggled for leverage. "I bet Aunt Ma doesn't even know you're over here."

He ignored this challenge as well and took her hand, tugging with his scratchy red mitten. "Come look. It's snowing."

"I know!" She saw from the beginning that he would try to take control of the relationship if she didn't resist.

His floppy black rubber galoshes, the tops wrapped twice around his ankles, left rippled white treads on the floor as he herded her to the window and gestured outside, past the gray mottled branches of the old sycamore that reached long arms toward her room, arms made even more ghostly because of their cape of snow. "Grandpa Tat knows when snow's coming," he said. "He feels it in his cut-off leg. And look at it come!"

Despite her huffy "I know!" Noni had never before seen this much snow. When her father had kissed her goodnight, the lightest flurries had just started and he had predicted they would never stick, but now there was at least a foot on the ground and snow was still falling. Whiteness everywhere made the dark brighter than moonlight. White sparkles floated, flying in all directions, up into the night and down to settle on the lawn and fields and woods of Heaven's Hill as far as she could see. Everything familiar to her—shrubbery, urns and fences, cars, brick garden walls and rows of outbuildings—all were changed by the snow into a wonderful strangeness.

Under the window she and the boy kneeled on the hope chest that had been her mother's and her grandmother's. Side by side they looked silently at the snow falling. After a while, he stood on the chest to lean out the window. "Be careful," she said. "That's my hope chest."

This aroused his curiosity and he bent to examine the highly varnished wood. "What you do? Write your hopes down and stick them in there?"

She giggled. While she'd never questioned why the chest was called "hope," she knew it wasn't for as vivid a reason as he imagined. "No! You save sheets and tablecloths and things for when a girl gets married."

"Oh." All interest vanished. He tilted upside down and scooped a handful of snow from the porch roof, deftly squeezed it into a small round ball, and instructed her to take a bite. It was like ice cream but not sweet.

"What's your name?" she asked him as she ate, politely offering her own name first. "I'm Noelle Katherine Tilden, but everybody calls me Noni except my daddy. He calls me Princess. Noelle means Christmas."

He made a huge show of raising his eyebrows. "My uncle got a cocker spaniel and he named her Princess. That's a dog's name."

"No it's not."

He pulled off his red cap, shaking snow into her room. "That's a dog's name."

Frustrated, she scooped up the ridged snow prints left on the floor by his galoshes and threw them out the opened window, then she jumped up at the window sash, pulling it down, for cold air had filled her room. "You ever heard about Princess Grace?" she asked. She suspected he hadn't, but he nodded his head indifferently. "Well, she's a movie star and she married a prince. She's my mama's 'beau ideal.' That means somebody you think is great. Jackie Kennedy's her other one. My mama's a Gordon. This is my house."

"I know it. 'Cause my people worked here before you were even born, before your mama was even born. I'm a King. You want to ride on that sled?"

She was outraged by this claim. "King? King of what?"

"You don't know anything. That's my name, John Montgomery King, but they call me Kaye."

She felt she had him back now and quickly said that she knew a girl in school named Kay. Kay was a girl's name.

"That's a different kind of Kay," he told her blandly, with another of his immense insufferable grins. "I'm named K-A-Y-E for King. That was my grandmama's name, King, 'fore she married Grandpa Tat."

"Now her name's Fairley, Mrs. Tatlock Fairley. And her real name's Amma." She was glad to display at least some knowledge.

"Why you call her Aunt Ma and call him Uncle Tatlock? They're not your family."

With a frown, she answered him carefully, with the answer she'd been given when, last year, she had asked the same question herself. "It's what my mother told me to call them, it's what she calls them because when Aunt Ma was young she helped raise my mother and when my mother was a baby she heard *her* mother calling for 'Amma,' and she thought it was 'Mama' and tried to call her 'Mama,' but she wasn't her mother and they changed it to 'Aunt Ma,' and now everybody calls her Aunt Ma."

This complex explanation seemed to satisfy the boy for he nodded, then returned to his earlier question. "You want to ride that sled?"

"Did you get a sled for Christmas?"

He snorted with derision. "Me? No sir re bob." (She had noticed that he frequently used expressions that she had heard Uncle Tatlock use—like "no sir re bob," and "dead to the world," and "smoking like a chimney"—as the old man sat in his wheelchair telling her stories. Maybe that's why the phrases sounded so funny; she was accustomed to hearing them in a rumbling low grandfather's voice, not this sharp young one.) "I don't need a sled," the boy added, hopping up on her bed, bouncing as he talked. "I keep on asking for a puppy but I can't have one 'cause I got to go back to Philadelphia with my mama and we can't have any dogs or cats in our apartment. Plus my mama's not feeling too good and she can't be taking care of any dog. So I got to get something little from Santy so I can carry it back on the train." He jumped down from the high four-poster.

The boy had given her a great deal of information, and as she moved backwards to absorb it, she stepped into one of his snow prints. Shocked by the feel of ice on her bare foot, she fell against his shoulder; the brown scratchy car coat still held the smell of the cold caught in its big collar.

He elbowed her away impatiently. "Let's go ride your sled."

"How come you think I've got any sled?"

He gave the girl a bossy nudge toward the door. "'Cause Santy Claus is come," he told her with conspiratorial glee, "and left you a red sled with your name on it under the tree, left you a lot *more* presents too, a whole shithouse full of presents, all over your living room floor."

His casual curse stunned Noni. While she'd heard the word before, it always came in a hiss or a shout, came when her mother was tense as hot wires, or when something annoyed her brother Wade, which was most of the time. But this boy said it without aggression, said it for a joke.

"You sure the sled's for me?"

He didn't reply as he picked up from her dresser a blue bankbook with Moors Savings Bank stamped on it in gold. "Grandmama's got one of these," he said.

"It's my savings book, it's where I keep my money."

He shook the passbook as if he expected cash to fall out; it was clear to her that he didn't know what savings even meant, but while she was still thinking how to confront him with his ignorance, he passed on to study the photographs of her parents and her brothers and herself in silver frames. He examined not the pictures but their frames. "I'm giving my mama a picture of JFK in a *gold* frame," he said. "Me and my grandmama got it at Woolworth's. You ever heard of him? The president? He's my mama's…" He scrunched his face searching for the new phrase. "He's my mama's 'beau idea.'"

Of course she'd heard of JFK. Just last month, someone had shot President Kennedy while he was riding in a convertible. Miss Pratt had run out of the classroom and then come back sobbing out loud, which no one had ever seen a teacher do; she told them that a man had killed the president and it was a national tragedy. But that night some friends of Noni's older brother Gordon had driven him home from the nearby university, blowing their car horn, weaving onto the grass and shouting, "The son of a bitch is dead!" Gordon was in the back seat and looked upset; he said these boys had had a beer party in the front yard of his new fraternity house to celebrate getting rid of JFK. He'd whispered to Noni that he'd had it with his frat brothers and, indeed, the "whole establishment."

"President Kennedy," Noni nodded. "He's dead."

Suddenly the boy put down one of the pictures (her family in front of their Christmas tree last year, when Gordon hadn't abandoned them but looked from his scowl as if he wished he had). Pulling his metal flashlight back out of the baggy pocket, he raced with it into the hallway. She hurried after him, for he was already trotting along the wide shadowy second-floor hall, shining his bouncy light at the tall white closed doors of unused guest rooms. Running quickly, she passed in front of him and sped down the slender steps of the staircase, swung around the walnut ball atop the newel post, and skidded into the foyer.

Her father's still damp hat and coat lay where he had tossed them on the green leather bench when he and her mother had come home late from their party. She saw that he'd thrown his kid gloves into the huge blue Chinese jar on the console, knocking over the little Christmas sculpture of a jeweled partridge in a malachite pear tree that he'd given her mother before they were married. His cigarettes and lighter and car keys had fallen out of the long camel-hair coat onto the parquet floor. The boy picked up the silver lighter, flicked it inquisitively on and off, and placed it back on the floor.

The Heaven's Hill living room had windows as tall as doors on two of its pale yellow walls, and through their panes the snow threw light onto an enormous Christmas tree whose angel stretched her red velvet wings to touch the ceiling and whose large colored lights winked brightly. Noni's father had forgotten to turn them off, and they shone glittering red, green, blue, and amber on the tinsel and glass balls and beaded garlands that crowded every bending branch.

The boy had not exaggerated. Presents of all sizes, some of them in gold paper with gold bows, more of them unwrapped, lay thickly piled everywhere, arranged on brocaded chairs and stacked against the tall Sheraton breakfront, so many gifts that they spilled all the way across the old Persian carpet, and under the black grand piano that no one played but Noni herself, and over to the edge of the fireplace where five fat red stockings hung bulging from the high mantel.

Instantly Noni took in the particulars of her own presents; most of them she had expected—the immense wooden dollhouse, the pink bicycle, the metronome for the piano, the Easy Bake Oven, the white leather roller skates: things she'd asked for in her obligatory letter to Santa. But the sled, the red wooden sled scrolled with her name NOELLE in gold, she had not known to ask for that, never suspecting a world of snow. And so it seemed magical that a sled should be waiting under the tree, just when for the first time she'd needed one. Noni didn't imagine a bearded Santa Claus had climbed down the chimney with this sled. She knew the magician was the father whose Princess she was, for it was already clear to the girl that he would deny her nothing, unless he'd forgotten that she wanted it.

"I told you," Kaye was saying. "Didn't I tell you? Santy didn't even have time to wrap most of 'em." From the couch of presents, he picked up a red Swiss Army knife, and with an adroit precision he opened, then closed all its little blades.

"The gold presents are just from my parents," Noni explained. "If they're unwrapped, they're from Santa. Those are all Wade's." She pointed at the array of objects near the couch, in whose profusion could be seen an air rifle, an ACC basketball, a small pool table, and a madras golf bag filled with clubs wearing little tasseled head covers. "This side is mine. But," she added with a flippant shrug, hoping to convey a sophistication as blasé as his curse, "I don't even believe in Santa Claus. There's no such thing."

It was true that her brother Wade had disabused her of faith two years ago by sneaking her down the stairs to watch as her parents quickly disposed of the milk and cookies left for Santa, after which they had yanked unwrapped gifts out of huge shopping bags and tossed them around the room as fast as they could.

The boy was waving his flashlight in broad arcs back and forth across the floor full of presents. "Well, Santy or somebody. Could be it was the Baby Jesus did it. 'Cause this sure is a *lot* of stuff. Put on your coat. Let's ride this sled or I got to go home."

She always remembered that she didn't hesitate. That she said yes. Over the years she would often wish that she could have lived her whole life that way, saying yes or no without fear, without qualification.

Together they struggled to carry the sled into the hall. Turning the old black iron key, she unlocked the door so slowly that the boy snatched at her hands in his eagerness. But she swatted him away, carefully pushing the door so there wouldn't be the loud screeching squeak that it made if thrown open. A swirling gust blew snow into the foyer. "Wait on the porch," she whispered. She helped him haul the sled through the door down the stairs, then closed it behind him.

❊ ❊ ❊ ❊ ❊

In her blue winter coat and her white angora cap and mittens, Noni slipped out onto the porch minutes later to find that the snow had slowed so that it no longer blew crazily in all directions but fell unhurried straight downward in large, soft, lazy drops. But the boy was gone. The sled was gone, too. Running to the snowy stairs, she skidded down them, fell, bounced to the bottom step, and sprawled in the foot-deep snow, her heart pounding, nearly in tears. She ran to one side of the house, then the other.

And suddenly, off beside Aunt Ma's house, she saw the beam of his flashlight through the floating snow. The boy was drawing circles of light around her, again and again, until she waved that she could see him. Coughing, struggling—her white rain boots, too large even with her jeans stuffed in them, were hard to lift out of the deep sinking snow—she labored across the lawn to where, holding the sled by its rope, he stood beside the door of Clayhome, the white-frame "servants' house," which abutted the building that had once housed carriages and wagons and was now the garage. All the windows at Clayhome were dark but there was a light above the front door, where a wreath of holly, mistletoe, and pine, tied with a shiny red ribbon, hung on a nail.

"Watch out!" the boy called, pointing.

Noni looked down. She was about to step inside a square of earth that was protected under the eaves of the house. It was outlined by an odd assortment of stones and bricks now half covered by drifting snow. Inside these borders, sticking up from the snow in rows, stood a dozen or more little crosses, each about four inches tall, made of Popsicle sticks bound intricately together with different-colored rubber bands. Names and dates had been written in black ink down the sides of the crossed sticks. She could read only some of the names.

"Are they pet graves?" she asked, thinking the crosses might be for goldfish or canaries; they were too small for dogs or cats. But the boy said no, the crosses belonged to his mother, that she always brought them with her and stuck them in the ground when she came to visit. He said that every year on New Year's Day she would start assembling a new collection of these grave markers, then she would pack all but one of the previous year's crosses into a shoebox that she called "The Promised Land." Each year she saved one cross from the previous year and put it with the other saved ones, and she set them out with the new ones in her cemetery. They were, she said, "reminders."

"Reminders?" Noni asked.

Kaye looked away, then turned back to her with a dramatic nod. "Like your mama's 'beau ideas,'" he said. "These are my mama's."

Pulling her down to her knees beside him, shining his flashlight on the strange little crossed sticks, he began reciting from memory, as he might a school lesson. "Emmett Till, 14 yrs old, Aug 27, 1955, beaten to death." He moved the light's beam along the row. "Willie James Howard, March 12, 1944, lynched to death." "Harry T. Moore and his wife Harriette, Christmas Day, 1951, bombed to death in bed."

In the front row of the cemetery all the sticks had this year's date on them, 1963. Kaye quickly bounced the flashlight beam at each cross: "June 12, 1963, Medgar shot." "Nov. 22,

1963, JFK shot."

There were four crosses close together side by side that all said Sept 15, 1963. The boy read out their inscriptions: "Addie Mae Collins, 14 yrs old, bombed." "Denise McNair, 11 yrs old, bombed." "Carole Robertson, 14 yrs old, bombed." The fourth cross had fallen over. He brushed off the snow and stuck it back in the ground next to the others. "Cynthia Wesley, 14 yrs old, bombed." Noni didn't know how to respond; she wasn't sure what any of it meant, except that somebody had killed these people, children too, and that as a reminder the boy's mother had made these peculiar little stick crosses—which was a very strange thing to do—into a sort of doll's cemetery. She said, "They're very nice," which was all she could think of to say.

Kaye stood, brushed snow from his knees. "My mama's been in marches and sit-downs, too."

"Sit-downs?"

"You sit down and the police can't make you get up. A policeman hit my mama in the head." He ran his hand across the top of his head. "She'll show you the scar. Well, my grandmama says," and he spoke with a sad matter-of-factness that Noni recognized as Aunt Ma's voice. "Says my mama takes things too much to heart, and she takes any more, she's gonna bust in two. You want to see something else?" Before she could answer, he slipped inside the door and vanished, leaving her huddled beside the cemetery. He was back within minutes, awkwardly holding a long narrow cardboard box. Holding it out across his arms, he told her to open it. "You're gonna see something you *never* saw!"

In this prediction, the boy was absolutely right. For inside the box there were human bones wired together. The bones of a big foot. And the bones of half of a long leg. "Now how 'bout that!" he asked her, eagerly grinning.

Noni was speechless. She could only nod.

"My Grandpa Tat keeps this box hid in his closet, but he

showed it to me. He made the V.A. hospital give him back his leg they cut off, and me and him wired it back together just like a jigsaw puzzle and now he's gonna use it to make his case."

"His case?"

But Kaye was busy thrusting the box back inside the door, and after he closed it he seemed to be finished with the subject for he didn't answer her. "You want to ride that sled?" he said again.

Beside Clayhome, the hill swept widely down through a meadow where in summer wildflowers grew. Toward the bottom, the slope plunged steeply through the knolls and gullies left by century-old earthen terraces falling to the edge of the dark woods that guarded Heaven's Hill.

Noni was upset to see that, without waiting for her, the boy had already taken her sled for a ride down the long slope. All the way to the woods, two blades had cut deep, straight parallel lines into the snow; running beside these tracks were the scuffled tracks of his boots climbing back to the top, dragging the sled behind. "You already went," she complained.

"Sit down," he told her, carefully maneuvering the sled into position, patting the seat and tugging on her coat.

She wanted to protest his preemptory orders, remind him that she owned this sled, that she'd take charge of it now. But she wasn't exactly sure what steering might entail, and finally she decided to wait until after the first run before she demanded the return of her property. Before she had even a second to settle herself with the towrope he'd handed her, he was at her back pushing, his thin shoulder leaning sharply into hers, shoving the sled hard, snow flurrying around them, and then he was jumping on behind, bumping her forward with his body, his legs straddling hers, his feet in their floppy galoshes stretched out to each side of the wooden steering bar. He was shouting, "Hang on!"

Down the hill they flew, fast, faster still, faster than skates or bicycle, so fast that her mouth opened, not to scream but to laugh. And she laughed all the way down the long steep slope until they skidded to a stop at the edge of the woods against a snowy bank. Back they ran, without talking, hauling the sled up the hill, then again she sat and again he pushed and down they flew once more. The third time, he said, "Your turn," and sat down himself; she pushed, leapt on, and steered with her feet, and they shot away, at first a little wobbly but then as fast as ever. Over and over, moving along the rising for fresh snow, heated now inside their coats but their hands and feet wet and chilled, they rode the red sled down the slope for which her house had been named, hundreds of years ago, Heaven's Hill.

During the hour they were sledding, the snow slowed to a few drifting flakes, then stopped. Above the white trees, the gray sky grew luminous. Years later she would remember that it was Kaye who wanted to quit first, although they would argue this point like the others for decades. But it was her clear memory that although she was very cold, she begged for one last ride down the steepest edge of the slope, and that he was steering this last time, and that they both screamed all the way down with the thrill of the speed.

The knoll racing toward them was too high, the ditch behind it too soon, too deep, and the sled tilted, tipped, and flew away spinning, and they toppled out, rolling together down the bank, stopping in a tangle, as high over their heads snow fell on them like a wave at the beach, but not scary like a wave. Soft and thrilling. It was then that his lips, chilled and soft, brushed against her face, so that in her memory he had kissed her. And it was then, as he struggled across her, that his cold cheek moved against her lips so that in his memory she was thanking him with a kiss.

But both were later memories only, not really thought of by either of them in the moment. At the time they were laughing in a loud manic delight, as they rolled out from under the snow slide. Then side by side, they moved their arms up and down, making angels, angels like paper dolls tied at their wing tips.

"I got to go," finally he said, checking his enormous watch. So they tugged the sled out from under the snow where it was buried and ran with it, both of them pulling the towrope, across the lawn to her front porch where, straining against the weight, they hauled it up the steps.

"You want me to carry this on back under your Christmas tree?" he asked her. When she said no, without a word he ran away, through the deep dragging prints they had made in the snow together.

"Good-bye," she called. "Merry Christmas." But he didn't answer her.

❄ ❄ ❄ ❄ ❄

Alone in the living room, Noni looked at the presents poured out across the floor. Her mother hated to wake up in the morning, even on Christmas; her brother Wade always sneaked downstairs and played with his toys for hours before making Noni go ask their parents to come begin the day. Wade had even boasted that rising early he had often stolen gifts from her pile and from Gordon's pile and had added them to his own, and that their parents had never noticed his theft. She wasn't sure if this was true. It was flagrantly true that Wade stole, but he also lied and he took a perverse pride in boasting of exaggerated misdeeds. On the other hand, her parents were so careless that it was possible, even probable, that they would never notice that a few gifts were missing from the haphazard display.

On the floor of the hall closet she found a shopping bag and began to fill it. In the morning, when Aunt Ma arrived at Heaven's Hill to make their breakfast, and when she asked why these gifts had been left for Kaye at Clayhome's door, the girl would explain (if need be, explain to her mother as well) that the presents were only a few little things of her own that she'd wanted Kaye to have, as she'd wanted to share her sled with him during his visit. Noni's preoccupied mother never paid much attention to what her daughter said—nor to what Aunt Ma said either—so she anticipated no awkward questioning. And Aunt Ma would say Noni was sweet and that would be the end of it.

She chose small gifts, mostly from Wade's pile but a few from her own and a few from Gordon's stocking (he wasn't even home anyhow), easy-to-pack objects that Kaye could take back with him on the train to this place called Philadelphia—the Swiss Army knife, cards, an Astronaut's belt, a book, a Beach Boys 45, Silly Putty, a Frisbee. One by one she placed the gifts in the shopping bag, took a red crayon, and wrote on it, "To Kaye. From Santa." Then she carried the bag out to the sled, which she'd left on the porch. On the seat of the sled, with a black crayon, she printed beneath the ornate gold scrolled script of her own name, the words "and Kaye."

Noelle
AND
KAYE

She left the sled in front of Clayhome, beside the little cemetery of sticks made into crosses to remember the dead.

The Second Day of Christmas

❄

December 25, 1968
The Piano

Earlier in the week, Noni had left a red envelope inside the screen door of Clayhome addressed to "Mr. John Montgomery King." Kaye's grandmother had shaken her head at the waste of the unused five-cent stamp. The envelope contained a stiff creamy card with a drawing of Heaven's Hill on it. "You are cordially invited," the printed handwriting began, and it went on to request Kaye's company at a "Holiday Open House" on December 25 from two to five.

It was now two-thirty, Christmas Day.

"We're not talking about it. You're going and you're not going empty-handed," Kaye's grandmother Amma told him matter-of-factly. "Those poor people have had a terrible loss and Christmas just makes it worse."

Kaye, twelve today, replied with ironic movements of his eyebrows and lips. "Right, and what the whole Tilden family's waiting for is me to come over there with these dumb cookies and make their lives just perfect again."

Amma Fairley turned her quiet dark gold eyes on her grandson, glancing from his braided headband to his peasant shirt and the colorfully embroidered vest that his mother had made him up in Philadelphia, copying a picture he'd shown her of Jimi Hendrix. "Tell you what I'm waiting for, Mister I-Know-Everything—you putting a civil tongue in your head before the only place you're going is up those stairs." She pointed through the sweet-smelling kitchen to the narrow steps whose edges had been worn by time as round as river stones; they led to the room that was now going to be Kaye's.

"Fine!" He crossed his arms emphatically. "Fine! That's the only place I want to go. You think I want to go watch Aunt Yolanda wait on those people? You're the one making me show up where nobody gives a rat's—" The gray-haired woman held up a warning finger and the boy closed his mouth over the last word of his sentence. "You're the one," he repeated in a stubborn mutter.

"That's right. I'm the one." Carefully smoothing the wrinkles from a piece of used green tissue paper, she pushed it across the tabletop at him. "Here. Wrap that candy up." On a card she wrote in her flowing formal schoolhouse script, "Merry Christmas from Aunt Ma, Uncle Tatlock, and Kaye."

It was Kaye King's fifth holiday trip down to North Carolina since he'd met Noni, but this Christmas everything was changing. This time there would be no train ride back with his mother to Philadelphia after New Year's; instead he would stay in Moors and live with his grandparents. Nineteen sixty-eight had been a hard year for Kaye's mother, with losses too fast and too deep for her cemetery of sticks and rubber bands to contain—in the end, a harder year than the boy could hide from those who would separate them.

Finally in November, when the sky in West Philadelphia was always gray and the days too quickly gave way to night, his mother gave way as well, retreating to a darkness from which, despite all the tricks his years with her had taught him, he could not bring her back. After she was carried strapped on a gurney to a hospital, her sister, unable to support the boy, called home to North Carolina for help. Amma Fairley sent Kaye a train ticket.

Now his grandmother watched him as he turned the radio dial from a choir on her church music station singing "Jesus the Light of the World" over to loud Motown on the rock station, in order, she knew, to keep her from talking. Abruptly, Aretha Franklin shouted, "R-E-S-P-E-C-T / Find out what it means to me!" The old radio spluttered static as if indignant at the change.

Kaye hit the plastic box hard with his fist, then yanked out its plug.

"What you so angry about, Kaye?"

"Nothing."

But that wasn't true, although he claimed otherwise, even to himself. Kaye was angry. Angry with his mother for choosing madness over him, with his aunt for choosing her own children. Angry at his expulsion from the urban turbulence of the world he knew, where—despite his small size—he'd won, with his fearless audacity, a place for himself. He was angry with his grandparents for living in the South where he would have to fight alien battles on a foreign terrain with unfamiliar weapons.

He didn't want to live in Moors, North Carolina, and go to the Tildens' holiday party at Heaven's Hill. He dreaded entering a new school where he would have to explain details about his parents to strangers. What was wrong with his mother? Where was his father? He didn't want to admit that, as far as he knew, his parents had never married and that he'd never laid eyes on his father, although he did have a snapshot of this young man, taken at a march in Montgomery, that he kept with his mother's Popsicle-stick crosses in her shoebox called "The Promised Land."

Kaye had brought this shoebox with him on the train with his large duffel bag. That's all he'd brought. What few toys he'd had, he'd given away to friends. He'd returned his books, his sports gear, and his used violin to the school that had lent them to him. He didn't want to play the violin down here in Moors. He didn't want to start school at Gordon Junior High in a room of white southerners, only one of whom he knew and that one a girl. Kaye hadn't spoken to Noni Tilden since his arrival at Clayhome three days earlier and he didn't want to speak to her.

It was the first Christmas in Moors that he had felt this way. While he and Noni had never so much as written a postcard or said a word on the phone during the full year between each of his earlier trips South, still, in the past, he had always been glad to see her and to renew their disputatious conversation. From the moment his uncle drove him through the brick gates of Heaven's Hill, he had always stared eagerly out the rear window of the black taxi, searching for Noni, readying himself to come bounding out the door to challenge her with new knowledge. And he knew that just as eagerly, Noni had started in right after Thanksgiving asking Aunt Ma almost daily, "How long before Kaye's coming?" and that she'd be waiting to see the old black taxi bring him in through the white stone drive.

It was true that each Christmas it had taken them a little longer to recover the freedom that they'd felt riding together on the sled the night they'd met—as if they were moving backwards, away from intimacy. Still, this was the first Christmas Kaye had felt that he didn't want to see Noni at all. In fact, he'd pretended not even to notice her as she'd run waving behind his uncle's taxi. This was the first time he'd stayed obstinately locked in his room—listening loudly to Hendrix's *Electric Lady-land*, or reading one of his mother's books, *Soul on Ice* and *Man-child in the Promised Land*—whenever he heard Noni downstairs in Clayhome's kitchen, hoping, he knew, to visit with him.

But now Kaye's grandmother was making him go to the Tildens' annual Christmas party, making him help bake the candies and cookies he was to take there as a gift. It was the last thing he wanted to do.

In pressuring him to attend this party, Amma Fairley was not motivated by awe or fear or even respect for her employers, but by a kind and generous pity. The Tildens' oldest son Gordon had been killed in Vietnam the previous February, almost a year ago now. But this was their first Christmas, their first social gathering, without him.

"Noni lost her brother. She needs your help," Amma said. "Or she wouldn't have come over here with that invitation, not with you looking through her like she was a old piece of glass. And no grandchild of mine's going to treat his friends that way."

"She's not my friend," snorted Kaye. He dropped the warm white sugar balls and dark almond chocolates into a drawstring cloth bag with a sunflower sewn on it. He wrapped the bag in the green tissues and held the twisted top while Amma ran red paper ribbon between scissors and thumb so the tips sprang into festive curls. "My friends all live in Philly."

"Well, those Philly friends of yours didn't invite you to a party and she did and she's the one with a big brother that got killed and you're going and you're taking these sweets with you."

Since her teens, Amma Fairley had worked as a maid at Heaven's Hill, and while in those forty years she had never been invited to a party there, on many occasions she had cooked for and cleaned up after the Christmas Open House. In the past few years, she had turned those duties over to her step-daughter Yolanda, whose husband also ran errands for the Tildens in his taxi, but from past experience Amma knew that guests would be expected to bring small gifts, usually of holiday food or drink, to this party. She also knew that the most courteous guests came neither too early nor too late; she was keeping an eye on the metal clock above the stove to make sure that her grandson left Clayhome just before three o'clock to cross the lawn to Heaven's Hill.

As for any further attempts to persuade Kaye to wear his new brown wool suit, a birthday present from her, instead of the bizarre and jarring outfit he had on, or to let her trim what he called his Afro, Amma had never been one to waste precious energy on futile desires. It was enough that he should go pay the Fairleys' respects to the Tildens at their Open House. And go he would.

She watched the boy with an appraising eye as he swiftly moved the cookie cutter over her sheet of gingerbread dough, leaving behind neat rows of brown Santa Clauses. "You got busy hands like me," she told him. "I never had any use for an idle hand." Amma nodded with tolerant disappointment at her husband Tatlock out in the living room in his wooden wheelchair, asleep in front of the large brown television set where he'd been watching news of the astronauts circling the moon in Apollo 8 the night before. The three astronauts were taking pictures of the earth rising behind the moon. Everyone was worried about them because Apollo 1 had blown up in January of 1967 and killed the men trapped inside.

Kaye gave a studied look at his grandmother's second husband, overweight and crippled in his chair beside the black iron coal stove. Grandpa Tat watched the news morning, noon, and night. Kaye didn't like the news; the news had driven his mother crazy. But unlike her, Tatlock listened to the goings-on in the great world with absolute impartiality and no emotional investment whatsoever. The news was his way out of the house, but it didn't touch him, not the way his own troubles did. His own troubles were his chief interest and chief conversation. With endless fascination he would recount the minutest details of his physical condition, with a ghoulish emphasis on how he'd "lost it all. Toes. Foot. Leg."

Tat had worked outdoors for thirty-five years on the grounds crew of the nearby Haver University, had built big walls and roads and fences, dug big ponds and cleared big trees. Now, he was shrunk into a wooden wheelchair in a low room, a sufferer with diabetes and, according to him, a victim of prolonged medical neglect for which, as he endlessly vowed, he would someday get a lawyer and bankrupt the veterans hospital.

Amma was saying, "That man tells me he can't do nothing 'cause he lost his leg to the Sugar. What's his leg got to do with his hands?"

Kaye shrugged. "He's got disability. You want him to get a tin cup and beg on Main Street?"

Her eyes—the strange dark amber that Tatlock called cat eyes—flecked gold. "Kaye King, don't make me think you're calling my table sales begging on the street."

"No, Ma'am." But in fact that had been what Kaye had meant. His grandmother's street vending embarrassed him; she resembled too closely the beggars on the sidewalks of Philadelphia. Amma spent evenings at her sewing machine, making place mats, dishcloths, aprons, tea cozies, guest towels, and such. On these objects she had started sewing, at Tatlock's suggestion, large yellow sunflowers that served as a kind of logo of her craft. In good weather, she sold them from a table set up in front of Moors Savings Bank, where Noni's father Bud Tilden worked for his father-in-law. She sold them as fast as she could make them. She also sold her candies and cookies, her pickled fruits and canned vegetables, cut flowers and dried herbs and willow baskets. For decades now she had sold anything she could think of to make or grow and she kept the money in a savings account at Moors Bank.

Kaye echoed his grandfather's perpetual lament. "What's he suppose to do? Thanks to that V.A. hospital he can't even walk."

"There's a million things Tat could do." Amma scooped the gingerbread Santas onto the baking sheet. "Help me with the million things *I* do. Sit behind my sales table in his wheel-chair and free me up to do my work. He could help me sew. A man can sew, same as a woman."

"You said he was a hard worker."

"I don't say him no. He worked long as somebody told him what to do and handed him money to do it. Minute that job quit, he quit too."

Kaye stepped into the other room and watched the great hewn coal-black slabs of Tat's hands as they floated, folded, atop his rising belly. "He'd look silly sewing. He's too big." Examining himself in the mirror over the blue threadbare vel-vet couch, the boy stretched up his shoulders, arched his feet, and then went back into the kitchen. "Was my real grandpa, was Grandpa King big or little?"

"Big." Amma closed her oven door, took Kaye's hands in her own, and held them up to his face. His hands were like hers, a light cinnamon brown with broad palms and long slender fin-gers. "Kaye, you stop all this worrying about being tall. Look at these hands of yours. You got big hands. Big feet too. You gonna be big as Tat there, big as Bill King. I married two big men.

"But I tell you one thing, son, the biggest man I ever knew in my life was my daddy and he was the runt of his litter. My daddy Grover Clay was no bigger than you are now the day he died."

This was news to Kaye, and the first positive thought he'd had about the forced move to Moors: that there were useful discoveries to be made here. "What was your daddy like?" He sat down, hoping for a story.

But Amma looked at her kitchen clock, handed Kaye the wrapped gift, and motioned him to the door. "Like your mama," she said, chagrin and pride in her voice. "He was like your mama. Just 'cause he couldn't win didn't mean he wouldn't fight. Get on over there." She plugged back in her radio, found her station, and began to hum along with the choir, "Jesus, Oh What a Wonderful Child!"

As Kaye left Clayhome, he put two of the bumper stickers he'd brought from Philadelphia into his pocket: STOP THE WAR and IMPEACH NIXON. (Even though Nixon wouldn't even be inaugurated until January, his mother had already wanted to impeach him.) He'd give the stickers to Noni as a way of demonstrating that he was, as always, far ahead of her.

❊ ❊ ❊ ❊ ❊

Despite the season, the day was warm and sunny, with a mild breeze that swayed the Victorian kissing balls hanging on red ribbons from the porch cornice of Heaven's Hill. The wide white door opened just as Kaye reached it and Noni stepped out to welcome him. He could see her whole face lighting up as if bright candles were shining through it. He also saw that she was still taller than he was. Standing as straight as he could, he took solace in his grandmother's prediction about his large feet and hands. "Merry Christmas," he said, frowning. "My grandmama sent me over here."

"Merry Christmas." Noni's smile faltered in response to his scowl. "Happy Birthday."

"Yeah, you too." He looked at her, then looked at the porch roof, then sighed, making a loud noise through his lips. "Listen, I'm sorry about what happened to Gordon."

Noni nodded slowly, swallowing the abrupt tears that always came whenever anyone was kind to her about her brother's death.

Kaye frowned. "Gordon was okay."

"He liked you a lot."

"I liked him too. So, I guess you heard…" Kaye made a face, pointed at Clayhome.

All of a sudden Noni wasn't sure if she should mention Kaye's mother's hospitalization. His loss was oddly more complicated, more private, than hers. Anxiety heated her hands and face as she fought to find the right words. "Aunt Ma told me you were going to stay down in Moors and go to school here and you probably wish you weren't but maybe it won't be so bad."

He shrugged. "Yeah, it will."

She felt for a moment defeated by his certainty. Then affection rushed through her. "Kaye, I'm so sorry about what happened to your mother."

He nodded, looking away until he gained control, then he spoke in the tone that Noni came to think of as his Philadelphia voice, the voice of the alien place called "the Street," the place that excluded her. "Well, my mama always said, 'You fight Whitey, he'll take you out. Jail you, shoot you, bomb you, drug you.' That's how they got her."

Noni wanted to protest that all whites wouldn't do those things, but she thought she might offend him. Instead she asked, "Don't they think your mother'll get better?"

He shrugged again. "¿Qué se?" Then he shook himself, literally shook himself free of memory, and smiled ironically, holding out the candy. "Well, I'm not here empty-handed."

She took the tissue-wrapped bag. "Thank you."

For a while they both looked at the porch floor. He noticed that she wore boots and it occurred to him that maybe they added to her height. High white boots with white tights on her thin legs and a lime green miniskirt as short as summer shorts, and over it a bulky red sweater that had Christmas trees knitted across the front. To his surprise, she had cut her blonde hair short, like the girl in *Rosemary's Baby*, and she was wearing makeup, at least black eyeliner and black mascara.

Finally, with a trace of his old flamboyance, he pointed at her head. "What happened to your hair? Get caught in a lawn mower?"

She looked at him for a minute, and then suddenly relaxing, grinned back. "What happened to yours?" She felt happy that he'd challenged her in that aggravating manner. "Your hair's as big as...as...a beach ball."

He twisted the psychedelic peace symbol pinned on his headband. "A beachball? You think Philly's on the beach? You think I even know what a beachball is?"

"It's a big round rubber ball as big as your hair."

"You ever see a black beach ball?" He crossed his arms and grinned at her with that irrepressible ebullience. "You ever hear a beachball say, 'Shout it loud, I'm black and I'm proud!'? You ever hear that?"

"No." Her smile widened.

"Who are you suppose to be anyhow—Twiggy?"

She mimicked his comic exaggeration, crossing her own arms as she said, "I am supposed to be me, myself, and I!"

All at once they both burst into laughter in the old way, as they'd laughed on the sled the night they'd first met.

It was at this moment that Noni's seventeen-year-old brother Wade, wearing his gray cadet's uniform from his military school, slammed out of the front door and, shoving his way between them, snarled, "I'm getting the hell out of Munster Lodge."

Wade Tilden looked like his mother; he had her milky skin dotted everywhere with red freckles and her strawberry blond hair—although his was almost shaved. He was tall with dangling arms and his tight gray jacket was covered with gold braid and brass buttons sticking out from his thin chest in flat straight rows. Ignoring Kaye completely, he added with a casual belligerence, "Noni, you don't want to wake up dead, tell Mom I went to see *2001*. They're just looking for any excuse to treat me like a dumb baby." Wade was pretending to be going to the local movie theater, when in fact he and his friends were driving his new Mustang to Charlotte three hours away to attend a rock concert.

Alarmed, Noni pleaded with her brother. "Mom said you couldn't go to Charlotte. Please, Wade, don't upset her."

"If she doesn't get off my back, I'm joining the fuckin' Army! Maybe I can get myself killed like perfect old Gordon. Maybe if I'm dead I can catch a break from those two!" Wade shouted this at the closed front door.

Mrs. Tilden, having lost her older son Gordon to friendly fire in the Tet Offensive, lived in terror that freakish violence would rob her of her younger boy as well. Had it been possible, she would have kept Wade by her side waking and sleeping, locked away from the risks of life. Nothing frightened her more than his new driver's license. Their embattled negotiations over the Mustang that Judy's father, the bank president R.W. Gordon, had ridiculously bought his grandson (as a bribe to finish school) were as prolonged and labyrinthine as a war treaty, with peace never coming closer.

"Just keep Mom off my back before I kill her and you both." Wade repeated the warning without affect or without elaborating on how his twelve-year-old sister was supposed to accomplish this urgent task.

Kaye stood there, still invisible to Wade. He could tell that the way Wade ignored him was embarrassing Noni. So he walked away, over to one of the green rockers on the porch, and sat down in it. Kaye had always felt a physical dislike of Wade; it was as instinctive as the affection he'd felt toward Noni's other brother, the older Gordon. While over the years he'd encountered Gordon no more than half-a-dozen times, his memories of him were warm and rich.

Gordon had once told Kaye he "was taking a slow soul train to freedom," and by his last year at college had quit his fraternity, grown his blond hair down to his shoulders, started playing the harmonica, and stopped wearing shoes. Kaye could remember seeing Gordon's long dirty white feet hopping warily over the icy lawn to untangle the Tildens' old setter Royal Charlie from a prickly holly bush. He could remember the wry sweetness with which Gordon had winked at him once, making him feel grown-up and smart, as the college senior had been arguing about the Vietnam War with his nasty-tempered grandfather, R.W. Gordon, in the Tildens' driveway. The old man had shouted at him, with his typical coarseness, "Don't shit where you sleep, boy. You know how rich I am?"

Gordon had smiled, winking at Kaye. "Depends on what you mean by rich, Grandpa. Martin Luther King's the richest man *I* know."

Listening now to Wade whining at Noni, Kaye was thinking that it was Wade, not Gordon, they should have named after the bank president, for Wade far more resembled R.W. Gordon in both his irascible personality and rigid politics than his gentle older brother ever had.

Two years ago, Kaye had heard from Noni about how Gordon had gone off to fight a war he didn't believe in because Mrs. Tilden had made it clear that serving his country was expected of someone with the Gordon name. It was too bad, Kaye was thinking, it was a real shame that it had been Gordon and not Wade on whom a bomb had landed out of the Asian sky back in February.

As if Wade had overheard this thought, he abruptly wheeled around in Kaye's direction. "Hey, Sly," he said, "why don't you just make yourself at home on my porch?"

Noni said, "Wade!"

Kaye rocked with exaggerated contentment in the green rocker. "Thanks, I will."

"If you're looking for your Aunt Yolanda, she's inside serving our guests."

Noni said, "Wade, stop it!"

Kaye stood up, staring at Wade, grinned as he extended his middle finger, and then slowly turned his hand and formed the peace sign. "Mustang Sally, I'm just here to date your sister."

Noni said, "Kaye!"

Fists tight, Wade lunged toward him. Kaye raised his own fists and grinned, "Come on."

But just then the door opened and Judy Tilden's head leaned out, her strawberry blonde hair pulled back by a burgundy velvet headband that matched her short burgundy velvet dress and burgundy satin pumps. She ignored Kaye and Noni both. "Wade, I need to speak to you for just a minute, sweetheart, right now." Her head disappeared. The military cadet spun around, his face enflamed with rage as he slammed into the hall after her. "Great! What did I do wrong this time?!"

A little while later Wade stormed back outside and bolted down the porch stairs. Noni now sat in the swing that was hung by chains from a high bough on a huge oak near the driveway. Standing behind her, Kaye pushed on the wooden seat. Noni was laughing with her hands over her mouth.

Wade growled, "What's so funny?"

She shook her head, laughed harder and harder.

Wade picked up river pebbles from the driveway and gratuitously hurled them at the two doves sitting, as usual, in the dogwood near the house. Then Noni and Kaye watched as he flung himself into his Mustang and went squealing away fishtailing, tires spitting gravel behind him, unaware of the stickers on either side of his front bumper—IMPEACH NIXON and STOP THE WAR.

Noni couldn't stop laughing. "Asshole," Kaye said, mimicking Wade's furious stomping around the yard flinging pebbles.

"Don't make me laugh, or I'll, I'll…"

"Pee?"

"Yes!" She couldn't believe she'd admitted that. She ran off and left him. When she returned, he got off the swing and sat her back down in it. Pushing hard with her feet, she began to pull herself back and forth.

Kaye grabbed both chains. "Hang on!" He hauled the swing back, further and further, high over his head, as high as it could go, until Noni was almost tilted out of the seat. "Kaye, stop!"

"Hang on!"

Then Kaye pushed hard, running forward as fast as he could. Noni felt his shoulder against her back, and suddenly her body remembered the sharp feel of his bone as he'd raced her down the hill on the red sled so long ago.

Now he was running all the way beneath her swing, pushing her as hard as he could when he ducked beneath. She arced skyward, legs pumping, laughing, free.

❄ ❄ ❄ ❄ ❄

In the wide front hall of Heaven's Hill there were willow baskets of poinsettias lining the parquet floor and holly wreaths with plaid bows on the doors. Christmas cards hung from swags of white pine on the banister. Presents from guests had piled up on the green leather bench and on the cherry console. Chocolates in gold boxes, champagne in silver boxes, a camellia in red foil. Noni placed Kaye's candies among the gifts between the little pear tree and the blue antique Chinese jar.

As they moved together toward the living room, Kaye felt himself pulling inward, making himself completely still in the way he had always tried to do whenever confronted with something he wasn't sure of. He felt Noni sense this tightening as she took his arm. At first he resisted her, but then his muscles relaxed beneath her hand.

Gently she squeezed his arm. "Don't worry about it if you don't know anybody. They're mostly jerks anyhow."

He mugged in his cocky way. "You're the worrier. You're the one hid under the covers the night I met you."

"I did not."

"You're the one was scared to sled down the hill."

She smiled, happy to feel close to him again in their old joking way. "I was not. You wanted to quit before I did."

Kaye looked into the living room of Heaven's Hill, smoky and crowded with white people, mostly middle-aged. He wagged his eyebrows, grinning, and spoke again with the bravado of that alien Philadelphia "street" voice. "Hey, long as they don't sic their dogs on me, long as they don't call in the Fuzz, they don't worry me at all."

"Most people aren't like you say." She felt she had to protest. "My parents' friends aren't like you say."

"Sure they are."

Swarming out of the living room with its tall windows and old Persian rugs rushed a loud hum of laughing voices. Two small children sat at the grand piano banging on the keys until a woman in taffeta bell-bottom pants ran over, slapped them on the hands, and pulled them crying away. Another woman sat down and with one finger began to play "Scarborough Fair." A man with a plate of little biscuits leaned over and sang in her face, "Parsley, sage, rosemary, and thyme." His red tie said, "Ho Ho Ho," all over it.

Another man in a shiny plaid jacket ran at a woman shouting, "Here come the judge!"

Kaye noticed that the red velvet wings on the angel atop the fourteen-foot Christmas tree were the same color as Mrs. Tilden's dress. He noticed that hanging from the mantel above the fireplace were five now empty red stockings, five—even though Gordon had been dead for almost a year. He wondered if they had filled Gordon's stocking this year, and if so, who had taken out all his gifts?

Behind a table with curved legs stood Noni's father with his handsome blond head and his son Gordon's soft sweet smile. He sang, "God rest you merry, gentlemen!" and called out "Peace on Earth, Ladies!" over and over as he poured eggnog from a huge scalloped silver bowl into small silver cups and handed them to the men and women buzzing around him. He wore a beautiful dark green jacket, and the color of the jacket matched his soft silk tie. Kaye noticed that Mr. Tilden filled his own cup with bourbon whenever he added more to the punch bowl.

"Hey there, Princess. It's been a hard day's night."

"I know, Daddy."

Noni's father pulled her under his arm and kissed her hair as he reached to shake Kaye's hand. "Hey there, Kaye! Peace and brotherhood, man."

"Peace and brotherhood, Mr. T." The boy noticed the beautiful gold wristwatch Tilden always wore and then saw a swollen scab on his wrist; there was a red streak running from the sore up under his shirt cuff. Kaye pointed at it. "Something looks bad on your hand."

Laughing, Noni's father pulled up his cuff and showed a red streak following the veins of his arm. "Unscrewing a light bulb and it broke off." He handed eggnog to a tall thin homely faced man in a pearl gray Nehru jacket listening to their conversation with an unlit cigarette in his mouth. "Hey, Jack, let me light your fire."

Tilden reached toward him with his silver lighter but the skinny man brushed it aside, then took the swollen hand and pulled it close to his face. Tilden winced when he poked at the sore and told him, "Bud, this kid's right. You got blood poisoning here that'll be headed straight for your heart if you don't look after it. I'm giving you a prescription for antibiotics. Start taking them tomorrow."

"Oh sure."

The homely man turned to Noni. "And you, kid, you're anemic. Eat more spinach." Grinning, he pulled forward a tall, well-built teenaged boy standing bored beside him in a blue blazer and striped tie. "And will you tell my son the jock here to treat me with a little more respect? I'm a doctor, for Christ sake!"

Noni smiled shyly at the older teenager. "Hi, Roland."

"Tell him," nudged the thin man.

"Treat your dad with a little more respect. He's a doctor."

The handsome boy grinned, brushing back his black curls, looking her over. "Sure thing, whatever you say, Noni."

Noni explained as she and Kaye moved on through the crowd. "That was my godfather, Jack Hurd."

"And his son the jock."

"Roland's okay. Doctor Jack delivered me. He calls himself my 'Deliverer.' He's nice. He runs OB/GYN at the medical school."

Kaye wasn't precisely sure what the letters OB/GYN stood for, and would be certain to check them out later. "Infections can go straight to your heart," he told her. "Your daddy better be careful."

"I know." Noni led Kaye into the crowd. "My mom met Doctor Jack in college before she met my dad. She said Doctor Jack wasn't her type. He was a Roanoke Scholar; that's the best thing you can be at that university. They pay *everything* for you."

"Who, your dad?"

"No, Doctor Jack. My dad played basketball. That's the *real* best thing you can be. You're not tall, or you could try it."

"I'm planning to be tall, lot taller than you," he told her. "But not so I can jump around swatting at orange rubber balls." Kaye took a handful of peanuts from a silver bowl. "I'm not gonna sing, I'm not gonna jump, run, grin, Watusi, I'm not gonna jive."

A girl near them said, "Right on. Me either."

Noni introduced Kaye to the girl, her school friend Bunny Breckenridge, plump and colorful in a yellow muumuu with six strings of bright beads around her neck and ostrich feathers hanging awkwardly from her wild frizzy light brown hair. Bunny felt the braid on Kaye's embroidered vest. "Holy shit, Jimi Hendrix, hunh? Cool."

"You too," Kaye pointed at the girl's feathers, thinking she looked a little like Mama Cass and that she had smart eyes and that she at least had recognized a Jimi Hendrix record cover when she met one. "Bunny, hunh? Is that your real name?"

"I know, isn't it stupid? But my real name is Bernice and that's not any better. So, Kaye, Noni talks about you all the time."

"I do not!'

While the three stood there, Kaye saw his Aunt Yolanda in a white uniform making her way through the room, holding out to guests her tray of deviled eggs with their tiny Christmasy bits of red and green peppers on top. Yolanda noticed but did not acknowledge Kaye. Embarrassed for them both, he led Noni away from Bunny, across the room toward the blazing lights of the extravagant tree.

Some of the guests, he saw, were looking askance at a black youngster moving through the crowd with his Afro and red embroidered vest, arm in arm with Noni Tilden. But most were too busy trying to talk to each other over the noise to pay much attention. Their conversations floated past him.

—Who *is* that boy with Noni? —
—His folks work here. You know, Judy's Aunt Ma?—
—The one that does those pretty things with the sunflowers? I love those.—

—Don't let Bud Tilden tell you anything except how to make a good martini.—

—God rest you merry, gentlemen!—

Talk on the silk couches and brocaded chairs drifted by:
—Judy's doing it. It's called aerobics.—
—Well, that little Bunny Breckenridge ought to

try it. How can her mother let her eat those
eclairs, look at her! Is it the same as jogging?—
—Sort of, but you don't go anywhere.—
—Oh, with this Weight Watchers you go to
meetings and they clap for you.—

—Parsley, sage, rosemary, and thyme.—

And around the Sheraton breakfront:

—Well, if Judy doesn't hide that bourbon bottle
from her husband, he'll be headfirst into what-
ever's next to him and I hope it's me.—
—Becky!—
—Frankly, Bud Tilden, you just be my guest!—
—Becky! You are bad! Isn't Bud your cousin?!—
—Oh good lord no. Judy's my cousin.—

—Here come the judge, here come the judge.—

—Parsley, sage, rosemary, and thyme.—

Kaye stood listening as Noni showed him her favorite
ornaments from her childhood on the huge twinkling tree. "So
what'd you get for Christmas? A Thunderbird?"

"No, I got that for my birthday," she grinned, looking at
him. "For Christmas I got my own private jet."

"Ho ho."

"Ha ha." She held up the gold watch that she'd received
"from Santa," and noticed that he still wore the flat black plastic watch he'd proudly displayed that night in her room back
when they were seven.

Kaye examined her new watch dismissively. But she held
onto his hand to study the handmade ring of silver coils that

he now wore. "Where'd you get that?"

"A friend in Philly gave it to me."

"A girl?"

"Yeah, a black girl. That's the only kind I'm ever going to date. You think a boy gave me a ring?"

"What girl was it?"

"What's it to you?" Actually Kaye had bought the ring for himself on South Street and he wasn't sure why he had told Noni a girl had given it to him.

"Nothing. It's a nice ring."

Suddenly he became aware of her hand holding his. In a strange and oddly heightened way, he could feel the skin and bones of her fingers as they touched his. He looked curiously into her eyes and when he did she blushed.

Noni was still holding his hand when, glancing away from her, he saw her mother threading her way toward them with her unhappy smile.

"Montgomery, may I help you?" asked Mrs. Tilden, her voice pleasant as a breeze, her eyes desperate. "Is there some problem at Clayhome?"

Noni's face tightened, flushed. "Mom, I invited him."

Mrs. Tilden stared at her daughter, then she smiled her unhappy smile a little more rigidly. "Oh, you did, sweetheart? Well, that's very nice. Are you ready to play for our guests?"

"Please, please, do I have to?"

"Noni, are you ready to play for our guests? Excuse us, Montgomery."

From his place by the over-laden tree, Kaye watched Mrs. Tilden thread her way back with Noni to Bud Tilden, who shrugged sadly as he embraced his daughter. Her mother then clapped for attention and announced that Noni would play for them the Chopin Etude in C Minor, after which she would take their requests for Christmas carols.

Noni's father pulled back the embroidered bench for her
at the long shining black piano. Its top was up; to Kaye it
looked like a big black curving wing shadowing Noni, blocking the winter light from the window. The guests started
shushing each other until the room was quiet. Seated at the
bench, Noni ran her fingertips back and forth over the gold
letters of the piano's name, like a blind person trying to read.
She held her hands above the keys, took them away, put them
back, and looked up for her father who kept smiling at her his
sweet helpless smile. Then, finally, Noni struck the first
chords of the etude and then she kept going, the cascade of
notes beautiful to Kaye. He watched the red flush spreading
from her face to her neck, her hands dead white and shaking.

He hadn't known she could play so well. He found the
music sad; it gave him strangely the same tight feeling in his
chest to which thoughts of his mother gave rise. It was a feeling like a big wave that could knock you down, and that power
made it seem very dangerous. Kaye wanted to feel only what he
could stand up to, only what he could turn his back on and
walk safely away from.

When Noni finished the Chopin, everyone clapped and
Bud Tilden shouted, "Brava brava brava!" Then the woman in
the red taffeta bell-bottoms yelled out, "Joy to the World!"
Hurrying over, Noni's mother placed the book of carols on the
piano in front of her daughter.

As the singing started, Kaye pushed a pathway through the
guests and left the party. No one tried to stop him. They were
talking all around the room.

—Oh Becky, stop it!—
—Well, it's true! How can a stick like Jack Hurd
produce a gorgeous boy like Roland? Sugar, you
think there's a law in this state against seducing a
fourteen-year-old?—

—Peace on Earth, ladies!—

❊ ❊ ❊ ❊ ❊

Later that night when Kaye answered the knock on Clayhome's door, there stood Noni holding a large wicker picnic basket in both hands. "Why'd you go?" she chastised him. "You just left and didn't say good-bye. You're always doing that to me."

He shrugged and stared off at the moon behind her.

"I wanted to give you your present." She handed him the basket. "Happy Birthday."

In his arms the basket shook and a mewling cry came from within. When he opened the top, a little black puppy struggled to its feet, then fell over. "What's this suppose to be?" said Kaye, although he knew why she'd done it.

Noni smiled. "You were always telling me, 'I want a puppy but I can't take one back to Philly.' So now you're staying here, so now you can have one."

"Where'd you get it?"

"It's a boy. My dad and I bought him at a pet store. He's a Labrador."

Scowling, Kaye put down the basket, pulled the puppy out of it, and examined him as the little dog tried to gnaw on his fingers. "What? You picked him 'cause he reminded you of me 'cause he's black?"

Noni stamped her foot in exasperation. "No. I picked him 'cause he reminded me of you 'cause he was an asshole who doesn't even know how to say thank you." She turned and marched off across the lawn.

Kaye watched her go. When she was halfway across the lawn he called out into the dark, "Thanks."

"You're welcome!" was shouted back.

❊ ❊ ❊ ❊ ❊

On Monday morning of the following week, Wade was driving Noni to school, in order, he told her, "to score Brownie points" with their mother before she saw his fall semester grades. As they started out, he was saying how, at the rock concert in Charlotte, some creep had defiled his Mustang with hippie bumper stickers. Noni was worrying that Wade was trying to trick her into admitting the vandalism, when suddenly she was thrown forward as he slammed on his brakes.

The entrance to Heaven's Hill was being blocked by a yellow school bus. While Wade was cursing the bus, Noni saw Kaye stepping stiffly into it, his hands jammed down in the pockets of his pea jacket. Before she could think, she leapt with her notebooks and her purse out of the Mustang, calling back to Wade, "Nevermind, I'll take the school bus." She ran between the driveway columns over to the yellow vehicle, banging on its door just as it was closing.

At first the driver, a plump sour woman, didn't want to take on a passenger of whom she had no record. Noni spoke to her quickly (fearful that Wade would storm the door), but she kept her voice as quiet as her mother's. "I go to Gordon Junior High. I live here at Heaven's Hill." She pointed up the driveway at the enormous house. "I'm Noelle Tilden. My mother's Judy Gordon Tilden. My mother told me to take this bus." While Noni was talking, she glanced back into the body of the bus, quickly spotting Kaye, the only black person on it (there were only four blacks in the whole school, for all the others who lived in Moors lived in a different district). Two-thirds of the way down the aisle, he sat alone in a double seat, pressed against the window, ignoring her.

Silently the driver struggled with the girl for authority but finally she decided against taking the risk of trouble, with the house up that hill looking so large, and the name Gordon dropped so significantly. Besides, the horn of the Mustang was beeping non-stop, presumably because she was blocking the driveway. So with a shrug, she pulled the lever that closed the door and told Noni to sit down.

Noni knew many of the students riding the bus, and more than that number knew her. She was aware that her name gave her power, made her popular. Everyone knew that Noelle Katherine Tilden lived in Heaven's Hill and wore stylish clothes, that her grandfather owned the bank and much of the town's real estate and had the same name as the school. Several seventh-graders greeted her as she passed them and offered to share their seats. She could feel them craning their necks to gawk back at her when she sat down beside Kaye.

Staring out the window, he didn't turn his head, but as the bus moved bumpily forward, she could feel a little of the tightness give way in his arm and she could feel his shoulder turn almost imperceptibly toward her. She leaned against him. "How's the puppy?"

He just shrugged.

She tried a few casual comments, but it became clear that Kaye wasn't going to talk to her. So she opened her music book. She struggled to study the notes of a Schumann piece she would have to play for her teacher after school, but instead she found herself thinking, on the slow ride through Moors, about the last conversation she'd had with her brother Gordon.

They'd been at the airport, the whole family. Gordon, in his new lieutenant's uniform, was going overseas, leaving his hometown—although none of them knew it—for the last time. He'd asked the ten-year-old Noni to come have a "private Coke" with him.

It was then that he'd told her about a September morning back when he'd been a high school sophomore. The first Negro students were entering the segregated Moors High School that day. There were only two, he said, a girl and a boy. The girl wore glasses and a starched white blouse and the boy had on a navy blue suit and a tie. Yelling at them from the sidewalks were thirty or forty white parents. (One of these red-faced women—Gordon told Noni that he'd emphasized this fact to their mother to make her sympathetic to the Negroes—had been smoking in public, and wearing a quilted bathrobe.)

He said three police cars sat parked at the curb in front of the school, but the policemen didn't get out of them or try to stop the crowd of adults from screaming at the two children. But five members of the student council organized by Mindy Breckenridge (Bunny's older sister) were waiting on the sidewalk with two teachers, the music teacher Miss Clooney and the English teacher Mr. Altman. And they made what Miss Clooney called "an honor guard" ("And the honor is ours," she'd said) around the two Negroes and they'd walked them past the shouting parents and into the school. Gordon, the sophomore class vice president ("and that was a joke"), was one of this honor guard.

Day after day these school officers met Dorothy and Arthur after their classes, walked with them through the halls, sat with them in the cafeteria, walked with them out of the school and into the bus.

"You know what, Noni?" Gordon told his little sister as they drank their Cokes in the airport. "It's the only thing in my life I'm proud of. That I showed up that morning when Mindy called me. The only thing."

Upset, Noni tried to make her brother feel good about himself. "Aren't you proud to be a soldier?"

"No. I just don't have the guts to fight Mom and the rest of it. That's what I'm telling you, Noni. It's so damn easy to give in. They make it so damn easy. So don't get scared. Don't let them."

Unsure of what he meant, she ran around the chair to him, hugging him tightly. "Oh, Gordon. Please don't go!"

"I've got to. You take care of Dad, okay? You know what I mean, the drinking? Nonibaloneymacaroni?"

On the bus ride now, Noni was thinking about Gordon's funeral, how the rain was falling from the shiny brim of the honor guard's hat in St. John's Cemetery as he handed the American flag to their mother. And how their father had cried so terribly, his face twisted in a way she'd never seen before, when he put his hand on Lt. Gordon Tilden's rose-covered casket. She was wondering now whether the young black woman she'd seen that day standing under an umbrella next to an ivy-covered tomb of another Gordon who'd died in a war, Capt. E.D.R. Gordon Jr., C.S.A., 1842–1864, whether the woman had been the girl Dorothy, beside whom Noni's brother had been so proud to walk.

When the school bus stopped, Kaye pushed around Noni out of their seat and hurried up the aisle. She had to move quickly to stay at his side as he strode straight through the cluster of teenagers on the lawn and climbed the stone steps of Gordon Junior High School.

At the top of the steps, he turned and found her beside him. "I named that dog Philly," he said. "I'll see you."

Inside the school corridor, Noni watched as he pushed open the door labeled "Principal's Office."

When finally Kaye walked out, she was still there in the hall, waiting for him.

And she walked with him from class to class, from locker to lunchroom, throwing the power of her name over him like a cloak. He didn't ask her to do it, he didn't acknowledge that she was doing it, but she knew that it would make a difference and that it was something, it was some one thing she could offer him.

And in a strange way it was also a means of her keeping close to Gordon, of keeping Gordon alive.

After school, Noni's mother drove up in their Lincoln to take her to her piano lesson, and although Noni looked in the

bus windows as fast as she could when they passed it, she didn't
see Kaye inside.

That evening, back at Heaven's Hill, Noni tapped at the
door of Clayhome. She could hear the radio inside, a woman on
it singing, "He's got the whole wide world in His hands!" While
she waited for someone to answer, she looked down and saw
that there was a new cemetery of Popsicle sticks beside the
door, inside their old border of stones and broken bricks. This
time the plot was more crowded with the little black-marked
crosses than Noni had ever seen it before. But why would the
sticks even be here when Kaye's mother was in a hospital in
Philadelphia, when she couldn't have brought her crosses down
to Moors this Christmas as she had done on previous years?

Kneeling, Noni read the names on the sticks: there were
crosses for Che Guevara, for Black Panthers "Shot by the Los
Angeles police," for Bobby Kennedy, for Watts and for Czecho-
slovakia and for Hue. There were dozens and dozens of crosses.
And in their center was the one that Kaye had told Noni had
burst in two his mother's heart.

Black words filled both small sticks of this cross:

> Apr 4, 1968, Martin Luther King, Jr., 39 yrs old,
> shot to death. I may not get there with you, but I
> want you to know tonight that we as a people will
> get to the promised land.

"Noni? What you doing, baby?"

The girl stood, brushed soil from her white tights. "Hi,
Aunt Ma. I was looking for Kaye. I wanted to know how it
went, the rest of his day at school. I didn't see him on the bus."

Amma told Noni that her grandson hadn't come home
yet, that he had gone off with his Uncle Austin to try to find
a part-time job at the taxi company. "You want to come in and
see that cute little dog Philly? He is a devil."

"Thank you, but I have to practice." Noni pointed at the cemetery. "Is Kaye's mother down here now?"

The woman shook her head. "No. Kaye stuck those sticks in the ground himself. He brought all that stuff with him in her old shoebox. Kaye and his mama are real close, always were. It's tough on a only child."

"If she gets better, will he go back to Philadelphia to be with her?"

Amma gave Noni a long look. "Kaye's going to stay here with us. And I'm glad he's got you for a friend. Now don't stand out here in this cold damp without your coat on. Go on back home and get warm. I'll tell him to call you."

Noni lifted her thin shoulders, let them fall. "He won't."

Amma took the girl's flushed face in her broad strong hands. "Go on home."

The Third Day of Christmas

❄

December 21, 1972
The Chinese Jar

In Heaven's Hill, fifteen-year-old Noni walked tentatively and loudly on her new clunky platform heels down the front stairs into the hallway and looked in the mirror at the gown her mother had chosen for her to wear to the Senior Class Christmas Dance, to which she'd been invited although only a sophomore. From the den, where her father had begun spending his evenings, she could hear Walter Cronkite tell the country about casualties in Vietnam.

Then she heard the chinkling ice in the bourbon glass.

"Daddy?"

Noni's father moved into the foyer and propped himself against the console with the easy grace that wouldn't desert him until the fifth or even the sixth drink. "Look at you. Who's the lucky fellow taking the Princess to the Ball?"

"I already told you, Roland Hurd."

"Ah." He raised his crystal glass. "Doctor Jack's handsome boy. The running back. The senior. The Princeton man. The pick of the mothers."

"Come on, Daddy."

"Well, would you please go get a ten out of my wallet by

the bed? In case the Son of Dr. Hurd runs out of gas."

"He's not going to run out of gas." She bent down, brushed her father's cigarette ashes from the parquet marble. "Daddy, be careful, you're getting ashes on the floor."

Bud Tilden kissed his daughter's nose and she turned her face from the familiar smell of bourbon and tobacco. "These days, honey, even a princess should carry cash." With his soft smile he spun her in a waltz step and told her that she was perfectly beautiful. For Noni, the compliment was both sweet and meaningless. Her father had always said she was perfectly beautiful.

"Mom?"

From the living room came the thin mellifluous voice of Joni Mitchell singing a carol on the radio. Noni found her mother in the room alone, hanging tinsel strand by careful strand on the giant Christmas tree; Mrs. Tilden kept at the decorating task for days, long after everyone else lost interest, adding glass balls beside porcelain bears beside painted nut-crackers, adding ornaments old and new, until all the green was gone. She was proud of the tree, which was so famous in Moors that photos of it appeared in the *Moors Mercury Gazette* almost every year.

Near her, a silk couch was crowded with shiny rolls of wrapping paper, boxes of ribbons. Beneath the tree there were already dozens of beautifully wrapped presents spilling out across the floor. Among them was Noni's gift for Kaye, a fountain pen she'd bought at the Moors jewelry store with money from her savings account.

Tightening her tortoise-shell barrettes, Mrs. Tilden sat down at the piano bench and carefully studied her daughter. She turned Noni, arranged the fabric in her dress, coiled an elaborate curl in her hair. Then with her unhappy smile she said that Noni looked very nice but that she might want to consider not wearing those clunky shoes and she might try just a little more lift to her bodice, by which she meant the rubber pads she'd left on Noni's bed, and that a little less eye shadow might make a nicer impression. She pinched Noni's cheeks, told her to pinch them again from time to time to give herself "a little more color."

These suggestions, which carried far more weight than her father's compliments, sent Noni back up the stairs, on the verge of tears, and caused a fight between her parents. Their argument—Noni's father's charge that her mother was judgmental; Noni's mother's charge that her father was passive and weak and gave their daughter none of the guidance necessary to help her make her way in life—was a battle carried on in the hallway in complete silence through facial expressions that they both understood.

Upstairs, Noni passed Gordon's bedroom where the door was always open, his childhood books were always dusted, his khaki pants and ironed blue shirts were hanging in the closet and his old loafers with their crushed heels were under the Hitchcock rocking chair with the cane seat. Even his cherry-wood baby crib that had belonged to the Gordons forever still sat there against the wall. Sometimes Noni would find her father in Gordon's room, sitting in the little rocking chair, quietly looking out at the night.

Thinking of Gordon, Noni could no longer hold back her tears, and she ran into her bedroom, where she stared sobbing at herself in the mirror of her vanity table and agreed with her mother that everything was wrong and nothing would ever be right. Then she told Gordon's silver-framed photograph that she hated her mother and that she hated herself as well; she told him she felt as if the floor were cracking open underneath her and that she was falling down through nothingness forever. In the old days, Kaye would have listened to how she felt, but now Kaye never seemed to want even to be around her, much less talk about anything that really mattered. Noni flung herself onto her four-poster bed, threw the rubber breast pads on the floor, and crushed her face into the pillow. Finally when the tears did stop, she moved over to sit on her hope chest and stare out the window at the moonlit sycamore boughs. She tried to make the tree look like a ghost again, the way it had transformed itself in her childhood, but now it only looked like a tree.

After a while, she heard the doorbell ring downstairs. Changing into the satin shoes that her mother had left in a box of gold tissue papers on the little pink couch, she washed her face in her bathroom, applied less eye shadow than before, and hurried the length of the hall to her parents' room.

On her mother's bedside table, beside the Tab can and the Kleenex and hand cream and the bottles of Vitamin C and sleeping pills and amphetamine diet pills (to which Wade had no doubt helped himself), and the stacked hardcover library books—*Jonathan Livingston Seagull, Love Story, Watership Down*—there was a Christmas photograph of the three-year-old Noni in a green velvet dress; she was sitting on her mother's lap, with Gordon and Wade, both in green velvet jackets with plaid bow-ties, on either side of them. Noni had a fleeting urge to smash the picture on the corner of the table, but the impulse faded before she even touched the frame.

On her father's side of the bed sat his perennial aspirin bottle and Rolaids, an empty crystal glass, a leather tray strewn with loose coins, cuff links, wooden golf tees, and the wallet where he always kept at least a dozen ten-dollar bills. The wallet was empty.

Noni stormed back along the wide hall to the "children's" wing of the house. She didn't knock on Wade's door because Wade only locked it when he was in there, talking on the phone to his idiot girlfriend or looking at *Playboy* and playing with himself under the covers so hard that Noni had heard the bed thump. His room was freezing now because he left the windows open while he was gone, to get rid of the smell of all the pot he smoked. Noni went straight to the huge poster on the far wall of the Olympic swimmer Mark Spitz in his tiny bikini trunks with gold medals strung around his neck. She slipped her hand behind the poster and pulled out four of the stolen ten-dollar bills.

Three of these bills she had just returned to her father's wallet when Bud Tilden himself wandered into the room looking for her, holding her new floor-length fitted wool coat. "Doctor Jack Jr.'s downstairs. The Princeton man. You look like a Christmas dream come true, the first Noelle, the last Noelle, the best Noelle."

Noni didn't tell her father that Wade was robbing him, but showed him that she had placed the ten dollars in her small velvet purse.

He smiled. "That's right, Princess. Powder room." She wasn't sure what he meant.

As they started back down the stairs together, she took Tilden's arm and turned him so that he would be next to the banister but so that it would look as if he were escorting her, rather than she guiding him. It was a trick she'd seen her mother use.

In the foyer, her mother was telling Roland Hurd that the orchid corsage he'd brought Noni would go perfectly with her dress. Looking nothing at all like his homely father, Roland was tall with black shiny curls and skin that always looked tan. He was—she was amazed to see—larger than her slender father. Over his tuxedo he wore a gray wool coat that made him appear completely grown-up. His eyes were as blue as the under glaze of the Chinese jar on the console. The first time she'd seen those blue eyes burning into her, last August at Pinky Mann's pool party, she'd felt as if her legs were melting. To avoid his stare, she had abruptly dived into the pool and then had swum underwater until she had stopped feeling as if she had been stung by bees. The second time, he was holding in the crook of his arm his white football helmet and when he called, "Hi Noni," up into the stands, she saw that his eyes were the color of the blue hawk on his helmet. Roland Hurd was so handsome and so popular that when Noni had phoned to tell her friend Bunny that he had asked her, although she was only a sophomore, to the Senior Christmas dance, Bunny had said, "No way." And another friend had screamed so loudly into the phone at the news that it had hurt Noni's ear.

"Look here at my princess," her father told Roland, handing her over at the foot of the stairs. "Have you ever seen anyone so beautiful in your whole life?"

Roland, whose perfections she could read in her mother's eyes, politely said that he never had.

* * * * *

Each night when Amma Fairley left Heaven's Hill, she walked through its galleries and hallways and up and down its stairs and turned off all the lights in its empty rooms. Each night, an hour or two later, when she looked out across the lawn from Clayhome as she was looking now, all the lights were back on and the big white house was blazing out at her as if the people living inside it had set it on fire. All these years and she couldn't teach the Tildens to stop wasting electricity. They were careless, or they were scared of the dark, or maybe they were both. Even when Judy and her husband had been living alone in the house, when Wade was off in college and they'd sent little Noni up North to that boarding school after Judy'd said she didn't think much of the Moors schools anymore; even then the two of them had kept the lights on in almost every one of the seventeen rooms in Heaven's Hill, even the children's rooms.

Amma sat by the lamp at her kitchen window sewing her sunflowers onto the aprons she'd made. Pulling off her glasses, she threaded the needle with yellow thread. From the next room came the bland murmur of television voices, Tat listening to his programs with the Labrador dog, Philly, lying on the floor by his wheelchair. Amma had her old radio on beside her, Mahalia Jackson singing "Go tell it on the mountain."

Of course, she thought, when you lose a child like the Tildens had lost Gordon over in Vietnam, it makes you so scared about the others you need the lights on. Even four years later. When that phone call had come that Gordon was gone, Amma and little Noni had grabbed Judy just in time as she dropped straight to the floor. After that it was like Bud and Judy Tilden just didn't have the strength to come through things together. It was like that news about Gordon took all the hope out of their marriage. Amma could see how they blamed each other and how they blamed themselves. She could see Bud Tilden turning more and more to drinking alone. She could see Judy just freezing up, like she'd packed her heart in ice so she'd never have to feel it again.

It was Mr. Tilden who took the call, three years back now, from that school up North about how they'd had to rush Noni to the hospital with pneumonia just a few months after she'd gotten there. Twelve years old, up North by herself, alone in that hospital. Now Noni's mama Judy had been sick all the time when she was little, but Amma hadn't even believed all those illnesses of Judy's were real; they were just a way for Judy to get attention from her busy daddy and mama. But Noni had been truly sick; she had almost died. The Tildens had brought her home to Moors from the airport in an ambulance bed. And then it had taken the child another month lying in her room before she could start back to school at Gordon Junior.

Amma would say this for her grandson Kaye, back then he'd brought over his books and helped Noni with her homework evening after evening that whole spring. Every day before he hurried off to his job dispatching at the taxi company, he was over there at Heaven's Hill helping Noni. Bud Tilden had treated him like his own son, he was there so much. Kaye had been a good friend to Noni.

And Noni had been a good friend to him. When her health got better, the two of them started spending every evening here at Clayhome, laughing, listening to those rock and roll records, learning some new dance or other that they'd seen on television. Back in Philadelphia, Deborah had taught Kaye to love to dance, and he and Noni got to be really good at all their fast steps and combinations, though they never did seem to do any dancing anywhere except here in Amma's house.

Funny, Kaye loved to dance but he wouldn't have a thing to do with music any other way, even though he had a nice voice, tenor like Amma's daddy Grover King. Noni had found out how Kaye had played violin in Philadelphia back in the fourth and fifth grades, and she'd kept at him and gotten Amma to keep at him to join that little school orchestra she was in at Gordon Junior. Amma had taken Tatlock to one of their concerts where Noni had the solo on the piano. But it wasn't too long before Kaye quit his violin. And not too much longer before it seemed like he'd just about quit Noni, too.

Now all Kaye could talk about was how the Tildens were the problem with America and how everybody else was the problem, except for the people he had pictures of covering the walls of his room. Bobby Seale, Huey Newton, and such. These last few years Kaye had stopped making new Popsicle stick cemeteries for his mama and instead had started taping up all these newspaper photographs on his walls until his room finally looked to Amma like the shotgun house Tatlock had grown up in out in the country, wallpapered with tin signs and pictures cut out of store catalogues. After Kaye taped the pictures to the wall, he wrote things in black marker on them, just like Deborah had written on her little crosses. Soledad

Brothers, ACQUITTED. Angela Davis, ACQUITTED. George Jackson, KILLED. ATTICA.

A few months ago Noni had told Amma that she never saw Kaye much at school anymore; somehow both of them had started running with their own crowds and had drifted apart. Noni said that their friendship had gotten harder to keep up anyhow: Kaye acted so angry with her every time he told her about something he'd seen on the news. But how was Noni supposed to make up to him for the last four hundred years of American history? Why was he taking it out on her?

Amma had hugged Noni and told her that the past was a heavy thing, too heavy to lift unless everybody lifted together. It would all work out in the Lord's good time. "The Lord's too slow for Kaye," Noni told her.

Deep down, Kaye's grandmother had thought maybe it was just as well that he'd stopped spending so much time with Noni. She had always wondered if the real reason Judy had sent Noni up to that New England school hadn't been to get her away from Kaye. And if the child hadn't gotten so sick up there that first semester, Judy could have kept them apart, too, that way. But if that had been her plan, it had backfired. Noni came home and the teenagers had gotten closer than ever. It was clear to Amma that Judy didn't like her daughter's friendship with Kaye, or her husband's affection for him either, not one bit.

Of course, if those children did fall in love, the world wouldn't be easy on them. Love was hard enough without adding in other people's nastiness about race. It was probably all for the best. And both of them were too busy to get serious anyhow; children didn't used to keep so busy. Kaye had two jobs and a dozen or more after-school projects on top of his sports programs. And Judy kept Noni wound up tight enough to snap a watch spring. She couldn't have worked her harder if she'd been planning to enter her in a pet show. It had been just the same with Judy's parents pushing her when she was little:

Judy had to come in first in every swim meet, win the blue at every horse show.

Noni was a sweeter child than her mother had ever been. Sometimes Amma felt like she could see Noni's heart right there in her face. She could see Noni's heart filling up with all this love she wanted to give folks. But folks wouldn't take enough of it to give her ease. Noni was all feelings, always had been. She was like her brother Gordon that way.

Wade now, he was a different story. Ever since Gordon died, it was like Wade had joined hands with the devil, like he'd decided that if the Good get killed, he'd better be as bad as he could be. He'd flunked out of one military school and got himself thrown out of another one. Then the university here turned him down, in spite of how they still had Bud Tilden's shirt hanging from the rafters of their stadium, in spite of how some Gordon or other had even built them their library. Now Wade was home for the holidays from the pokey little college in Atlanta where they'd had to send him. Home and up to worse than his mama knew. Vodka bottles in the trash and old marijuana butts in ashtrays under his bed with a bunch of filthy magazines. Pills of every color rolling around in his sock drawer.

Getting into college, thought Amma, that's not something I'll have to worry about with Kaye. Not with his good grades at Moors High, not the way he'd scored on that test they'd had to drive to Raleigh for. Plus, once Kaye had gotten his height—just like she'd told him he would—once he'd shot up all that way—Kaye had sports going for him, too. Or could have going for him, if he'd cared anything about it and could learn to stop his back-talking the coach.

"Your boy's got an attitude problem," the coach came over to Clayhome to tell her and Tatlock. "And he's got a motivation problem. We need to motivate that boy's passion for the game of football." Well, all the man had heard in reply was a long speech from Tatlock about how, back in his teens, he'd played the best football, baseball, *and* basketball the town of Moors, North Carolina, had ever seen, but because of his color he'd never a chance to show what he could do. Which was possibly even true, for Amma could remember to this day, even in love with Bill King as she'd been at the time, how that Fourth of July at the town park the muscles ruffled in Tat's big back and arms, and how his skinny bat slung around and how the baseball flew like a white bird off into the blue cloudless sky.

But none of Tat's horn-blowing about the past was any use to Kaye, who might need a push from that football coach if Amma's savings wouldn't stretch far enough to get him through college. Bills were high, money hard to come by. And her daughter Hope, with six kids, Hope and her husband both working, a good man, but they could always use a little extra help. Plus, Amma was still trying to catch up to what she'd put away three years ago that she'd had to use traveling with Kaye by plane to Philadelphia. But after Deborah had got hold of those pills in the hospital, Amma wasn't about to stay home; she had to be there at Deborah's side to pull her through, even if it broke her heart when she saw she might as well have been a stranger off the street to her own daughter.

Yes, Amma thought, I sure do worry more about Kaye since I lost my poor child Deborah, because I've lost her sure as if I'd lowered her into the ground. And a child's a child, in their thirties, their twenties, or even a baby taken from you before you gave birth, like she'd lost two before Deborah came. A child's a child.

Amma finished stitching the sunflower to the third apron. Well, Noni looked so pretty tonight and let's hope she has a happy time at that school dance—even if Kaye and his friend Parker put it down the way they did. Tat asked them why *they* weren't going to the dance, and of course, the truth was they couldn't have gone anyhow because they weren't seniors and they weren't dating seniors, but Kaye started in on Tat about how this was no time to be dancing.

"You think they're 'dancing' in Hanoi with those B-52s carpet-bombing them day and night?! You think Vietnamese children are 'dancing' down the roads on fire with napalm?! You think with the world blowing up I want to go boogaloo with a gym full of bubblehead crackers like Roland Turd?"

Tat told him, "Boy, I'd boogaloo with Mrs. George Wallace I had my legs. And old George Wallace would cut in and grab his wife back, he had the use of his. And look at us both stuck in these wheelchairs. You don't know what life's going to do to you, Kaye King." Then Tat just wheeled himself over to the TV and turned on the news, while Kaye muttered at his back, "Life's not gonna do anything to me, old man, I'm gonna do things to life."

Well, Amma thought, probably he will. I'm not worrying about Kaye. She folded the finished apron and took another one from her stack. Her grandson wouldn't be waiting on life to come smack him from behind, and even when life inevitably did, it wasn't going to knock him over like it had his poor mama. Kaye always bounced back. He reminded her of that plastic punching bag he used to love that would pop back up at you. Bounced back and talked back and wouldn't stop talking, that was Kaye. 'Course, he could always get you laughing sooner or later. Yolanda said that's why he'd been made night dispatcher at Austin's taxi company, young as he was. He made the drivers laugh with his voices and jokes. Plus he could always get the cars to the customer, like he had all of Moors County on a map inside his head. She wasn't going to worry about Kaye.

Amma heard heavy shoes come running down the stairs, young male laughter, then she felt a kiss and the brush of a moustache on the side of her neck.

"Stay cool, Grandma." Kaye stood there at the opened refrigerator with his skinny school friend Parker Jones, both of them in solid black, head to toe, with big black circles of hair on their heads. Kaye pulled off the legs from the Cornish game hens left over from the supper Amma had made for Heaven's Hill. He gave two to Parker, ate two others himself.

"You turn off those lights upstairs?"

"Yes, ma'am."

"Well, go turn off those tree lights, too. Tat's not looking at that tree, he's looking at that fool television."

Kaye's dog Philly ran into the kitchen to see what the noise was about and followed Kaye back into the living room.

Amma slapped Parker's fingers off a cake. "Leave that alone. Parker, you weren't upstairs messing with Tat's leg box again?"

For years Kaye's friend had had an insatiable fascination with the bones from Tatlock's amputated leg, and had loved to look at them. Parker had even borrowed the bones once to terrorize his sister into believing that he'd dug up a murdered man in their crawl space.

"We got better things to do than play with old bones," Parker told her. "Times are changing, Grandma."

"That so?"

"Yep, the black man's time has come."

"Um hum."

Kaye returned and spun the radio dial to the Motown station where the Drifters were singing "White Christmas." He shook out one of his grandmother's aprons, held it so the sunflower spread across his chest. "Outta sight. I'm telling you, slap these sunflowers on wild-color T-shirts, you can sell 'em, make some bread."

"You can sell 'em," agreed Parker. "Every jive turkey in town be wearing a big yellow flower."

"Flower power to the people, Grandma. Later." Kaye tossed the apron back on her table and pulled Parker with him across the room.

"Kaye! You come back in here and put on a coat. It's cold out there. Kaye!"

The door slammed as she turned up the radio. Tat yelled, "I can't hear my program in here," and turned up the television. A TV voice was singing, "Here comes Google with the goo goo googly eyes" about that horrible chocolate and vanilla peanut butter that Tat would eat right out of the jar with a spoon.

Amma turned off her music and went back to work. She pinned a sunflower onto an apron bib, smoothed the cloth under the foot pedal of her sewing machine, and looked out the window at Heaven's Hill where all the lights were still on.

❄ ❄ ❄ ❄ ❄

At Moors High School gym the spinning planets were deflating and the sparkle lights were blinking out in the fiberglass snow of the Stardust Court. Hands held tightly between them, Noni and Roland were slow-dancing to the last dance, John Lennon's "Imagine" without the words. Inside her head Noni was singing the words about imagine all the people living life in peace, while the outside of her head was pressed into the silky lapel of Roland's tuxedo. She could feel his warm breath in her hair as he whispered, "You're the most beautiful girl here. I'm a lucky guy."

This conjunction, or disjunction, between imagining world peace and feeling Roland's breath was symptomatic of how Noni had felt through the entire Christmas dance—Stardust on Mars, it was called—as if she were looking at the gathering through peculiar binoculars that caused her to see completely different scenes through each of the lens, one far away, one very close. Far away, the dance looked like the tacky Snowland at the mall, a row of cheap plastic Christmas trees in front of which children got their pictures taken with Santa, with the odd addition here in the gym of a solar system of painted balls hanging from the ceiling representing the planets (in the wrong order). Far away, girls without their dance partners looked miserably perky laughing together in corners, while the boys who were supposed to be dancing with them ran outside to drink or do drugs; teachers didn't notice, or pretended not to. Far away, Noni could imagine Kaye's look of exaggerated comic horror at the poor dancers, or the talentless band, which played everything from David Bowie to the Allman Brothers in the same thumping style. Far away, she could imagine the speech on archaic sex roles delivered by her best friend Bunny Breckenridge, who had gone tonight to see *The Garden of the Finzi-Continis* with "The Outsies," the group of self-described hippies and nerds with whom she and Noni had picketed the Moors draft board to protest the Vietnam War.

But close-up, Roland Hurd, who would never picket anything, was leaning down to kiss Noni sweetly on the face and then on the lips. "My dad's so right," he whispered. "You're the best of the best." Close up, other senior boys were cutting in on Roland to dance with her. Senior girls ran over to ask her where she'd bought her dress. Roland did, well, not real dance steps like the ones Kaye and she had choreographed together, but Roland moved his body in ways that felt very pleasant. He had no doubts when he danced, which made it easy to give in to him.

Indeed, Roland Hurd appeared to have no doubts about anything in the world, including facts that Noni was fairly certain he'd gotten wrong and opinions she knew she would have argued against if Bunny, for example, had expressed them, or if she'd heard them from Kaye. In fact, she was far more sympathetic to Kaye's views than Roland's—even if Kaye drove her crazy by the assertive way he insisted on knowing things. Roland, on the other hand, had an unsettling manner of making outrageous claims so coolly and blandly that they sounded like incontestable clichés.

Roland's lack of investment in what he said was very different from Kaye's and Bunny's ardent quarrels with the world, and somehow Noni couldn't bring herself to fight with Roland the way she fought with her friends. Somehow she didn't want to. Roland took away her will to fight, the way her mother did, but without the tension and the anger. As if weight had lifted from her, she felt herself floating toward him, like a leaf blown against the side of a building, until she was pressed against his chest, warm and close, and with no desire to argue.

But, at the same time, through the other lens of the binoculars, far way, she could see another Noni, the Noni she'd been before Roland, and that Noni was shrinking into someone small and quiet as a mouse. It was all very strange.

The dance ended. Noni was saying good-bye to some friends when Roland sauntered back into the crowded lobby of the gym and draped her long coat around her shoulders. Then to her shock he suddenly moved his hand under the coat and cupped her breast in his palm. He squeezed, not hard enough to hurt, but not at all in a way she liked. He smiled until, frowning, she pulled away.

"What's the matter?" he asked, staggering slightly against her. His blue eyes, she noticed, now had little red lines in them. Throughout the night, Roland had "stepped outside" with the other boys, although only when another boy had cut in to dance with her. And now as he whispered, "Noni, wear my varsity ring," pressing his lips into her neck, harder and less pleasantly than when they'd been dancing inside, his words were slurred and she could smell the whiskey strongly.

But it was a familiar smell to Noni, even loved.

✳ ✳ ✳ ✳ ✳

Kaye and Parker hadn't had much luck with their evening, although it had started well. Still a few days short of sixteen, Kaye had borrowed his Uncle Austin's taxi by assuring him that it was legal for him to drive with a learner's permit as long as a licensed driver (Parker) was in the car. They'd driven into

Hillston. Because state troopers were always pulling over young blacks, Kaye had put Parker in the back seat as if he were a customer; he figured that cops wouldn't bother a taxi, because they'd assume there must be a white person in the back seat.

But at the new mall, when they strolled through a department store where Kaye was looking for a present to give his grandmother, an old lantern-jawed guard began following them up and down the aisles. Finally, as Kaye was searching for an open cash register to pay for the purple down-filled coat in his hand, the man had growled at them, "Put it back and move along, boys,"

Curses rose quickly to Kaye's lips, as strong as bile, but he stopped them before they escaped. Two years ago, he hadn't always managed such control. And as a result, he'd once been physically shoved out of a store by a security guard. He'd once been forced by the Gordon Junior High football coach to stand on a chair in the middle of the boys' locker room for an hour as a punishment for "back talk."

"Pick your battles," his grandmother Amma had told him after that incident. "Some things just not worth what they cost. Fight to win, Kaye, not to fight."

He heard her voice now as he restrained Parker with an arm, then with an elaborate shrug of his shoulders, tossed the down coat onto a table of sweaters. "Just cost your boss a sale," was all he said to the guard.

The man repeated, "Move along," as if it were the only phrase they'd taught him.

Afterwards, the new Chinese restaurant on University Street where Kaye wanted to try something called "Szechwan" didn't have any tables and apparently didn't plan to have any for the rest of the evening. So the two young men strolled among the college shops and hippie sidewalk venders. Kaye bought a silver chain and had his present for Noni wrapped in

Christmas paper for fifty cents. Then they bought hamburgers and sneaked them in when they went to see *The Godfather*, which Parker found hilarious.

After the movie, Kaye and Parker drove to the Underground Railroad, a college dive in an old Pullman car near the train station. It stank of beer and urine but had a young racially mixed crowd and live folk singers—mostly white local dropouts, who sang, Kaye said, with weedy voices and loud guitars about social and personal horrors they'd never experienced. Parker said, fine; he didn't want to hear folks singing about horrors they *had* experienced. All he wanted to hear about was good times and fast women.

Kaye had never been carded at the Underground because of his size and his moustache and the fact that the bartender thought he was a cab driver. But this time the bartender asked Parker for his ID, and as Parker wasn't carrying his driver's license, they'd been thrown out. Worse, their expulsion had been observed not only by three attractive black girls in a booth, who'd agreed to let Kaye and Parker join them there, but by Wade Tilden, who'd taken to hanging out in funky places like the Underground where the drug dealers could be found. Wade's hair was now almost as big as Kaye's, a fluffy red Afro, and he wore a tight gray leisure suit that resembled a space suit and accentuated his skinniness. Kaye told Parker that Wade looked like he was on his way to the moon. When Kaye had first spotted him over by the bar, he was buying a dime bag of hash from one of the bearded folk singers.

It was embarrassing that just as Kaye, with a grin, was dramatically pantomiming at Wade the smoking of a joint, Parker should get them bounced so that Kaye had to endure not only the three girls' mocking waves but also Wade's smirk as he mouthed "bye-bye" when they left the bar.

"Parker, would you carry your fucking driver's license with you?" Kaye stormed across the parking lot.

"No, thank yoooou." Parker was actually eighteen although he attempted to stop anyone in authority from finding out his age. His teachers at Moors High School (where he was still a sophomore) thought he was stupid and kept him back, which was fine with him, and part of his plan for "flying under the radar screen" of the Moors draft board. "I'm not about to be the last nigger Huey'ed out of that jungle stuffing his guts back in his stomach."

"No," said Kaye. "You're gonna be the last nigger sitting in the 'leventh grade right beside your own grandchildren."

"That'll be just fine with me."

Parker wanted to check out the Christmas Dance at Moors High, to which a few of his friends, being seniors, had taken dates. Begrudgingly, Kaye drove back to Moors in a cold misty rain and detoured over to the high school. As they slowed going past the parking lot, Parker rolled down his window to see better. "Man, that Stars on Mars dance is already let out." He pointed at dozens of prom-goers heading for their cars. "Look over there. Somebody puking on his Corvette. Ten-four, good buddy!" He leaned out the window. At the Corvette, the boy's date was holding onto him, trying to turn him away from his car hood.

"Hey, Kaye, there's that girl lives 'cross your yard from you."

"What girl?"

Then Kaye saw Noni as she was struggling to get out of a blue GTO. Someone inside the car was holding her back by her long coat. With a yank, she broke loose, staggered, stepped away, clutching at her dress. Then the other person jumped out of the car as well, grabbing her again. Kaye recognized the tall man in the tuxedo as the senior halfback, Roland Hurd.

Slamming hard on the brakes, spinning the old black taxi around, narrowly missing a car speeding out of the parking lot, Kaye sped over the sidewalk onto the asphalt and

squealed to a stop beside the GTO. Startled, the girl at the
Corvette, still holding onto the boy who'd been sick, suddenly let him go and he bounced off the hood of his car and
fell onto the pavement.

"Kaye, where you going?"

Kaye ignored Parker as he hurried toward Noni. He saw
that her hair was disheveled and that she was holding her coat
tightly closed. He saw that Roland was squeezing her tightly by
the upper arm, that he was swaying, and that his words slurred
as he kept repeating. "Jesus, what's the matter with you, Noni?
What did I do?"

"Please just leave me alone please."

"Leave you alone? What the hell you crying about?" Roland
saw Kaye approaching from the black cab. "Jesus, you called a
taxi? When the hell did you call a taxi? I don't believe this."

"Noni?" Kaye stepped beside her. "You need a ride?"

Roland moved between them. "She doesn't need a *cab!*
This is my date. How do you even know her name? How does
this cab driver know your name?"

"Noni? You need a ride?"

Struggling not to cry, she nodded.

Other students had heard Roland's raised voice and had
drifted over to see what was happening. Kaye recognized two
seniors, one of them a fat defensive tackle, as teammates of
Hurd's. The two football players shoved to the front of the
group. The fat one had a nasal way of talking that squinted his
nose up to his eyes. "What's the deal, man?"

Kaye said, "Well, the deal is, the Marlboro man here is
loaded. So I'm taking her home."

Roland Hurd shook his head at his two friends in amazement. "This is mind-blowing. Where'd this cab come from?"

The other senior said, "Hey, Rol, we know this guy. He's
not a cab driver. What's your name? JV running back. Rol, we
know this guy."

"My name's Kaye King. I'm a friend of Noni's."

Behind them Parker got out of the taxi and stood beside the opened back door.

"Excuse me, please, I'm sorry," Noni said. It was hard to know if she was talking to Kaye or to Roland or to the dozen students now milling around them in the parking lot in the soft rain.

"Noni, honey, come on!" Roland reached for her but she twisted away from him. Then abruptly she ran to the black taxi and jumped inside the back. Parker shut the door behind her, calling over to Kaye. "Move it, man!"

Roland's two teammates crowded on either side of Kaye, then they turned to Roland for a lead on what to do. But the tall, handsome senior was staring at the cab into which Noni had disappeared. Then he turned back to Kaye. He and Kaye just stood in the soft rain, looking at each other for a while. Finally the fat tackle with the nasal voice hit Hurd on the shoulder with his huge fist. "Roland, hang on, you gonna let this nig—, oh sorry, this black person drive off with your date?"

Kaye did a perfect imitation of the tackle's scrunched nose and twangy voice as he pointed at him and the other senior. "Where are y'all's dates? Oh hang on, maybe some black person already drove off with them. Or oh hang on, I got it, y'all are dating each other! Far out!" So uncanny was the mimicry that a few students snickered before they could stop themselves.

Seated in the driver's seat of the taxi with the window down, Parker mumbled, "Shit, don't pull a knife. Shit, don't pull a knife."

Noni saw with horror that Parker had taken a pistol out of his jacket and was resting it on the open window. "I'm going to get a teacher," she said.

Parker reached over and pushed her back into the seat, told her to sit still. He turned on the car radio. The news came on saying that the trial of the Watergate Seven would start in January. Incongruously, Noni found herself thinking that Kaye would be happy to hear it.

Suddenly, the fat tackle lunged at Kaye and just as suddenly Roland threw his arm in front of his teammate to block him. Roland was so drunk that the sudden movement threw him off balance too; he lurched forward and fell down onto the wet asphalt. Quickly, his two friends pulled him back to his feet.

Kaye hadn't budged. He nodded at Roland. "That's right. You want her to get home to her folks safe and that's what I'm going to do."

Roland stared at Kaye, motionless for a moment, then he nodded at him. "Okay." He turned to the two seniors. "He knows her. His family works for hers."

"What's her problem?" asked the tall senior.

Roland shrugged. "Okay," he mumbled at Kaye. "Just take her home."

"That was the plan, man." Kaye turned and walked to the taxi.

Parker blew out a sigh as Kaye drove them from the parking lot. "Don't *do* that to me."

Kaye sneered. "Me? Talk to Miss Stardust Ballroom here in the back seat."

"Please stop it, Kaye." Noni hit the back of the seat beside his head.

"You stop it. And stop bawling back there."

"I'm not bawling! I just *feel* like bawling!"

"Well, stop feeling like it!"

"*Do* you have a knife?"

He threw something into the back seat. "Yeah. Be my guest."

Noni felt around on the seat. Surprised, she saw a red Swiss Army knife like the one that she'd given Kaye from "Santa," back on the first Christmas they'd met. "Is this the one I gave you all those years ago?"

"You want it back?"

"I'm sorry. I thought Parker was telling me you had like a *switchblade*. I was scared somebody was going to get hurt."

Parker wheeled around on her. "I didn't mean Kaye. I meant *them*."

"A switchblade?" Kaye made his raspberry noise. "Who you think I am, James Dean at Hollywood High?"

"You two are weird," Parker muttered. "Just let me out of here at this corner. Let me out! I'll walk the block. Y'all are too weird."

After they dropped Parker off, Kaye asked Noni if she wanted to go to the hospital. "Why?" she asked.

"Did he rape you?"

"No! How could you say that?"

"How could I *say* it?"

She was profoundly, horrifyingly shocked. Roland had simply tried to "go too far" —as her girlfriends had told her, as her mother had told her, all boys would always try to do—by trying to undo her bra and touch her breasts. And she had stopped him—as her girlfriends, as her mother had told her all girls must always try to do in order to be respected and ultimately married to the boys they'd stopped from touching them.

Kaye and Noni didn't speak again until they were driving through the brick columns guarding Heaven's Hill. Then she said, "Parker has a gun."

Actually it was the first Kaye had known of it, but he masked his surprised shock with a shrug. "Yeah, so what?"

"So what? He could get killed. You could get killed."

"That's the least of my worries." Kaye laughed, struck that she hadn't said, "He could kill someone, you could kill someone." The white stone drive curved like a river to the house where dozens of lights were blazing, even at one in the morning. "Your folks are up."

"They just leave the lights on."

"Is Wade back?"

"Wade's over at his girlfriend's. Her folks went to St. Thomas." Noni's careful curls were now wet and disarrayed. She'd buttoned her coat to her neck. "Kaye. You don't need to come in with me….I'm sorry—"

"Oh shut up. Here." He handed her a small present elaborately wrapped in shiny red paper. "I won't be around Christmas. I'm going to Philly to see my mama. So Happy Birthday, et cetera."

"Oh thank you. Let me get yours under the tree."

"Good luck finding it." He followed her to the big white front door that was never locked. She opened it quietly and slipped inside.

Kaye was waiting at the door when a small cry came from the hallway, like grief caught in her throat. "Oh….Oh."

He hurried in to find Noni kneeling on the parquet floor in the midst of broken blue pieces of pottery. The Early Ming Dynasty Chinese jar that had always sat on the console lay on the floor smashed into fragments. Leaping up, Noni ran down the hall. Following her, Kaye noticed a path of small red smudges on the wide floorboards leading into the den.

There, on the far side of the handsome paneled space, Bud Tilden lay on his red leather couch, dressed in his perfect soft wool gray slacks and his cashmere sweater, but with bloody bare feet. A spilled glass was tilted in his hand. A record album lay on the floor, *Where Are You?* On its cover, Frank Sinatra hunched over, sadly smoking a cigarette, wearing a green V-neck sweater very much like the one Bud Tilden had on. Nearby, built-in shelves showed off trophies with basketball players on them; others held hundreds of vinyl records—classical Romantic music mostly, and pop vocalists. Other shelves held dozens of matched sets of "good books"—like the Meditations of Marcus Aurelius, the poetry of Keats, *Ivanhoe*, and *Arrowsmith*, that Tilden read in the evenings.

A large trophy, a silver loving cup commemorating Tilden as player of the year, sat on the coffee table near him. It was filled with tennis balls, and other tennis balls lay on the floor around it. It looked as if Tilden had been throwing the balls from the couch into the trophy. A television was on without the sound, showing a test-pattern. The stereo turntable was on too, the needle rasping again and again at the end of the record. Kaye clicked the machine off.

"Daddy?"

Tilden groaned softly, rolled to his side, deep in drunken sleep.

"He's hurt himself," Noni whispered. She ran to a small sink that was set in a bar in a corner, noticing as she wet a cloth there that the bottle of bourbon beside the sink was empty. Tilden winced and twitched as Kaye carefully washed away the blood from his bare feet. The long pale feet reminded him of Noni's brother Gordon, of how Gordon had made a stand in college by not wearing shoes but had gone to Vietnam wearing stiff shiny boots.

Pulling out a tiny sliver of the broken jar, Kaye cleaned the sole of Tilden's foot. "He's okay. He'll be fine. Where's your mom?"

Noni gestured above to the ceiling. "Upstairs. But she won't wake up." Noni didn't want to say that her mother took sleeping pills. "She's a heavy sleeper."

"I guess your dad was wandering around in the hall, knocked that blue bowl off." Kaye didn't want to say that her father had obviously been drunk and had now passed out.

"Mom loved that jar. Her grandfather brought it home from China. I hope she didn't hear it break, I hope she didn't." Tears fell from Noni as she leaned over her father. One of the tears struck Tilden in the face and he brushed at it with his hand. She smoothed the tear away from his cheek. Then, taking a plaid throw from an armchair, she floated it over him, softly tucked it in around his legs, kissed his forehead, and turned out the lamp in the den. "Everything's breaking," she said quietly in the dark.

The phone rang, terrifyingly loud, on the table right beside the couch. Tilden didn't stir. Noni quickly picked it up before it could ring again. It was Roland Hurd, wanting to know if she was all right.

"Yes, Kaye got me home," she said stiffly. "I'm fine." Kaye saw her take a large gold sports ring from her coat pocket, look at it, then return it. "No, I still have it," she said. Kaye left the room as Noni kept talking into the phone, "No, you can't come over…."

When she returned to the hallway, she found Kaye kneeling on the parquet floor, collecting the broken pieces of the jar into its jagged base. Still in her long buttoned coat, she knelt beside him to help.

Kaye looked at her. "He apologize?"

"Yes. He apologized."

"Good."

"He'd had a little too much to drink."

"Um hum. 'A little.'" Kaye shook his head. "What does he do to his date after he's had a 'lot'?"

"Can we forget about Roland?"

"That sure would be my advice. Find me some good glue."

They walked through the house back to the large kitchen. From the living room, the hundreds of lights on the huge tree blinked on and off in complicated sequences. Kaye wondered if the Tildens just plugged in the lights and left them on day and night from December 5 to January 5. They never seemed to be turned off.

The long pale green–painted pine table and pale green chairs and the enormous sink and enormous refrigerator were all familiar to Kaye. While his grandmother cooked or cleaned, he had often waited in here, studying the new appliances and gadgets that Judy Tilden was always buying.

When Noni came back from the bathroom, she'd fixed her prom dress and her hair. She sat down at the table and watched Kaye start to sort the pieces of the jar. There must have been twenty or thirty broken shards.

"Aren't you going to help me?" he asked.

"It's stupid. You think my mother's not going to notice?"

"So what, it'll be fixed. Come on, we can fix this. We can fix this as good as new."

She rolled her eyes. "It's an antique, Kaye! It's early Ming Dynasty!"

He grinned at her. "We can fix this as good as old."

Noni couldn't stop herself from smiling.

He looked up from his neat pile of sorted chips. "Why do you always cover your mouth like that? You've got a pretty smile."

The compliment astonished her. Embarrassed, she began examining the broken pieces. She found one that fit to the base and handed it to him. When she found the adjoining piece, he glued them together.

"Nice smile, but look, kid, you're anemic," he added, mimicking the way Dr. Jack had once always been telling her that. "You need to eat more spinach, get some iron in your blood. I know some black people, they want to be whiter. But you are *too* white. You need to get a little more colored blood in you."

"I probably have plenty."

"You probably do."

"Maybe as much as you do."

"Now that's not happening." Grinning, Kaye took a small mirror off the wall and brought it over, held it in front of her, pressed his head against hers so they could see both of their faces in the narrow glass: her pale cheeks, blonde hair, his cinnamon skin, black Afro, his gold-flecked eyes ironically asking her gray-blue eyes to laugh with him. But then as they kept looking at each other in the mirror, they became suddenly aware of their closeness. The laughter left his eyes and her cheeks flushed. They looked away and then they moved apart.

"We need to fix this bowl," Kaye gruffly announced, returning the mirror to the wall.

An hour later, with the meticulous precision that she'd noticed in him from the beginning, he had put most of the Chinese jar back together. While they worked they drank Cokes and ate brownies. Mostly they didn't talk. But suddenly out of nowhere he said, "That asshole Coach Ross, he's always telling me how I need to get 'a passion' for football. I said to him, 'You think a black man's got to dance in the end zone, is that what you think? How 'bout if I got a passion to be a rocket scientist?'"

"Do you?"

Kaye didn't answer. Instead he attached another piece to the jar. "And I don't want you turning into a zombie."

"What in the world is that supposed to mean?"

"It means, tell me something *you* want. You want to marry Roland Turd?"

"Don't call him that."

"Sorry. So, what do you want?"

It was disturbing that the image invading Noni's mind was of Roland kissing her sweetly on the dance floor, early in the dance, before he'd "stepped outside" too often. Then bizarrely Roland was turning into Kaye and Kaye was kissing her. But of course she couldn't say any of that out loud. So she said, "For one thing I want people I care about not to drink so much." She hoped Kaye would think she meant her father. And she did mean him. But she also meant Roland.

Kaye made his raspberry noise. "Not what you want for somebody else. For *you*."

"That's what I want."

"Nope." He shook his head at her.

"You can't just tell me, 'No.'" But Kaye kept waiting, gesturing "Come on," with his hand, and, finally, exasperated, she blurted out. "I want to go someplace where they can teach me to play the piano better."

"You play the piano fine. You just play scared."

"Oh, you think you know everything."

"I do," he grinned.

"At least I play the piano. At least I love it. You just use everything you do as something to put on your college applications. Football. Violin. Science Fair winner. Paper editor. He does it all. You're just collecting medals."

"Damn straight I am. I need all the medals I can get, need the Medal of Honor, for me to get anywhere in the old U.S. of A."

She watched him maneuver the piece he'd just glued into place. "I know I play scared. Don't you ever get scared?"

Slowly he pulled at the glue stuck to his fingers. The silence stretched until she was sure he was going to ignore her question (as he often did). But then he said, "You grow up in the streets, in Philly? You don't let it show. You blink, and you're lucky, you're lying on the sidewalk and you hear the sirens come. You're unlucky, you're lying on the sidewalk and you're wearing a toe tag." He made this comment with his usual braggadocio, as if boasting about a violent cityscape she could never know.

"When were you the most scared?" she asked. "I was the most scared when they told my mom Gordon was dead."

Now he spoke in a different voice, softly rubbing at the old black Timex watch that he'd had since childhood, whose square face had once looked so large on his wrist. "My mama. When she didn't make sense, that scared me," he said quietly. "The first time when they tied down her hands and stuck needles in her and rolled her out to the ambulance and wouldn't let me come too, that scared me bad. I was seven. I got on a bus but I couldn't find the hospital so I kept on riding because I didn't know what to ask for. Then the driver started in about calling over a cop so I ran off. Except I got lost in downtown Philly, and I got so tired and cold I just went to sleep on a grate next to this stinky old man." Kaye glued the edge of the blue broken piece and then pressed it into the top of the jar. "That old man gave me part of his blanket. Could have been a rapist, killer, anything. But he was just a nice old man. You need luck, too. Or angels."

"You believe in angels?"

"When I was little, my mama used to tell me I had angels fighting for me, not sweet little nice angels, but warrior angels with great big swords. She showed me pictures of them and told me they were always on watch up there, looking out for me. Anybody messed with me and these angels would whack off their heads. You remember those crosses she used to put out in the yard here?"

"Her 'beau ideas'?"

He smiled. "That's right."

"You used to keep them in the Promised Land shoebox?"

"I still do. I still got 'em. Well, those folks she made the crosses for? They're the ones, she said, that went up to heaven and got to be the angels with swords. And you know what? I always did used to feel like they had their eye on things for me."

Only one more piece and the jar would be whole again.

Noni watched Kaye working. "Sometimes I'm jealous of everything you've been through. I know that's awful, but it's like if you wake up on a grate and it's morning and you're alive and see how you can go ahead with your life, well, then I bet it stops things from being so scary."

"Noni, I wouldn't waste much time wishing you were homeless." He shrugged. "Poor people know about being poor. Rich people know about being rich." He turned the jar slowly, smiling at her. "Good as old."

"You like to put things that get broken back together. Like Uncle Tatlock's bones."

"Oh lord, those bones of his." Kaye laughed. Noni laughed too. She touched the jar and as she did so, her fingers touched his. Neither moved. Then softly his hand slid over hers. She looked into his eyes. Again his eyes stopped laughing but this time he didn't look away. She looked at him, kept looking and deep at her heart's core she felt something lock into place. She felt that the Noni she was seeing reflected in his eyes was the truest part of herself.

Kaye looked back at her, kept looking until he felt a wave of feeling that was big enough to knock him down, coming closer, too high, too close. He had never wanted to feel so big a wave of feeling, one too high to beat back. But in Noni's eyes he suddenly saw that the wave would do him only good. The moment lengthened.

Then the beautiful old French clock off on the dining room mantel chimed midnight, echoing through the house. Kaye looked at his watch. His voice was thick. "I better go."

Noni felt she had to say something. "Anybody who likes to put bones together would probably make a good doctor. You ever think about that?"

"Yeah. I have." He glued the last piece into the rim of the blue jar.

"I can see you doing that."

In fact, Doctor Jack had told him several times to "think about medicine," and his chemistry teacher had once said that she bet Kaye would do very well in med school, and once, seeing the movie M*A*S*H, he had thought that being a surgeon would be a cool thing to do. And while he hadn't focused yet on a career, still, as soon as Noni had said he'd be a good doctor, Kaye thought that maybe she was right. Suddenly he saw a whole possible future to consider.

"Well, think about it," she said.

He went to the sink, washed his hands. "I'll think about it."

Noni was wondering, as she kept trying to come up with something to say, that maybe she'd been wrong to believe Kaye had been looking at her in a different way just a few minutes ago. He seemed so preoccupied now. "So, say you were a doc-tor, what kind of doctor would you be?"

Kaye was still shaking off the surge of feeling about Noni that had taken him by surprise. He was pulling himself back as fast as he could into the safety of his bravado. "I could be any type of doctor. Okay, the richest type. A surgeon."

"What kind of surgeon?"

"A heart surgeon. How's that?" As he dried his hands, he looked over at her with his irresistible grin. "You get your heart broken, Noni Tilden, you come see me."

Three days later, on Christmas Eve, when Kaye was back in Philadelphia visiting his mother at the hospital, Noni opened her gift from him. The box held a silver heart.

Noni's mother frowned seeing it, biting on her lip when Noni told her the gift had come from Kaye. But Mrs. Tilden said nothing as her daughter put the small silver heart hanging from its silver chain around her neck.

On the card, Kaye had written that he'd made the heart from a dime, the cost of a phone call. There was a quote on the card, "Come on girl, reach out for me. I'll be there," from the Four Tops song. It had been one of the records with which in his grandmother's kitchen they had taught each other to dance so well together.

The Fourth Day of Christmas

❄

December 25, 1974
The Porch Rocker

The Tildens were having Noni's godfather, Dr. Jack Hurd, for Christmas dinner this evening. Noni, just turned eighteen, and her mother were setting the table with the holiday china. Mrs. Tilden had invited him, she said, because she felt sorry for Doctor Jack, whose wife had left him for a dentist.

"That's a real come down all right," agreed Bud Tilden, passing by on his way to the den where he was pasting photographs and souvenirs—invitations, programs, ticket stubs—into enormous vinyl photo albums. Because he and his wife were the last of their two families, he had whole generations of Tilden and Gordon photographs stored in large boxes beside him, and he now spent his evenings filling book after book with their pasts. But to his wife's distress, there was no organizing principle behind the way he pasted together the family story. In fact, she couldn't bear to look at the chaos he was making of their history. On one double page, for example, he had glued a Hilton Head golf scorecard, the puppy Philly sleeping on the now deceased Royal Charlie's neck, R.W. Gordon on a camel in front of the pyramids, thirteen-year-old Noni and Kaye dressed like the Mod Squad at Halloween, his great-aunt's wedding announcement,

Gordon's baby footprint, nametags from Parents Day at Wade's military school, and a daguerreotype of his wife's twice-great grandfather on the porch of Heaven's Hill in 1860, a baby held in the arms of a black slave wearing starched white clothes.

While Mr. Tilden worked on the albums or read his Great Books, often until the early hours of the morning, he listened to classical music like the Warsaw Concerto or what he called "the old-timers"—like Nat King Cole and Doris Day—sing sad songs, or he listened to Noni playing the piano across the hall. What he liked most was romantic piano music that had been turned into the kind of songs Frank Sinatra sang—like Rachmaninoff's "Full Moon and Empty Arms" or Chopin's "I'm Always Chasing Rainbows." Noni was happy to play for him; she practiced the piano three hours a day now. Her teachers thought she had a very good chance of being accepted at the Curtis Institute of Music in Philadelphia. She would find out in April.

In the dining room, arranging the silver flatware at each place setting, three forks, two knives, three spoons, Judy Tilden told their daughter Noni that she didn't know what her husband meant by "a real come down." Did he mean that Doctor Jack was a better person than the dentist even though the dentist was better looking? Or that Jack (head of OB/GYN at the university medical school) had a better job than the dentist and made more money? If the latter, then did Bud really mean that she, Judy, was a snob? She suspected that's what he did mean, although she wasn't sure what he meant by it.

Mrs. Tilden corrected her daughter's positioning of the three glasses at each setting as she confessed that she almost never knew what her husband meant anymore, if indeed he meant anything. He sat in the den reading from the matched sets of famous books of poetry and philosophy, writing down passages from them on scraps of paper that she found rolled into little balls in his pockets or on his dresser. He wandered the house for hours as if he were looking for something he could never find, talking softly to himself, smiling. She suspected that somewhere along the years he'd decided that life was a joke it would be inappropriate for him to share.

Nor did Judy Tilden imagine her father the bank president would think the joke were funny if he'd happened to overhear it at Moors Savings. Judy's father was losing patience with Bud. Not only was his son-in-law making odd remarks to wealthy customers, he was giving loans to people who had no collateral. Fortunately, Bud's secretary was devoted to him and Judy had taken this woman to lunch to ask her to keep an eye on her husband, to check his desk drawers for bourbon bottles and report back. The secretary had been so noncommittal that Judy had felt obliged to point out that if Bud were forced to leave the bank, the secretary would also be out of a job.

There would only be five for dinner at Heaven's Hill tonight—Noni and Doctor Jack, as well as Mrs. Tilden, her husband Bud, and her cousin Becky—whose attempts to seduce her husband Bud had escaped Judy's notice. (Bud had noticed the overtures but had politely sidestepped them.) Since Becky and Jack Hurd were both divorced, Mrs. Tilden planned to play cupid, she told Noni, and bring the couple together in a non-dating venue to see if they had chemistry.

Wandering back through the dining room with his chinkling bourbon, Bud murmured, "Sure, why not?" He was wearing his sunglasses in the house, which he had taken to doing lately, as if there were nothing he cared to see and no one he wanted seeing him.

"Bud, let's make this a fun evening for Jack and Becky," his wife called after him.

"Why not?" he said again.

The Tildens' son Wade was having Christmas with his wife's family and had invited his grandfather R.W. Gordon to join them. A few days earlier, in a "blow out," as Noni had described it to Kaye, Wade told them he would rather be with his wife's family than his own because he was sick of everybody's sitting around wishing Gordon were alive, or wishing Wade were Gordon. (Everybody told him it wasn't true, but in a way it was.) Wade then called his father a loser and a drunk, an assessment with which Bud Tilden declined to argue— although Noni had done so, and had added that Wade made her sick when he advised their mother to "wise up and get rid of Dad."

Wade was twenty-three now and his red hair was once again very short. He wore three-piece suits and wide paisley ties and played golf all the time with his grandfather. He already had not only a wife (Trisha), but a new business (the first two had failed despite his grandfather's friends) and a baby—a little girl with whom Trisha had been pregnant when they married.

Noni didn't think her mother knew that Trisha had been pregnant at her wedding. But maybe she did; maybe she also knew that until a few years ago Wade was popping pills, smoking pot, sniffing cocaine, and stealing from his parents to pay for it all. But Noni didn't think so. She didn't think her mother knew that Gordon had only gone to Vietnam because she had made such a big deal about how the men in her family had always served their country and how she would be ashamed of him if he dodged the draft. Noni doubted her mother knew that Wade had bullied his first fiancée into having an abortion and had cheated his way through two mediocre colleges (the first expelled him), or that Noni had lost her virginity last summer to Roland Hurd.

But maybe Mrs. Tilden did know all these things and just pretended she didn't in order not to crack the smooth mirror in which she needed to view their tranquil lives in order to keep herself from going to pieces. She said she could stop worrying about Wade now that Trisha had him firmly in hand. She was confident (using current lingo like a tourist with a phrasebook) that "Wade has his act together and Trisha's the chick to thank." Bud Tilden thought it was not so much marrying Trisha that had turned Wade around as the failing health of R.W. Gordon, who'd bluntly told his grandson to "get his ass in gear in a goddamn hurry" or he could expect to inherit from him "a big fat goose egg."

"Trish," said Bud Tilden, "you nabbed Wade on the rebound from R.W. Gordon."

"Oh Poppy," smiled Trisha but it was not really a smile. "Don't tease Wade."

"I'm teasing *you*," he told her, but she knew better.

In many ways, thought Noni, Trisha was very much like Mrs. Tilden, both of them piling sandbags of rules and amenities against a rising, flooding chaos, both at war against imperfection, their faces composed, their eyes desperate.

Noni's mother had wanted to invite Jack's son Roland to this Christmas dinner tonight as well but Noni had stopped her by threatening to "talk politics" at the table. Mrs. Tilden was unhappy because Noni had once again broken up with Roland, but she didn't want to risk her dinner party. She had no patience for "things nobody cares to hear about"—like the resignations of Agnew and Nixon or the disastrous war in Vietnam—and she was horrified when she learned that Noni had been going to peace marches and civil rights meetings and was in a high school "women's lib group." She blamed Noni's friends Kaye and Bunny for her daughter's even knowing the words Wounded Knee, Karen Silkwood, and Rap Brown.

But there was a deeper, blacker terror in Mrs. Tilden than even a child's liberal activism. It bubbled up like oil in her sleep, churning and spuming at her the word "Kaye." What if her daughter and Kaye should fall in love? What if they already were in love but didn't know it? What if they did know it? What if that silver heart that Noni still wore on a chain around her neck were a secret token of a love all too requited?

Asked whether he also worried about Kaye and Noni's relationship, her husband Bud replied, "We should be so lucky," which was scarcely any comfort. Then he added as he wandered away, "Kaye's Noni's only brother." She wasn't sure exactly what he meant by that, except that it was a slap at Wade, which was scarcely any comfort either.

Noni and Roland Hurd had been dating off and on for two years but now was one of the off times. Last month they had had a fight about Roland's possessiveness, how he constantly wanted to know where she was and what she was doing. He said everything he did just meant he loved her. Noni assumed she was in love with Roland, too, but sometimes she wasn't sure she wanted to be. Although she felt her future floating inextricably into his in a slow strong relentless tide, there was a way in which over the past two years she hadn't altogether minded his long absences from her daily life.

Everyone at Moors High knew she was going steady with a sophomore at Princeton, and as a result she had both status and freedom from the dating competition that so pressured her friends. Admittedly she had applied to Curtis Institute of Music mostly because Philadelphia was less than an hour from Princeton. She knew that the proximity of the Institute to Roland also made it a more appealing college possibility to her mother—who otherwise (terrified by memories of Noni's illness in her boarding school, coming so soon after the loss of Gordon) had opposed all choices beyond the borders of North Carolina.

Noni had also, like Kaye, applied to Haver University, only an hour away from Moors. As she was not merely a double legacy but a Gordon legacy, it was inconceivable that she wouldn't be admitted. But she thought it would be easier to keep her independence living an hour away from Roland in Princeton than an hour away from her mother in Moors. She had already flown to Philadelphia to audition at Curtis; she had played the hardest Liszt her teacher could find and on her own had added some little Bartok songs. It had been nauseating to perform under the terror that she would fail her mother, but she got through it and one of the judges even told her she played the Bartok beautifully, and that nobody should try a Liszt *Transcendental* Etude unless he or she had to, because there was too much else in the world to play and most of it was a hell of a lot easier. For the first time Noni began to think studying music could be fun.

"Noni, move those candlesticks a little to the right." Mrs. Tilden rearranged the centerpiece of fruits so that a tapered bunch of black grapes spilled over the edge of the silver plate just as she had seen in a photograph of a painting in the Prado. Mrs. Tilden loved to look at paintings in museums, or even pictures of paintings. Despite her family's wealth, she hadn't traveled much (except for trips to New York City as a child) because extensive foreign travel wasn't something Southern girls like her had done at the time. They'd gone to college, found husbands, and had children, just as Judy Gordon had done. But she had always tried to make her home a museum and to turn its furnishings into the kinds of paintings she might have seen if she had traveled.

The table was now perfect with red candles surrounded by evergreens and special Christmas china. When she looked at the table, the tight bands that were always around her chest slightly loosened. It wasn't much, a beautiful table setting, but it was something. A stand, even only for a moment, against the world's continual collapsing.

She turned her attention to Noni, who was wearing a black velvet pantsuit with a tuxedo jacket that had wide satin lapels. Under the jacket was a shirt with huge white ruffles. Noni's hair was long now and fell in two straight blonde parts over her shoulders. Mrs. Tilden smoothed the hair and fluffed the ruffles on the blouse, her hand tensing as she saw the little silver heart on the silver chain.

Later, at 6:45, the doorbell rang. "Please get that," Mrs. Tilden called to Noni, who jumped from the piano where she was playing for her father, and closed her sheet music inside the black leather folder embossed with her name, "Noelle Katherine Tilden." Kaye had given her the folder for her birthday. She hurried into the hall, thinking about Kaye, wondering what he was doing tonight. Behind her she heard her mother say, "Damn it, why is he always early?" as Noni opened the door to Roland's father, Dr. Jack Hurd, hoping he hadn't heard her mother's remark too.

The porch was garlanded in swags of ribboned pine; there were holly balls and wreaths hanging everywhere, and a large fanlight over the door was decorated with fruits and nuts. Dr. Hurd stood there shaking his head at the display. "You know your mom's a little compulsive?" He smiled at Noni.

"Think so?"

Under his Burberry raincoat, Dr. Hurd had on almost the same velvet pantsuit Noni did—except instead of ruffles he wore a claret-colored shirt. "Wow," he said as they went into the hall. "You look great. Merry Christmas and Happy Birthday. Don't you hate them dumped together?"

She hugged her godfather. "Yes, I do."

"Looks like Santa came in an Italian sportscar." He pointed outside.

"Oh, you know my dad."

He hung his coat on the Victorian hat rack. "You know what I think it is? Bud can't spoil you so he just keeps trying.... Still mad at Roland?"

"Is that what he told you?"

"Please forgive him. Please! I know he's a jerk but I'm counting on you to change all that. Don't forget, you owe me. Who delivered yah, baby?"

"You did. You're my Deliverer." She took his armful of presents, put them on the console by the mended blue Chinese jar and the jeweled metal pear tree. "So I'm warning you. Mom's setting you up with a blind date tonight."

"Who? Farrah Fawcett?"

"Close. Mom's cousin Becky. Becky Van Buehling." (Becky had big streaked blonde hair rather like the actress Farrah Fawcett.)

"Oh lord, her. I'm too old. Maybe I'm too young. You know she married Bob Van Buehling for his name? Her name was Becky Nutt. That's true, that's what your mom told me, Becky Nutt, and now it's like she's got a castle on the Rhine. Rebec-cccaaaa Vannn Buehlllingkkk." He turned Noni's face from side to side, examined her pale skin.

She smiled. "I know. Eat more spinach."

"Liver. Eat somebody's liver every other day."

Noni had always loved her godfather, with his thin homely face and his gray ironic eyes, so unlike Roland's cool blue ones. And although she thought Doctor Jack a little silly in his youthful faddishness, and naïve in his effervescent good will, she also thought him a smart, generous man. She tried not to wonder whether she didn't see, and love, more of the father in his son Roland than was actually there.

In the hall that smelled festively of pine garlands, Hurd pulled her down beside him onto the green leather bench. "Have I got some great news for Kaye! Hubba hubba."

One of the things Noni liked most about Doctor Jack was the interest he had taken these past years in Kaye; the time he had spent talking with him about his going to medical school. Now he whispered dramatically. "Quick, before everybody shows up. I got a call from a guy on the Roanoke committee. It's not official and I'm not supposed to say anything."

Noni leapt to her feet. "Tell me! Did Kaye get it? Did Kaye get it?"

Jack Hurd laughed, kissed both her hands, his gray pony-tail flopping over the wide collar. "He got it. The first black ever."

Noni was so happy she bounced up and down as she corrected her godfather. "Afro-American, we're supposed to say Afro-American."

"Christ, I can't keep up."

They heard Judy Tilden as she closed the door from the dining room with a swirling full turn copied from her mother who had gotten it from Loretta Young. "Keep up with what?" she called.

"Shhh," whispered Noni. "Don't tell her about Kaye."

"Kaye who?" grinned Doctor Jack.

❋ ❋ ❋ ❋ ❋

By ten o'clock, across the lawn from Heaven's Hill, Kaye and his grandmother had almost finished the dishes. Amma returned bowls and platters to their places on her shelves. Kaye took back the chairs he'd brought to the dining room table for the big family meal. Most of the chairs, discarded, donated, forgotten, had come over from Heaven's Hill sometime in the last century and a half. Whenever the big house had redecorated, so did Clayhome. The chairs were all different. There was an eighteenth-century Windsor chair whose spokes sometimes fell out, a 1940s metal chair, a black lacquer Depression Modern chair with three burled legs and one makeshift pine leg, and a Victorian throne-chair with a plush purple seat into which Tatlock Fairley was transferred from his wheelchair for the special meal.

This afternoon, Amma had served Christmas Day dinner to her three brothers, their two living wives, three of their grown children, those children's children, as well as Tatlock, his daughter-in-law Yolanda, his son Austin, Kaye, and herself.

Her brothers had never felt about Clayhome the way Amma did, so hers was the first generation since 1840 when a male Clay hadn't made the place his home, when the house hadn't had a "Clay" in it to pass along its name. "The end of our line on this land," Amma said every year. But her brothers and their children and Kaye didn't share her love of Heaven's Hill. "Clayhome was never ours anyhow," they told her. "It's just where the hired help lives."

Amma had always felt the land *was* hers, or maybe more just that she and the land belonged together. She felt it today as her family crowded round the dining room table, with the children at a card table nearer the living room so they could see the tree twinkling with the ornaments they'd made. Everyone had been given a place mat and napkin with Amma's signature sunflowers on them. As he had every year, Tatlock presided with his customary *noblesse oblige* over a holiday feast he had neither prepared nor paid for, passing around roasted chicken and buttered yams, collard greens and mincemeat pie with a garrulous sovereignty, talking mostly about the case he planned to bring to court to reclaim land where his Algonquin Indian ancestors on his mother's side had once lived and where developers were now building condominiums they called Algonquin Village.

Everyone told him, "You're right," and, "You do that," and, "Is that so?" But none of Tatlock's "cases" had ever ventured beyond the walls of Clayhome and the family didn't expect this one to either.

Now the dishes were cleared and the Fairley relatives had all gone home. It was dark and drizzly outside; Tatlock was asleep in his wheelchair with his long arms around the big portable radio that Kaye had given him for Christmas, a "boom box" Kaye had told his grandfather to call it, but Tatlock had said he wasn't going to. He liked it though. He was glad to have the kind of radio he could take with him when he rolled his wheelchair outside and slept in the sun of the yard. Gently, Kaye eased the boom box out of the old man's arms and brought it into the kitchen, turned it on to the quiet jazz station from the university. Finally, he and his grandmother had found a station they could agree on. She liked the jazz station because it featured so many natives of North Carolina, like John Coltrane—whom she had met once at a picnic.

Amma was sealing with wax paper the last of the scalloped oysters, a dish she had first cooked on Christmas Eve for the Tildens. "That was a sweet thing, Kaye, helping Yolanda's kids make something special for the tree." Their tree in the living room was decorated with ornaments Kaye had created over the years out of pieces of tin, old buttons, parts of toys, and empty thread spools. Today he had organized his small cousins into an assembly line producing dried cranberry garlands and strings of paper angels. "They look up to you and you can be an influence on—"

He interrupted her. "Don't you ever get tired of Tilden left-overs?" Annoyed, he gestured at the oysters, then around the house filled with Tilden furniture and thrown-away Tilden clothes and uneaten Tilden food—here was a gift box of grape-fruits sent to Bud Tilden, here were fur-lined gloves that had once been Judy Tilden's. The American Empire dining-room table with its matching sideboard was a castoff of Judy's mother's, who'd given it to Amma's mother in 1927 so she could replace it with something more modern. "This whole house is nothing but their throw-aways."

Amma kept patiently wrapping leftovers for the refrigera-tor. "What you rather do with good food, son, toss it in the garbage? You rather chop up that nice old table for firewood?"

"Hey, they just tore down Moors Savings Bank and it wasn't as old as that table."

"Too much wasting in this world. And too much of it over there across that yard, and I'm not adding more. Now let's sit down. "As if to symbolize her refusal to waste, Amma pulled on a long cardigan sweater that years ago she'd knitted for Tatlock but which he'd outgrown ("out-eaten," she called it). Amma

Fairley's own weight hadn't changed in twenty years. In fact, to Kaye, everything about his grandmother looked exactly as it had on his first Christmas trip to Moors eleven years earlier, except that her then peppery hair was now white. Firm and sturdily built, with her smooth long-fingered hands and strong-muscled arms and her braided coils of hair, Amma Fairley seemed to have rushed early to a certain place in her life and then stopped there forever.

Sitting at the kitchen table, she took a flat square packet wrapped in Christmas paper from her pocket and placed it carefully and precisely in the center of the cleared table.

Kaye assumed it was an envelope holding twenty or forty dollars in spending money, for she had often given him money so that he could "buy for himself, since Lord knows nobody else can get it right." It was true that Kaye took a great deal of care with his clothes, and liked to choose his own. Tonight he was wearing a full-sleeved dark green silk shirt with a turquoise tie and the turquoise cuff links that Noni had given him yesterday (their birthstone) and which he loved. But if the gift were money, Kaye wondered why his grandmother hadn't presented it this afternoon when they'd opened all the other presents—both for Christmas and his birthday.

"Kaye, let's us talk for a minute."

Now he knew why she had waited. She wanted to preface her gift with a sermon. For that invitation to "talk for a minute" was always the preamble to something serious, often critical or painful, and rarely brief. He looked studiously at his watch, his customary response. His watch was now digital, with an alarm, not that setting the alarm would shorten his grandmother's lecture. He predicted that she would begin in her usual way with a summation of his blessings. Then she would narrow in on some failure of his to capitalize on those blessings.

"Kaye," she said, true to form, "God has given you so many gifts."

"I wish He'd given me that green sports car somebody over there got for Christmas today."

"You got a good brain, a healthy body."

"Grandma—"

"You've been a good steward to your talents. And even though sometimes you been cheated and set aside—" Amma was talking here about school prizes that should have come to Kaye but didn't; a school election he had probably won but was told he'd lost. "—Every time they slapped you down, you got up and kept coming on."

"Thank you."

She patted his hand. "And you got a real kindness in you. You always pretending like you don't care, but you got a good strong heart."

He grinned at her, stood, threw his hands to his hips in his old comic way. "Aren't you going to tell me I'm good-looking?"

"You already got enough people telling you that." Amma said this flatly, not as a joke but as beside the point. Kaye was in fact secretly called, by the eleven Afro-American girls in his senior class, "The Catch." He dated often and variously, only Afro-Americans; that was a rule of his, much debated among his friends. But he took a kind of pride in the fact that he was not in love and was too busy to be interested in falling into such a state.

Amma was going on, commending him for keeping his grades high despite his night job at the taxi company and for sticking with football even though he didn't like it—

He interrupted her again. "Grandma, am I going to have to hear one more time how much money O.J. Simpson got to play for the Bills? When are you and Grandpa Tat gonna believe me? I am not going to make my living in their black box, running, jumping, dancing, or singing. And even if I wanted to, I'm not that talented!"

"Your coach says all you needs a passion for the game."

"What do you think talent is? It's a passion for the game!"

"Kaye. I'm trying to talk to you. You know I admire how you been working for the advancement of the race even when it wasn't appreciated."

Now Kaye snorted at her loudly. "Can we call it a little more than 'not appreciated,' when the police bash your head open?"

She held up her hand. "I don't want to talk about Parker or about your mama either."

"That's right, because you know it's true and you don't want to think about it."

Somehow lately it always came back to Kaye's friend Parker when he and his grandmother argued. Parker had been in prison for a year, convicted of possession of marijuana, of resisting arrest and even of assaulting a police officer. Summer before last, Parker and Kaye and a friend of Parker's had fought with half-a-dozen young whites outside a disco club in Mill-grove (the section of Moors known—until the city council changed the name in 1958—as "Africa"). The whites (county boys, high school drop-outs mostly) had decided to retaliate for a race riot in another state that they'd seen on television by trying to run down with a pickup truck the first group of local young black males they came across. Kaye and his friends had gone to the club after taking part in a civil rights demonstration earlier that day, and the stickers on Kaye's car had drawn the whites' attention.

Kaye had protested to the police that they'd only been defending themselves against drunks who were backing them into an alley, swinging bats and chains. The police arrested the three blacks anyhow, in fact arrested only the blacks, though they'd been outnumbered two to one. Amma had hurried to the police station the minute Kaye had called her; she'd brought Bud Tilden and they'd gotten Kaye out on bail.

Then Amma had hired a lawyer, a man who'd repre-sented Moors Bank and who had always stopped at Amma's sidewalk table outside the bank and joked with her. This lawyer had quickly arranged to have all charges against Kaye dropped. He told the judge Kaye King was a straight-A student and a first-string running back and that if he had seemed to be talking back to the arresting officers, he would apologize for it. The judge already knew Amma Fairley; she was a town landmark. The police accepted Kaye's apology and agreed that they had made a mistake in this one case.

But Parker's friend was not so lucky. And Parker himself unluckier still. The police claimed he had pulled a knife to stop them from entering his car where he had hidden half a kilo of homegrown marijuana. Parker said that the police had planted the drugs in his car but nobody but Kaye believed him. It was true that Parker had pulled a knife; what was remarkable to Kaye was that he'd had the strength to do it after one of the policemen had beaten him to the ground with his nightstick.

"Parker fought back," Kaye said stubbornly now to his grandmother. "And it's like Mama used to say, white people don't do time and rich people don't do time and the only poor black people that don't do time—" Kaye thumped both fists on his chest. "—Are the ones with the right connections. The lucky ones like me. But Parker still fought back. If you don't fight back, you're already dead. It was your daughter Deborah taught me that, Grandma!"

Amma nodded slowly. "That's true. Your mama was always saying, 'Fight. Fight.' Well, son, like I keep telling you, you can fight and lose every time—"

"Doesn't mean your fight wasn't right—"

"No it doesn't. But it means you'll end up like your mama. Or my daddy, shot through the head and nobody ever even arrested for it. Or your friend Parker in jail with blood still running down his face." Suddenly Amma pushed the present across to him, slid it under his hands. "I want you to fight, Kaye." She touched the card. "But I want you to win."

He strode back and forth, urgent to make her listen. "We *are* winning. Segregation. Gone. Death Penalty. Gone. Vietnam War. Gone. Nixon and that whole gang of crooks. Gone. We did that. A whole generation did that."

"Well, let's hope so, son. But I'm not talking about any generation. I'm talking about *you*. I don't want there to be nobody can set *you* aside. Nobody in this world." She moved the wrapped packet. "Open it."

Kaye sat down, opened the Christmas wrapping carefully, as she had taught him, so that the paper might be used again. Inside bound together with a rubber band were three blue pass-books gold-stamped "Moors Savings Bank." On the inside cover, each book had "John Montgomery King College Account" written in Amma's beautiful ornate script. Every page of each book was filled with entries of small deposits, usually weekly, going back for decades. He saw one entry for $2.13. The current total was $38,798.96. Kaye was amazed by the amount his grandmother had saved. All this from sunflower napkins, from pickled okra and willow baskets, all this from eighteen years of her resourceful labor.

Slowly he grinned. "…Damn!" He jumped up and kissed her, hugged her raucously. "Look at you, Grandma. Look at you."

"Don't be fooling with me." She freed herself from his embrace, pushed him back into his seat. "Kaye, you're already gonna get yourself into a good college. You did that on your own." She held the savings books up before him. "This gonna keep you there. Oh, I know, they all saying at Moors High how you'll get some scholarship. But they're the same ones said how the student with the highest grades was going to give that valedictorian talk at Gordon Junior and then they took that away from you, son, and gave it to a white girl. This way we don't even need them, no sir." She squeezed his hands in hers, his hands so much larger than hers now. "This is how you gonna fight for your mama." Tears lightened her amber eyes to gold.

"This is how you gonna win. You not going to end up a little cross tied with a rubber band lying in some shoebox."

Kaye couldn't swallow fast enough, so he swiped tears away with his fist, and Amma thought that it was just what he had done as a child because he'd never wanted to cry. "You know I love you, Grandma?"

She blew her nose in a handkerchief she took from the sweater's pocket. "Yes, I do."

He turned the radio to an Oldies station. Fats Domino was singing "My Blue Heaven," one of the songs Kaye's mother had taught him to dance by when he was six years old. He pulled his grandmother out of her chair and jitterbugged her around the table. "Yes, she does!"

She tried to pull away. "Kaye, Kaye, you stop it and turn that mess down!" The black Labrador Philly galloped into the kitchen, leaping and barking to join the dance. From the living room Tatlock yelled, "I'm trying to watch my program in here!" although he'd been fast asleep and the television wasn't even on.

Through the noise came the sound of someone knocking at the front door; Kaye two-stepped Amma, protesting, over to open it, as Philly jumped around them.

❊ ❊ ❊ ❊ ❊

Mrs. Tilden's dinner party had officially ended and Becky Van Buehling, the divorcée intended for Doctor Jack, had rushed away in order to make it home before her ex-husband returned their children as arranged by their lawyers. The minute Doctor Jack managed to get Mrs. Van Buehling's mink coat on over her immensely wide-shouldered red sequined dress, she'd hurried out into the rain, but before he could follow her, Mrs. Tilden had pulled him into the living room and sat him down beside the huge dazzling tree.

"What's Rockefeller Center doing without its tree?" he'd joked.

But Mrs. Tilden had no time for his humor. "Did you like Becky?" was all she wanted to know.

"I'll marry her tomorrow."

"Will you stop joking? Why does everybody think life's a joke? Life's not a joke."

At the same time Bud Tilden carefully (after three bourbons, five glasses of champagne, and two snifters of brandy) was making his way to the den to listen, while pasting the past into photo albums, to the record of Chopin piano music Noni had given him for Christmas.

At the same time, unnoticed, Noni raced, under her father's huge white golf umbrella, through the rain across the wide lawn between Heaven's Hill and Kaye's house to tell him the good news.

As soon as the kitchen door of Clayhome opened, it felt to Noni as if the celebration of what she'd come to announce had already started. "My Blue Heaven" played loudly on the radio. Kaye and Aunt Ma whirled about. So happy did Kaye look that Noni wondered if Jack Hurd had phoned him while she was walking across the lawn. "Merry Christmas!" she shouted.

Kaye pulled her into the circle with Amma, moved them both in a swing step across the kitchen floor.

"Do you know?" Noni shouted over the music.

Amma fought free of the young people and fell breathless into a chair while Kaye danced Noni around her in one of their old intricate shag combinations. "Know what?" he grinned. "What do I know? I know everything!" They knocked into the table, oranges and grapefruits rolling onto the floor.

"Did he already call you?"

"Who?"

Noni held Kaye with a fierce hug, tightly linking her arms behind his back. "You got a Roanoke Scholarship! Listen to me. You won the Roanoke, Kaye, you won it!"

Kaye stopped dancing, broke her embrace with his hands, backed her off so he could look at her. "...You're kidding?"

"No! Doctor Jack just told me. He found out early. It's true. He's sure." Noni turned to hug Amma. "He got a Roanoke, Aunt Ma. That's the best thing you can have at Haver. They pay everything, tuition, room, even your books and your food for the whole four years."

Amma stared from Noni to Kaye. "He got one of those?"

Noni explained how the Roanoke was a full four-year scholarship to Haver University, how there were only two awarded each year and that Dr. Jack Hurd, who knew someone on the committee, had told her that this year Kaye would be one of them. They would send him a letter on January 10 telling him so.

Kaye repeated, "You're kidding me?" Laughing, he dropped theatrically into the chair beside his grandmother. Then he nodded with the old childhood grin, quietly cursing in amazement.

Amma had opened one of the passbooks, was looking at the neat rows of figures, was seeing—Kaye knew—eighteen years of sewing, weaving, canning, and baking, eighteen years of smiling beside the doors of the bank. She said, "Now, that's, well, something, ain't it? They can give you all that in a letter, what I spent so many years piecing together." Neatly gathering together the three passbooks, she handed them to Kaye. "Honey, these are still yours."

"Grandma, Grandma, you know what these are for?" He waved the three blue bankbooks in front of her, kissed them one by one. "These are for medical school. For medical school! That's when you really need money. Not college, that's nothing! But the money it takes to go to medical school! And

money's what you got! You are a Mama Moneybucks!" He
flipped the bankbooks in her face like cards between his long
dexterous fingers. "Why, I'm going to learn everything in that
medical school. I'll make Grandpa Tat a new leg so amazing
you two'll be doing the Watusi at the Indigo." He rushed at her
chair, started tickling her in the sides. "I'll cut open your chest
and fix your heart so it will never stop working!"

Amma slapped at his hands, laughing. "There's nothing
the matter with my heart!"

He kept tickling her. "I know there's not. That's why I
want it to go on thumping away forever and ever and ever and
ever. Why, you listen, my operations'll be so famous they'll be
on TV, have their own show." He moved around behind her,
hugged her back and forth in her chair.

"That's the last thing I want to see, isn't that right, Noni?
Kaye cutting up some poor soul's heart and making jokes while
he do it?"

Noni took in everything—the Christmas paper, the gold
letters spelling Moors Savings Bank on the passbooks. She
bent on the other side of Kaye, embracing his grandmother.
"Oh, aren't we proud of him, Aunt Ma? Aren't we proud!"

"We sure are, honey."

Smiling at them, Kaye checked his watch, looked out the
window. The rain had slowed to drizzle. "Hey, Noni, come on.
Let's go to the Indigo and celebrate." He pulled on her hand as
if they were going right out the door that minute. She was suddenly strangely reminded of the first night in her bedroom, the
feel of his scratchy red mitten when he had pulled her to the
window to look at the snow. He was still holding her hand as he
said, "Now, here's an idea. Forget Curtis. Why don't you come
to Haver in the fall too? You know you'll get in. And believe me
you don't want to go to any school in downtown Philly. Believe
me that place is too hard for somebody like you, isn't that the
truth, Grandma?" He dropped Noni's hand to turn to Amma.

Amma laughed. "You talking about Philadelphia or that Indigo Club? I don't think she ought to go to either one." Indigo was a black dance club, a low, sprawling frame roadhouse on the old highway leading out of Moors. From the forties to the sixties, Indigo had had live bands, some of them good bands touring the South, and it had catered to hard-drinking, hard-dancing couples who dressed for the occasion; now it had disc jockeys and served beer to young locals and college students. Noni had never heard of it.

"I'd love to go," she said. "I just have to tell my folks."

Kaye rolled his eyes. "I wouldn't be asking them if you can go to the Indigo Club."

"How dumb do you think I am? I'll just say I'm going out."

Amma held up her remonstrating hand. "Noni, don't you be lying to your mama and daddy. Are y'all even old enough to go to the Indigo?"

Kaye told her they only had to be eighteen, which they now were.

Noni said, "Let's take my car."

Kaye pretended to look out the window. "Don't tell me that green Alfa Romeo belongs to you? That Spider? That's what your old pal Santy gave you for Christmas?"

She smiled, mimicking his flamboyantly crossed arms. "So? Santy just gave you a scholarship worth forty thousand dollars."

Tatlock Fairley rolled lumbering in his wheelchair into the kitchen, the old weakened floorboards trembling with his weight. He shoved himself over to his radio, turned it off, hugged the large metal box to his stomach. "Y'all all lost your damn minds? What's going on out here? Who got forty thousand dollars?"

Noni hurried to him as Amma slipped the bankbooks into her sweater pocket. "Oh, Uncle Tat, Kaye's won a scholarship that's going to pay every penny of his college education. He's a Roanoke Scholar."

"I'm a Forty Thousand Dollar Man!" laughed Kaye.

Tatlock's big dark head swayed in thoughtful assimilation of this news. "Good. 'Cause I got too many other things to worry 'bout to be paying Kaye's bills." Then he sighed. "They'd made me one of those Roanokes, I mighta had a chance to get somewhere. Wouldn't be long they'd be calling me 'Six Million Dollar Man,' much less Forty Thousand."

Noni kissed his wide gun-black cheek. "I bet they would, Uncle Tat."

Amma turned the wheelchair toward the living room, leaned over Tatlock's broad back, rubbed her chin in his shoulder. "Come on, Six Million. Let's us go to bed, let these young folks have their time."

He reached up his hand, cupped her face in it. "Had us ours, didn't we, Lady?"

"I guess we did." She leaned her face into his hand as she rolled the chair from the kitchen. "Y'all don't stay out too late. And be careful driving in that rain."

Together Noni and Kaye stood outside the door of Clay-home under her father's big white golf umbrella. Their hands entwined, she struggled to keep control of the umbrella handle but he wrestled it away, telling her she was too short and that she was holding it so his head kept getting caught in the spokes.

"Let us remember," she said oratorically. "That I was taller than you for a long, long time."

"I don't remember that."

Laughing, her arm through his, they ran together across the wet lawn to her new car, the green Alfa Romeo Spider. Noni slid into the passenger seat and gestured for Kaye to take the driver's, watching him as he quickly, appreciatively studied the instrument panel, the wood gear-shift knob, the leather-wrapped steering wheel. The key was in the ignition and Kaye started the engine. The sports car leapt forward.

"Kaye, what are you doing?"

"Hang on!"

They raced along the oval driveway, the white stones flying away under them, the little car cornering tightly as Kaye sped around the circle faster and faster, again and again.

"Last lap," he shouted. "We're in the lead!"

"Kaye, you're crazy!" But Noni was laughing.

He braked to a stop in front of the bright lights of Heaven's Hill and opened the car door for her with a grandiose bow, holding the umbrella over her. Just as they reached the porch steps, they heard another car crunching in the white stones up the slope of the driveway. It came floating over the curve and was caught in all the sparkling white Christmas lights strung in the dozens of crepe myrtles and tall Savannah hollies. Both Noni and Kaye recognized the blue GTO that Roland Hurd still drove.

"I thought you two broke up," Kaye said, closing the umbrella and stepping away from Noni's side.

"We did." She watched Roland run around the hood of his car, his Navy blazer pulled over his black curls.

"Noni. Hi, Noni. Noni, please, my dad got home and said you were here…listen, I've got to talk to you. I love you, baby, this is just crazy." Roland registered that she was standing there with Kaye. Distracted, he shook Kaye's hand. "Hi. Excuse me, but I really need to talk to Noni, okay? Excuse me." He reached for her hand, drew her across Kaye toward him.

Noni pulled away. "Kaye and I were just going out to the Indigo."

"The Indigo?" A twitch briefly decomposed Roland's regular features. "That roadhouse?"

Kaye shrugged. "Yeah, well, you know, I thought we'd go there first, get bombed, then maybe drop by an opium den, check out a whorehouse—" Kaye thought he heard a chuckle somewhere in the dark, but it certainly wasn't coming from Roland.

"Not funny, man." Roland's voice tightened in a low whisper. "Noni, please, please, just talk to me. You know anything I say, anything I do, it's 'cause I love you and need you. Please." He reached for her again and this time she didn't resist, although she kept her face toward Kaye. "Noni, just take a little drive with me. Just give me a few minutes. Come on, let me give you your birthday present."

Noni kept looking at Kaye.

Kaye thought he saw Roland pull a ring box from his blue blazer, squeeze it, jam it back in his pocket.

"Kaye?" Noni turned to him.

Kaye leaned against one of the porch's big white columns, shrugged. "No big deal. You guys go ahead. We'll do the Indigo some other night."

Noni was aware of too many feelings inside her and suddenly remembered a moment when she was a child and a bird flew through her window. The bird had panicked when it found itself trapped indoors and had hurled itself crazily at the walls. Amma had run into the room, thrown a blanket over the bird, then shaken it free outside the window. But there was no way to shake these feelings free now. She was glad to hear Roland say he was sorry and that he loved her, needed her. Wasn't it what she wanted, to be loved, needed?

But the thought of hurting Kaye by not celebrating his triumph with him was a hot pain in her throat. Yet maybe it was conceited of her to think Kaye cared whether she went to the Indigo with him or not. He had never invited her there or anywhere else for at least a year, and he almost always said no when she and Bunny asked him to go any place other than a political rally with them. He usually ignored her at school and he treated her most of the time with a casual irony that she took for affection, but perhaps she only did so because his irony had been in her life so long. He'd certainly never said he needed her, and probably he never would.

Roland pulled her hand to his cheek, kissed her palm. "This is the most important night of my life," he told her.

She turned again to Kaye. "If I got back in fifteen minutes, we could still go, okay?"

Kaye shook his head. "Let's make it some other time. I don't even know they're open on Christmas. Stay cool." He walked past them down the steps and around the GTO. The rain had stopped as suddenly as it had begun. He was halfway across the lawn when he heard the GTO doors shut and the tires crunching through the white stones, circling him, speeding down through the columns and into the night.

❉ ❉ ❉ ❉ ❉

Kaye was almost home when he realized he still had Noni's father's golf umbrella. Turning back, he ran to the porch of Heaven's Hill, leaned the white umbrella against the front door.

A voice softly called out of the dark. "You ever drink a Sazerac?"

Startled, Kaye peered into the dark, saw a shape in one of the green rocking chairs in the far corner of the long wide porch. It was Mr. Tilden, holding out to him a small crystal glass.

"Hey, Mr. Tilden, Merry Christmas." He pointed at Noni's green Alfa Romeo Spider parked where he'd left it in the driveway curve. "Nice car."

"Yeah, you two looked like you were having fun. But hey, it's a thing. The world's full of them."

"That just makes folks without money want them more."

"Oh, you'll have money, Kaye, and it won't make you happy. Just like they say. Merry Christmas. Taste this."

Kaye sipped the pleasantly bitter beverage. "Um hm."

"I've had the Sazeracs at Galatoire's, and this is a good one." Tilden had a wire golf basket filled with tennis balls on his lap and he suddenly threw one of them the length of the porch. It landed in the silver loving cup with his name on it that usually sat on a shelf above his stereo in the den. He threw another and it missed the cup, rolled under the rail and off the porch. Shrugging, he took back the drink. "Kaye. There was one thing that twenty years ago I was really excellent at. And that was throwing a ball through a fairly high net." He tossed another tennis ball; it dropped into the silver bowl. "Twenty-eight points in the national semifinals. You may think that's a silly thing to brag about, smart guy like you."

"No, it's a gift."

"You can marry a Gordon with it, that's for sure." He threw another ball into the bowl. "Well, now there're two things I do really well, Kaye. Mix drinks and tie a Windsor knot." Tilden pointed at the neat knot in his soft gold silk tie. "Some men go to the moon. Our pal Jack Hurd says I tie the best tie in Moors, North Carolina."

Kaye pointed at the drink. "Sazerac. So you up to 'S'?"

"Um hm." Tilden took a swallow. "Not looking forward to those Singapore Slings." He coughed, shivering in the cold damp in his white dress shirt.

"Why don't you skip 'em?" In the dark, Kaye sat down in the rocker beside Noni's father.

"Can't do that. Can't cheat." For a few years now, in addition to assembling photo albums, Bud Tilden had taken up the hobby of making his way methodically and alphabetically and daily through a comprehensive bartender's guide, drink by drink.

They sat together a while. Over the rise of Heaven's Hill, somebody set off fireworks. Clusters of blue and red sparks flew up into the night, then spilled away. Tilden took a bottle of aspirin from his pants pocket. "Kind of an early start on the New Year." He called out to the darkness, "What's your rush?!" He opened the cap of the pills with his teeth and almost choked on it. Kaye jumped from his rocker to help him just as the inebriated man spat out the plastic cap.

"You okay, Mr. T? Don't scare me like that."

"Fine. I'm fine. But if I wasn't, you'd be the guy I'd want." In a while, to his surprise Tilden added, "Got a girlfriend, Kaye?"

"Two or three," he answered. It was true.

Tilden shook a finger solemnly. "Two or three's the same as none. Take it from me."

Kaye worried that Bud Tilden was referring to his extra-marital affair with his secretary at the bank, about which Kaye had overheard his grandmother fretting to Grandpa Tat. His grandmother had said Mrs. Tilden and Noni had no idea about it.

To forestall any unwanted confession, Kaye took one of the tennis balls from the basket and tossed it at the silver bowl. It missed. Tilden put another ball in Kaye's hand, showed him carefully how to hold it, how to release it. Kaye tried again, still missed. Tilden showed him once more. This time Kaye's ball bounced into the silver trophy. "So, what you doing out here on the porch so late, Mr. Tilden?"

"Listening to the rain. Rain on a metal roof sounds pretty." The tall man pointed across the lawn at the copper roof of Clayhome.

Kaye did a loud drum roll with his fingers on the rocker's arm. "Not if your bed's less than a foot away from that metal."

Tilden leaned forward to look at Kaye, nodded apologetically about this unconsidered drawback. He tipped the rocker so far that he would have fallen out had Kaye not caught him and settled him back in the chair. "Birds too. Lot of night birds calling to each other out here if you just listen."

"Like owls?"

"Sure, owls. All kinds. Talking to each other, working things out."

"I saw this really nice letter in the Moors paper about birds working things out and why can't the human race. It was signed 'Night Owl.' Was that you?"

"That was me. You didn't think it was dumb?"

"It was great. I loved the way it ended with that Gandhi quote. 'Somebody asked Gandhi, "What do you think of Western Civilization?" And Gandhi said, "I think it would be a good idea."' Why didn't you sign your name to it?"

"You know who owns the *Moors Mercury Gazette*? My father-in-law."

"So what? What would he care?"

"Mr. R.W. Gordon likes Western Civilization just as it is. Well, just as it *was*. I think he really resents them freeing the slaves." Tilden tried to light a cigarette; his hands were shaking.

Kaye asked where Mrs. Tilden was, worried that she ought to get her husband out of the cold.

"Gone to sleep. Oh, about ten years ago. This'll amaze you, Kaye. When we got married we were in love. I sure was. First time I saw her she was swimming in a race at the Haver pool. She won. Beautiful stroke, just beautiful. But now she doesn't like me much. You notice that?"

Kaye felt uncomfortable with such personal talk. He offered his great news as a distraction. "I'm going to get a Roanoke Scholarship to Haver, Mr. T."

"You are? That's wonderful!" The man beside him reached over, pulled Kaye's head close, and surprisingly kissed him on the side of his face. "That's wonderful! Congratulations, Kaye. Jack'll go nuts! Noni too. You tell Noni?"

Kaye just nodded, not wanting to expose her, or Doctor Jack either, for releasing the news too soon, or for excluding Tilden from their happiness.

The tall man patted his knee. "Well, son, that's a start. That's a real start. You keep going."

"I'm going to."

"I bet." Noni's father sat silent for a while, drinking his cocktail. Finally he said, "She's the one thing in the world makes sense to me. Sometimes I think we're the only ones that get her, Kaye."

Kaye knew he meant his daughter Noni. "Um hm."

"The thing about Noni, if you thought of any situation and you imagined her in it, you could count on what she'd do. She'd do the good. Know what I mean by that?"

Kaye nodded. "But you got to include the good for yourself. You think she does that?"

Another long silence before Tilden asked, "You like Roland?"

Kaye thought about lying but decided not to. "No."

"He's probably okay. Don't you think?"

Kaye didn't reply.

"I want someone to love her who knows who she is, knows what they're getting."

Kaye didn't reply.

Finally Tilden sighed. "Sure. It's none of my business.... You play golf, Kaye?"

"Nope."

"This spring we'll play some, all right? I'll teach you. I'm not bad."

"That'd be great, Mr. T."

"Isn't your name John really?"

"John Montgomery King."

"That's what I thought. We've got the same name. You know my name's John, too? John Fitzgerald Tilden. But nobody ever called me anything but Bud."

"You're kidding? John Fitzgerald, like Kennedy?"

Tilden laughed. "Right, Fitzgerald was my mother's name. But, hell, maybe that's why Judy's stuck with me as long as she has. She was crazy about JFK."

Side by side on the dark porch the two rocked slowly back and forth, listening to the screek of their chairs, the soft fall of cold rain on the distant metal roof.

The Fifth Day of Christmas

❋

December 26, 1976
The Hope Chest

Noni was twenty years old and everyone said she was beautiful. The old rector, Dr. Fisher, said she was the most beautiful bride in the history of St. John's Episcopal, a history that was longer by ten years than that of the nation itself. And although Kaye would not smile at her, and although Noni's mother, on her knees arranging the train of the wedding gown (itself half-a-century old), quickly demurred that all brides were beautiful, Noni felt on this day that Dr. Fisher was absolutely right. She was beautiful in her grandmother's satin gown with its French lace and beaded pearls.

On either side of the choir stall the four small Christmas trees, completely bare of any decoration, looked perfect. The violins and trumpets were playing Purcell, and every pew was happily filled, everyone a sharer in today's love.

Except Kaye, who would not smile at her.

In the vestibule, Dr. Fisher was telling Noni that they had had some sad times together at St. John's. Nodding, Noni looked into the church. At the end of the center aisle was the gold-filigreed rail in front of which she had seen the coffins of the dead, most recently that of her maternal grandfather, the bank president R.W. Gordon, who had died of a stroke back in May. But this man had been so bad-tempered that Noni had cried at his funeral only because her mother had been crying; certainly not because she was going to miss a horrible old bigot who'd yanked at her hair and pinched her arms in an excess of affection whenever he went past her and who'd told her she was his favorite grandchild and that her brothers ought to be drowned, as if he'd thought she would happily agree that they should do away with her brothers.

For Noni, the only unbearable coffin had been the one draped with the American flag, her brother Gordon's, that rainy February afternoon eight long years ago. Gordon's coffin, that had buried so much of their family with it in the wet red ground.

Reverend Fisher was squeezing her hands. "But happy times, too, Noni?" Pointing at the worn white marble baptism font near the doors, he recounted once again how as a baby Noni had grabbed the baptismal candle right out of his hand when he'd held it up to her, telling her to behold the light of Christ. She didn't remember the moment, of course, but had always liked that adventurous image of herself snatching greedily for illumination.

Now she looked up the length of the church at that familiar nave, at the altar cushions on which she would soon kneel. When they were confirmed, she and her friend Bunny Breckenridge had knelt there, struggling not to giggle as the bishop pressed his hands fiercely onto their heads, crushing their garlands of daisies and pink sweetheart roses. Today, Bunny, the maid of honor, and all the bridesmaids made a bouquet of red roses in their crimson taffeta dresses. Today, Noni felt that she was like a white camellia at their center.

"Today," Dr. Fisher was saying as he kissed her on the head, "today will be the happiest day of all. I wouldn't have missed this day for the world. Now I can retire." Dr. Fisher was in fact retiring in the spring, to be replaced by a younger priest (practically handpicked by Judy Tilden, chair of the calling committee). But Dr. Fisher's step was bouncy today as he left Noni to join the groom.

A few minutes later he hurried out from the side vestry door to the front of the altar. Beside him stood the best man, a Haver University Kappa Delta whom Noni had never much liked. And then, into a paradise of red roses, stepped Roland Hurd, smiling, his eyes as blue as heaven, waiting for Noelle Katherine Tilden to come walking with her father up this aisle to him.

Today, two days after her birthday, the day after Christmas (Boxing Day, Mrs. Tilden liked to call it), St. John's was still festive with its holiday decorations and was now also luminous with hundreds of white candles glowing on banks of red roses and white camellias. Flowers and evergreens were heaped upon window ledges and choir stalls and edged along both sides of the aisle up which Noni was just about to walk with her father. Noni's mother had designed the wedding and chosen the day as an especially good date, not only for a wedding but also for a large wedding reception to follow, for everyone was home for the holidays and almost everyone at leisure. All Noni had picked was the music, and even then Mrs. Tilden had insisted on Mendelssohn's "Wedding March," which she felt was really the only appropriate piece of music to which a young woman should walk down a church aisle. The violin and cello were playing Fauré's Pavane as the last guests found their seats, and Noni was wondering if Kaye were listening to the violin, wondering if he ever wished he hadn't so long ago stopped playing that instrument himself.

Bud Tilden smiled at her. He was handsome in his gray cutaway and his smile was sweet, although a little sad. Noni's father lived alone now, in Algonquin Village, the new stucco condominiums near the new shopping mall. He and Noni's mother had separated. Last August, Mrs. Tilden had asked for the separation, after she'd found out about her husband's (actually long-ended) affair with his secretary, whom she'd mistaken for an ally, or at least a nonentity: the woman hadn't even been that attractive; her only asset was kindness. Or maybe, Noni thought, her mother had known all along about her father's affair, but had been waiting until after the woman had moved away from Moors (as the woman had done), or she'd been waiting for R.W. Gordon to die before taking any public step, fearing to risk his disapproval. She certainly had not told her father, or anyone else in Moors, about the affair, and in fact almost no one knew.

R.W. Gordon finally had died of a stroke, as everyone had impatiently predicted he would for decades, because of his apoplectic tirades. Most of his fits had been against blacks who didn't know their place—presumably slavery—and against the Supreme Court justices who had stirred them up, against hippies' hair and the draft-dodging socialists who'd destroyed Nixon, against women's-righters. (When Noni had first heard him use this phrase she had thought that it was women writers who had so enraged her grandfather, and she had asked him if he realized that George Eliot—whose *Silas Marner* he'd so preferred to "the crap being written today"—was a woman.)

In any case, three months after his father-in-law's death, Bud Tilden quietly moved out of Heaven's Hill, which Judy had inherited (conditionally). She had also acquired (conditionally) a great deal of bank stock (Moors Bank was now a branch of a large chain), and newspaper stock and rental properties and her mother's jewelry and her mother's trust fund. Judy Tilden was now a wealthy woman.

To Wade's dismay, the real surprise of the will had been how much Grandpa Gordon had left Noni. On Judy Tilden's death, Noni would inherit the furnishings of Heaven's Hill, as well as the use of the house and land itself during her lifetime, after which Heaven's Hill would go to any living male heir of her body. If Noni never married, the house and land would go to Noni's brother Wade or to any sons of his. As for Mr. Gordon's own house in the country, and its two hundred acres of rolling fields and riverbank, the bank president did leave that to Wade, with the terse instruction in his will, "Make something of it."

This house, named Abbotsford by Mr. Gordon (a fan of Sir Walter Scott), was a huge, ugly fake chateau with conical towers, mansard roofs, and Greek Revival porches; he had built it in 1950 for his wife, who hadn't liked it. But then, Judy Tilden's mother hadn't liked much of anything subsequent to the night when she'd danced with Charles Lindbergh at her debutante's ball. Wade Tilden had immediately moved into the house with his family and begun making something of it, by turning it into the centerpiece of a gated community he christened Gordon's Landing. With his new partner (Trisha's brother), Wade began dredging the river behind the house to build a marine landing for the luxury homes he planned to cluster about the two hundred acres. Wade's earlier subdivision, on which investors had lost a great deal of money when lawsuits forced them into bankruptcy, consisted of two streets of small cheap houses that looked as if they were going to fall apart, and which had done so. Gordon's Landing would be big, expensive houses that wouldn't look that way.

Wade had not spoken to his father since a fight in which he'd blamed Bud Tilden for breaking his mother's heart—to which charge Tilden had replied, "I don't want to be unfair to your mom. Why don't we say Life did the breaking? To both of us."

"Just shut up, Dad. You don't make sense."

"I have the same feeling, son. I'm sorry."

"Calling me son is a joke. You had one son, Gordon, and he's dead. Unless you're counting Kaye Wonder Boy King as number two."

"I'm sorry, Wade. I haven't been much help to you."

"You want to help? Stay out of our lives."

And Tilden had pretty much done that. For example, he no longer worked at the bank. The new president, from Dallas, had never watched Bud Tilden winning basketball games for Haver, much less been his father-in-law; he fired him after a few months of watching him wander around the new building, quietly talking to himself. But Tilden had always had many friends in Moors, recipients of his hospitality at Heaven's Hill. Three of those friends owned Algonquin Village. They had made him sales manager there and given him a very nice model condominium in which to live. Although he didn't like the condos, he actually did very well selling them. Not only were his manners lovely and his athletic fame lingering, but he seemed to care so little whether people bought the units or not that they assumed they would be getting fantastic deals if they did so.

Noni's father and her brother were both standing in the vestibule with her waiting to enter the church, but Wade was acting as if he'd never met Bud Tilden and never wanted to.

"Dearly beloved, we are gathered together here…"

As she waited, Noni kept saying these words like a prayer, over and over. "Dearly beloved. Gathered together." All her life it had felt as if she were trying to gather her beloveds together, trying to lift them all in her arms at once, as she'd done with her dolls when a child. That was the family story, this picture of little Noni struggling to carry all her dolls at once from place to place, leaving none behind, clutching a dozen or more under her arms and chin and to her chest. But her family had never seemed to realize that she was always trying to do the same thing with them—gather them together. All her life, she had been tugging on their hands to join them, pressing on their faces to make them smile. All her life, trying to please her mother, hiding the empty glasses that set her mother against her father. All her life, hiding Wade's lies, healing the loss of Gordon, making Kaye a sharer in her unearned bounty and privileges (beginning with the night that she'd written his name with hers, NOELLE AND KAYE, on her new sled).

The prayers she had prayed in this church, year by year, kneeling on these cushions, seated in these wood pews, came back to her now. Prayers to be of use, to be good, to be brave, to meet her mother's expectations, prayers for her father, for Gordon's life, for Wade's soul, prayers that Doctor Jack was right and that she could "save" Roland, prayers for the world to give Kaye all he deserved and didn't trust the world to give him.

If only Kaye smiled at her now, even if just for this one moment, then Noni could feel that she had finally managed it, that she had gathered all her dearly beloveds in her arms and had brought them together here, to this church, to this wedding on this day when she had finally, finally, succeeded in making her mother happy.

Noni peeked out from the vestibule and saw Aunt Ma on the bride's side, in a bright green dress, bent over the pew's back, praying. Nearby, a beaming Tatlock had stationed his wheel-chair under the Tiffany stained-glass window of a blue angel welcoming Noni's great-grandmother into heaven. Beside Uncle Tat, Kaye looked anything but welcoming. Dressed in black, head to foot, black tie, black shirt, black suit, Kaye was like a monument to grief in the midst of this celebration of love.

Noni and Kaye—of this she had no doubt—had been from the beginning of their relationship so attuned to each other that she knew that if she stared long and hard enough right now at the back of his head, he would turn around and look at her. She had done it before, had made him turn to her across the width of the Gordon Junior High auditorium, when they had announced the votes for the class presidency, when she had wanted Kaye to see in her face that she knew they had cheated him out of the election.

Finally Kaye did turn around in his pew at St. John's, but
when he saw her, the coldness of his face was chilling. It was
the same cold face he'd shown her a month ago, the night after
her bridal shower, when she had asked him, in tears, "Why are
you saying such horrible things?" And he'd told her.

✳ ✳ ✳ ✳ ✳

The wedding shower had been on Thanksgiving weekend.
Kaye was at Heaven's Hill that afternoon carrying away a half-
dozen boxes of food left over from the party. His grandmother
Amma had been helping him pack the surplus to take to the
soup kitchen at her church, but she had left Kaye to finish
alone, out of patience with his sarcasm about the wasted
cheeses, crudités, dips, patés, pastries, and cakes. Sarcasm like
"Who did those twelve skinny women expect to show up here
and help them wolf down all this junk—Bangladesh?" And
"Those two homeless potheads y'all are putting up at Redeemer
A.M.E. gonna love these little quiche Lorraines." And so on
until finally, pulling on her coat, Amma told him to load all the
boxes in his car himself and drive them to Redeemer because
she wasn't going to listen to any more of his mess.

Noni was in the yellow living room when she saw Kaye
walk through the front hall with a cardboard crate of soft-drink
bottles. She was sorting through her shower presents and stor-
ing some in the hope chest that had been carried down from
her bedroom. Friends and relations and friends of relations had
given her a great many pieces of china, crystal, gold, silver, and
linens, all of which had been suggested to them on a list prepared by Noni's mother and registered at the best department
stores. There was far too much for the small one-bedroom
apartment in which Roland and Noni would be living in
Princeton, so she was going to leave most of the gifts at home
until they moved into their first house.

Kaye stopped in the doorway. "Why don't you just pack your-self up in that hope chest too, lock it and throw away the key?"

On her knees on the Persian rug, surrounded by lingerie, sheets and tablecloths, candlesticks and coffeemakers, Noni looked up at his hostile face, then turned back to wrapping sil-ver salt and pepper shakers in their gray velvet bags.

"Why don't you stuff that piano—" He pointed at the black grand Steinway in front of the tall windows. "—In your hope chest too, 'cause you can bet your butt you can kiss that piano good-bye." (Because of her marriage, Noni had decided to take the spring term off from Curtis Institute of Music, where she had already completed almost half of her four-year program.) "Kiss that B.M. good-bye too. 'Cause B.M.'s exactly what that Bachelor of Music degree's turning into."

Noni stared at Kaye. He stared back, anger in his face, and she felt a tear on her cheek. Furious at herself for crying, she suddenly shouted at the top of her voice. "Why are you saying such horrible things?"

"'Cause I don't like what you're doing to my friend. And I don't like why you're doing it. Your mother's manipulated you, and Jack Hurd and his asshole son have manipulated you into this whole thing, and you don't even know it!"

She shouted again. "I'm just taking a goddamn term off! Two years ago you were *telling* me to go to Haver. That's where I'm going after I take one goddamn term off!"

"Oh sure," he nodded, juggling the crate onto his shoulder to open the front door. It was Noni's father's phrase, but in Kaye's mouth its irony was much sharper, quick and hurtful like a paper cut. "Maybe you'll graduate in time for your fifti-eth birthday," he called over his shoulder.

She yelled after him, "We can't all be king-shit from turd-ville genius Roanoke Scholars like you!" (By adding to his courses and going during the summers, Kaye had sped so quickly through Haver that he was already a senior and taking a graduate course at the medical school.) She ran after him into the hall. "We can't all grow up in ghettos and never know our dads."

"Right. That was so easy. Fuck you." He slammed the door. She opened the door behind him and shouted. "Go to hell, you conceited asshole!"

Noni's mother came running downstairs, expecting—she didn't know what—but some cataclysmic disaster, for Noni had never been known to scream curses in her life. Noni was the one in the family who didn't shout or fume; she was the peacemaker. So out of the ordinary was the shout that Mrs. Tilden feared that her daughter had for some horrible reason suddenly broken off her engagement to Roland Hurd, less than a month before their very large wedding. Or that Roland Hurd had broken it off for some embarrassing cause, maybe because of Mrs. Tilden's separation from her husband. The news that it was only a quarrel with Kaye King was a great relief.

In fact, despite the shock, it was a relief to Judy Tilden that Noni, in tears of rage, *was* quarreling with Kaye and had called him a "conceited asshole." For Mrs. Tilden had never stopped having those awful nightmares of a romance between her daughter and her maid's grandson. Indeed, her fear had actually been intensified by Kaye's academic accomplishments, in which she perversely also took a kind of family pride. So it was satisfying to hear that Noni was no longer blind to the young man's insufferable self-assurance. The way Kaye King behaved around Judy Tilden was not the way black people of any age had ever acted around her, much less one so young, and it was, to say the least, discomfiting.

For example, Mrs. Tilden had once gone out of her way to praise Kaye at the Moors High commencement, where he'd won so many plaques, cups, medals, and letters that the Fairleys were having to carry them home in shopping bags. When she'd walked across the gym lobby to offer her congratulations, Kaye had actually grinned at her with unmistakable mockery and said, "Yep, I'm Sidney Poitier all right and I guess if I get the Nobel Prize, you'll be Katherine Hepburn." She wasn't exactly sure what he meant, but she knew it wasn't flattering and, having seen *Guess Who's Coming to Dinner*, she was briefly and irrationally panicked that he meant he'd already secretly married Noni.

So, on this Thanksgiving occasion, having heard Noni curse Kaye, Mrs. Tilden offered up to her daughter the young man's earlier quote about Sidney Poitier, as a way of agreeing that Kaye was a, well, an a-hole, only to have Noni burst out, "Oh, Mom, he's giving you too much credit. I don't think even the Nobel Prize would do it for you."

And Noni had then run upstairs, leaving Mrs. Tilden to hope the next month would pass quickly, after which these strange volatile moods of her daughter's would be Roland's problem, not her own.

❋ ❋ ❋ ❋ ❋

In the vestibule of St. John's Church, Noni was thinking about that Thanksgiving scene, first the fight with Kaye, then the exchange with her mother. She was thinking that she hadn't practiced the piano much lately. No doubt the birthday present that Kaye had left at the house yesterday, a record set of Rubenstein playing piano concertos, was just his sarcastic way of scoring another point about how she'd sacrificed her music to Roland. Although she'd sent a note thanking Kaye for the gift, he hadn't acknowledged the cashmere sweater she'd given him. He hadn't spoken to her since the fight after the bridal shower.

The day of the shower had certainly not been the first time Kaye had claimed to know more about her than she knew herself. He'd done it from the first moment they'd met when he'd told her her own parents' first names and her own brother

Wade's secret vices, when he'd told her that she was getting the red sled for Christmas. Kaye always claimed to know more.

Their other really bad fight about Roland had taken place years earlier, the August of the year she'd graduated from Moors High. The fight had ended with Kaye's talking her out of her spur-of-the-moment decision to elope with Roland.

* * * * *

It was a day heavy with a wet heat that clung to her skin as she and Roland had sat by the pool at Heaven's Hill on a weekend when her parents were away in the mountains trying to save their own marriage. Finally he had worn her down with his persistence and she'd agreed to elope now so they could live together up at Princeton in the fall. As soon as he'd left to go home to pack, Noni had called Bunny Breckenridge and told her that she was driving to South Carolina with Roland, that they'd go to a justice of the peace and get married. Would Bunny come along on the drive and be her witness?

Bunny had shouted no, she would not, and had immediately called Kaye with the news, and Kaye had immediately come pounding on the door of Noni's bedroom at Heaven's Hill. It was the first time he'd been inside her bedroom since, as a child, he'd crawled through the window the night of the big snow. The room hadn't changed much in the decade since. The four-poster was still piled high with white-laced linen pillows and coverlets, and the vanity table was still crowded with framed photos, though now many of them were of Roland. Noni was sitting on her hope chest by the window looking out at the sycamore tree, fearing (although she would never admit this to Kaye) that she'd made a terrible mistake by letting Roland talk her into driving to Myrtle Beach to marry him. What was the matter with her that she couldn't bear to say "no" to anybody she cared about?

Kaye flung himself down on her little pink couch at the foot of her bed, shoving her suitcase aside, and yelling at her without any preamble that she was about to do a very stupid thing. Marrying Roland at all *ever* would be a stupid thing. But marrying him before she'd even *started* college, marrying him by running off to a cheap beach motel on a whim was monumentally, disgustingly, self-destructively idiotic!

There were only three possible reasons for Noni's moronic behavior, he said.

One, she was pregnant.

Two, she was trying to wiggle out of going to the Curtis Institute the following month because she was scared that she'd fail there.

Three, she was trying to spite her mother by frustrating Mrs. Tilden's dreams of a big wedding for her only daughter.

Emphatically, Noni denied these charges. She didn't at all think she'd fail at Curtis; she'd gotten over the worst of her stage fright about playing the piano in front of people when she'd realized (at her audition) that no one, not judges, not audiences, could ever make her feel any less adequate about her musical ability than her mother had.

Nor was she pregnant. Although she didn't tell Kaye this, she'd briefly thought she might be, but she wasn't.

Arms crossed, ironic, Kaye nodded at her. "So it's three. You're just eloping to spite your mama? Don't give her a big wedding? Show her you're not scared of her?"

She yelled back, "I'm *not* scared of my mother."

"You're scared of letting her down. Just like you're scared of letting Jack Hurd down and letting Roland down." Kaye reached over to the vanity and grabbed a picture of Roland and his father taken with Noni and her parents; they were all wearing tennis clothes and having lunch outside by the courts. "If they asked you to jump off a building for them, would you do it?"

Noni was startled because she'd just been asking herself why it was so hard not to do what people asked her to do. She didn't want to admit this, so she said, "Why are you turning on Doctor Jack after he's been so good to you?"

"He's not being good to *you*, conning you into thinking you're going to save his son for him."

Noni jumped up from the hope chest and snatched the picture back from Kaye. "You're crazy."

"You're chicken."

Noni started to argue with him but suddenly fell silent. Kaye was annoyingly right. She *was* scared. In fact, in the last year nearly everything had begun to feel scary to her. Except, strangely enough, Kaye himself. Kaye didn't scare her. Despite his boasts of how he'd frightened her that first night of the snowstorm, he hadn't scared her then, he didn't scare her now.

Then, as Noni looked at him, sitting there on her pink couch, suddenly he grinned at her and crossed his eyes. And despite herself, she started laughing.

Everything but the laughter left her body—the tension, anger, dread. That was it. She could laugh with Kaye. And she could shout at him, too. And he was the only one. She trusted Kaye with her laugh and her anger, and she always had.

Noni told Kaye that maybe he was right; maybe she *had* wanted to thwart her mother's chance for a big wedding. Maybe, if her mother wasn't even going to keep her own marriage together, Noni had asked herself why she should have to fulfill her mother's social dreams?

Kaye nodded. Then he suggested that maybe she'd had the exact opposite hope. Maybe her eloping was a weird way of trying to make her parents' marriage hold together because she couldn't stand the thought of her dad's being unhappy.

As Noni was absorbing this idea, tears starting again, the young black man suddenly stood up in the middle of her bedroom, grabbed her suitcase off the couch, and flung it over his

head so that all her clothes flew out in the air. Brushing off
underwear and nightgowns that had landed on him, he started
to laugh, and his laughter started her laughing again. Then
Noni ran to Kaye and hugged him, and then she started to cry
with her head pressed into his shoulder.

"You are such a crybaby." He patted her mockingly on the
top of the head. "Poor, poor little crybaby."

"Oh, shut up, Kaye."

He handed her the box of tissues on her vanity table.
"Blow your nose. So tell me ten things you're scared of." And
he sat down on her hope chest to listen. "I bet you're scared of
ten things for every one that I'm scared of."

She said she was scared of what people said to her or
didn't, of what she said or didn't, of her own body, the cars
around her on the road, standard tests, the weather, ghosts,
noises, animals, Roland's moods, everyone's anger and unhap-
piness, of the way her mother treated her father and the way
her father ignored it and poured another drink.

"Stop, that's more than ten."

"Tell me one thing you're scared of, Mr. Perfect."

"Werewolves. You scared of werewolves?"

She laughed. "No."

"You're scared of ghosts but you're not scared of werewolves?
Man, there's a full moon, I want you to walk me home. Deal?"

Noni wiped her eyes with a tissue. "I'll think about it."

"You think about it."

Then Kaye, with his typical, outrageous appropriation of
control, closed her empty suitcase and slid it under her bed.
Passing her vanity, he saw the old silver chain with its dime
heart that he'd given her long ago (the heart with its message,
"Reach out, I'll be there") now hung from a knob of the mirror.

He tapped the chain so the little silver heart swung back
and forth. "You should have called me. That's the point. Reach
out, I'll be there."

"I should have."

"But I figured you called Bunny to get her to get me to come over here and stop you. Now, go eat some spinach. You're so pale, if you were lying around naked in the snow, you'd be hard to find."

"Yeah, right, I'm going to be lying around naked in the snow."

"It wouldn't be any dumber than eloping with Roland Hurd."

An hour later when the phone rang, Noni told Roland that she'd changed her mind and didn't want to elope.

* * * * *

On her wedding day, Noni wore Kaye's silver heart around her neck. It was the something old she wore. Her shoes were new. Her prayer book was one she had borrowed from Bunny. Her little sapphire earrings, her birthday gift from her father, were blue.

Noni's bridesmaids gathered around her with their bouquets of roses and camellias floating red silk ribbons over their white-gloved hands, and she was glad that she could no longer see Kaye's angry face. Wade's wife Trisha hurried to part the bridesmaids so that Wade could escort Mrs. Tilden to her seat in the front pew. "Let's go, Grandma Judy," Trisha said.

Mrs. Tilden didn't really like being called a grandmother, but she was too happy today to let it bother her. She looked beautiful in pale rose silk and dark rose hat and ropes of perfect pearls that would come to Noni someday, just as the wedding gown had come to her. Noni's mother kissed her daughter and told her how happy Noni had made her; she even kissed Noni's father on the cheek, but she didn't look at him when she did it.

Suddenly Wade snarled at his father, whom he had ignored until now. "Just try to keep it together, okay?" Actually Bud

Tilden looked so perfectly together that he could have been the handsome mannequin in the window of a formal shop.

The music changed, and it was time to begin. Wade's wife gathered the ring bearer and flower girls. And although Noni's mother (even at the moment when Wade was trying to walk her down the aisle) whispered to his four-year-old daughter Michelle, "Now make a good impression, honey," as she straightened the child's sashes and fluffed the rose petals in her basket—even that phrase, echoing down Noni's own childhood, could not ruin this day.

With hushed giggles, two by two the bridesmaids streamed like flowers from the vestibule into the aisle behind the ring bearer, Roland's sister's son. Wade's wife hastened those in the procession who were too slow, held back the too eager. Two by two the bridesmaids floated into the church. Noni quickly retied the undone sash on the gown that was almost too small for Bunny, her still plump maid of honor.

Bunny embraced her. "You look so beautiful," she whispered and for once Noni accepted that it was true. "I'm going to miss you so much."

Miss me? Noni didn't know what Bunny meant. In fact, by marrying Roland she would soon be much closer to home than Bunny herself, who went to college at Mount Holyoke, all the way up in Massachusetts, whereas Noni would be back in Moors, or at least in the next town over, by the following summer. For Roland was a senior at Princeton, and they would be coming home so that he could attend business school at nearby Haver University in the fall. Noni, midway through her sophomore year at the Curtis Institute of Music, would transfer to Haver herself. But was that so horrible? Wouldn't she still be studying music when she returned to Moors, wouldn't she finish her degree? What did Bunny mean, I'll miss you? How could Kaye tell her, I don't like what you're doing to my friend? Shouldn't they have faith in her, hope for her?

Now the trumpet and the organ played the opening chords of the Mendelssohn "Wedding March."

"Ms. Tilden, I love you." Her father held out his arm. "May I have the honor?" He kissed her nose, the old familiar woody smell of his bourbon absent today, his gift to her, for his face was pale, his hand trembling as he touched the hand she placed on his arm. Ms. Tilden? Not Princess. He had never called her Ms. Tilden before. For the first time he had called her by a name she would give away when they reached the altar.

Together they started down the aisle, her arms chilled, her face warm. Everyone was standing, everyone was gathered together. Her mother was smiling. At the front of the church, next to Dr. Fisher, Roland shifted from foot to foot, like a bored handsome thoroughbred. But he smiled too, urging her forward.

There on the groom's side was Noni's godfather, Dr. Jack Hurd, Roland's father, who had wanted for so long that she should marry Roland. He was seated next to his ex-wife and her new husband the dentist. Doctor Jack wore a blue velvet embroidered waistcoat with his suit and still kept his silvery hair in a short ponytail, although he was now Dean of the Medical School.

There, in a red silk suit jacket open to the red lace of her bra, was Noni's mother's cousin Becky Van Buehling, who was no longer dating Doctor Jack but was engaged to her estate planner.

There was Wade with his wife Trisha, both tense because their four-year-old daughter Michelle was throwing rose petals at the guests in their pews.

There sat Aunt Ma and Uncle Tatlock, even though Wade had tried to stop Noni from inviting them. "I don't see why we have to have the maid's family at your wedding."

Noni had actually wanted to respond, "I don't see why we have to have *you*." But she hadn't said it. When she was a baby, Wade had played with her. When she was a toddler, he had let her follow him around. He had been in her world from her birth. If she couldn't love her own brother, her only surviving brother, how, she thought, was she going to come anywhere near doing those hard, those impossible, acts of love Christ asked of us, remarkably proposing that we be as perfect as God? "For if ye love them which love you, what reward have ye?" When Dr. Fisher had read that passage out in church, Noni had felt a shiver of guilt about Wade. Not that she could honestly say that she had ever felt much love coming from him in the last ten years or so, but maybe it was her own failure, maybe she shut him out. When she'd been five, he had pulled her around the driveway in his wagon. That must have been love.

Noni glanced over at the new stained glass window, purchased to replace the one that had been broken last summer by vandals; Mrs. Tilden had just given it to St. John's in simultaneous honor of her son Gordon Tilden and her father R.W. Gordon. The window showed Christ benevolently patting on the head a small boy, one of the little children suffered to come unto Him. Noni found the choice ironic, since Gordon had to be physically forced anywhere near the vicinity of his grandfather, and had once told her that as a child he'd always worn a baseball cap around the old bank president to forestall the man's rubbing his knuckles into his grandson's crewcut hair.

Walking down the aisle, Noni glanced over at Kaye. His eyes were on her and she looked straight at him, kept looking, slowed down as she passed, pulling back slightly on her father's arm, so that she could keep seeing Kaye, keep willing him to look at the love in her face, keep willing him to show her that he wanted her to be happy.

"Come on, Kaye," her father startled her by whispering. Looking up, Noni saw that her father was staring straight at Kaye, too.

Noni kept smiling at Kaye. And then suddenly she crossed her eyes at him. And just before Kaye passed out of her view, suddenly, undeniably, she saw that he couldn't stop himself and was grinning back at her.

Dearly beloved, we are gathered together here in the sight of God, and in the face of this company, to join together this Man and this Woman in Holy Matrimony.

Noni and her father stood in the nave with the flower girls and bridesmaids, the best man and groom. Noni felt her father loosening his hand over hers and suddenly she wanted everything to stop, to reverse steps like a waltz he had taught her, to go backwards into the vestibule, back in time to last month, last year, back to her childhood when she was only a Princess. She held tighter to her father's arm. Everything was floating quietly in a bank of red roses. Dr. Fisher was talking, and then Roland said, "I will."

Now the minister was calling her name "Noelle," and she rushed back into the present. "…Comfort him, honor, and keep him in sickness and in health; and, forsaking all others, keep thee only unto him, so long as ye both shall live?"

"I will."

"Who giveth this Woman to be married to this Man?" Dr. Fisher looked around the church as if he didn't already know the answer. Bud Tilden placed Noni's right hand in Roland's. Then he kissed her cheek, and then he was gone.

And then Noni was making a vow, trembling with its solemnity, her unguarded earnest eyes searching Roland's blue ones, pledging all that she was to him. "I, Noelle, take thee Roland to be my wedded Husband, to have and to hold from this day forward, for better for worse, for richer for poorer, in sickness and in health, to love and to cherish, 'til death us do part…."

Bunny handed her the gold ring and it slid perfectly, just as they'd rehearsed, onto Roland's fourth finger. His fingers were

big and square, and it was very disconcerting to Noni that
looking at Roland's hands in the middle of her wedding she
should suddenly think of her hand touching Kaye's fingers as
he pressed in place the blue pieces of the broken Chinese jar,
his long brown slender precise fingers trying to help her gather
the pieces and put the jar back together.

Dr. Fisher tied her hand to Roland's in the white silk stole
and said to everyone that she and her husband could not be
put asunder, that he could not be left behind, that she could
not fall like a doll from the gathering arms of the beloved, who
now kissed her, and Noni hoped that everything Dr. Fisher said
turned out to be true.

❋   ❋   ❋   ❋   ❋

—No, you throw them away. Disposable. Wait, it
won't be long, everything'll be disposable. Just
like my last husband.—
—Oh Becky, stop it!…Wasn't Noni beautiful?—

—Okay, Wade, you tell me how we can walk
around on the moon but we can't make eighteen-
and-a-half minutes disappear off a damn tape
machine without the whole country finding out
about it.—
—It's the damn press. I'm telling you, Roland, buy
the press. That's where we ought to be putting our
campaign money. Buy the press.—

—Everybody, everybody! Noni's going to dance
with her Daddy now. Trisha, where's that photog-
rapher? Get him over here. Honey, be careful that
Daddy's shoe doesn't catch in your hem.—

—God rest you merry, gentlemen! Peace on
Earth, ladies!—

The reception at Heaven's Hill was hosted by Bud Tilden,
even though he no longer officially lived here—a fact that was
not generally known beyond the inner circle of Moors society.
Mrs. Tilden felt that since her (presumably soon to be ex-) husband (although she had taken no steps to divorce him) would
be necessarily a part of Noni's wedding, he might as well serve
the punch as he had always done at their Christmas Open
House, which a dinner reception for two hundred was replac-
ing this year.

Heaven's Hill looked as if a Renaissance war was about to
start on its lawn, where three enormous white tents flew red
banners. The tents were resplendent with holly balls and pine
garlands and each tent had its own dazzling Christmas tree.
Fortunately the tents were heated, since the temperature—
guaranteed by the weather report to be in the sixties—had
plunged thirty degrees, a breach of promise that had incensed
Mrs. Tilden against both God and the local news. But the special heaters worked wonders; so did the fifty cases of champagne and the twenty tables of hot catered food and the band
that made up in tempo what it lacked in skill. Drinking, dancing, eating, everyone stayed warm.

Noni's father was trying to keep up a cheerful appearance.
He joked that, thanks to the speed of the band, their father-
daughter dance had been more of a fox-gallop than a fox-trot.
As he returned her to Roland, he joked that the song they'd
danced to, "Love Will Keep Us Together," had said the
opposite of what was going to happen, hadn't it? Love—her
marriage to Roland—was going to keep the Princess and her
father apart.

"No it's not, Daddy. I'll come see you all the time."

"Oh sure." He kissed her cheek and that was the last time
she saw him at the party.

After Bud Tilden (hoping for the best) watched his daughter dance with her new husband, he walked over to find the Fairleys, to offer to roll Tatlock across the lawn in his wheelchair whenever he and Amma were ready to go.

Tatlock had been having a wonderful time drinking champagne, eating jumbo shrimp by the dozen, and having conversations with a variety of guests, including two lawyers with whom he had discussed possible legal cases against the V.A. hospital (for amputating his leg) and against Algonquin Village Condos (for stealing his ancestral home). But Amma was tired. The Fairleys and Kaye had been the only black guests at the reception, and that hadn't felt very comfortable. Plus, it had been wearing to worry about Noni, about Kaye, about Bud and Judy Tilden, about the mess the caterers were making of her kitchen at Heaven's Hill and the slowness of their service and the mediocrity of their cooking. She wanted to go home and go to bed.

—Kaye, you avoiding me?—
—Kind of am, Dr. Hurd. Sorry.—
—What's the problem?—
—It's a little personal.—

—Everybody, everybody! Noni and Roland are going to cut the cake now. No, honey, cut from here first.—

—Peace on Earth, Bunny! Hey, listen, you're the economist. How can we be in a recession and an inflation at the same time? —
—I'd tell you, Mister Tilden, but if I don't go take off these shoes, they'll have to use a blowtorch on them.—

Bud Tilden was about to leave too, when he saw Noni walk over to where Kaye was standing alone beside one of the Christmas trees decorating the tent. Noni was clearly asking him to dance with her—a fast dance. At first Kaye appeared to resist her, but finally Noni pulled him by the hand onto the floor. They spun and turned faster and faster, beautifully together, so smoothly together that they might have been dancing on ice. Noni was smiling and then she was laughing the way she had once laughed as a little baby; Tilden remembered how Noni's baby smile had turned the whole world to sunshine.

He noticed that Kaye almost never looked back at Noni as they turned and stepped in the complicated patterns they seemed to know so well. And then when the song ended, Kaye simply walked away from her and she stood there alone in the beautiful white satin dress, watching him go. Tilden stepped forward to go to her, but then his little granddaughter Michelle ran over to her, and Noni leaned sweetly down and picked up her niece and danced her around the floor.

Tilden felt suddenly so tired he had to sit down in one of the little white wooden chairs with their white satin bows. He wanted to go home and listen to his old records. Today, for Noni's sake, he had been without alcohol longer than at any time in the past twenty years, and he didn't like the feeling.

He was terrified that his daughter had married the wrong man. Why hadn't he helped her say no, why hadn't he done more? How sad to think he had failed her, failed them all, would go on failing them, how sad. Tilden lit a cigarette, reached for an opened bottle of champagne on the table beside him, poured himself a glass.

—Hey, I'm with you, Wade. Why bomb Cambodia, why bomb Laos, whoever heard of them? Let's bomb the damn Arabs next time they cut off

our oil! Thirty-five cents a gallon one day and it
doubles the next!—
—You being sarcastic, Dr. Hurd? Because I seriously don't want a fifty-five mile-an-hour speed
limit.—
—No, I'm seriously with you, Wade! Hell, I go
fifty-five miles an hour in my own driveway!—

—Everybody, everybody! Noni's going to throw
her garter now. No, honey, turn around and throw
it over your shoulder. —

Wade and his wife Trisha wanted to go home because
they'd been insulted. Their exhausted, over-stimulated daughter had had a temper tantrum, and Trisha had heard Bunny
Breckenridge say that the child looked like something out of
The Exorcist.

—Oh, Judy, I thought that was a sex thing, the
Peter Principle, like fear of flying. You know, you
keep getting guys with bigger and bigger ones
until you can't—
—Becky, if I ever thought you meant a word you
say, I'd, well, I just don't know what I'd do.—

—Roland, do you know how lucky you are?—
—'Course I do, Dad. Take it easy.—

—Everybody, everybody! Noni's going to throw
the bouquet now. No, honey, wait, let the girls get
in position. Where in the world is Bunny, doesn't
she want to get married next?!—

Roland wanted to go, not home, but to the airport so that

he and his new bride could fly to St. John's, to the Bitter End Yacht Club, and sit on the beach and drink champagne. (Drinking champagne was what Roland was doing at the moment, in fact he could barely walk, and Noni could scarcely understand what he was saying about how they would soon be drinking champagne on the patio of their tropical honeymoon cottage.) He hummed in Noni's ear as they danced in the huge heated tent: "They long to be dah dah de de close to you."

She was thinking that all she had to do was figure out how to make Roland so happy that he wouldn't need that extra drink. Her mother hadn't figured it out because she hadn't loved Bud Tilden enough. But Noni had enough love to save Roland, didn't she?

> —Everybody! Everybody! Noni and Roland are leaving now!—
> —Merry Christmas! Happy New Year!—
> —Congratulations!—

Kaye didn't want to go home because he didn't want to think about the day, didn't want to sort out his feelings about Noni's marrying Roland. He decided that instead he would go back to campus, to the medical school where he had a friend who worked nights in one of the autopsy labs. Dissecting bodies didn't bother Kaye at all; he liked it. But dissecting his response to Noni's marriage, pulling back layers of his emotional skin and muscle, probing nerves, that prospect was so daunting that, rather than begin it, he told himself, as he'd told Bunny Breckenridge a few minutes earlier, that he didn't care.

"It's nothing to do with me," he'd told Bunny. "Okay, it's a little worrying our friend just married a jerk, that's all, no big deal."

"Talk about jerks," Bunny had said and left him standing at the center of the tent, staring at the sparkling Christmas tree.

Now he heard the motor and the tires of the limousine on the pebbled drive as Noni was driven away with Roland. Suddenly, that wave that Kaye dreaded came out of nowhere and knocked him down and he couldn't pretend everything was fine.

Mrs. Tilden suddenly appeared beside him and put her hand on his arm. It struck him that she had never touched him before. Kaye noticed that she still wore both her engagement diamond and her wedding ring although she had moved Bud Tilden out of her house. "Merry Christmas," she told him. "And thank you for coming, Montgomery. You've always been a special friend to Noni and you must be so glad to see her looking so happy and so in love."

"I hope so." Kaye kept looking down at the woman's hand until she removed it.

"Hope so? We are all just crazy about Roland."

"Are you?" He said this in that unsettling matter-of-fact way that so infuriated Mrs. Tilden—as if he were deliberately but unprovably accusing her of lying. Once, years ago, she had told him to take down an antiwar banner he'd hung from a Clayhome window—which was, after all, her property— because the banner was an insult to her son Gordon who had chosen to fight for his country. In just the same way, Kaye had responded, "Did he?"

He said it again now. "Are you? All of you are crazy about Roland?" And he walked away from her.

But, a flush rising in her pale freckled face, Mrs. Tilden followed Kaye to the edge of the tent where she silently handed him the small piece of wedding cake she carried. Then she smiled. "Would you like some wedding cake? To remember the day."

He looked into her eyes and kept looking. Mrs. Tilden's pale blue eyes were at the same time desperate and triumphant and cruel.

"No, thank you," he said. "I'll remember the day."

Kaye walked off into the dark with the walk Noni used to call his "Philly strut," walked out of the heated wedding tent and across the cold winter lawn of Heaven's Hill.

The Sixth Day of Christmas

❆

December 25, 1979
The Silver Trophy

Nineteen seventy-nine was a hard year for everyone.

Hard on Noni's mother. Only three years since their wedding and Noni had already left Roland Hurd. That was a shock to Mrs. Tilden, although she remained confident that she and Doctor Jack could persuade her daughter to return to her husband.

Bud Tilden's recent heart attack was also a shock, especially hearing about it not from Bud himself but from Kaye King, who'd happened to see Noni's father being discharged from the hospital. Kaye drove him home to Algonquin Village, and then came to Heaven's Hill to tell them about it.

The heart attack was apparently mild, but Mrs. Tilden nevertheless was flooded with the commiseration of her friends, who emphasized how easily she might have lost Bud forever. While it could be said that, having evicted him from their home three years earlier, Bud Tilden was already lost to her, he was still legally and socially her husband, and all the public sympathy she received actually made Mrs. Tilden feel as if his death would have been a devastating blow. She didn't ask him to move back in, but she didn't proceed with the divorce either.

Having left Roland, Noni was staying at Heaven's Hill, which never seemed to change, no matter who came or went. The married Noni's room looked much the same as it had when she was a child there. So did the married Wade's room (of course the hidden drug paraphernalia and pornographic magazines were gone). Even the long dead Gordon's room hadn't changed. Nor had Bud Tilden's den, except that all his records of the old timers singing sadly about love had been replaced on the shelves by his wife's collection of mechanical music boxes, and all his matched sets of the Great Books were also gone. But his vinyl photo albums were still there—thirty-five of them—as if he'd done an album for each year of his and his wife's married life, except that every album was as randomly helter-skelter as the first had been.

Sometimes Mrs. Tilden thought she would make it her project to tear out all the photos, programs, tickets, and souvenirs, and put them in chronological order, beginning with the old sepia daguerreotypes of nineteenth-century Gordons picnicking in Tuscany in top hats and lace umbrellas, and ending with little Michelle's seventh birthday party at Disney world.

But the task overwhelmed her; each page was like a disjointed nightmare into which it exhausted her to try to read meaning. For example, on the last page of the last album her husband had glued all the photos of Judy Tilden herself, had pasted her life into a chaotic jumble—Judy in a wedding dress, Brownies uniform, baby-doll pajamas, cap and gown, poodle skirt, horse-show outfit, swimsuit with a racing number, Givenchy strapless formal, bathrobe when she'd been too depressed after Gordon died even to put her clothes on, and in the middle of them all, her earliest naked baby picture, lying helpless on her back like a turtle.

Bud Tilden had taken only books and records with him when he left, not these albums nor his basketball trophies, which still filled the same shelves, just as the same family

Christmas ornaments crowded the branches of the enormous spruce tree. Just as the same five red stockings hung by brass holders on the living room mantle and were still beautifully embroidered with the words BUD, JUDY, GORDON, WADE, NOELLE.

Judy Tilden had never discussed tough times with her maid, but 1979 had been hard on Amma Fairley, too.

Amma's daughter Deborah, Kaye's mother, had died the previous summer from a rapidly critical pneumonia. On Kaye's last visit, shortly before her death, his mother had been well but tired and withdrawn; he couldn't persuade her even to discuss leaving her sister Hope's house and moving down to North Carolina where Kaye could help care for her. Two months later she was in the hospital; after three days there she was dead.

Kaye flew with Amma to Philadelphia where he caused a scene at the hospital, accusing the staff of homicidal negligence and threatening a lawsuit. But in his heart he thought his mother had just given up fighting. And fighting had always been her reason for living.

He brought her ashes back South and put some in a small alabaster case in the shoebox called "The Promised Land." The rest he drove to Alabama where he sprinkled them off the Edmund Pettus Bridge in Selma; it was from that city that Deborah King had been so proud to march with Dr. King to Montgomery. Kaye watched her ashes float down into the river from the middle of the bridge where Alabama state troopers had long ago beaten Selma marchers with clubs and the world had seen them do it. Kaye let himself cry because no one could hear him. People in cars rushing by stared at the man on the bridge, but they couldn't see his tears.

While in Alabama, Kaye attempted to locate his father through the one photograph he had of the young protest marcher. He wasn't successful, but he hired a private investigator to continue the search.

In the autumn, Kaye had a call from the investigator telling him that his father's name was Joe Wesley, that he'd been drafted and that he had died in an ambush in the Mekong Delta. He'd been twenty-five, which meant he'd been only seventeen or eighteen when he'd fathered Kaye. The man returned the photograph, which Kaye put with his mother's ashes in the shoebox.

Amma's other daughter Hope and Hope's family left Philadelphia and moved to California, looking for work. Amma never saw them.

At home, Amma had been having troubles with Tatlock as well. Warned by his V.A. doctor for years about the dangers of his diet, he still blamed that doctor when he lost his other leg to diabetes. His convalescence was long and cantankerous. Amma's own medical bills, for she had to have cataract surgery, had forced her to borrow from Kaye's savings. (It had never occurred to Judy Tilden to provide Amma—who had worked for her family for almost half a century—with health insurance or social security or even a week's paid vacation.)

When the Fairleys' old Dodge gave out for good, Amma said she was starting to feel about the same. Even with the furnace heat in Clayhome turned down to fifty-two, she couldn't pay the bills. In a single year, oil prices had gone up 50 percent and inflation in the U.S. was high. For warmth, Amma kept a fire going with wood that two of her brothers had split for her from fallen oak and pine trees in the forests of Heaven's Hill. When Wade Tilden heard what they were doing, he told his mother that she ought to charge Amma for the wood—firewood cost a hundred fifty dollars a cord—but Mrs. Tilden wondered what people would think if she did that to her Aunt Ma after all these years. Noni said she was stunned that Wade would even *think* of it, much less say it.

Noni had had a miscarriage in the spring.

Nineteen seventy-nine was a hard year on everyone.

❋ ❋ ❋ ❋ ❋

On Christmas Day, smoke floated up out of the chimney of Clayhome and mixed with snow floating down.

From Tatlock's bass to a grandchild's treble, a dozen voices sang "Happy Birthday, dear Kayyy-yuh, Happy Birthday to you."

When the Clayhome door opened, the song reached Noni as she crossed the white lawn, pulling her niece Michelle on the red sled. She saw Kaye's old friend Parker retrieving an ice cooler from under the house's eaves. It was the first she'd known that Parker had been released from Dollard Prison. This had been his second stay there in seven years; he'd been sent back for violating parole after his first incarceration. Parker was a Muslim now and wore an embroidered fez. Years of weightlifting in prison had changed his once skinny body into bulky, oddly bunched muscles as if he'd been injected with plastic that had hardened in clumps.

Noni waved at Parker and he shouted back, "Hey there, Disco Lady!" (Years ago, she had gone to a party that Kaye had given at the Indigo Club. There she'd done the Hustle with Parker, who ever since had called her Disco Lady, or Disco Duchess, or some variation thereof.)

"Merry Christmas!" she shouted.

He pointed at the sky. "Snow!" He tilted his head back, stuck his tongue out, and caught snowflakes as they flurried around him. "Free and snow! Life is good!"

Last week, the week before Christmas, it had snowed four inches and hadn't melted. Now it had started snowing again, on Christmas Day, for the first time since 1963. But this wasn't the soft wet thick snow of that memorable storm when drifts had reached two feet high. These were sharp icy little mean snowflakes that bit at the face and lay in a thin sheet on the ground. Noni was outside, with her long scarf wrapped to her nose, pulling the bundled seven-year-old Michelle across the driveway on her old sled, which she'd found behind some stored porch windows. Noni was baby-sitting Michelle for a week and they were going to take a sled ride down the hill. An ardent aunt, she was happy to care for the child. Nor did she have any other particular plans that would interfere.

Noni had promised Roland and her mother not to file for divorce quickly but to "think about it" a while. In fact, she was trying not to think about it.

"Please, please, please listen to Judy," Roland had begged; "Judy" was what he called Mrs. Tilden, his best ally. "Promise me you won't do anything crazy, Noni. You know I love you." Then Roland had flown off to Houston to train with a large commercial real estate corporation there.

Their marriage had lasted only twenty-seven months before the separation—long enough to put an end to Noni's graduating from Haver: complications from the miscarriage had kept her in the hospital during her spring senior term. But not nearly long enough, according to Noni's mother, before her daughter had decided to abandon "a commitment to God made in a church in front of everybody we ever met." Mrs. Tilden frequently pointed out that she herself "stuck with" her husband Bud for twenty-seven *years*, not twenty-seven months, and that she herself still hadn't rushed into a divorce even after three full years of separation.

Mrs. Tilden had no patience with Noni's plans for divorcing Roland; indeed, she became quite exercised when discussing the matter: "Noelle Hurd, don't you dare talk to me about your husband's so-called drinking problem after I watched my whole life get poured down the drain with a glass of Kentucky's finest bourbon. Did *your* husband dive into your swimming pool in a tuxedo at *your* twenty-fifth wedding anniversary and crack his head open in front of everybody you ever met?"

Noni never answered these outbursts by saying that she'd rather not watch her own life be thrown down the same drain as her mother's, if in fact that's what had happened to her mother's life. She didn't want to explain how her case might be even worse than her mother's, for her father was a sweet and gentle man, drunk or sober (if she'd ever seen him sober), whereas on the (admittedly infrequent) occasions when Roland drank too much, he changed as abruptly and as roughly as a werewolf in a movie. Noni had often thought back to when she'd told Kaye that werewolves didn't scare her, because she now knew better.

The best Mrs. Tilden would ever say was that if Noni had to leave her husband, maybe it was better she'd done it sooner rather than later since sooner she might still be attractive enough to find somebody else.

And Noni, a tall slender young woman, was attractive. Just turned twenty-three-years old the day before, she had large wide quiet gray-blue eyes and silvery straight blonde hair that she wore pulled back with a ribbon or barrette. Despite two decades of her mother's commands to stand up straight, there was a slight bow to her back, a curving in toward others as she listened or spoke. She had a kind mouth that she thought too wide, just as she thought her nose too long, her breasts too small, her flesh too pale. Noni had been taught to be hard on herself. But in fact people had always thought she was "pretty," although they were more likely to talk about her "goodness" than her looks. They had always said there was not a mean bone in Noni Tilden's body, that she was always thinking of others, that she was the sweetest soul.

That was exactly what her sister-in-law Trisha, Wade's wife, had said early this Christmas afternoon, when dropping off Michelle with her suitcase. "Noni, honey, you are the sweetest soul and Michelle that little bitch loves you more than she loves me anyhow, I'm just teasing."

Then, after hurrying through their Christmas presents, barely ahead of the snow, Wade and Trisha had flown off to

Cancun and taken Mrs. Tilden with them. According to Wade, she (his mother, not his wife) had needed a break. Wade and his mother were very close now and worried all the time about each other's well-being; each thought the other "took on too much." Mother and son had always looked alike, with their curly strawberry-blonde hair and milky red-freckled skin, but now that Wade had "gotten it together," they thought and acted alike as well. "Mom's overdoing it," Wade bragged. It was true that, with her planning board, altar guild, preservation society, garden club, book club, investment club, and yoga, Judy Tilden did keep busy. So busy in fact that she didn't seem to have time to find a replacement for her husband Bud, or, despite a three-year separation, to find a lawyer to divorce him.

Both Mrs. Tilden and Wade would have been upset if they'd known that Noni had invited her father over to baby-sit for Michelle at Heaven's Hill. While he did so, she would make an appearance at a Christmas party that her friend Bunny Breckenridge was giving that evening. Although Noni had presented the baby-sitting to her father as his favor to her, her motive was actually to make it possible for him to spend a little time with Michelle, his only grandchild, for Wade never invited him over to their home in Gordon's Landing.

This wasn't the first time Noni had made these secret arrangements for her father to see Michelle. As it happened, the little girl was crazy about her grandfather, who appeared to have all the time in the world for her and, unusual for an adult, absolutely no preoccupations. Sometimes when Tilden visited with Michelle at Heaven's Hill, Noni found them together in Gordon's room. Her father would be sitting in the black Hitchcock rocking chair with the little girl on his lap, reading to her from one of Gordon's children's books that still filled the shelf above his dresser.

Michelle shrieked with pleasure as she flew on the sled alone down a short, shallow slope. Noni knew that Wade and Trisha would be upset about this sledding too, for life appeared to strike them as a risky business and they tried on their daughter's behalf to avoid as much of it as possible. Also, if Wade and Trisha hadn't been standing right there beside their Land Rover when Amma Fairley had walked over to invite Noni and Michelle to share Kaye's birthday cake, Noni would have taken her niece to the party at Clayhome. But Wade had said that Michelle couldn't go—adding, after Amma left, "Don't you think that's a little much, the maid inviting you to a birthday party?"

Noni had said only, "Jesus, Wade."

But Trisha had told her husband briskly, "Babe, don't get me started. That old woman's been taking advantage of Grandma Judy forever. But what can we do? Go put her bags in the trunk." While Wade did so, Trisha had given Noni a long list of instructions about their seven-year-old's diet, clothing needs, sleep schedule, allergies. Then Trisha had made such a production of their departure that Michelle was sobbing by the time they drove away.

Now, halfway down the hill, the child, swaddled from head to toe in padded clothing, tumbled off the sled, rolled into a fallen tree, and started crying again. She was surprised when her bawling did not bring Noni running. Instead, her aunt called cheerfully down to her, "Come on, Michelle, my turn, bring that sled up here! Go go go go go go go!"

Michelle was so surprised that she started to do as asked. But she stopped suddenly and pointed. "Somebody's here." Noni turned to look. It was Kaye.

The sudden sight of him made a pulse leap in Noni's neck and her cheeks flush. He looked different. Had he always been so good-looking or had he changed? His cinnamon-colored face was thinner, so the soft full lips and gold-flecked joking eyes seemed to stand out more. Snow looked very white in his short tight black hair and on his long curled eyelashes.

She had missed him. She hadn't known how much she'd missed him, but she had. He smiled the old smile, walking toward her in sweater and slacks, no coat, ignoring as usual the bitter cold. He was leaner now than in his football days and Noni couldn't believe that he wasn't freezing.

She shivered herself. "Kaye! Aren't you cold? You've got to be cold."

"Where's your coat?" Michelle echoed.

"Hey, you two sound like my grandmama." Kaye helped the child pull the sled back to the hilltop. "Y'all having fun on my sled?"

Michelle was indignant. "It's not your sled, it's my Aunt Noni's sled. She's had it since she was a little girl."

With a grin for Noni, Kaye brushed the icy crust from the red paint, pointed. "See what that says? 'Noelle and Kaye.' I'm the Kaye part."

Pushing her hat up and pulling her scarf down from her eyes, Michelle studied the tall young man; she had seen him before but not often, and she was puzzled that a black person should share a sled with her aunt. She dropped into the snow to study the crayon letters. "K-A-Y-E" she spelled aloud.

"That's me. Me, myself, and I." Kaye winked at Noni. "Dr. Kaye King."

"You're a doctor?"

"Amazing, hunh?"

Kaye had been over at Heaven's Hill, talking with Bud Tilden, and he had come to tell Noni that her father was looking for her.

Michelle ran forward, saw the tall blond man waving from the porch of the big house. "Grandpoppy!" she screamed and raced slipping through the sleety snow toward the big white house.

Kaye picked up the sled's towline. "He says he's baby-sitting for her and you're going to Bunny's. Want a ride? Oh and happy birthday."

"Happy birthday. Welcome to twenty-three. Better late than…"

"It's pitiful you have to gloat about being a few lousy hours older."

"Face it. I'm older. I'll always be older. How have you been? *Where* have you been?" It was the first time she'd seen Kaye in a month. Aunt Ma said she never saw him either these days because he was always at the hospital, always told her he had no time for anything but work. "Aunt Ma thought you weren't going to be able to come over here even on Christmas."

Kaye shrugged. "She made such a big deal about it, I did a trade with somebody."

"Well, it made her very happy." Noni stepped closer, studied the shadows under his eyes. "You look so tired, Kaye."

"Tired?" He playfully slapped himself on both cheeks. "Come on! You're supposed to say I look so battle-fatigued and burned out that after a few years of this I *deserve* to charge you ten thousand dollars for an hour of my time. I'm in a macho rite of passage here. 'Course I look tired."

Kaye had just sped his way through medical school at the university and was beginning an internship in cardiac surgery, living in a rented room close to campus. To supplement his income, he did research late at night for a book his advisor was writing. Although Kaye was accustomed to staying up late because of his years as night dispatcher for his Uncle Austin's cab company, lately he had been working so hard and sleeping so little that sometimes walls seemed to him to move, colors to change, words to turn into senseless squiggles on the page. Sometimes in class or over his cafeteria tray his head dropped into sleep, jerked out. He knew other last-year medical school students and interns who used pills or cocaine to keep alert, but he had a horror of drugs, of how they'd been used to control his mother.

Noni and Kaye reached the porch of Heaven's Hill and he pointed across at his car, a rebuilt cherry-red 1967 Thunderbird Landau with whose engine he had once endlessly tinkered. "You want a ride to Bunny's? I'm not too tired to party."

"I'd love a ride to Bunny's."

He looked at her, struck by the warmth of her voice. He had always loved her voice, which was low and soft and Southern in its long slow vowels. It struck Kaye now that everything about Noni was like her voice; her generous mouth and blushed cheeks, even her clothes, all were perfectly Noni—gentle and warm and fine. The gray-blue cashmere scarf curling around her shoulders was the color of her eyes, the soft silvery blonde fur-collared ski jacket she wore was the color of her hair. Suddenly he leaned down and kissed her on the cheek.

Her face brightened. "What was that for?"

"For thanks." Suddenly embarrassed, Kaye retreated to his mocking grin. "Thanks for that present you gave Grandpa Tat. He loved it!"

Noni touched her cheek as if to keep the kiss there. Then she looked over to Clayhome, smiling. "I thought he would." This year Noni's Christmas present to the cranky legless Tatlock Fairley had been a large assortment of art supplies: oil paints, brushes, canvas, and easel.

Kaye laughed. "That old man's already got all that stuff out all over the kitchen table and he's already painting a canvas. He calls it 'Tatlock Fairley at Home,' and it shows him looking at the whole town of Moors, like he owned it. What in the world made you think of paints?"

Noni's enthusiasm flushed her face into the look that had made Amma call her "Sunshine" as a baby. "Well, you know how

Uncle Tat's always doodled all over things and how he loves colors. But one night I saw him watching *Lust for Life* on TV, that movie with Kirk Douglas about Van Gogh? And he was going on about how he could paint just as well as Van Gogh if only—"

"He had his legs?"

Noni laughed. "No! His 'chance.' You know, his chance."

Kaye imitated Tatlock's grumbling bass. "I bet it was the V.A. hospital cut off that painter Go's ear and they covered it up to keep the law off 'em and told the world the man was crazy. I sure wouldn't cut off my ear or my legs either, 'less I *was* crazy, and I'm not, no sir re bob. I am the Six Million Dollar Man. Anybody can paint some old pot of flowers like Go did. Me? I could of carved the Venus de Milo if I'd just had my chance, and she would have had the full use of her arms too—"

Noni covered her mouth. "Stop, Kaye, stop, don't make me laugh."

"Why, you got to pee?"

"Yes!" She ran away, pulling the sled behind her.

At six that evening, when Kaye came back to collect Noni, he heard piano music and stopped on the porch to listen before ringing the bell. He recognized the melody as one of those sad pretty Romantic pieces that her dad liked so much.

Noni was in fact playing Ravel's "Pavane for a Dead Princess," although she hadn't told her father the name of the piece, knowing its title would bother him. Beside the huge Christmas tree, Bud Tilden lay on the living room floor listening to the music, smoking a cigarette, looking up at the twinkling lights (they were no longer different colors but all tiny and white), while Michelle marched her new model horses across his chest. The five red stockings hung from the mantel behind him. There was a cocktail glass on the Persian carpet beside his ashtray.

"Brava, brava!" Tilden clapped when Noni finished the pavane. Michelle clapped too, then leapt up and raced to the door at the sound of the old-fashioned bell. She returned with Kaye behind her. Bud's lovely smile welcomed Kaye as it always had since the boy had met him.

"Sorry I'm late," Kaye said, holding up his wrist to show the digital watch. "Damn thing's battery died."

Bud Tilden sat up, cross-legged on the rug like a boy, and unbuckled the leather band of the old beautiful gold watch he wore. "Here, take this." He held it up to Kaye. "You're young, you care about time. I don't have—" He smiled. "—the slightest interest. But, Kaye, if time matters to you, don't turn it over to a battery. Pay attention. Wind it."

Kaye backed away. "I'm not taking your watch."

Noni said, "Forget it, Daddy, Kaye's a nightmare to give a present to."

Tilden kept holding out the watch, looking up at the young black man, smiling. "Kaye's not going to hurt my feelings. He knows it means a lot to me to give him something when he's given me so much. He knows that."

Finally Kaye moved forward, bent, and took the watch. "Thank you." He nodded at the man.

"Thank you."

"Well, Daddy, how'd you manage that?"

Tilden rolled back down onto the rug. "I'm a night owl, right, Kaye?"

"Right." Kaye took off his plastic watch and replaced it with Tilden's. "A wise old night owl."

Noni picked up her coat and gloves from the couch. "Kaye and I are going to Bunny's now, all right? I'll be back in a couple of hours. Michelle goes to bed at eight. Eight, no later."

"Oh sure sure sure."

"Oh sure sure sure," repeated Michelle.

"And Daddy, if you do get hungry, the refrigerator's stuffed. Mom'll never notice."

"I remember." Tilden propped his still blond head on one elbow, looked at Noni and Kaye with the old lovely hapless smile. "You two," he nodded to one, then the other. "You two are my favorite people—did you know that?—in the whole wide world."

Michelle bounced a plastic black stallion up Tilden's chest and poked his chin with it. "What about *me*, Grandpoppy?"

"You're my favorite little girl." He made no effort to stop her from dancing the little horse's hooves across his face. "You and the Princess."

"Who's the Princess?"

Tilden pointed at Noni. "She is."

Noni crossed to her father, knelt, brushed his hair back from his forehead, and kissed the familiar scent of alcohol and tobacco. His skin felt cool and smooth as marble. She picked up the drink from the rug. "Please eat some food, Daddy. Do you want me to make you a sandwich?"

"Hey, I was making sandwiches before you were born. Taste that, Kaye," he pointed up at the glass Noni held. "That's a Zombie."

Kaye took the drink from Noni, sipped it. "Zombie. You're getting to the end of the list here. You gonna start over?"

Tilden shook his head. "No, I think I'll call it quits. Zombie sounds like a good place to stop." He rolled onto his stomach and Michelle crawled onto his back. "Kaye, soon as spring gets here, let's play some more golf. Take care of my Princess in this snow."

"Always, Mr. T."

❋ ❋ ❋ ❋ ❋

In the old rebuilt Thunderbird, Kaye and Noni were bringing Parker along with them to Glade Lake, the affluent neighborhood where Bunny's parents, the Breckenridges, lived, and where (home for the holidays) she was having her party. Parker hadn't been invited, but Noni (who had called ahead to ask if he might come) told him that Bunny had wanted to invite him, just hadn't been sure if he'd be in Moors for Christmas.

Parker laughed. "If Allah's into white chicks in heaven, He's sure gonna make you one of them. 'Cause, Lady Disco, you are lying like a rug on a rich man's floor."

"No, it's true!" Noni turned around in the cracked red-leather bucket seat to protest.

"Oh sure," said Kaye in her father's voice of soft skepticism.

When the three arrived at the huge modern glass and red-wood house, the party was a loud crush of people, mostly, like them, in their twenties. The Breckenridge parents had abandoned their home and fled to relatives in Raleigh. Many of Bunny's guests were old high school classmates who hadn't seen much of each other in the last five years and had in common little but that shared past. The boys who'd had long hair in high school mostly had short hair now; the ones who'd had short hair then mostly had long hair now. Fewer of them smoked.

In large part the group was welcoming to Parker, although most awkwardly avoided questions about what he'd been up to since the old Moors High days.

Parker, who had a shaved head and a Kung Fu moustache, told Bunny he remembered her in the junior talent show, playing the guitar and singing. "You were whapping on the side of that gittar, doing this big voice Odetta/Georgia chain gang shit. 'Huh. Huh. Huh! Oh Rosie oh Lawd gal, the Man done killed my convict pal. Huh. Huh. Huh!'"

Bunny laughed. "Was I awful?"

"Oh Lawd, gal." He ate the Brie-filled mushroom she handed him. "But I gotta say, you had guts, those crackers guffawing at you." Parker told Bunny he had converted to Islam in prison and was getting ready to change his name to Kareem Aked.

Bunny, who had wild frizzy long mousy-brown hair and wore loose black caftans to hide her weight told Parker she was working on her Ph.D. in economics at the University of Chicago, and that she was keeping the name "Bunny" although it made her sound like someone who worked in a Playboy Club, because every time she heard it, it was a battle cry to war against the patriarchy.

Parker said, "Kick ass, Sister!" but declined her offered glass of chardonnay. He was a teetotaler now.

Bunny's older sister Mindy (the one who so long ago had asked Noni's brother Gordon to help escort the first black students into Gordon Junior High) was here from Atlanta with her husband; they manufactured something called "software" for computers and were doing quite well. She told Noni that sometimes she dreamt about Gordon.

From speakers embedded in the ceiling, music pulsed loudly: Elton John, the Pointer Sisters, Blondie, Carly Simon. Noni fast-danced with Parker, and slow-danced with a pleasant young lawyer named Lucas Miller, who confessed that he'd had a crush on her in high school. He wondered if she'd care to go out with him now. Noni thanked him, but said she was still married, although separated from her husband. He apologized for asking.

There was paté and a roast goose with ribbons on its legs and there were white pizzas. One of the pizzas had spinach on it and Kaye left the two other medical students he'd been talking with beside the huge raised fireplace in order to bring Noni a piece, making Doctor Jack's old joke about how she needed to eat spinach to build up her iron.

Noni was dutifully finishing the pizza slice when the Four Tops' "Reach Out, I'll Be There" began. Kaye looked at her, then held out his arms. "I bet I haven't danced in a year or more."

Noni smiled, stepped into his arms. "It'll come back. You can do anything, remember?"

They danced so well together that people stopped to watch. They danced with the old rapport that they had had, practicing in Amma's kitchen when they were thirteen. Their bodies remembered more than they did.

But there was a difference now and they both felt it; those bodies had changed, felt less familiar, and the two of them were strangely more conscious of each other's hands, arms, hip bones, the small of her back, the length of his leg. They looked at each other, then they looked away, the intimacy in their eyes suddenly too strong for easy dancing.

Noni thought back to one of their practices in the kitchen at Clayhome, how Kaye had choreographed them in his bossing way. What had that song been? He'd mapped out every step. "All right. On 'time goes by so slowly,' we open out like this. Got it? Outside arm out. We lead with the outside foot. Walk, walk, walk, walk. 'Time goes by so slowly / And time can do so much.' Walk, walk. That's right. Good. Now, we spin on 'Are you still mine?' Spin spin, 'Are you still,' now I'll dip you, '*mine?*' 'Are you still mine?' Got it? Great, that's great. Boy, we're good."

Around them as they danced at the Breckenridge house, the party went on. There was talk of whether Noni had left Roland or vice versa, and why. Whether their former class president was gay and if he was not, why was he still living with his college roommate? Whether their former head cheerleader was pregnant.

Kaye and Noni slow-danced while around them there was talk of Three Mile Island, new Swedish stoves, *Apocalypse Now*, pocket calculators, the Sugar Bowl, the Pritikin diet, the new discount mall, whether sexual fidelity was unnatural to the human species, and what the meaning of happiness might conceivably be.

Kaye and Noni fast-danced again while there was talk of whether Parker (or rather Kareem Aked) was guilty of what he'd gone to prison for, and if so what exactly had it been? Whether Kaye—who certainly had turned out a more handsome man than they had thought to conjecture—was involved with anyone, and if so, who.

There was talk about whether Bunny had slept with Kaye, with Noni, or with Parker; if with Parker, it might explain why he had come to this party, even if guilty of whatever crime had sent him to the state prison, if in fact prison was where he had been.

In fact, Parker *wasn't* at this party anymore, at least Noni and Kaye couldn't find him when they stopped dancing, although they searched through the house. They needed to leave so Noni could drop off a Christmas gift for Reverend Fisher who lived in the next block. She worried that perhaps she and Kaye, dancing, had paid too little attention to Parker, and that, feeling uncomfortable, he had left Bunny's without telling anyone, although he was miles from his own neighborhood and without a car.

But after another search through the house, and with Kaye's assurances that Parker could take care of himself, she finally agreed to go. The truth was, she wanted to get back to Heaven's Hill to check on Michelle and her father. She feared, not that her father would overdrink when in charge of the child, but that Michelle would talk him into letting her stay up way past her bedtime, just as Noni herself long ago had talked him into it.

✳ ✳ ✳ ✳ ✳

Michelle was actually sound asleep in Noni's four-poster bed. Amma Fairley had come over to Heaven's Hill and found the child sleeping on the red leather couch beside Bud Tilden; *A Christmas Carol* was showing on the television. Amma had brought Tilden a bowl of her Brunswick stew, which she knew he loved. In the past, she could always get him to eat her stew when nothing else would tempt his appetite.

Turning off the set as Ebenezer Scrooge leapt happily through the streets of London with Tiny Tim on his shoulder, Tilden lit a cigarette and gestured for her to sit down with him.

"Amma," he said, "I've got a serious question for you." He wondered if Amma wouldn't agree that we don't need ghosts, like the ghosts who visit Scrooge, to show us visions of our ruined pasts and our unhappy present and our doomed futures.

She told him she wasn't sure what he meant.

"I mean, don't we have those visions with us all the time anyhow? All the time. And you know what, our knowing what we've done, what we've left undone—it doesn't help one bit, Amma, it doesn't change us at all. There's a book," he pointed at the shelves where rows of music boxes had now replaced his collection of Great Books. "A Greek philosopher said, 'To know the good is to do the good.' But, Amma, who was he kidding?"

Amma carried Tilden's untouched cocktail from the coffee table and poured it down the drain of the wet bar sink. "Well, Mr. Tilden—"

"How many years have we known each other? Thirty?" He took her hand. "Thirty? Do I call you Mrs. Fairley?"

Amma patted his hand, removed hers. "If you knew what the right thing to do was, why wouldn't you do it?"

He laughed, put out his cigarette. "Oh, Amma. You'd do the right thing. That I do know. Noni'd do the right thing. But that's all I know on earth and all I need to know. You think Noni and Kaye'll ever get together?"

She stiffened, stood to leave. "I don't know if they will or not."

"But you think they shouldn't? Hang on, don't go. Hell, they're probably seventh cousins anyhow. What do you bet?

You know damn well, Amma, your family and Judy's family have been all mixed up together for the past two hundred years."

Amma did know this, knew that in the long oral history of the Clays there were tales of nocturnal visits by Gordon men to Clayhome women. She had been told that her great-grandfather was actually, secretively, a Gordon, and that was why her eyes were amber and her skin cinnamon. But Amma said none of this, and didn't want to. All she said in the doorway was, "Mr. Tilden, you carry this child up to bed for me and then you come on down to the kitchen and eat some of my stew. You're not looking too good."

Giving up the conversation, he sweetly smiled. "Oh sure. Thanks for the stew. I love that stew."

"I know you do."

Half an hour later, Amma returned to the den from sitting beside Michelle's bed. She found the stew bowl on the kitchen table empty and Bud Tilden gone.

He was nowhere in the house, but she heard the stereo playing loudly, an orchestra.

Rachmaninoff's *Piano Concerto No. 2* boomed out from the speaker Tilden had moved to face through a window onto the porch so that he could listen to it while outside.

By the lights on the front porch and by the Christmas lights hung on the shrubs and bushes bordering the circular drive around the lawn of Heaven's Hill, Amma could see Bud Tilden out there in the icy slush, throwing a basketball into an old ratty hoop on a backboard that he had set up in a corner of the yard a long time ago.

Amma remembered watching him out there, way back twenty years or more, when he'd been running around under that hoop with little Gordon sitting high up on his shoulders so the boy could drop the ball through the rim. She remembered long summer twilights with the two of them playing with that basketball. Gordon shrieking with pleasure and Bud Tilden shouting, "Another one! You're so good!" A long time ago.

She watched Tilden now through the living room window. Over and over the tall slender man leapt in air, arced the ball over his head, threw it, raced to catch it under the net, spun, and threw it again. Usually—and this surprised Amma—it dropped right through the rim and into the net.

Amma walked out onto the porch. She saw Tilden's big silver basketball trophy sitting on the top step with a bottle of champagne in it, packed in snow. She called to him over the sweet sad music to come on inside, that it was too cold and icy to be out in the yard throwing a ball around at night in just his pants and that thin V-neck sweater.

Jogging through the slush to the foot of the porch, he asked her please if she couldn't stay with Michelle just a few more minutes. Just let him do a dozen baskets in a row if he could, let him do thirty-five, please. He smiled as he lit a cigarette, then picked up the trophy and showed her the champagne bottle. "If I make it, here's my victory cup. We'll celebrate, you and I, Mrs. Fairley, okay? Thirty-five in a row. Thirty-five married years, thirty-five baskets."

Amma went back inside and returned with Tilden's fleece jacket. "I'll stay a little while more. Tat's sleeping and I've got stuff I need to get done here. But you put this on."

He ground out the cigarette, took the jacket, slipped into it. "That twenty-fifth anniversary party was some disaster, right? Remember that? Poor Judy. She hung in there as long as she could, don't you think?"

Amma zipped up the jacket as if he were a child, the way she used to do for Kaye. "For better, for worse, the Book says. You got to decide what that means to you. I didn't leave my husband Bill King 'til I left him in the ground at the cemetery. And I'll leave Tat Fairley the same way. Or he'll leave me.

Whatever God decides. 'Til death do us part. That's what it means to me. And that's what I plan."

He smiled at her, tucked the silver cup under his arm. "Oh Amma, sometimes death just gets to be too long to wait."

She watched him from the porch for a while. It had stopped snowing, and he didn't seem to have had all that much to drink tonight. He looked as if he might be enjoying himself, and heaven knows, the man could use a little happiness. Not a bad man, not mean, not cheap, not hard. Not hard enough maybe. Too soft anyhow to keep Judy from feeling like she had to be so hard herself. He must have been good with that basketball in his day, thought Amma, as she walked back to the kitchen to clean up the meal she had talked him into eating. As she dried dishes in the kitchen she thought of as hers, she sang:

> *When that first trumpet sounds, I'll get up and walk around.*
> *Ain't no grave can hold my body down.*

Out on the lawn, Bud Tilden stopped for a moment, looked up at the great endless night where the sky now sparkled with infinite millions of disinterested stars. He thought something he had never believed before, about his connection to this universal dome above him: he thought not how small he was in relation to it but that he was a part of it, that he was a piece, even if broken, of a lovely and eternal wholeness. He felt in harmony, like the music he was listening to. He saw Noni playing the piano, her face so beautiful, so filled with the beauty she heard.

He ran faster, leapt higher. Again and again the ball dropped through the hoop.

❖ ❖ ❖ ❖ ❖

Kaye's red Thunderbird was parked in front of the ivy-covered stucco house where Dr. Fisher lived; Kaye was waiting for Noni who was inside giving a Christmas gift to the elderly minister. Snow on the lawn was thin, and there were icy patches on the walkway and the sidewalk.

Suddenly he was startled by a bright light in his eyes and a loud rapping on his car window. It was a Moors policeman. The officer shined his flashlight into the front and back seats of the Thunderbird. Kaye rolled down the window but didn't speak.

The policeman, young (Kaye's age), white, stone-faced, said, "What're you doing here?" Not, thought Kaye angrily, "Can I help you, sir?" Not even, "Sorry to bother you, sir, but what are you doing here?" Not even, "Sir, what're you doing here?"

"Waiting for a friend," Kaye replied. He could have said more but didn't.

"Can I please see your license and registration?"

"I'd need to know why you want to." Kaye saw another policeman suddenly run out from the side of a nearby house, slipping on ice as he headed up the sidewalk toward them, looking into the dark yards with his flashlight. "I'm legally parked. My plates are in order. What's your probable cause, officer?"

Now the policeman opened Kaye's door. "Step out of the car please."

In part Kaye was thinking of Amma's rule, "Save it for when it's worth it." In part he was watching the other cop ring the doorbell of the house next to Reverend Fisher's, and in part he was wondering where Parker had gone when he'd left Bunny's party. Meanwhile he slid from the Thunderbird, and without looking at the young policeman handed him his opened wallet. In the wallet, facing the driver's license, was a photo card identifying John Montgomery King as a doctor at

University Hospital. Kaye was interested in whether the cop would notice the ID and, if so, whether it would change things.

It changed things immediately. The policeman returned the wallet. "We've had a report of a suspicious person in the neighborhood, sir, and a possible attempted break-in."

The other officer had now disappeared inside the house next door.

Kaye asked, "How would someone define 'a possible attempted break-in'? Would that be a black person slowing down in a white neighborhood?"

Doctor or not, his tone was too much for the young officer whose face returned to stone. "I need to see your registration."

As Kaye reached for the glove compartment, he saw a sight that surprised him and probably, he thought, surprised the policeman even more. Out of the gray stucco ivy-covered Georgian house walked three people: old Dr. Fisher in his clerical collar and a baggy cardigan sweater, Noni in her beautiful gray cashmere coat, and, with Noni's arm through his, Parker Kareem Aked Jones.

Noni waved at Kaye, calling to him as he stepped around the car toward her. "Oh, Kaye, here we are. We're so sorry to keep you waiting, aren't we, Reverend Fisher? Parker and I just lost track of time." Tightening her arm, Noni pulled Parker closer to her. "Didn't we, Parker?"

"Just lost track of time," repeated Parker. "Talkin' 'bout church and stuff like that."

Dr. Fisher reached Kaye, touched his shoulder. "Everything all right?" He turned to the young policeman, touched him as well. "What's the problem here, Officer? Dr. King have car trouble?"

"Report of a suspicious person in the neighborhood." The cop stepped back as Noni moved next to the passenger door where she stopped expectantly. She waited a moment, then gave the cop a cool expectant look and he jumped forward to open the door for her.

"Good gracious," said Dr. Fisher, "on Christmas? What kind of 'suspicious'? Oh, excuse me." The old man leaned into the front seat, kissed Noni's cheek. Then he opened the back door, gestured for Parker to get in. "Noni, good-bye, thanks so much, you and Parker, for my present. Merry Christmas. Merry Christmas, Kaye." The old minister led the policeman along the sidewalk away from the red Thunderbird. "So, Officer, who saw this suspicious person?"

Kaye started his motor and drove away as Parker blew out a great long sigh, then a cascade of curses, then lay down laughing in the back seat. "Disco Queen, you too much. And that little old priest ought to be on TV."

"Parker, shut up! What's going on?"

Together Noni and Parker explained. Noni had been in the old minister's backyard, hanging up on a hawthorn tree the new bird feeder she'd given him for Christmas. Suddenly she'd spotted Parker running as hard as he could out of the yard next door. She'd jumped in front of him and grabbed him; when he'd said the police were chasing him, she'd hurried him inside Dr. Fisher's house.

Watching out the living room window, they'd seen the officer interrogating Kaye, and seen the other officer knocking on the neighbor's door. They had decided to walk out of the house together as if Noni and Parker had been paying a social call on their pastor.

Kaye wanted to know why the police were chasing Parker in the first place. Why was Parker running through strangers' yards at night? Why had he left the Breckenridge party without telling them?

Parker said, "I felt like a rabbi at a redneck pig picking. But I didn't want to bust up your fun the way y'all were dancing like you were trying out for American Bandstand. So I was gonna walk to where I could get on some bus line and go home, but I got lost and I didn't wanna ring, know what I mean?, bells in Lake Glade, so the more I walked the lost-er I got and then, Jesus fuck, I see this cop shining his flashlight round those yards like he's gonna find gold with it. And I say, Kareem kiss your free ass good-bye, 'cause my parole officer is a fucker. Then I swear it was like there's Noni like Allah dropped her out of the sky…"

As Parker went on with his story, Kaye was thinking that he didn't believe it. The saga of looking for a bus, of being lost and too wary to ask for help, was too much like the Philadelphia incident from Kaye's childhood, a story he had often told his friend. But maybe Parker wasn't lying; maybe he wasn't casing houses to rob them. Maybe it was true that he was looking for a bus, or maybe he was just wandering around, glancing in the windows of safe, comfortable, unfamiliar lives, intriguingly unlike his own.

Parker was still congratulating Noni on how she'd cowed the policeman by the way she'd looked at him as she'd waited for him to open her car door. "That's class. You can't learn that. You gotta be born thinking you're higher up."

"I don't think I'm higher up!'

"Sure you do." Kaye pulled in through the brick columns of Heaven's Hill. "Parker's not saying you think you're better, just higher up."

"Well, I don't know what you mean."

"That's why I love you, Duchess." Parker hugged her from the back seat. "Let's us three go to the Indigo!"

Disappointed that Noni and Kaye said they didn't want to go dancing with him, Parker finally hopped out at Clayhome to pick up his sister's car.

"Go home, Parker," Kaye told him.

"How 'bout you, Lady Disco? Change your mind. You and me and night fever."

"Thanks, but I've got to check on my niece. Merry Christmas."

"Y'all are drags," lamented Parker. "Come on, Doctor Feelgood, least meet me later."

"I'll think about it."

Parker waved goodnight as he climbed into his sister's old Pinto. Kaye and Noni stood together waving as he drove away.

"Thanks," Kaye told her. "Even if he wasn't trying a breakin, they'd have probably nailed him."

"You don't have to thank me. Parker's my friend."

Kaye stared at her. It was true, and odd that he'd never thought it. Parker was her friend.

He walked Noni across the long icy lawn toward the big house.

Only when he stumbled over the silver trophy and the champagne bottle rolled out of it did he see the human shape lying, arms and legs at odd angles, in the snow near the basketball hoop.

He ran toward the body so fast that he'd already had time to discover that Bud Tilden was ice cold and blue in the face before Noni was near enough to see her father.

Kaye jumped up and ran back to her before she could come closer. "Call 911! Go call 911! Now!"

Her voice was terrible. "Is it Daddy?" She tried to twist around Kaye, but he blocked her, turning her toward the house, shaking her.

"You've got to call 911! Now! Hurry!"

Noni ran, slipped in the snow, fell to her knees, ran again, up the porch stairs and inside Heaven's Hill.

Kaye blew again and again into Bud Tilden's mouth, hit again and again on Bud Tilden's chest. After a while he was pretty sure there was no use, but he didn't stop.

Even when the ambulance wailed in through the gates of Heaven's Hill, even when the medics tried to pull him away from the body while his grandmother Amma shouted at them, "He's a doctor!"—even then he wouldn't stop trying to make Bud Tilden breathe again.

Kaye wouldn't stop until Noni knelt down in the snow beside him as he pushed against her father's still heart and breathed into her father's still mouth. She put her arms tightly around Kaye, telling him, "It's all right. It's all right. You can stop. It's all right."

The Seventh Day of Christmas

❄

December 24, 1984
The Wedding Band China

It was Christmas Eve, and Noni had invited Kaye to have dinner with her at Heaven's Hill to celebrate their birthdays. Just the two of them.

In its slow indifferent turning, the world had changed seasons, changed lives, and five long years had passed since the death of Bud Tilden.

The first year was hardest. It took Noni months to forgive her mother, whose public widowhood, modeled on Jackie Kennedy's, had begun with ostentatious weeping behind a black veil at the funeral. Watching Mrs. Tilden receiving the condolences of friends, as if she'd never thrown her husband away, so upset Noni that she had refused to join her in greeting guests at the open house at Heaven's Hill after the burial.

But in the end she could not stiffen herself against her mother's uneasy solitude, her desperate busyness, and they reconciled.

It had taken longer for Noni to reconcile with her brother Wade, who had rushed home from Cancun and blamed her for allowing his daughter Michelle to spend time with her grandfather and as a result to be grief-stricken by his sudden death. Wade had also raged at Amma Fairley for letting Michelle run out of the house and so see her grandfather's dead body. (It was to this disturbing experience that Wade was later to attribute his daughter's refusal to become a social star at her elementary school.)

According to Wade, Noni and Amma had acted irresponsibly, first for allowing Tilden ever to visit Heaven's Hill; second, for "abandoning the man to his own wacko devices." While for years Wade had shown little interest in whether his father lived or died, and was persuaded that his father felt the same about him, Bud Tilden's death, shooting hoops in the snow after forty years of heavy smoking and drinking, had so incensed Wade that he tried to evict the Fairleys from Clayhome for causing it. Only his mother's distress (how could she manage without Aunt Ma?) stopped him. He then demanded that she at least charge the Fairleys "the going rent for a house that size in the best neighborhood in Moors."

Noni told her mother that it would be indecent to ask her lifelong maid for rent on a house that Clays had been living in since 1850. Mrs. Tilden agreed that people might think ill of her if she did it.

Wade told Noni her priorities were screwed up. Noni told Wade that all her life she had tried hard to love him but that it was no longer possible for her to like him.

His response was, "You always liked black people better than whites anyhow."

At the funeral reception itself, Wade had accused Kaye of killing Bud Tilden by performing "voodoo mouth-to-mouth" on him. An enraged Kaye flung him against the wall in the foyer. When Wade covered his face with his hands, Kaye told him he was too contemptible to hit, and he walked out of the house with Wade yelling after him that he was going to call the cops. Kaye knew he wouldn't. It would embarrass the family.

Kaye tried hard to talk his grandmother into moving off the Heaven's Hill property, but Amma refused. Clayhome was her home, as it had been her daddy's home, her granddaddy's, her great-great-great-granddaddy's, and she would stay as long as she was able.

As for Roland Hurd, he had immediately flown back to Moors from Houston as soon as he'd heard of Noni's father's death. At the graveside he'd pleaded with her to salvage their marriage "for Bud's sake." It was a low but effective strategy. So was Roland's claim that he couldn't live without her, that he needed her to get through life.

Doctor Jack also begged Noni to return to Roland. "Noni, you've got to give love a second chance. Roland'll fold without you. It was when your mom quit on him that your dad folded." This was also a low blow, but very effective, for not only did Noni love Doctor Jack, she believed deeply that what he'd said was true. You should never give up on love.

So she agreed to think about a reconciliation with her husband, although in truth she couldn't think about anything yet. She asked for time. Roland returned to Texas for three months. When he came back to Moors, he brought with him a promise. He would quit drinking. He didn't know why Noni thought his social drinking was such a problem; nevertheless, to please her, he'd quit. Noni accepted this promise, one that her father had never made. Maybe her father hadn't been as strong as her husband. After all, Roland had quit smoking (which her father had never done). Why shouldn't he quit drinking, too?

Part of Noni's decision to try to save her marriage was her great desire, after her miscarriage and now that she'd lost her father, to have a child. She wanted to be pregnant with new life before the anniversary of Bud Tilden's death the following Christmas. Having a baby growing would help, she hoped, fill the awful emptiness that his death had left inside her.

"I have to try to make *something* last," she'd told Kaye the morning she left Heaven's Hill. "Don't make it worse."

Kaye pressed his fist hard against the living room mantel. "Jack's talked you into this. Jack and your damn mother. He's using you to prop up his drunk of a son. And your mother's doing what she spends her whole life doing, polishing the family name—"

"Please, Kaye." Noni took his hands, squeezed them tightly. "Please."

"—So why are you turning your life over to other people?"

"Don't tell me I'm stupid or wrong or dreaming or throwing my life away. Just tell me, 'Good luck.' Please."

Kaye stared at her a long while. Then with his forefinger, he tapped the heart made of a dime that he'd given her and that she was wearing on the silver chain around her neck. "Good luck." Then he walked out of the room. He didn't look back. He never did.

> On the right of the old lace-bordered place mat, a
> silver meat knife, fish knife, teaspoon, soup spoon.

It was April of 1980 when Noni moved to Houston. Roland bought them a brand new Dutch Colonial with a pool on a cul de sac.

That year Noni sent Kaye a signed first edition of Martin Luther King's *Stride Toward Freedom: The Montgomery Story.* The birthday card said, "From one Dr. King to another, with love, Noni."

Kaye sent Noni one of Tatlock's oil paintings, with a card saying that Noni had unleashed the Afro-American Van Gogh. In the year since receiving her gift of art supplies, Tatlock had taken up painting with a gusto he'd shown for nothing else—except food and imaginary litigation—in his entire life. He painted at least eight hours every day in his wheelchair, painted on canvas, cardboard and siding, on old doors and pieces of tin. All his paintings were blazing with bright clean colors, straight out of the tubes and mixed with linseed oil to make them shinier.

The picture Kaye sent Noni was called (they all had their titles painted on them) "HOME ON A NICE DAY." It was a colorful canvas showing Tatlock himself, with his legs restored, standing beside (and the same height as) Clayhome, wearing one of Amma's sunflower T-shirts and drinking an old-fashioned green soda bottle labeled "The Real Thing." The lawn stretched away from him in a flat sheet of green, with camellias, red bud and apple trees, asters, peonies, petunias, and rose bushes all in simultaneous bloom. Across the lawn, but no taller than the sunflowers that surrounded it like a gate, stood Heaven's Hill. The painting, said Kaye's note, was to remind Noni of home.

She hung it in the empty room off the den that Roland called "hers," the room they hadn't gotten around to decorating yet.

Heaven's Hill felt far away from Houston, where Noni was trying hard to make a good life for Roland, who worked all the time brokering real estate deals. She studied fashionable recipes and served them to his colleagues and their wives, she planted bulbs, pickled walls, made duvet covers, joined a gym and a church and a book club. But Kaye was right. Heaven's Hill was home and she missed it. She even missed that hard first winter she'd spent there after her father's death, the winter when she couldn't believe in spring, the winter eased only by her playing her piano and by the long chilly walks she took with Kaye in the countryside around Moors. She missed Kaye.

On the left of the place mat, a silver salad fork, dinner fork, fish fork.

In March, Noni had a second miscarriage, a girl. Reassuringly, the doctor told Roland there was no reason for them not to try again with every expectation of success. Roland's pledge to quit drinking lapsed, but he promised that he didn't have a problem. It was only social, only relaxation.

That year, 1981, the Hurds flew home to Moors for the holidays. Against Roland's advice, Noni decided to give what she called a reconciliation dinner at Heaven's Hill. She did it while her mother was away in New York City with her granddaughter Michelle. They'd gone to stay at the Plaza and to see the Fifth Avenue Christmas windows, just as Mrs. Tilden had once done with Noni, just as her own mother had once done with her.

During her mother's absence, Noni invited Wade and Trisha to come "bury the hatchet" on her birthday, Christmas Eve. They accepted and brought with them Trisha's unmarried brother, Chadwick, Wade's business partner. Noni had also invited Kaye and Bunny Breckenridge. Roland drove Noni's old Alfa Romeo over to Hillston and bought some excellent wine for the meal.

Gathering everyone at the table that night, Noni said she did not like making speeches but that it was important to her to have her family, her husband, and her best friends together here. These were the people she loved most, in the place she loved most, here at Christmas time, when both the happiest things (her wedding, Kaye's and her birthdays) and the saddest (her father's death) had happened. She hoped that they could all try to be kind to one another, to forgive one another, to give one another a chance.

Despite Noni's plea, the peace party was not a success. Roland did not resist the impulse to say 'I told you so.'

Both Bunny and Trisha's brother thought they were being set up for a date and both resented it.

Wade hugged his sister as if nothing had ever gone wrong between them, but he completely ignored Kaye, even when Kaye, trying hard, asked him a direct question. And when

Noni inquired about Parker (for whom Kaye had found a job at the hospital ER), Wade was snide: "I thought your friend Mohammed was back in Dollard Prison, Noni."

"His name isn't Mohammed, Wade, stop it."

"Sorry."

"More wine, anybody? It's a nice white Burgundy." Roland poured himself another glass.

Wade's wife Trisha asked Kaye an endless stream of questions, but they were all about Afro-Americans; her eyes widened in bafflement when he didn't know details about Diana Ross's relationship to Michael Jackson, Kareem Abdul-Jabbar's real name, the actors who played the Jeffersons on television. And Kaye's response to her query about whether he counted Indian doctors at University Hospital as blacks was to ask her, "Do you count Italians as Chinese?"

To which Trisha replied, "Wade, could I have a little more of that whatyoucallit, ratatootie? Noni, you have certainly turned into some kind of cook here, all these strange-tasting things. But good! Wade won't eat a thing but meat and potatoes, will you, Wade? I don't think he ever ate duck before." Trisha went on to ask if Noni had read *When Bad Things Happen to Good People*, which Trisha had given Grandma Judy to take with her to New York. "It really will help her," she assured Noni.

Noni said she found it curious that people continued to think of Judy Tilden as a widow tragically bereft of a cherished spouse, forgetting that she had evicted her husband from the house years before he died.

Wade muttered that he didn't want to hear Noni start insulting their mother.

"It's just the truth, Wade."

"Let's change the subject," Roland said. "More wine?" He began a long account of how his Houston corporation had been "cutting the fat off the staff" by firing a third of its low-level employees.

Bunny, next to Kaye, interrupted to ask Roland to listen to himself. We were in a recession, she said, a severe recession caused by President Reagan's idiotic trickle-down theory, because what was trickling down was a national deficit of hundreds of billion of dollars, a deficit landing on the heads of the poor.

Wade said he was sorry to have to suggest that Bunny didn't know what she was talking about.

Kaye said he was sorry to ask why—since Bunny taught economic theory at Columbia University—Wade assumed he knew as much about economic theory as Bunny did.

"Excuse me, I was talking to Ms. Breckenridge here," Wade snapped.

Kaye folded his napkin. "Actually, I believe it's Dr. Breckenridge, right, Bunny?"

"I don't care what she calls herself, or you either. I'm a businessman, I know business."

Kaye slid his napkin back through its silver ring. "I guess so. You bankrupted two. That must prove something."

"Whoaaa," said Roland. And then the table fell silent.

Finally, at Trisha's indignant prodding, Wade stood up and said, "I think you ought to leave now. Tell you the truth, King, I'll never understand why you even get invited."

Roland laughed. "Wade, come on, Jesus!"

Noni stood up and said that she was sorry; it wasn't Wade's house, it was their mother's house, and that she (Noni) was hostess here in her mother's absence and that Kaye was her guest and that she trusted her brother to be polite to him.

Wade told his sister that if she didn't ask Kaye to leave, he and Trisha and Trisha's brother were all walking out right this minute.

"Are you really sure that's how you feel, Wade?" asked Noni quietly.

"Honey." Roland reached for Noni's arm to sit her down but she shook him off. He shrugged and poured himself another glass of wine.

Trisha said, "It's exactly how Wade feels."

"I'm so sorry to hear it." Noni held out her hand to Trisha's brother. "Good night, Chadwick. I apologize, but Wade feels he has to leave now. Thank you so much for coming. It was a pleasure to see you again. Merry Christmas."

And that was the end of the peace party.

By New Year's, everyone had calmed down and Trisha even invited Roland and Noni to their home at Gordon's Landing. They all tried but it was hard work. Roland vowed he'd rather drink jug wine from a cardboard box than spend another holiday at Heaven's Hill. He didn't like what it did to his wife. "One day here, and your family turns you into a stress case, baby. They don't deserve you. And I know Bunny and King are your buds—"

"They're my best friends."

"Okay, but I mean, give me a break from the left-wing soapbox. Plus your brother's a cheap son of a bitch. No way I'm ever eating flank steak and drinking rotgut at his house again."

In Noni's view, the serving of "rotgut" wine to Roland was the least of her brother's sins. But he was right that Wade was as stingy as he was narrow-minded. Investing in real estate and the stock market, he had grown rich, but he didn't feel that way. Sometimes Noni despaired of ever reaching the heart she had been sure Wade had. Could she be wrong that everyone had the same heart, deep down?

She sat in the kitchen with Amma Fairley, and told her how guilty she felt to stay so angry with her brother.

Amma told her, "Honey, you can't forgive somebody if he don't think he's done a damn thing wrong."

Still the failure hurt. She and Wade almost never saw each other anymore.

Above the place mat, a silver dessert spoon, a dessert fork.

The following Christmas, 1982, Noni stayed in Houston. She sent Kaye a new machine called a CD player, and with it she sent a CD set, *Twenty-Five Years of Motown Hits*, that included the song by the Four Tops, "Reach Out, I'll Be There." She didn't hear back from him.

That year she and her husband celebrated her birthday and their anniversary by going skiing at Squaw Valley with Doctor Jack and his new family. Doctor Jack had recently married a widow with three teenaged children and moved them out to California, which he loved. He was dean of another medical school, lived in a big house with a hot tub overlooking the Pacific, and was an expert on Napa Valley wines.

At the lodge restaurant, Roland drank too much champagne (a special reserve estate California vintage chosen by his father for their celebration). Then he started sarcastically teasing his young step-brother, despite Noni's whispers that he was upsetting the boy. Then he accidentally bruised Noni's wrist by squeezing it when she tried to leave their table. In their room the next morning he confessed that he didn't remember the events of the previous night. He was profoundly apologetic about her wrist. All right, he hadn't quit drinking, but the truth was, he didn't see why he should have to go cold turkey. But he would cut back. He promised "never again" would anything happen like the accident at the restaurant. He also spontaneously offered to go get tests done to see if he might be the reason they weren't getting pregnant. Noni was his angel, she knew that, didn't she?

> *Above and to the right, her mother's mother's Hawk crystal. Water glass, red wine glass, white wine glass, dessert wine glass.*

In 1983, Noni received a Federal Express package from Clayhome: a Christmas wreath made by Amma Fairley of

Heaven's Hill holly, ivy, mistletoe, and magnolia leaves. To the wreath was tied a gold box. Inside the box was a gold charm bracelet. On the bracelet was a single charm, a tiny gold grand piano. The gift was from Kaye, she knew that, but there was no note.

For weeks Noni found herself touching the charm on her wrist like a bead on a rosary. Finally she sat down with the Yellow Pages, found a music store, and rented a spinet piano, which she moved into the undecorated room called "hers." She put nothing in the room but the piano and Tatlock's painting, "HOME ON A NICE DAY."

At a local college she found a teacher and started taking lessons again.

It turned out that the problem wasn't specifically with Roland's sperm count. There just seemed to be an incompatibility between his sperm and her eggs. The doctor started Noni on a rigorous graphing of her ovulation, which proved to be remarkably regular. She became so sensitive to her body temperature that she could often identify the rise of a few degrees.

Napkins, Irish linen soft with age, pulled through old silver napkin rings with a baroque G for Gordon ornately engraved.

In June of 1984, Noni flew home to Moors at her brother Wade's request. He'd had several phone calls from Amma Fairley about "Grandma Judy," who was having "a bad patch." According to Amma, it was little things: Mrs. Tilden had forgotten to turn off a burner of the gas stovetop, which had burned all night, although luckily there'd been no damage done. She had lost two sets of her keys and accused Amma of taking them. She had left her purse out on the St. John's altar after finishing her floral arrangement for the altar guild. When the handbag was brought over to Heaven's Hill by the new rector, she tearfully told him that her daughter-in-law Trisha had stolen it. She'd called Amma from the Moors Library and said someone had taken her car. It was right there in the parking lot.

Mrs. Tilden's family doctor said she was suffering from depression, a delayed "and all things considered, natural mini-nervous-breakdown." This was more of a problem than Wade, with his busy business, and Trisha, with the heavy schedules of their two children (they had a little boy now), could deal with. They needed Noni to come take care of her mother.

Over Roland's objections, Noni flew to North Carolina. A week at Heaven's Hill was enough to make it clear that her once purposeful mother was growing at times (though not at all times) strangely distracted and forgetful, as if she were much older than her sixty years. She would buy new clothes identical to clothes she'd already bought and never worn; a third of the articles in her closet still had their price tags on them. She would buy new sheets and towels, put them in the kitchen pantry with the canned goods, and then burst into tears because she couldn't find them in the linen closet. Often she accused people (usually Amma) of stealing things. She would drive off in her large Mercedes sedan, forget where she was going, turn around, and drive back to Heaven's Hill.

But if Mrs. Tilden periodically lost focus, at those times she also lost the angry tension, the endless criticism that had made it so painful to be around her when Noni was growing up. Occasionally there was now a vague softness to her. Noni noticed that in these gentle moods her mother wanted to be near her or near Amma, accompanying them through the house as they worked. She also spent long afternoons with her granddaughter Michelle and was more patient with this child than she'd been with her own.

Noni studied her mother as she stood looking at objects in her hand as if she couldn't imagine what one did with them, as she sat for hours in the den on the red leather couch, listening to her mechanical music boxes. The little machines she collected were all toy pianos: uprights, spinets, embellished harpsichords, black enamel concert grands. Once when Noni came upon her mother in one of the gentle moods, listening to a Chopin *Nocturne* phrase repetitively played on a music box, she asked if she would like her to play the whole piece on the piano for her.

"Oh, yes, please," said Mrs. Tilden. "I wish I could play like you. You have such a beautiful touch."

Noni had to leave the room she was so moved. It was the first unqualified compliment she could remember her mother ever giving her.

Over Roland's escalating protest, Noni stayed at Heaven's Hill almost a month. The most pleasant time of the day was early evening when Mrs. Tilden would sit with her chamomile tea on the yellow couch in the living room and listen to Noni play the piano. It was the closest she was ever to feel to her mother, who in the long gold light of those summer evenings never told her what to play, nor corrected how she played it, but just listened.

During that month, Mrs. Tilden began again to work on the photo albums that her husband had left behind when he'd moved out. But when Noni looked at the albums, she saw that all her mother had done was cut her own face out of all the photographs in which she'd appeared. Noni found all the small circles of faces floating like confetti in the swimming pool behind the house. She cleaned them out before Michelle arrived for Mrs. Tilden to give her her swimming lesson there the next morning.

During Noni's long visit, Kaye would occasionally drop in to see how she was doing. A few times, she walked with him while he played golf, as she had done long ago with her father. When he had an evening off, he took her out somewhere to give her a break; once they drove Kaye's vintage Thunderbird to a jazz concert at Haver, once they went out with Parker to the Indigo Club. Mrs. Tilden became very upset whenever Noni left her alone to go off with Kaye, so much so that Noni would sometimes wait until her mother was asleep before leaving the house.

Nor did Kaye come to the house often to visit, not only because he kept very busy at the hospital, but also because Mrs. Tilden appeared to be frightened of him and would nervously leave the room whenever he'd ask her things about her health, like whether she had headaches ("All my life"), whether she had dizzy spells ("All my life"), had trouble seeing, had trouble swallowing. Instead of her old patronizing attitude toward Kaye, there was now an uneasy dread, as if she were scared he would find out something about her.

One night Kaye watched her teaching Noni how to play bridge, a game in which Noni had never had any interest. Once a ruthless and formidable contract bridge tournament player, Mrs. Tilden grew flustered at her inability to remember the rules of the game, and finally ran from the room, screaming at Kaye that he was deliberately making her confused by staring at her.

"Her doctor says she's depressed," Noni explained.

"What's this doctor's name?" Kaye asked.

The following week he dropped by to tell Noni that he'd spoken with Dr. Schillings and that he was concerned that the elderly family physician was not treating Mrs. Tilden adequately. Even if her problem were in fact depression, she needed medication for it. But frankly Kaye didn't think depression was the cause of her behavior. He had begun to suspect that Mrs. Tilden was showing symptoms of either early-onset Alzheimer's or of some other dementia caused by neurological necrosis.

It was also possible, he warned Noni, that her mother had suffered a stroke (both her parents had died of strokes), and if so, the sooner they knew the facts, the better her chances for avoiding or surviving a second stroke. At the very least, she needed treatment for what he was sure was high blood pressure.

Noni said she'd talk to Dr. Schillings.

Mrs. Tilden began to spend most of her time in her sitting room. She had a pretty little writing desk there and a television hidden in a painted armoire. She liked to sit at the desk with its view from a bay window over the Heaven's Hill woods to the meadows and river that had all once been Gordon property. Sometimes two swans, wild descendants of swans brought there by Noni's great-grandmother, floated past together on the river, and whenever Mrs. Tilden saw them, she always commented on how swans mated for life and then she started to cry, lamenting that Bud had died and she was all alone.

At her little desk she wrote endless thank-you notes, some for recent gifts, but more of them acknowledging occasions from the distant past. Noni would find these notes addressed but never stamped and sometimes not even finished before Mrs. Tilden placed them inside the thick creamy envelopes engraved:

JUDITH GORDON TILDEN
HEAVEN'S HILL
MOORS, NORTH CAROLINA

Dear Mrs. Hadlemeyer,

My husband and I acknowledge with gratitude your donation to the Gordon Tilden Memorial Children's Library at Moors Elementary in memory of our son. Gordon often spoke of his hope to teach the young children of…

Dear Sunny and Derek,

What a wonderful time Bud and I had at your Halloween costume ball. It was a great idea for a party—

come as your favorite song—and you two looked adorable as "Mister Sandman" and "How Much Is That Doggy in the Window?"...

One day Noni's mother handed her a half-dozen envelopes, asking her to mail them. But two of the people to whom they were addressed Noni knew to be already dead.

So she went herself to talk with Dr. Schillings, who (being of the old school) was thoroughly unaccustomed to being questioned, much less advised, by a younger doctor, much less a black one, much less by his patient's daughter at the instigation of that young black doctor. Somewhat petulantly, Dr. Schillings told Noni that if he'd thought an ultrasound or angiography or an EEG or a CAT scan would serve any purpose other than enriching the people who'd performed the tests, he'd have ordered them. Judy Tilden was depressed and why shouldn't she be? She'd lost her son, her father, and her husband. That was enough to depress any decent woman. There was nothing else wrong with her.

When Noni asked Mrs. Tilden to go with her to see another physician recommended by Kaye, her mother refused; even the suggestion agitated her. She blamed Kaye for "stirring Noni up for no reason." When Dr. Schillings told her that Kaye was questioning his treatment of her, she flew into a tantrum. Why, Doctor Schillings had treated her all her life! Hysterical, Mrs. Tilden begged Noni to keep Kaye away from Heaven's Hill.

At a loss, Noni called Jack Hurd out in California; Doctor Jack called Schillings and persuaded him to put Mrs. Tilden on blood-pressure medication and on antidepressants. Noni was able to get her mother to take the drugs by having Doctor Jack telephone her. After a few days, she did in fact appear to be responding to them.

Kaye and Noni were having dinner at the new sushi restaurant in nearby Hillston (the first in the area) when Noni

told him happily of Doctor Jack's intervention. She was surprised by how deeply the news upset him. He grew quiet and
withdrawn. It took her half an hour to prod out of him why he
was angry. His answer came out in an intense low voice that
she almost couldn't hear: her choice to rely on Jack Hurd's
medical advice rather than Kaye's own, her decision to trust
some older white authority rather than someone who was sup-
posedly her closest friend, meant that in the last analysis she
didn't trust him any more than her mother did. Noni was
always turning to Doctor Jack, Doctor Jack practically ran her
life, Doctor Jack had guilt-tripped her into marrying Roland
and into going back to Roland and…

And at that point Kaye abruptly stopped, carefully, precisely, crossed his chopsticks on his plate, and shrugged. "Sorry,
it's your business, not mine. Ready to go?"

Noni grabbed his hand and shook it furiously. "It's not that
I *won't* listen to you. It's that she *will* listen to him. Jack got her
to take the pills. You want me to just let her die?"

"Let's drop it."

"Kaye, come on!"

"Fine. She's your mother. Let's go."

And so they left it at that.

It was ironic to Noni that when she returned home that
night after such a bad fight with Kaye, she'd had a phone call
from an indignant Roland, his third—he said—in as many
hours. She was supposed to be taking care of her sick mother, not
be out partying all night with her "quote best friend unquote"
Kaye King. She'd been gone for a month and Roland needed her
back in Houston. It wasn't fair for him to have to do without her.

"Have you been drinking?" she asked him.

"I just want to know what the fuck is going on," he replied,
and Noni hung up on him.

He called back an hour later and apologized, assuring her
that everything he said was because he loved her so much.

During the next week, her mother looked to be feeling better—she said she was her old self again—so much so that Noni made plans to return to Houston. Wade agreed to hire a niece of Amma Fairley's to sleep at Heaven's Hill every night to keep an eye on Mrs. Tilden while Amma was at Clayhome. Yolanda (Tatlock's daughter) already did the cleaning for the Tildens, Lanie King (Amma's sister-in-law from her first marriage) did the ironing, and McKinley Clay (Amma's baby brother) took care of the yard. Amma still cooked, and still did what she called "watched over" Judy Tilden. Amma told Noni, "Honey, you either get out of that marriage or you go be with your husband. I watched over your mama since the day she was born and I guess I can keep on."

"Get out? You always say marriage is for better or worse, Aunt Ma."

"Noni, everybody's got a different better, got a different worse. You figure out yours."

In the center of the place mat, her father's mother's Limoges wedding band china, white bordered in gold. Dinner plate beneath salad plate beneath fish plate beneath soup bowl.

After her return, life in the Houston Dutch Colonial on the cul de sac felt smaller and tighter and sadder. Whenever Roland drank too much and lost his temper, he apologized with an excuse: he was under a lot of stress, this wasn't an easy time, the pressure was on. The problem was always just this particular deal, this individual meeting, this specific boss. When Noni suggested that maybe the problem was the way Roland reacted to the problem, he said she had no idea what the real world was like "out there."

She couldn't argue. Her world inside the Dutch Colonial felt very unreal; the very knobs on the closet doors felt unreal.

Then one morning in early December, Wade called to say that their mother was in the hospital. She'd apparently had a stroke. Noni immediately bought a ticket to North Carolina on a flight leaving late that same night. When after dinner she told Roland that she was flying home, he exploded. "*This* is your fucking home," he told her. "Wade says she's fine. Let somebody else handle it. Let Wade and Trisha. You're two thousand miles away, for Christ sake. Why do you have to take care of everything and everybody?"

All of a sudden Noni had the strangest sensation that she was walking quickly down a long corridor at the end of which someone whom she couldn't identify stood waiting for her. On the sides of this corridor, tall old doors and broken wooden shutters, of the kind stacked in a smokehouse at Heaven's Hill, swung slapping loudly shut.

Carefully she put down on the table the dirty dinner plates that she had started to clear. She looked at her husband, sitting across from her, pouring another glass of wine, until he looked up. His eyes were still as blue, his hair as glossy black, his shoulders as broad as the day he'd called up to her in the stands of the Moors High stadium. But Noni realized that even when Roland looked right at her, he wasn't looking at her at all.

Collecting their napkins, she dropped them onto the plates. "I'm sorry. You're absolutely right, Roland. I don't have to take care of everything and everybody."

Walking to their perfectly coordinated bedroom, Noni picked up her already packed suitcase from their king-sized bed and took it to their perfectly appointed country kitchen where she put on her raincoat. She checked that her ticket was in her purse. From the dining room she could hear Roland still talking. "We aren't even going to discuss this. Just call Wade and tell him you're not coming."

The kitchen opened into the two-car garage. Noni took the BMW convertible, not because she liked it but because

Roland had always referred to it as "hers."

She was a mile away, headed to the airport, before Roland stormed into the kitchen to see why she wasn't answering him. She waited until just before her plane left before she called the house to tell him where she'd parked the car. He wasn't there. He was driving around and around the winding roads of their subdivision looking for her. She left a message.

Arriving at Heaven's Hill, Noni moved into her old childhood room and made the house beautiful for her mother's homecoming. Mrs. Tilden's time in the hospital hadn't been so bad. Everyone had come to see her, filled her room with flowers and balloons and baskets of fruits. The retired rector Dr. Fisher brought her communion and said she looked ten years younger. But it would take a while, everyone warned, for her "old stamina" to return. Noni said it was all right; she wasn't going anywhere.

The sound of the phone ringing became to her the sound of Roland's voice. His angry calls insisting that she return to him finally led her to install an answering machine.

A week after her return, in a bookstore, she ran into Lucas Miller, the man she'd known at Moors High who was now a lawyer, the man she'd danced with at Bunny's party years ago. He said he was still unmarried and still had a crush on her. She told him that she didn't want him to ask her out but she did want him to help her file papers of separation from her husband.

Beeswax candles in four tall silver Georgian candlesticks. Candles in two candelabra on the mantle. Candles in sconces on all four walls.

And now it was Christmas Eve. The French clock on the Heaven's Hill mantel chimed eight o'clock and Kaye would be coming at any minute. Noni was setting the dining room table for two. She moved the place settings to each end of the long polished table. Then she moved them to the middle of the table across from each other. She had red wine decanted, white wine chilling.

There was no illumination in the dining room but candlelight. In the center of the table a silver Tiffany platter was held aloft by two silver mermaids. On the platter sat red apples and green pears, red and green grapes.

"Oh my god," whispered Noni, shaking her head as she adjusted the grapes. "I am my mother's daughter."

At this moment, her mother, she hoped, was upstairs asleep. Mrs. Tilden slept at odd times, and ate, when she did eat, at odd times too. After dark she usually went upstairs and ate her dinner in the sitting room next to her bedroom. She hadn't been told that Kaye was coming over, but she wouldn't come down even if he weren't.

Today Noni was twenty-eight while Kaye was still twenty-seven. She had a surprise gift for his birthday tomorrow that she was eager to give him. There was soft Mozart music playing on the speakers in living room. Violin music. That was a part of her plan.

✳ ✳ ✳ ✳ ✳

The doorbell rang. Noni felt oddly warm, and she glanced in the mirror above the Sheraton sideboard, but she didn't look flushed, in fact she looked pale. She was slender in her favorite black dress; her hair was up, a silvery blonde twist. She wore the tiny gold grand-piano charm on the same wrist as the bracelet of sapphires that her father had given her, with the small sapphire earrings, on her wedding day.

Noni bit her lips, rubbed hard at her cheeks, then laughed at herself. What was she doing, dressing up for Kaye? Kaye who'd known her forever, who knew how her mother would pinch her cheeks when she was young to give her "a little more color." Kaye who once when she'd come back from a beach trip boasting "Look how much color I got," had teased her: "Better watch it, Noni. My people started out white as you, just went to that beach too much, trying to get a little more color."

The doorbell rang again and she hurried into the foyer.

"Hey there, Dr. King. Merry Christmas. Don't you look nice."

Holding two of Amma's large wicker baskets, he stepped inside. "Merry Christmas. Happy Birthday. You look nice too, Mrs. Hurd."

"Stop it."

Beneath his long flowing cashmere coat, Kaye also wore black, a black linen shirt, black pleated trousers of thin Italian wool, black woven leather slippers. Amma had told Noni that it sent a shiver through her how much money Kaye spent on his clothes. But all of a sudden he had the money to spend. In his first two years in his private cardiology practice he had made more, Amma speculated, than Tatlock Fairley had made in two decades on the grounds crew of Haver University.

Of course, as Amma complained, what was the good of Kaye's having money when he wouldn't give himself a life to have it in. Her grandson performed heart surgery on eight or ten people a week and charged them thousands of dollars each for doing it. But it was all he did. Nothing but work. So who was he to tell Amma to quit working and let him buy her and Tatlock a nice new house somewhere? Of course Tatlock was all for the plan but Amma would not leave Clayhome where she'd been born and had lived all her life. Not unless the Tildens threw her out. And that, Noni swore, would never happen in her lifetime.

In the doorway by the console where the old blue Chinese jar sat beside the metal pear tree, Kaye leaned over, kissed Noni's cheek. "Been pinching your cheeks again?"

She ignored him, took one of the baskets; there was a covered cake stand and a covered salad bowl in it. In the other basket there was a large enamel cooking pot. "So what's this? Did you really make this?"

Their agreement about their birthday dinner tonight was that they would each contribute half the meal. He followed her along the front hall. "What was the first thing I told you the night we met?"

She placed the basket on the sideboard in the dining room. "That it was snowing, which was obvious."

"What was the second thing?" He stopped and looked around the candlelit room at the gleaming crystal and silver of the table setting, the red tapers and green pears, the low leaping flames of the gas fire in the fireplace. With a bow, he applauded her.

"Thank you." She curtsied.

"So what was the second thing I told you?"

"How to run my life. Oh, I don't know."

"I told you I can do anything. And that includes cook." Kaye pushed past her into the kitchen, placed the pot on the stovetop.

She took the lid off the pot and the smell of hot delicious soup floated up. "Oh, you didn't make this. This is Aunt Ma's she-crab soup."

"This is *Kaye's* she-crab soup." He crossed his arms in the old flamboyant way. "You don't say those were Rockefeller's oysters you and I ate last night. You say those were your damn oysters. Well, this is Amma Fairley's recipe and it's *my* soup. 'Course Grandpa Tat says," and Kaye lowered his voice to his Tatlock rumble, "'If I'd just had my chance, I'd of proved I invented she-crab soup and *he*-crab soup both, and every other kind of soup Campbell's stole from me, and I'd of been the richest Indian in America, if I'd just had my chance to prove I was an Indian.' Okay, Noni, stop that laughing, you're going to pee."

"No, I'm not."

"Yes, you are."

"Nope, it's not going to work this time. I'm over it."

"Oh, no, you're not."

After she poured the soup into the tureen, Kaye brought it to the dining room table. Both were suddenly made strangely formal by the setting. "Madame," he smiled and pulled back her chair for her and she sat. She could feel his breath near her hair as he pushed the chair in.

She toasted them with the wine. "To us. To Christmas past and present…"

"And future." He handed her a bright red ribboned box. "Happy Birthday." In the box was another charm. This one a little gold telephone. "You remember that silver dime shaped like a heart I gave you a long time ago?"

She gestured out to the foyer. "It's upstairs in my jewelry box."

"Well, you can't call anybody for a dime anymore, no matter how bad you need them." He held up a quarter.

Noni reached across the table, touched his hand, then took the quarter from him. "'When you feel lost and about to give up, / Cause your life just ain't good enough,' reach out for me too." She smiled back at him. "'Course, Kaye King, I know you never would be about to give up and you never would feel life just wasn't good enough, but just in the remote, remote, remote possibility—"

"You like the soup?"

"The soup is delicious."

Back in the kitchen, Noni watched Kaye's long fingers cut precisely and perfectly through the melon, then carefully drape prosciutto over it. His hands had always been beautiful to her.

As they ate the melon, they talked about Parker, who'd been fired for insubordination from the job Kaye had helped him find at University Hospital. Kaye feared that Parker might be back on drugs that he'd gotten addicted to in prison. Parker and Kaye were drifting apart. Parker had accused Kaye of thinking he was too good for him, but Kaye said it wasn't personal. He really had no time these days for anyone or anything but medicine. His life was his work.

Noni rolled her eyes. "Of course it's personal. It's about drugs, it's about what happened to your mother. It's too painful for you to be around Parker. So you avoid him."

"Sure sure sure."

"Well, why can you have theories about me and my mother, but I can't have theories about you and yours?"

Kaye watched Noni squeezing lemon into olive oil. "You've got wonderful hands," he said. "It's in your hands that you can see how strong you are."

She smiled, wiggling her fingers. "Fingers of steel. All that Chopin. Thank you."

As they ate the sautéed shrimp, they talked about Bunny, who, despite her professional success—she was the youngest full professor in her department at Columbia—was unhappy because she still couldn't find the right man, or even—as she joked—"the wrong man." Noni said that Bunny was thinking of having a baby by herself.

Kaye gave his parodic eyebrow bounce. "That'll be a first. Didn't even Jesus's mother need an angel or a bird or something to help her out?"

"Don't even try, you're not getting my goat tonight."

He grinned at her. "Okay, not your goat. How 'bout your lamb of God?"

"That is so bad. That is really wretched, even for one of your jokes. And don't start in on St. John's."

"Did I say anything?"

"I could see it in your eyes." Noni told him that the truth was, sitting in church brought out the best in her—it was the place where she felt at peace.

"Bull," said Kaye. "It's the place where that fine old glorious Gordon past falls bong on your head with big gold *thunks*—

the altar rail dedicated to devoted wife Martha McAllister Gordon, *thunk*; the pulpit stand in loving memory of Shelby W. Gordon Jr., *thunk*; collection plate, stained glass, *thunk*, *thunk*, *thunk*. You need to get out."

"I got out. You don't think Houston is a long way from Moors?"

"No, I don't."

"You think you have such a life? You just told me you had no life at all."

"I didn't say that. I said my work was my life."

Noni raised her shoulders, held them arched and ironical.

"Don't get sarcastic with your shoulders," he told her.

"What? You don't like my shoulders as much as my wonderful hands?"

"Your shoulders are wonderful, too," he smiled. And then suddenly they were both embarrassed. "I'll tell you whose life is his work these days." Kaye changed the subject. "Tatlock Fairley, the African-American Van Gogh."

It had been only a few years since his grandfather Tatlock had started setting up his pictures beside Amma's sales table outside the bank. The first pictures he'd sold were paintings of vanished Moors landmarks, all with himself prominent in them: there was one of Tat and R.W. Gordon in front of the old Moors Savings Bank that had been torn down. One of Tat and Dr. Fisher in front of St. John's Church before they'd added the modern annex. One of Tat and a crowd of car buffs at the old filling station, another of Tat and shoppers at the dime store that was now a parking lot, another of Tat and the owner at a fruit stand that was now the site of the town's first ATM kiosk.

Not only had passersby immediately begun to purchase these paintings for twenty-five dollars each, one day a woman who owned a fancy art gallery over in Hillston had come to call on Tat at Clayhome. She'd picked out ten of his works, all kinds, big pictures on old doors, little pictures on tin boxes, telling him she'd give him fifty percent of what she sold them for, and that if this lot sold, she'd buy more. At first Tat had been indignant; why should the gallery owner keep half of his money? But when the woman had told him what she planned to charge for his pictures, "that old man signed so fast he smoked the paper."

"He's going to do a painting of me," Noni said. "'Noni at the Piano.'"

Kaye tossed the salad he'd brought. "I guess you'll be play-ing a duet then, 'cause you can bet that old man'll paint him-self right beside you on the bench." He served Noni's plate. "Spinach salad. Eat some. Anemic."

"You don't know that."

"I know—"

"Everything."

"Right."

They took their coffee to the living room where violin music was softly playing through the speakers. The only illumi-nation was the fire in the fireplace and the delicate shimmer of the white lights on the Christmas tree. Noni, not her mother, had put up the tree this year and it was the most perfectly shaped one that Kaye had ever seen there, a white pine beautifully tapered. It was also the least decorated tree he'd ever seen at Heaven's Hill. "So your Christmas trees *are* green," he grinned.

Some things had stayed the same. As always the five big red stockings embroidered BUD, JUDY, GORDON, WADE, NOELLE, hung from the mantel. Noni's suggestion that they leave the stockings packed away this Christmas had so distressed Mrs. Tilden that she'd withdrawn it. The stockings were only decorative now; there was no pretense of a Santa filling them.

But there were presents under the tree. Kaye's from Noni was in a large box wrapped in green. When he opened it, he saw a violin in a case, its beautiful reddish wood gleaming in the firelight. He was surprised into silence.

While Kaye had played violin in elementary school in Philadelphia, and again in the string orchestra at Gordon Junior High, he had never owned an instrument of his own, nor ever wanted to. "I'm not really into it," he'd told Miss Clooney when he'd reached high school.

"You're right about that, Kaye," the music teacher had replied. "You just don't want to feel what that violin makes you feel."

"You think you know me, Miss Clooney?"

Kaye had liked Miss Clooney, who called herself "the last of the burnt-out hippies" and who was the teacher who years ago had organized the student council into the honor guard for the first black students to integrate Moors High. Still, he had returned the rented violin and quit the program.

"What am I supposed to do with this?" he said to Noni now. "Hang it on the wall? I can't play this."

Noni threw up her arms. "I swear to god, Kaye, you are the absolute worst receiver of gifts I have ever met in my life. The absolute worst."

"I mean, thank you, it's beautiful, but I'm just saying I can't play it. I haven't played since ninth grade and I was terrible."

She took the violin from its case, strummed the strings, started tuning them. It was a gift of hers, perfect pitch; she had always had the burden of hearing disharmony and the gift of setting it right. After she tuned the violin, she plucked a melody on it as if it were a guitar, a simple melancholy Bach melody that they had played in the school orchestra. Bach's "Air on a G String."

Then she handed the instrument to Kaye, who held it uncomfortably. "Well, Dr. King, why don't you learn to play better? You're always telling me what to do with my life, so I'm going to tell you something. They call it *playing* music."

He looked at her quizzically. "So?"

"So you don't play anymore. I bet you don't dance. You

don't play golf even. Amma says all you do is make money."

"I fix hearts."

She smiled. "I used to love to play with you." Her face flushed. She closed the violin back in its case. "You think about it."

He followed her back through the dining room, looked at her, couldn't move his eyes away. The only lighting was the candles on the table, and in the wall sconces, and leaping from gas flames in the fireplace. From the living room softly came the violin music.

In the kitchen with its hanging lights and copper pans, side by side at the large gray limestone sinks they washed and dried china and silverware too old and fragile for dishwashers.

Washing soap from his hands, Kaye passed Noni the soup tureen to dry. "Have you worried enough tonight about everybody but yourself? Is it time yet for me to ask you what *you're* going to do? Can I nag you like you nagged me?"

Carefully she placed the china lid on the tureen. "Isn't that all you've ever done? What I'm going to do when?"

"From now on. I'll make it easy. Here're a few choices. One. I'm going back to Texas and chuck the rest of my life away on Roland. Wait, there's Two. I'm going to stay here at Heaven's Hill, even though my mother may be perfectly okay, or even if she's not, somebody could be hired to take care of her, or even if they can't, she could be placed in a facility, I'm going to personally be her nurse 'til one of us dies, preferably her.

"Or Three. Now listen carefully to Three. I'm going back to Haver University and finish my degree and do something with a talent I happen to have, that I just said was damn important, and that's a talent that not everybody's got." He handed her a platter. "You want some advice? Don't pick One or Two."

"What do you mean, 'do with it'? Like what, play in the lounge at the Pine Hills Inn?"

"Sure, why not? I don't know. You figure it out." Kaye

opened the door to the walk-in utilities closet. "Any matches in here? I need to light my pudding." He turned the light on. "Noni, look!"

Against the pantry wall, where Michelle had left it, stood the old red sled inscribed "NOELLE AND KAYE." The writing was faded, the paint chipped, the runners rusty.

"It's our sled." He brought it out to show her, held it up to his side. "It looks so small. Don't you remember it being a lot bigger?"

The sled reached no higher than Kaye's waist, rested against the soft fabric on his thigh.

Noni ran her hand along the runner's curve. "It was taller than we were, remember? We could both sit on it."

Kaye set the sled down on the kitchen floor and straddled it, his long legs stretching out on either side. "That was a long time ago."

She nodded. The room got quieter as he looked up at her, at the deep shine of the black silk against her slender collarbone. It was so quiet that Noni could hear her own heart.

Then suddenly, loudly, the oven buzzer blared at them and Noni jumped to turn it off.

Kaye put the sled back where he'd found it. Then at the green pine table, he stuck a holly twig atop his plum pudding and poured brandy over the mounded cake. "Now go sit down."

"Could you ever ask, instead of bossing me around?"

He put his hands on her shoulders, gently pushed her forward.

Noni was seated in the dining room when Kaye carried in the blazing Christmas pudding. He began singing as he held it out to her. "God rest you merry, gentlemen, let nothing you dismay."

He was shocked when her eyes welled with tears and she began to cry. Then instantly he remembered her father singing that carol, remembered how Tilden would sing that line festively at his guests, year after year, as he served them his holiday punch in the silver cups. "Oh, I'm sorry, Noni. I'm so sorry. I forgot. Forgive me."

Kaye set down the dessert in front of her and leaned over to embrace her as she sat with her head in her hands. He kissed her hair, then the side of her face, then he pressed his cheek to hers, wetting his skin with her tears.

For a long time he stayed there, their faces touching, neither of them moving.

Then slowly he reached across her, took the silver cake cutter, placed her hand on it beneath his. Slowly together they cut down a piece of the dark spongy dessert, then another piece.

Still neither of them spoke. The only sound was the violin music playing from the next room and the ticking of the old-fashioned French clock on the mantel. It chimed softly. Eleven times. Kaye listened to them, not moving away from her.

Then Noni stood and stepped back from her chair. Slowly she turned to him.

To Kaye as he looked at her suddenly the candle flames on the walls and on the table seemed to grow brighter and to lighten until the room glowed with golden halos, as if angels stood all around them.

They kissed. In his eyes Noni saw the walls of the room float backwards. She saw the walls turn to gold like the domed ceiling of a great church. The walls opened into a long empty corridor and at the end of it the person she saw was Kaye.

She moved into his arms. They kissed again and then they stepped back to look at each other. And what they saw was that they had left all questions behind.

Above them, the gold and red flames of the candles burned lower in the beautiful room.

❋ ❋ ❋ ❋ ❋

Kaye and Noni heard the quick racing footsteps above them on the second floor. The mantel clock was chiming again, over and over.

As they leapt to their feet, hurrying their clothes together, they heard the screaming. "Nonnniiii!"

Above them the footsteps rushed flying along the upstairs hall.

Together they ran into the foyer, smelling the smoke as they opened the door from the dining room. On the landing of the stairs above them they saw Mrs. Tilden spinning wildly, fluttering her arms at her sides as if trying to fly away from the flames that leapt up at her from the hem of her bathrobe. Her eyes were frenzied, the terror huge in them. "*Nonnniiii!*"

Kaye rushed ahead of Noni up the stairs, threw his arms about Mrs. Tilden, and pulled her with him down to the floor. He covered her with his body, and although she fought him frantically, he smothered the fire, beat it down until it was out. "Go check her room! She's okay," he kept shouting at Noni.

But as Noni struggled to move past them, her mother grabbed at her dress. "Noni, don't leave me, Noni!"

Below them the front door slammed open and Kaye heard his grandmother Amma running into the house gasping out, "*Fire!*"

"Up here!" Kaye pulled Noni down to hold her mother, who kept sobbing about how she'd only tried to do something nice. He raced up the stairs and along the second-floor hall. Pulling two quilts from an antique rack, he rushed with them to the wing where smoke was pouring from Mrs. Tilden's sitting room.

Below him as he ran, he could hear his grandmother on the hall phone calling for help. He could hear Noni's mother chattering hysterically about how she'd forgotten that she'd lit the candles for Noni's cake, that the curtain had caught fire and then everything was catching fire and she was sorry, she was so sorry. "Please don't be angry at me, Noni."

And down below him on the stairs he could hear Noni saying over and over, "Mom, I'm not angry, I love you. I'm not leaving, I love you."

The Eighth Day of Christmas

✳

December 24, 1986
The Hitchcock Chair

On a cold December night, starlight glimmered on the lawn and the sky was silvery with a big full moon that looked more like an autumn moon than a winter one. Amma Fairley paused in her preparations for her Christmas dinner the next day and wiped off her thick glasses. She put them back on and looked out the window of the Clayhome kitchen over to Heaven's Hill where she had left a light burning in the window for Judy and Noni Tilden's return home with Noni's baby. Amma couldn't wait to see that little boy. Poor thing, not even getting born in America. Well, they'd be here tonight from England in an hour or so, depending on traffic from the airport. For two whole years they'd hardly been home at all—not since the fire.

That fire.

The night of that fire it had been all they could do to keep Judy Tilden in one piece 'til the ambulance got there; the fire trucks had set her off screaming louder than the sirens. But those firemen had saved Heaven's Hill, no doubt about it. They'd hosed down the roof, beat back those flames 'til nothing was lost but the upstairs right wing. Things could have been worse. Somebody could have lost a life.

Where in the world had Judy hidden any cake after Amma had checked her sitting room that same afternoon? Lighting a bunch of candles on a birthday cake right next to some chiffon curtains, it was a miracle Judy hadn't burned herself worse than she did. Even so, she'd lost the use of her legs, not from the burns, but they thought maybe from a stroke, though the doctors couldn't seem to agree on anything.

Some of them thought Judy had maybe had two or three little strokes even before she'd caught the house on fire—TIAs Kaye called the little strokes—that nobody had noticed. The doctors said how she might even have had a stroke before the one that had put her in the hospital the year before that. Kaye explained how those little strokes were probably the reason why Judy had gotten so scattered and so raw in her feelings that year before the fire, to where one day she'd burst into tears if you said something nice to her, and the next, start screaming at you that you were robbing her.

But not walking was nothing compared to what that fire had done to Judy's spirits. Judy had turned into a child clinging to her mother night and day, and Noni was like that mother, never losing patience with her. Carting her all over everywhere, one doctor after another.

Well, it'd be good to have them home again. Amma and her niece Dionne and a few of the grandchildren had gotten the place all aired out and decorated. Amma had the heat on, and a little supper waiting to go in the microwave oven, although nothing would persuade her that any natural taste wasn't ruined by all that microwaving. Bad enough the way things tasted bought at the grocery store, not like in the old days when they'd grown everything they needed right here at Heaven's Hill. Raised all they needed too, her grandpa and grandma, her daddy and mama when they'd been working here. Chickens, pigs, cows, lambs, home-bred and home-eaten. Long after nobody else bothered.

Every day when Amma was little she would go off with her cousins May and Seka down the hill with their buckets to milk the cows, so early in the morning the grass was like walking through silky water. And in the summer they'd take the nickels they'd earned to Harmon's Drugs for ice cream. Amma would have to go in and buy for all three of them because when she was young she was light enough to pass. Even though Mr. Harmon knew who she was, he'd let her buy from his soda fountain counter because she was that light-skinned.

Back then you ate things in their proper time, fresh-killed, or ripe from the vine or the earth. Nothing tasted that good anymore, especially not coming out of some radiation machine like a microwave. Plus her eyes had gotten so bad, she couldn't read all the buttons and numbers anyhow.

But nothing ever changed in her kitchens, so she didn't need to use her eyes. Everything stayed right where it ought to be. Sewing, though, was too hard now; lately she'd had to give up her sewing. Still, like Kaye said, hadn't she sewn enough damn sunflowers on enough damn mats and napkins for one woman's lifetime?

Amma hummed along with Whitney Houston on the radio as she pushed her apple stuffing into the huge white turkey.

O come, let us adore Him,
Christ the Lord.

On the porch of Heaven's Hill, her grandchildren had wrapped evergreen garlands around the columns and hung one of her spruce and holly wreaths on the front door. In the living room they'd decorated a small tree with some colored lights and set it up in the corner. Nothing was as big or blazing as it used to be at the Tildens, but Amma had wanted Noni and Judy and the baby to have at least something looking a little cheery when the van pulled into the drive.

Tatlock, his son Austin, and Austin's son Zaki were going to pick the Tildens up at the airport, even though Austin never drove his taxis anymore, had ten regular drivers working for him now, had a shuttle van and a stretch limousine, too. Last July he'd driven Amma and Tat in that limo to the Peacock Room for their fortieth-anniversary party. But this evening the three Fairley men were going to the airport in Tat's personal van, because it was fixed up to handle somebody in a wheelchair, and Tat was going to take charge of showing Judy Tilden how to travel in one. And everything was ready at the house—now not just the one ramp they'd put in right away, but ramps off all three porches and an elevator from the first to the second floor so Judy could go back to her old wing of the house. Plus handicapped bathrooms upstairs and down. Money made things easier, that was certain.

It sure would be good to have somebody home over there across the lawn again. Especially a baby. Nothing was more lonesome than a house with no life growing in it.

And wonders of His love,
And wonders, wonders of His love.

✳ ✳ ✳ ✳ ✳

Carrying her sleeping son, now a little over a year old, Noni Tilden moved quickly beside the airline attendant as he smoothly hurried her mother's wheelchair along the ramp into the gate area.

Over the last two years, Mrs. Tilden had grown frailer and thinner, one side of her body weaker than the other, one side of her face slightly fallen. Were she not lifted and straightened in her wheelchair, she would sometimes slide down slumping into its corner. Fortunately, after Mrs. Tilden's hired nurse had gotten them situated at the London airport, the airline attendants had taken over the invalid and had been wonderfully solicitous to her throughout both long flights. Noni couldn't have managed without them.

Noni took her mother's hand, held it, walked beside her. "It's fine, Mom, we're right here with you."

In her cashmere sweater coat, heeled boots, jeans, and soft turtleneck, her silvery blonde hair loosely pinned, Noni was a very beautiful woman with no apparent awareness of the fact. A few of the men who'd appreciatively watched her as she'd played with her baby during the long flight from Heathrow had found themselves on the same plane with her from New York, too, and after a few more cocktails, had tried a variety of conversational gambits. Noni had politely ended them. Now they smiled at her as they went past. Busy with her son, she'd noticed none of it. But then her mother had often told her she didn't see that men were flirting with her even before she'd had her little boy.

Noni had named him John Gordon and called him Johnny; he was fifteen months old and eagerly walking. He'd exhausted her during the flights, making her walk him up and down the aisles of the planes, and now he was fast asleep, a heavy weight in her arms.

As soon as Noni turned the corner into the waiting room, she spotted Austin Fairley and his son Zaki standing by the counter in their down jackets, waving at her. At the sight of them, Noni's smile broke out like the sun. To see the Fairleys was to see Heaven's Hill, their shared home, and she ran forward to embrace them, waking the baby. "Austin, Zaki! I'm so glad, so glad to see you!"

"Noni, how's it going?" Zaki Fairley was fond of Noni, and not only because she'd given him her old green Alfa Spider two years ago when he'd turned sixteen. "Hey, this your little boy?"

"This is the one and only."

The little boy yawned widely when Noni handed him to Zaki, stared at the stranger hard, then snuggled his tight blond curls into the teenager's shoulder and went back to asleep.

Zaki's father Austin was grumpy. "We've been here a half-hour, no traffic at all. Pop Tat's waiting in his van out at the curb with a special lift for your mama, Noni. Let's get going. Hey there, Mrs. Tilden. Zaki, put that baby in his stroller and wrap him up. It's freezing out there." Austin took over the wheelchair and sped away.

As it turned out, there were only a half-dozen people at the gate, and few anywhere else in the terminal. Amma, who had flown on planes only twice in her life, both times to Philadelphia, had been wrong. Far from crowded, by seven P.M. on Christmas Eve, the airport was in fact nearly deserted.

As they waited for the bags, Mrs. Tilden grew querulous. She'd been on two long flights; her nap, the movie, *Hannah and Her Sisters*, and her book, *The Prince of Tides*, had not been enough to keep off the discomfort of even first-class seats. She complained now that her back hurt and the airport was overheated. Where was their luggage, how was she going to ride in this van of Uncle Tatlock's, how was she going to get up all the steps at Heaven's Hill?

Rocking the sleeping baby back and forth in his stroller, Noni answered each question with a patient matter-of-factness, only half listening. She was home. It was Christmas and she was home.

❋ ❋ ❋ ❋ ❋

The phone rang at Clayhome; it was the man selling Tat's paintings now; a "rep," Tat called him. Somebody from New York. Amma didn't like the man. She told him Tat was gone to the airport, and don't call him back 'til after Christmas. Christmas was a holy day and a family day. The man laughed like she was telling jokes.

Wasn't it something how, after all those years when you couldn't shove Tatlock Fairley out of the house with a bulldozer, all of a sudden he'd used his painting money to buy himself that big special van with all its lifts and levers and the fanciest motor-wheelchair you ever saw, one that would do just about anything you'd want it to except bake your bread?

Once he had those wheels, that man was gone like you'd shot him out of a cannon at the circus. And just as well, so she didn't have to listen anymore to him laughing 'til he choked over *Night Court* and those *Golden Girls* on TV, or watching the baseball games that had their own channels now. He had Austin's boy Zaki driving him all around the state meeting rich folks in the "art business," he called it, showing off his paintings to them. Take your breath away what people would pay for a picture of an old black man standing beside a pile of pumpkins painted on a piece of beat-up door frame.

Tat used to always be saying you never know what life was going to do to you. Well, he sure proved that right. Seventy-seven years old, no legs, and all of a sudden here he was, written up in a magazine. Plus, it truly made that old man happy painting those pictures of himself in front of everything ever built in Moors County and spending the money he got for them. His share up to three, four hundred dollars a picture now, sometimes more. And not just from folks that knew him—like Kaye and that girl Bunny Breckenridge—but from strangers. Tat had two of his pictures hanging right this minute on the walls of the new Moors Savings Bank. And you know old Mister Gordon would've had one of his fits if he'd lived to see a colored man's pictures up on the walls of his bank. Well, like the song says, it's no secret what God can do.

Tat got all his money in cash and kept it in a big iron safe he'd bought and hid in the bedroom closet. Mrs. Goldman at that gallery hadn't been able to do a thing with him about investments and taxes and all. And this New York "rep" didn't even try. Tat spent every cent he got. He had more gadgets than Kmart. Even got himself a telescope to watch Halley's comet coming back, not that the little blur he showed Amma through that thing looked like much worth making such a big to-do over.

A Child, a Child shivers in the cold
Let us bring Him silver and gold...

Amma slid her pecan pie into the oven, checking the clock above the stove. Yes, Judy and Noni and that baby would need a little Christmas to welcome them home after being gone so long and things so tough. Judy in the hospital with a broken collarbone after she'd had that fall down the stairs in their place in London. Somehow she must have lost control of her wheelchair while Noni was bathing the baby. It was hard to understand. Amma had been worried sick, despite Kaye's claiming how some hospital off in London, England, was going to be just as good as University Hospital in Hillston where everybody knew Judy's family.

But what with the smoke and water damage and the new construction, it had taken Carolina Restoration almost a year to get Heaven's Hill back in shape. And nobody could live in the house while they worked on it, and that's how the stay in California had gotten started. Judy didn't want to come back to Wade's—not that Wade probably even asked her—unless Noni would come too, and Noni and Wade just didn't get along. So they'd stayed out in California where Doctor Jack could talk Judy into better treatment than old Dr. Schillings had.

But then Doctor Jack sent Judy to see some expert back in Boston for a bunch more tests, and that man thought there might be something called Pick's Disease causing her troubles, so he sent her somewhere else. Judy didn't mind the travel. In fact, the more traveling Noni did with her, the better she seemed to like it. So bless Noni's heart, the whole first half of her pregnancy, she was taking Judy all over everywhere, getting her some test or other or seeing some new specialist. Nobody could have done better or sweeter than Noni, and Amma was sure it hadn't been easy, not with Judy getting so hard to manage. Sounded like those gentle moods of hers didn't happen much anymore.

Wrapping a cloth over the big turkey, Amma nestled it on its rack high on a counter where the dog Tina couldn't get at it. Tina was the daughter of the long dead black Lab Philly that Noni had given Kaye back when they were in seventh grade; Kaye had named her Tina Turner, because when she'd been a puppy he'd stand her on her hind legs and pretend like she was dancing. Of course, who'd ended up taking care of the dog because Kaye was never around?

Amma set the turkey aside, ready for the oven just before dawn. Nine for Christmas dinner. Not as many of her brothers' children as other years. But young folks have their own plans these days. Like Kaye's arranging his party tonight at his new house over in his fancy neighborhood in Glade Lake. Of course he had invited her and Tatlock, too. But she'd said no. What were they supposed to do over there with all that dancing and loud music and fast-talking young people not even half their age?

Here at Clayhome tomorrow they'd at least be able to hear each other speak when Kaye brought his girlfriend Shani over. Shani Bouchard that he'd met up in New York. She was so fast- and sharp-talking, it was hard enough trying to understand her even in the quiet. When Amma had gotten introduced to Shani's folks back at Thanksgiving, when they'd come down to meet everybody, they'd talked just like their daughter. The way they talked made everything sound like they were mad at you even though they weren't. Kaye could imitate them to a T. New Yoikers, he called them.

Of course, Tatlock had wanted to go to Kaye's party tonight. But he wasn't about to get back from the airport with the Tildens 'til eight at the earliest. Plus, even with Austin and Zaki right there helping with Judy's wheelchair and their luggage, even with Tat's special van, it was still going to take a while to get them settled in here. And you'd think—angrily Amma snapped off the tips of beans—you'd think that Judy's only living son, Wade, that had claimed to love her so much, would have put off taking Trisha and Michelle to Disney world (which he was doing just because he wanted to play golf anyhow) so he could be around to pick up his own mama and sister at the airport. 'Specially if his mama and his sister had been gone this long and had ended up stuck in a London hospital with broken bones.

But that was Wade. Love was just something for Wade to talk about at his Baptist men's prayer club breakfast.

Everybody talkin' 'bout heaven ain't goin' to heaven, heaven…

❋ ❋ ❋ ❋ ❋

"Noni? Oh my god, Noni! It's been forever!"

Noni turned at the baggage carousel and found herself in the arms of her old friend Bunny Breckenridge, just flown in from New York City, home for Christmas. Hair wilder than ever, wide warm smile, shawl dragging the floor, Bunny rocked Noni back and forth, then she bent down to the sleeping child in the stroller. "Oh my god! Is this your baby? I heard you had a baby in London!"

"This is Johnny." Noni knelt, pulled back the knitted blanket so Bunny could see the child's face, the tight blond curls and long dark lashes, the golden skin and tiny perfect features.

"He's beautiful."

"Yes, he is, isn't he?"

"Oh, you're lucky to have a baby!" Bunny hugged her. "Happy Birthday. It's your birthday today, right? How old are we?"

"I hate to be the one to tell you but we're thirty! Oh, Bunny, this is wonderful, how are *you?*"

Bunny's briefcase stuffed with books and papers slid off her shoulder with the shawl. "Sameo-sameo. Somebody told me you'd moved to London for good."

"No, no. My mom had a fall and was back in the hospital, so we had to stay longer than expected." Noni knelt again to let her mother know that this was Bunny, remember Bunny, her girlfriend from school? Bunny lived in New York now, she was a college teacher.

Bunny bent down to her. "Hi, Mrs. Tilden."

Judy Tilden covered the right side of her mouth with her hand as she always did, embarrassed by its drooping, when she talked to anyone but Noni. "Noni's friend, yes. Whom did you marry, Bunny?"

"Not a blessed soul." Bunny laughed.

Mrs. Tilden picked at Bunny's shawl. "Noni and Roland are divorced. You probably heard that. But at least she was already pregnant with Johnny when they separated and so we have my little grandchild."

"Well, he's sure a beauty." Bunny kissed Mrs. Tilden, who then started complaining that she couldn't breathe the horrible air in the terminal. She plucked at Noni. "Where's Wade? Why couldn't Wade come get me?"

Zaki Fairley, back from taking the carry-on bags to the curb where Tatlock waited in the van, offered to wheel Mrs. Tilden out there to see him. After they left, Noni asked to hear all her friend's news.

Bunny shrugged. "Still live on Riverside with a cat and a fish. Still looking for a biped. Still need to lose twenty pounds. Well, thirty. Still call myself a feminist, that's the kind of old-fashioned girl I am. But you, Noni, you look fantastic!"

"Oh god, don't be silly."

"So this is what having a baby and leaving your husband does for you? I gotta get married so I can get a divorce! How *is* Roland Turd?" She hugged her friend. "Oh, I'm sorry. Kaye and I were mean to call him that. We were probably just jealous."

Noni smiled. "It's okay. Well, let's see. Roland said I'd destroyed his life and he'd never get over it and then he married his CFO's daughter a month after our divorce."

"Holy shit, you just made fun of somebody for the first time in your life!" They laughed together. "But is it still Noni Hurd?"

"No, Noni Tilden. And the baby's John Gordon Tilden. John's my dad's real name."

"And Kaye's."

"John Gordon, for my brother and my dad."

Bunny studied her old friend. "So how does Roland fit into this?"

"I have sole custody of Johnny."

"You do? That's strange."

"But true. It's fine with him." Noni excused herself to check with Austin about the delay in the luggage.

When she came back, Bunny asked her, "Your mom's not getting any better?"

"No. She hasn't walked since the fire. One of the London doctors thinks she ought to be able to, but she can't. Some doctors we've seen say it's one thing, some say it's another. It's a long, slow process." Unconsciously, Noni clasped her wrist over the bracelet that Kaye had given her years ago; it still had only two gold charms, the piano and the telephone. "So you're in touch with Kaye? How's he doing?"

Bunny glanced puzzled at Noni. "He's fine. I saw him a few times in New York. It's great you're here for his party."

"Kaye's having a birthday party?"

Bunny frowned, her mouth awkward. "Tonight. His... girl...He's seeing somebody pretty regularly and she's moving down here."

"Oh....Do you know her?" Noni bent to pull a sock back up on her baby's foot.

"No, I never met her. He's got a new house. You knew he'd bought this house?" Noni shook her head, smiling, embarrassed. Bunny said she'd seen the place only once. "It's not that far from where I grew up, right on Glade Lake. Very modern, you know, lot of glass, lot of high tech, not much furniture. You two don't keep up?"

Noni was trying to imagine the house as she said, "I haven't heard from Kaye since the fire. I wrote him while we were traveling but, well, I guess he's been busy. That's Kaye."

"He did tell me he'd been mad at you."

"Did he tell you why?"

Bunny lifted her shoulders. "No, he didn't."

Noni blushed, her pale skin splotching with red. "It doesn't matter."

Stooping, Bunny began stuffing the scattered books and papers into the case. Noni bent to help her. "Come on to Kaye's party with me, Noni. We'll surprise him."

"No, I don't think I will. Thank you though, Bunny."

Then the buzzer sounded and bags began falling out onto the carousel.

"I don't know why you two won't admit you love each other." Bunny kissed her friend and, puzzled, watched her walk away, pushing the stroller with the sleeping child.

✳   ✳   ✳   ✳   ✳

Holy infant so tender and mild,
Sleep in heavenly peace....

Amma thought she heard car tires on the white stone driveway but it wasn't the van, whose sound she would recognize. She suddenly wondered if maybe Kaye was dropping off an invitation at Heaven's Hill for Noni to come to his party tonight. A week ago Amma had told him that Noni would be flying home from England on Christmas Eve. Even if Noni was too tired to go, it still would have been a nice thought to ask her. But Amma hadn't seen any invitation in the mail for Heaven's Hill; she'd have put it on the hall console by that blue jar where Judy Tilden had always collected her invitations.

The truth was, something bad had happened between Kaye and Noni around the night of the fire, and they'd never gotten past it. Something had closed them off from each other. Ever since they'd been seven years old, those two had had their ups and downs, the way friends do, but this was different, worse.

Amma took down the framed photograph on her kitchen shelf of the teenaged Noni and Kaye, arm in arm, wearing their Moors High School graduation gowns. She sat down at the table with the picture, took off her thick glasses, rubbed her eyes, put them back on. Look at those two, so young. Noni like ivory and Kaye like dark gold. Hugging and laughing.

Maybe somewhere along the way they had gotten closer than just friends, the way Judy Tilden had always been so scared they would do. No sense in denying Amma had thought it before, herself.

But who could tell what was going on with young people, even when they were under the same roof as you?

One thing she did know. Right after that fire, they'd had the worst fight she'd ever seen between them. Amma had heard Kaye yelling at Noni there in the hospital. It was the day they had released Judy, and Noni was taking her to California. Amma heard Kaye's voice in the hall outside Judy's room, and had stepped out to see what was wrong. What she saw was Noni throwing down all those flowers she'd carried from her mama's room, and then she'd ripped that little silver chain with the heart right off her own neck, the heart that Kaye had made out of a dime, and then she'd thrown it at him. Amma had shut the door so Judy wouldn't hear them fighting.

When Amma had opened that door back up, Kaye was sitting there on the floor of the hall, had just sunk right down there on the hospital floor, with his face as wet with tears as if you'd thrown water in it. She'd never seen him like that before or since. He was holding that little broken chain. Amma had gone in the ladies' room to get him a paper towel, and there was Noni, leaning against the wall, crying too.

'Course, Noni and Kaye had fought before; Amma had heard them right here in this kitchen at Clayhome time after time, arguing and arguing. But nothing like this. And it seemed like this time Life had gotten in their way too, and messed up any chance for mending things.

Just a few weeks before Noni had brought her mother back to Heaven's Hill from California and Boston, Kaye had all of a sudden won some prize for some little thing he'd invented to use in heart surgery and he'd gone up to New York City for the ceremony. And that's where he'd met Shani Bouchard, a doctor herself, and he'd stayed up there to go out with her, and then had gotten himself invited to teach a course up there and had called Amma and said he wouldn't be back for six months.

When Amma told Noni all this the day she got home, and told her how she'd missed Kaye by only a few weeks, the girl just fell apart. She'd said he hadn't answered her letters or called her or left her a message the whole time she'd been out in California. Amma couldn't get her calmed down.

That night when Amma was helping Judy get to bed, Judy told her Noni was "emotionally overwrought" because she was pregnant. Then Judy got all upset herself, talking about how Noni was going ahead with divorcing Roland even though she was having his baby.

The week after that, Roland flew to Moors and Amma heard him telling Judy he was going to fight the divorce. But then Roland and Noni went out to the pool for a long talk, and when they came back inside, Roland stormed up to his room, packed his bag, and flew off to Texas. He married somebody else as soon as his divorce papers came through.

By the time Kaye got home from New York, Noni had already left with her mama to take Judy to see that doctor in London. When Kaye heard Noni was having a baby, he'd looked disgusted in that nasty way he had, and said he was amazed she hadn't canceled her divorce, but figured she'd be happy with two babies to take care of, Roland's and her mother. He said she'd never stop throwing away her life on people that didn't deserve her. "Maybe Jesus told you to walk the extra mile, but when did even Jesus say you had to fly across the ocean with a woman who'd done nothing but make you feel lousy about yourself for the whole first half of your life! When did your friend Jesus say that, Grandma?"

"What Jesus said was, you don't quit on people you love. You never do. And, Kaye King, you ought to listen to Him. All Noni's trying to do is get her mama walking again."

That's when Kaye said the scary thing. "Well then she ought to take her mother to a good psychiatrist because I've seen her charts, I checked them out, I even called Jack Hurd out in California, and I don't think Judy Tilden's legs are the problem. As long as she can't walk, Noni can't walk out on her."

It was right after that when Shani Bouchard flew down for the first time to visit Kaye. Then Kaye started flying up to New York to visit her. And now Shani was moving in with him.

Kaye and Noni. Amma looked around her kitchen. Kaye and Noni. There were so many memories of those two in this room. All that dancing they used to do in here. All their schoolwork at this table. Making those election posters. Playing those violins. Filling out the college applications. Arguing about anything and everything. Laughing.

But, oh, who knew with young people? Maybe it was all for the best.

That Shani Bouchard was something. Long-legged and strong, just beautiful, like she'd walked right out of a red-clay country road, or out of the hills of Africa with her robes flying and her dark feet bare, not a fear in her face. But Shani had grown up her whole life a city girl. Born in Harlem with public school teacher parents and with sisters and brothers that still lived there. They were all so proud of her, a doctor, young as she was.

Shani would sit here in the kitchen for hours asking you about "Colored" water fountains and bathroom doors that said "Women" for blacks and "Ladies" for whites. Ask you about having to give up your seat on the bus to a white person, and not sitting at the lunch counter or having to go up to the balcony in the movie theater or the courthouse or the church. And you could tell it was like you were telling Shani something about Ancient China.

But the past wasn't that long ago. Amma's own grandmother Clay had been brought a slave child to Moors, North Carolina, by E.D.R. Gordon. That's how close the old times snuffle along at our heels.

Oh deep in her soul how Amma wished that Deborah could have held on to see her son Kaye grown into a fine doctor. Fine and free. With all that education and all that confidence so nobody could turn him around.

Just amazing how when you figure the world's never gonna change, it hurries on so fast. The longer Amma lived, the more change she'd seen coming, seen everything racing along faster and faster, doing good in the world, that was certain, but leaving folks behind, and losing things along the way.

✳ ✳ ✳ ✳ ✳

From the van window, with her baby asleep in her lap, Noni watched the dark pines and the gray trees rush by in the night. The red-clay earth was the right color now and she was going home to Heaven's Hill. From behind her came the soft murmur of her mother's unending complaints to Uncle Tat, who encouraged her to sue all her hospitals.

Noni closed her eyes, thinking back to the last time she'd seen Kaye, nearly two years ago, the day she'd taken her mother out of the hospital.

That day her arms had felt so heavy holding the flowers from her mother's room. Kaye in his long white doctor's jacket was pacing up and down the hospital corridor in a fury at her for going to California with her mother. "You're picking her. You're fucking picking her over yourself!" And he'd whirled around on Noni. "You're never going to *really* reach out for me. You're never going to use that dime for anything real. So why don't you just give it back? You're a coward!"

Noni had torn the chain right off her own neck, breaking it, burning her skin like a sharp cut in her flesh.

"It's not that I'm choosing my mother over myself, it's that you think I'm choosing her over *you!*" she shouted. "You sound like Roland!"

"That's right! You are choosing her over me. Just like you chose Roland over me! I told you not to marry him!"

"You never said it was because you loved me! If I'm a coward, so are you, goddamn it. All I'm asking you to do is just wait. Let me try to help her get well first. I can't just barge ahead with my own life now, not the way she is. Can't you just wait?"

He shook his head at her. "No I can't," he said. "I've been waiting four hundred years." And Kaye had turned his back on her.

Noni had run down the hall into the restroom, and when she came back out with Amma, Kaye was gone.

❈ ❈ ❈ ❈ ❈

The stars in the sky looked down where he lay,
The little Lord Jesus asleep in the hay.
Singing as she worked, watching for the van, Amma sprin-

kled little marshmallows over the yams and placed them in the
refrigerator for baking tomorrow. She thought she heard tires
as she pulled the steaming pecan pie from the oven and slid
onto the rack in its place a mincemeat pie.

She looked again out the window, but it was too soon.
That airport would be bedlam. Kaye had told her how three
days ago when he'd picked up Shani there, the place was "an
agoraphobic's worst nightmare," whatever that meant; sometimes he and Shani talked in a separate language they thought
was funnier than anybody else did, since nobody else knew
what they were talking about half the time.

She heard footsteps. Then the door flung open and she
knew it was Kaye before she saw him; he always burst through
doors like a jack-in-the-box. A second later he was in the middle of the kitchen, picking her up right off the floor, bouncing
her. Kaye in those soft slacks and jackets of his, and no over-
coat. Cashmere, Italian, he told her. And those shoes of his
that looked like bedroom slippers. Kaye, sweet-smelling, with
Deborah's pretty mouth and smart eyes and her little perfect
ears. Deborah's Kaye, a doctor, thirty years old, that she would
have been so proud of.

"You stop that! Put me down. What are you doing over
here? You and Shani not supposed to be coming 'til tomorrow."

"I know. And I'm supposed to bring the wine."

"If you want wine you better bring it. I don't care for that
stuff. She settling in? You need anything?"

"We're fine." Kaye kissed his grandmother. "I'm here to tell
you something, 'cause we're going to announce it at the party,
and since you're too stuck-up to come—"

She smoothed down the old long sweater of Tat's she was
wearing. "I'm too old. And it's too cold out there."

"You just want everybody to come over here to you at
Clayhome."

"Well, that's true, too."

Amma gestured for him to sit down. She already knew what he was going to say. She knew it the minute she heard the word, "announce." And sure enough, he took a ring box from his pocket and opened it for her. A big diamond in a strange-looking modern ring flashed out. She shivered to think what he must have paid for it.

"My my," she said. Then, "How you know Shani's going to tell you yes when you haven't even given it to her, and you planning on 'announcing' it tonight?"

Taking back the box, Kaye kissed the top of her head. "Grandma, it's 1986. Who you think picked this ring out?"

"Who?"

He did his old exaggerated mockery with his eyebrows. "'Who?' Dr. Shanila Bouchard, that's who. Where's Grandpa Tat? I want to show him this. I want to hear him say, 'If I'd had my legs and my chance I could of bought a diamond ring make this diamond ring look like some little old bug in a fly's eye.'"

"Don't make fun of your grandpa. Tat's gone to the airport in his van. Gone to pick up Noni and her baby and her momma. They're back from their trip tonight."

She saw Kaye stiffen. "Tonight?"

"I already told you that."

He pulled himself into that stillness of his. "Guess it didn't register. How's her mom?"

"Judy's still in a wheelchair. I told you that, too."

Kaye snorted. "Her and Tat both in wheelchairs, hunh? They drag racing around the airport or what?"

Ignoring his sarcasm, Amma busied herself checking her mincemeat pie in the oven. Finally she turned to him. "Noni know?"

Seeing the graduation photograph of himself and Noni lying on the kitchen table, Kaye picked it up and studied it. "Know what?"

Amma snorted. "Don't fool with me. About you and Shani

getting married." He shook his head. "Don't you think you oughta tell her?"

He shrugged, replaced the photo on the kitchen shelf with the other pictures. "Why should I? She didn't ask my permission to get engaged to that asshole she married. She didn't ask my permission to get pregnant when she already knew she was going to leave that asshole."

"You watch your mouth in my home." Amma raised her finger as she had when he was a child. "And we're not talking about permission. We're talking about treating your friend decent."

Kaye elaborately shrugged. "Was I right about Roland Hurd or not?"

"I just hope you're right about everything you think you're right about, Kaye King. I don't like waste. And you ask me, wasting love's the worst of all."

After Kaye left, his grandmother stared out the window at the lamp she'd lit in the window of Heaven's Hill, waiting for Noni and her baby and her mother to come home and be cared for.

❄ ❄ ❄ ❄ ❄

Oh the weather outside is frightful,
But the fire is so delightful…

Kaye's Christmas Eve party was a high hard hum of talk and laughter and seasonal songs like "Rudolph the Red-Nosed Reindeer" ironically playing from speakers embedded in walls throughout the house.

Young well-dressed men and women, mostly medical people, were celebrating with Kaye both his birthday and his engagement to Dr. Shani Bouchard.

Kaye held a champagne flute high above his head. "So in conclusion—"

"You promise?" Loud laughter and applause from the

circling guests.

"Thank you, thank you for keeping Shani from finding out in time she'd be crazy to marry me—"

"Hey, Shani, you'd be crazy to marry him!" More laughter.

Kaye gestured around the room with the glass. "Merry Christmas! Happy Hanukkah!"

"Happy Birthday!"

"Happy Engagement!"

Kaye's new house on Glade Lake was built on a ledge of land, with a high huge deck across its back overlooking the water. With only two bedrooms upstairs, it was not a large house, but as Kaye was telling a group of guests at his party, he had plans to expand. For one thing, he was going to terrace and garden the now steep overgrown path down to the water's edge, then he was going to build a gazebo and a dock on the lake bank. He was going to add a whole separate wing for Amma and Tatlock Fairley, everything on a single floor, everything handicap-accessible, and move them in as soon as he could talk his grandmother into leaving Clayhome.

Cool jazz, red wines, hot mulled punch and sparkling water, a three-tiered cake with two toy doctors on top, their faces darkened with a magic marker, platters of sushi and tapas, everybody laughing, talking.

—I've got a classroom full of fourth-grade kids watching the TV set. The *Challenger* blows up in their faces with a teacher on it. You think these kids want to be teachers when they grow up? These kids are going to be the Ayn Rand generation, trust me.—

—Good looks, good taste, M.D.s, fast track, Afro-American.—

—Who, Kaye and Shani? Not Afro, African.

African American.—
—Whatever.—

—Get in the Market! Come on, it's the eighties.
It's okay to make money.—
—Kaye, hey, doctors'll always make money.—

Santa baby, leave a sable under the tree, for me…

Here on the first floor there was, in addition to Kaye's
study, only one room. But it was an enormous open space with
a cathedral ceiling and a double-sided free-standing fireplace
and it served as living room, dining room, and kitchen all
together. The Christmas tree stood in a corner, a tall palm
strung with chili-pepper lights.

—You must be Shani. I'm Bunny Breckenridge. If
you need a break from Southernese, come see me.
I live in New York.—
—Oh, please, have you got a bagel on you?—
—I've got the *Times* in my car.—
—You've got a new best friend, too.—

Jingle bell, jingle bell, jingle bell rock…

No one noticed Noni walk into the house. It had been easy
to find the place with the address Amma had given her. Seeing Amma, Judy had burst into tears and then so had the baby.
Together, Amma and Noni had gotten Johnny to bed. Amma's
niece Dionne Fairley had been hired to nurse Judy; she would
sleep in the small bedroom next to Mrs. Tilden's suite. Amma
told Noni that she would help Dionne get Judy settled.

She said Noni ought to go over to Kaye's party, even just
for a few minutes, because all her old friends would be there.

Then Amma had hugged Noni and told her that Kaye was getting engaged.

Noni thought she'd done well. It was wonderful news, she'd said; she'd said that Bunny had already told her that Kaye was seeing somebody and so she wasn't surprised. She'd said she was very happy for him.

The house was only a few blocks from the old retired rector Dr. Fisher's home. Paper bags with lit candles in them lined the rails of the walkway and the deck. And there were cars parked all along the street. Although she had knocked, the music and talk were so loud that no one heard her; besides, the door was open and it looked as if everyone had just walked into the party on their own.

The first thing Noni thought as she stood inside the door was how open Kaye's new house was. There was one whole wall of glass, there were skylights in vaulted ceilings, space flowed over bare floors and spare contemporary furnishings. Even with so many guests clustered around tables of food and drink, there was a sense of great emptiness. It immediately struck Noni that everything was the opposite of Clayhome with its small doors and mullioned windows, its narrow, worn, winding stairs, all its small, low rooms with their wide-planked floors and bead-board wainscoting crowded with old tables and chairs and cabinets and couches.

The second thing Noni thought was how many friends Kaye had made here in North Carolina. Friends from the life he'd lived here. She saw people she knew from Gordon Junior and Moors High and Haver University, then more people she didn't know that she thought must be from Haver Medical School, where he now taught, or from his private practice in Hillston. The guests were from different races—black, white, Asian, Indian—and most looked to be around Kaye's age and, in their dress, like him, what he had once called "hip."

The third thing Noni noticed, as a group of the guests moved out of the center of the room, was the young woman who stood next to Kaye, her hand in his.

Long-boned and strong-featured, African-American, this woman wore a black silk caftan and a white and black silk scarf twisted in her hair. She raised Kaye's hand to her lips and kissed it, and as she did so, Noni saw the diamond ring on her left hand.

They know that Santa's on his way
He's loaded lots of toys and goodies
On his sleigh...

Noni was grateful that she was given a moment before anyone recognized her. For seeing this woman whom she'd never met, whose life was already joined to Kaye's, her heart hurt so sharply that she couldn't have kept the pain from her face if Kaye had seen her then. She just needed a moment.

The young woman saw her before Kaye did. She looked across the room at Noni and frowned. And then she stepped forward and smiled at her.

And by then Noni was able to smile back and walk toward her across the room, so that when Kaye first saw Noni she was coming toward him and she was smiling at the woman she knew must be his fiancée.

"You've got to be Noni. I'm Shani Bouchard." And the woman shook her hand kindly. "I've seen all these pictures of you."

"Yes, I'm Noni." She took Shani's hand in hers. Still holding it, she turned to Kaye. "You didn't tell me, no one told me. You're getting married. Congratulations."

Shani shook Kaye's arm as he stood staring at Noni. "Your best friend, you didn't tell her? I swear..." She turned back to Noni, shaking her head. "This man's a mess."

"You're back," Kaye said flatly to Noni.

Noni fought to keep talking, keep smiling. "Bunny told me you were having this party and Aunt Ma gave me directions to where you lived. I hope you don't mind."

Shani took her hands again. "Of course not. You've been living in London, right?"

Noni could tell that the woman was trying as hard as Noni herself was to make things all right.

Kaye muttered, "Shanila's an epidemiologist. Coming here to Haver Hospital. Yes, we're engaged."

"Shanila King. That's a beautiful name "

"Oh, just Shani. And I'm keeping my own name."

"Congratulations. Welcome to Moors."

"Thank you," Shani looked into a corner of the room. "Let me go help out Rana. She's stuck over there listening to Jim relive every tennis match he ever played." Shani hurried away, leaving them (Noni thought) alone to talk.

Kaye and Noni stood there in the middle of the room. Finally she said, "It was great to get home and see Aunt Ma and Tat."

"Where are you going next?"

"Nowhere. Home for good."

He looked at her a while. "So, I heard you had a baby."

"Yes. A little boy. Johnny."

"Oh. That was your dad's real name, right?"

"…Right."

"So. You and Roland working things out?"

"No, we're divorced."

"How 'bout your kid?"

"Johnny is just…mine."

Noni touched her breastbone with her fingers to press back her feelings. Tears welled in her eyes but didn't fall. "Kaye, you deserve all the happiness in the world."

He studied her seriously, started to say something, but didn't. Noni wiped her eyes with her hand. The bracelet he had given her with its gold charms, the piano, the telephone, slid up her wrist. She gathered herself, smiled, pointed over at the tiered cake on the table. "Your birthday isn't until tomorrow." Fighting hard, she folded her arms in an imitation of Kaye's old comic way. "It's my birthday. I'm older."

After a moment, a small smile flickered across his face.

"Well, you could offer to show me your house," she added. "How about a tour?"

And so he took her around the place, pointing out the unusual architecture. Everything blurred as she smiled and nodded.

As they came down the stairs, Bunny saw them and hurried over. "Noni, you did come! Excuse us—" She bumped at Kaye with her hip, and pulled Noni aside into the crowd. "I swear, I had no idea he was getting engaged tonight. I would have told you at the airport."

"It's okay." Noni felt flushed and heated. "Excuse me a second. It's jet lag. I want to get some air."

"Are you all right?"

"Bunny, please, I'm fine."

City sidewalks, busy sidewalks, dressed in holiday style…

—Get over it? Kaye, they indicted Poindexter!—
—Bunny, time to exit the Garden. People forget.
Kurt Waldheim is now president of Austria.—

I'll-uh have-uh a bluuuuue Christmas without you.
I'll-uh be so bluuuuue thinkin' about you.…

It was cold out on the deck, but the night was clear and brilliant. The air cooled her, made her shiver. Noni leaned over the rail to look at the stars; they shimmered in the black lake below as if someone in heaven were tossing them there like pennies in a well. Breathing deeply, she held open the

collar of her white silk blouse. All at once she smelled cigarette smoke.

From the dark end of the long deck she heard someone
singing to her.

Noelle, Noelle. Noelle, Noelle,
Born is the Queen of Heaven's Hill.

Parker Jones stepped out of the shadows, skinny and
hunched in the chilly air. "Hey there, Disco Lady."

"Parker! Oh, I'm sorry, Kareem."

"Naw, it's Parker again. Allah and me split up. I'm riding
with Jesus all the way to the finish line." He pointed with his
cigarette at his chest where a baggy T-shirt was in fact stenciled
with the face of Christ.

"You're not a Muslim anymore?"

"You go to Dollard Prison and get picked for a girlfriend by
enough brothers calling themselves Mohammed, it can make a
Christian of you, and that's a fact."

"Oh my god, Parker." She moved forward and hugged him,
shocked by the frail feel of bones thrusting from his ice-cold
skin. He wore a wool skullcap but only the T-shirt and jeans,
no coat. He weighed less than she did. "What are you doing
out here? You're freezing. Let's go inside."

Flicking the cigarette off the rail, Parker shrugged. "Naw.
That's not really my scene in there. I don't know those folks.
Kaye just feels like..." He stopped, shrugged. "I don't exactly
fit in, see what I mean?"

She nodded slowly. "You know what? I don't either."

"How you doing, Noni? Where you been so long?"

As she told him briefly of traveling with her invalid
mother and of her divorce and her baby son, she took in more
details of his appearance. There were deep hollows under his
eyes, and there were small dark sores on his face and on his
arms. Her heart struck hard against her breast. In all those
hospitals with her mother, she'd seen patients with AIDS. This

was what they looked like.

Parker gestured at the crowd inside. "Kaye's marrying another doctor." He chuckled. "Maybe I shoulda done that, least I coulda got an appointment every now and then." He tilted his head at her. "So how come you letting Kaye marry somebody else?"

She blushed. "What have I got to say about it?"

Parker frowned, shook his head. "Okay, never mind." And he shuddered in the cold. "I'm to the point where lying to yourself is hard to do, but you go ahead."

"Stay here."

"Where am I gonna go?" He gestured out at the black night of stars.

Noni stepped back inside the noisy cheerful room, found the mink coat she'd taken from her mother's closet because of the surprising cold. She filled a large cup with the hot mulled wine on the table.

Back on the deck, she put the long mink coat around Parker's shoulders and then handed him the warm cup of wine. "Or are you still a teetotaler?"

He smiled at her, his eyes bright and glittering in his sunken face. "A man's smoking on the way to the electric chair, you gonna tell him cigarettes are bad for his health? Man, this coat is warm. I love it. You see me in mink?"

Noni stepped closer, took his hands in hers. "What's the matter with you, Parker?"

He looked at her with his old silly sweet smile. "Besides dying, Duchess, nothing much…"

"Is it AIDS?"

"Well everybody's gotta die of something."

They looked at each other for a long quiet while. Then she leaned forward, kissed him on the forehead.

"You got a car?" When she nodded, he asked, "How'd you like to take me to the Indigo now? You, me, night fever?"

Noni squeezed his thin trembling hands. "I'd love to take you to the Indigo if you promise we'll dance."

"You're a good lady, Disco Queen."

"Merry Christmas, Parker."

❄ ❄ ❄ ❄ ❄

The stars in the sky looked down where he lay,
The little Lord Jesus asleep in the hay.

Amma had known as soon as she took the baby from Noni's arms and lifted him to her face. Maybe nobody else would see it in him, probably not, he was so fair and gold-skinned, curly haired but blonde, but then Amma herself had been blonde as a baby.

Amma had seen it, and she'd seen Noni watching her see it. Johnny Tilden had those same pretty little ears that Deborah had passed onto Kaye and the same soft full lips.

Maybe not even Judy knew the baby was Kaye's, and Judy would never admit it if she did know, she'd fight it forever. She'd say he was Roland's. And Roland had that black curly hair and olive skin. Folks would believe it. Maybe Roland believed it, but maybe not.

"This is my son, Johnny," Noni said. "Johnny, say hello to your Aunt Ma."

And in Amma's arms, the little boy had smiled in a way that was part Noni's sunshine smile and part that irrepressible grin Kaye had always had, and then Johnny had kissed her right on the lips, knowing she would love him. And Amma had loved him, right then and there, her old heart had opened to him and he'd looked right in it and claimed a place.

The rest of it came clear too, later on that same night.

Judy must have thought Amma was downstairs, or gone home. Dionne was sound asleep in the room next to hers. But Amma was in the other upstairs wing, the old children's wing, sitting in the dark in Gordon's room, sitting in the little cane-seated Hitchcock rocker, watching Johnny sleep in the old wooden crib where so long ago, just a girl herself, she had watched Judy sleep and then a generation later had watched Judy's children sleep. The boy lay on the bed just the way Noni had when she was a baby, with his fat pretty cheek resting on both his little hands. He moved his lips in his sleep, making that soft noise like he was looking for more people to kiss.

Amma heard the creak of the floorboard outside the open door and then heard footsteps hurrying away. Startled, she rocked herself out of the black cane chair and shuffled quickly to the door. And there, walking away from her, walking fast down the shadowy hall was Judy Tilden in her nightgown. No wheelchair anywhere around, no cane even. Judy Tilden walking the long length of that hall in her white nightgown.

Amma clapped her hands together. "Judy! What you doing?"

The woman turned, screamed once, her hand to her mouth. Then violently she shook her head and hurried along the hall. But Amma, breathing hard, caught up with her outside her bedroom and grabbed at her arms.

Sobbing, Judy threw herself against the old woman. "Don't tell her, Aunt Ma, please don't tell Noni and Wade. What good would it do now?"

Amma was so angry that she shook the woman. "What good! What good! How long you been able to walk, lying to everybody!?"

Judy pulled loose, then her face changed, hardened, and she stared at Amma like a nasty child. "Don't you tell her. Don't tell her or I'll kill myself and she'll think it's her fault." Then she pushed past Amma into her bedroom, slammed the door, and locked it.

Amma stood outside the door, breathing hard. "You go on and do it, you just go on."

The Ninth Day of Christmas

❄

December 28, 1992
The Music Stand

Year by year the clichés had proved mostly true. Time had healed some wounds and at least eased others. Around Noni in Moors, people did what they had always done—were born, grew up happily or unhappily; fell in love or didn't; made friends, families, careers, money, or didn't; grew old or didn't; died.

Year by year the seasons had sped more quickly by her, hurrying through six Christmases since she had come home with her mother and her baby from London to find herself unexpectedly at Kaye's engagement party.

Noni had been living those six years at home in Heaven's Hill. She rarely traveled anymore, except for occasional trips to New York; she felt no need to travel. Her life was in Moors and she was happy with it. Her son Johnny was the center of the circle, but the circle was large. Everyone invited her to their dinners and parties. Lucas Miller, the lawyer who had been in love with her since high school, and who had proved a good and loyal friend—and a very kind presence in Johnny's life—played piano duets with her and took her to concerts and out to the new restaurants. She worked hard as a teacher at the elementary school, she worked hard as a volunteer for causes that mattered to her. She was professionally and politically and socially active. In a small town, it was not a small life.

A few days after her thirty-sixth birthday, Noni knelt among the tombstones and marble orbs and granite obelisks in the Gordon plot of St. John's cemetery, next door to her home, where since her return she had visited her family's graves every Sunday after church. She kept the grounds of their graves, the old dogwood and apple trees, the azaleas and laurel bushes, beautifully tended. Two springs ago, she had planted hellebores, which Amma called Christmas-roses, in the plot, and she was worried about them, for an ice storm had swept through Moors the night before. But today the sun blazed out, hurting her eyes, bringing back one of the recent headaches, dazzling all the trees into boughs of bright glass.

Somehow the hellebores had survived, stronger than they looked, stronger than the couple who lay beneath the newest marble stone. Noni brushed ice from a white flower above her mother's grave. Judy Tilden had died a year and a half ago and was buried here with her husband, Bud. They lay together now under one headstone. It was what Mrs. Tilden had requested in her will, to the surprise of some (although most people seemed to have forgotten that they'd been apart for years when he'd died back in 1979).

JOHN FITZGERALD TILDEN
JUDITH GORDON TILDEN

"At least she didn't want it to read, 'Together forever,' or 'Devoted wife of,'" Noni said to her brother Wade.

"I don't see why you're taking that tone. Frankly, they shouldn't have been buried together. Lying there beside Mom is more than Bud Tilden deserves."

"Wade, for once we agree."

Three months after the engagement party, Kaye had married Shani Bouchard in the living room of their home, disappointing

Amma Fairley who'd wanted a church wedding in Holy Redeemer. There'd been no bridesmaids, no ring bearer, no minister, no Mendelssohn. Friends and family had sat on folding chairs in the large open living room and heard Kaye and Shani exchange vows of their own composition in front of a woman justice of the peace whom nobody knew. The Fairleys had all been there with an assortment of Kings and Clays with whom Kaye never socialized. The Bouchards had come down from New York. But most of the guests had been the couple's young medical friends from Haver Medical School or University Hospital, where they both spent most of their time, busy with their flourishing careers.

To Noni's shock, Kaye hadn't even invited Parker to the wedding. The two old friends had had a bad argument about Parker's refusal to "fight hard enough"—as Kaye called it—against his disease until science could figure out how to cure it. Kaye appeared to take as a personal affront Parker's "abuse of his body" (his smoking, misuse of medication, erratic trips to doctors), and had told him he was not about to sit around and watch Parker kill himself. Parker had yelled at his friend, "Hand me the cure for AIDS, King God, and I'll suck it down like a baby at his mama's tit. Come on, hand me the cure, God." They hadn't spoken since, and although Shani had sent Parker an invitation to the wedding on her own, he hadn't come.

At the reception, Noni had sat beside Bunny Breckenridge, who kept solicitously patting her until Noni finally had gotten up and said she had to get home.

On her way out, she had told Kaye, "Be happy. Please be happy."

And she'd meant it, hoped for his happiness even in the midst of a loss so deep that it felt, she was sure, like Tatlock's sense of his missing limbs. For in these six years she'd seen Kaye only occasionally and only in large groups, usually at a celebration or a funeral. Their old way of talking and laughing together seemed to be forever lost. He'd met Johnny at a gathering at Clayhome but he seemed to pay no particular attention to the toddler. And then, a year after his wedding, Amma had told Noni that Shani was having a baby.

Less and less did it feel right to throw everything into disorder by telling Kaye that their unplanned lovemaking had produced a child. Or was she being selfish not to? She wanted to do the right thing. But this time she wasn't sure what the right thing was. There was no doubt that Kaye was the father, but did that mean she should intrude herself, and Johnny, into a life he'd made without them? Often Noni thought of talking over her dilemma with Amma. Amma knew about Johnny, she was sure of that. But she kept putting off the conversation. Why place the burden on Amma?

The only person she'd told had been her mother, and she'd told her in England, the night Johnny was born. Mrs. Tilden had refused to believe the truth of the paternity. She had accused Noni of not really knowing the truth, or possibly even of deliberately lying just to hurt her. She begged Noni not to tell Roland. In the end, Noni had decided to tell Roland only that the child wasn't his. After Noni's divorce, she and her mother had never discussed the matter again.

The fall following her return, Noni had reentered Haver University. By the end of the next year she'd graduated, earned a certificate, and had begun teaching music at Moors Elementary School. The children she taught there called her Ms. Tilden and, as one of the parents told her, they played their hearts out to see her smile. By her second year at the school, she had a recorder group started for the first graders; by her third year, there was a little string orchestra playing a Christmas concert at St. John's.

By teaching children to play music with none of the dread she'd been made to feel as a child, Noni had hoped to find work that was as real to her as her son. That was how she'd first phrased it to Parker just before she'd started teaching.

✳ ✳ ✳ ✳ ✳

Noni was sitting with Parker on one of her evening visits to his room at Moors County Hospital where he was slowly, "too damn slowly for a fast man," he'd said, dying of AIDS.

She was telling him that she'd been offered a job teaching music to first through sixth grades and that she was going to take it. "I want something," she said, "as real as Johnny feels, like I used to be when I was little, playing with Kaye. I want to feel real."

"Don't pick this," whispered Parker hoarsely from his white tilted hospital bed, pointing a thin bruised finger at the I.V. needle in his hand, the oxygen tube in his nose, "but Lady D., this here is about as real as it gets."

Noni sat quietly, her hand resting softly on his thin arm. "You're doing better than anybody I ever knew."

Parker struggled to swallow. "Lucky I didn't go crazy, get myself strapped down. That's no way to die. Like having a fly on the end of your nose."

"You want some water?" She held up a paper cup.

"I want a big ole rum and coke, double Whopper, and some fries."

She smiled. "I could sneak them in tomorrow."

Parker looked up toward the ceiling where *Cheers* played silently on the small television. "Yeah, I'd like to hang in a place like Cheers where everybody knows my name and I'll be drinking a big ole rum and coke."

"I know."

"Least I got a bed. Lucky I had those comic books to sell or I'd of been dumped down a ditch like road kill. You tell Johnny, save those comics I gave him. Comic books are good as gold."

"I'll tell him."

"That's a cute kid you got but a smartass."

"He is that."

"Tell him, save those comics."

"It's good you did."

Six months earlier, having read somewhere that a copy of Superman's first comic book had sold for over eighty thousand dollars, Parker had asked Noni to put his extensive collection of Action Comics up for sale. With no family left, no money, and no health insurance, he had a terror of dying uncared for, and hoped this one asset, his rare comics, would pay his medical expenses. But when Noni had shown the hundreds of old comic books to the dealers she'd located, she'd learned that Parker's worn and tattered collection was worth only a few thousand dollars. Those big prices he'd read about were only for the very earliest comics, most of them published before Parker was born, and only if the copies were still in mint condition. She sold the collection for what she could get and paid his first bills.

She never told him when his money ran out. He always believed that his long months of expensive hospital bills were paid, not by her, but by his carefully saved *Batmans* and *Superboys* and *Amazing Spider-Mans*.

Two days before Parker died, he motioned for Noni to bring her head close, and he whispered that he needed a favor. He wondered if she could get Dr. King to come say good-bye to somebody he used to know.

"He'll be here," Noni said.

Parker held up his index finger, moved it weakly in a circle, the way he once had when they had danced together.

And she'd brought Kaye. He was there in Parker's room the next morning, because Noni wouldn't let him not be there, because when he hadn't returned her phone calls and when his nurses and secretaries had told her that he couldn't be disturbed, Noni had walked right into the middle of the seminar he was teaching at the medical school and had told him that he had to come with her right that minute. A block away from him, his oldest friend was dying. And even if Kaye didn't want to see Parker because he couldn't stop him from dying, he could goddamn well come say good-bye to him.

Noni had stood there, red-faced and breathing hard, until Kaye had shut off his slides and dismissed the startled students.

By that morning Parker could no longer talk, but when Noni kissed his hand, he lifted his fingers against her lips and she knew what he was saying.

Years earlier, when Noni had divorced Roland Hurd on the vague but profoundly accurate grounds of incompatibility, all she'd wanted back was what she'd brought with her from Heaven's Hill: her clothes and books and music, her china and silver and hope chest of linens. Her name and her child.

Of course, her lawyer and Roland himself had pressed on her a generous settlement. Roland had a horror of not appearing generous, and he wanted his largesse on the record. Besides, he had made a great deal of money in the eighties through his corporate real estate dealings, and although many of the Texas high rises that he'd brokered now stood almost empty, Roland's fees had gone into technology stocks, where they'd multiplied like dangerous cells, very fast.

Of course Roland could have gotten ugly about the divorce, and no one would have blamed him; he'd certainly gotten ugly in private once she'd said that he wasn't Johnny's father, and that she wouldn't tell him who was. In the end, as she'd known, the last thing Roland had wanted was for that news to become public. No more than Judy Tilden had wanted the news to become public.

Roland's father, Dr. Jack Hurd, had been baffled by Roland's complete disinterest in the baby and by his scathing animus toward Noni. Roland told him, "Maybe she's not the saint you think she is," but Doctor Jack decided not to ask him what he meant. Jack was divorced again himself (his second wife had left him for someone she'd met in her yoga class), and had recently returned to Moors and to Haver Medical School. He thought of Johnny as his grandson and visited him often.

Noni spent a lot of Roland's money on Parker, and gave the rest to AIDS research. The fact that Roland's settlement had paid Parker Jones's substantial medical bills was to Noni one of God's quiet ironies. She had heard Roland on the subject of AIDS victims and convicts and drug addicts and African-Americans, although the accusation that he was a bigot would have surprised him. (His rebuttal would have been, she knew, to point out that his lawyer in Houston was African-American, and that his new wife's brother had married a Mexican.)

She had seen Roland since their divorce only once, at her mother's very crowded and elaborate funeral. On the church steps after the service, Noni was receiving the condolences of her mother's friends who were telling her that Judy was now reunited with Bud in heaven at last. They told her that Noni was the daughter every mother dreamed of. "Thank you," Noni said, again and again.

Judy's cousin Becky Van Buehling (as she was once more calling herself, following the death of her second husband the estate planner), hugged Noni to her still partially exposed bosom and told her that Judy's funeral couldn't have been more like her. Becky hoped Noni would do *her* funeral if she ever died, Noni was so good at it.

Becky, who now had startling white hair, said it was probably for the best that Judy had gone so suddenly—even though it had been weird that she should have drowned in her own pool when she'd been a state champion swimmer as a girl, and even though it had been even weirder that she could have gotten out to the pool in her wheelchair and somehow rolled into it. And even though seventy-two years old was too early to go (Becky sure didn't want to go anytime soon), still, after all the personal tragedy Judy had suffered and all the years of pain in that wheelchair, death had to be some sort of a blessing.

As Noni was extracting herself from Becky's fleshy embrace, she saw her ex-husband, who had attended the funeral only because he was in town visiting his father and it had seemed the polite thing to do. Noni said hello. Everything about Roland had gotten thicker, she noticed, his waist, his fingers, his nose, his sarcasm.

"I don't think I have anything to say to you," he replied when she asked how he was.

"You 'don't think'? Gee Roland, don't you know whether you do or not?"

With a sneer, Roland had walked away without answering, leaving her standing on the steps with Doctor Jack. "What a jerk," said Roland's father.

Stooped and thin, with his bald crown and tufted white ponytail, Doctor Jack looked more and more like a strange old tall heron or crane. He pointed at his son talking to Wade Tilden; they seemed to be admiring Wade's Lexus. "Noni, can you ever forgive me?"

"For what?"

"Instead of telling you to save Roland, why didn't I tell you to save yourself? Some Deliverer, hunh?"

She rubbed his bony back. "You loved him. I loved him. He just got smaller instead of bigger."

"Yeah. Your mom would have admired that funeral, honey."

"I guess so. She left instructions in her will and I followed every detail."

Doctor Jack laughed. "You know, in the middle of the eulogy I actually thought I heard Judy's voice telling me that I ought to marry Becky Van Buehling. I hear she's roaming loose again."

"I've got a rule. I don't give marital advice."

"Don't rub it in."

Noni was staring into the grove of trees that separated St. John's from Heaven's Hill. "Jack, how do you think Mom could have fallen into our pool?"

"What do you mean? Don't they think she just rolled the wheelchair too close to the edge and fell in? With her paralysis, she couldn't swim, couldn't crawl out, and, well…" He sadly shrugged.

Noni walked Doctor Jack away from the church path where the crowd was clustered. "I mean, I don't see how she could have even gotten the wheelchair down there, down the stone walk to the pool, by herself. That path's long and it's steep and it's curved. And why'd she go out there at dawn? And take off her nightgown? I mean, does that sound like Mom? I just keep asking myself these things over and over."

Jack leaned his wrinkled tan face down to study hers. "What are you saying, Noni? Somebody stripped her and pushed her down those steps and flipped her into the pool? You're not saying that, are you?"

"No!" That wasn't what Noni thought at all; for one thing, who in the world would do such a thing to her mother? And for another, her mother would have screamed and someone would have heard her. Her mother had a very loud scream that had often brought Noni running in the past. "She liked to have me or Dionne push her in her wheelchair down to the swimming pool patio. She liked to sit there and look at the water. I just don't see how she got there by herself."

Jack suggested that maybe she'd asked someone to help her down to the pool. But Noni said she had checked with everyone who worked at Heaven's Hill and no one had taken Mrs. Tilden down to the pool. At ten o'clock that night, Dionne Fairley, Amma's niece, had helped the invalid into her nightgown and into her bed the way she always did, and after watching television, she'd checked on her at midnight and Mrs. Tilden had been asleep. At 7:30 the following morning, when Amma had gone to the cutting garden beside the pool to get some peonies for the breakfast table, she had seen Mrs. Tilden floating in the water, dead, the wheelchair sunk to the bottom of the pool.

Jack glanced back at the church. "How old is that woman? I saw her sitting in there with you and she looks like she's practically blind."

"Amma's ninety-one. Her eyes aren't very good."

"What's she doing schlepping down that walk herself?"

"She cuts flowers every morning before breakfast. She always has. In fact, usually it's much earlier than that. She said she'd slept late because she wasn't feeling well."

"Well, there's no way somebody in her condition could have gotten Judy down those steps in that wheelchair. But maybe one of those other people could be lying to you. Maybe one of them took her there and left her and felt too guilty to admit it?"

Noni said that none of the Fairleys or Clays would lie to her. "They're like family."

Jack smiled. "You think families don't lie?" And he hugged her. "Noni, you're too good for us. Not to mention, more beautiful than ever. You know, I honestly think you're the most beautiful woman I ever saw."

"Oh Jack, you're full of it. Becky Van Buehling will never be able to resist."

"Are you going to take care of yourself? I don't like to see you living alone."

"I'm not. I was alone when I was living with Roland."

"Worse, isn't it?"

"Much."

❊ ❊ ❊ ❊ ❊

Cleaning the graves, Noni heard young voices calling her from the brick path edging the St. John's Cemetery.

"Ms. Tilden, Ms. Tilden!"

It was the little Crossmore twins, both music students at Moors Elementary, both scheduled to play in the holiday recital this evening at St. John's.

"Hi, Madison! Hi, Laurel!" Waving, Noni pulled herself up from where she'd knelt at her parents' tombstone. She looked at her watch, waiting for the hands to come into focus. With these headaches, sometimes her vision blurred. Ten more minutes and it would be time for the rehearsal. The little girls, both carrying small violin cases and wearing satin baseball jackets over Edwardian-looking dresses, broke away from the woman bringing them to the rehearsal and raced toward Noni. "Ms. Tilden, Ms. Tilden!" They swung their arms about her and spun her into their circle. She hugged them together then let them fly apart. "You two stars ready? Brava, brava. Encore, encore!"

"There better be an encore." (For an encore, they would get to play the theme from *Star Wars*.)

"There'll be one, don't you worry."

With a loud world-weary sigh, Madison wiggled her fingers. "We're practicing and practicing and practicing 'til my Daddy just can't stand it one more minute!"

"Well, your Daddy is going to be so proud of you both."

"I hope," said Laurel, earnest, worried.

"Of course he is."

"Then we'll all do the men-you-et, right?" Madison began to pace out the steps, pointing the toe of her red rubber boot.

"*You'll* all do the minuet, and everybody will clap like crazy!" Noni took each child by the hand and danced them forward. "All the ladies will get to dance but me and I'll be stuck at the old piano bench, boo hoo!" She cried with a comical face until they were laughing.

"Where's Johnny?" Laurel asked. "Is he in the church?"

"Not yet. You go ahead and get ready. He'll be here. He just has to walk over from our house." Noni pointed at the roof of Heaven's Hill, visible through the winter trees.

They raced away through the wet muddy grass. The ice on the trees was melting so quickly now that it sounded like rain falling on the old slate shingles of the church roof behind her.

Noni held for a moment to the marble tombstone. She must have stood up too quickly. Then kneeling again, this time at Gordon's grave, she began cleaning fallen leaves and small branches from the holly that grew there, bright red berries in the deep green.

Bent to her work, she didn't see Kaye walking through the grove of old trees on the far side of the churchyard or her seven-year-old son Johnny running up the woody path behind him.

❊ ❊ ❊ ❊ ❊

Johnny was struggling to carry both a violin case and a thin carved wood music stand. "Hi, wait!" he yelled.

Kaye turned around and saw a small boy in parka and base-ball cap.

"You're Aunt Ma's son right?" the boy said.

"Her grandson."

"You used to be my mom's friend."

Kaye watched the boy run toward him, wildly swinging his violin case as if in greeting. "That's right," he told him.

"My name's Johnny Tilden. I live at Heaven's Hill." He pointed behind him. "You used to live at Clayhome."

"That's right." Kaye started walking again and the little boy hurried to keep up. Then Kaye stopped and looked down at him. His thin face looked tanned and his eyes large and wide-spaced like Noni's. "Actually I'm looking for your mother right now. My grandmama said she was over at the church. Here, can I help you with that?"

"Thanks." The boy handed him the music stand. "My mom forgot it. She says she'll forget her head someday, so she counts on me. Why are you looking for her?"

"To give her a birthday present." Kaye watched the thin little boy stick the violin case between his legs in order to rub his nose.

"You're too late. It was Tuesday. It's already over. We had a party, but Uncle Wade missed it because he went fishing in Florida. He has to go to Florida because Hurricane Andrew tore up his boat. I gave my mom a picture of her that Uncle Tat painted and I made the frame." Breathless, Johnny now ran in front of Kaye and then skipped backwards in order to face the tall black man. "What's your present?" Kaye didn't answer him. "Is it a surprise?"

"That's right. Do you play that violin?"

Johnny held up the case. "I'm the best one in the whole second grade." Suddenly the boy tripped backwards over a large gnarled root and fell hard against the base of a tree. His hat and violin case went sprawling. Quickly, Kaye reached down, lifting him up. "You okay?" The boy nodded, blinking away the pain, rubbing his head. Kaye noticed then how striking the child was, with his tan skin and tight dark gold curls and long-lashed dark gold eyes that were the shape of Noni's eyes. "That was some spill. You okay?"

"Sure." The boy scrambled away from him and crawled over to the violin, hurriedly opening the case.

"It looks fine to me," Kaye told him.

Johnny glanced up at him relieved. "I got to play this tonight. I'm the solo."

"Well, it looks okay." Kaye gave him back his baseball cap. "Yankees fan?"

"My Aunt Bunny got it. I went to New York and she took me to the game. You want to come hear me play? You could bring your little girl. Aunt Ma says you've got a little girl, and it's her *great*-granddaughter. Aunt Ma's the oldest person in Moors."

Kaye told him that yes, his daughter's name was Debby and that she was in preschool.

"I don't know her. I'm with the orchestra. I got to go." The boy closed the black violin case and raced away through the trees up the winding wooded path to the churchyard.

As Kaye came through the gate of the brick wall, he saw Noni kneeling, holding out her arms to the boy who was running toward her. She kept nodding as he talked, pointing back at Kaye. Then she looked up, shading her eyes, watching him approach.

"Hi, Noni."

Noni's smile felt like sunshine. It always had. "Hi, Kaye."

"How've you been?"

"Fine. God, it's been a long time." She held out her hand and he shook it a little awkwardly. Then he handed her the wooden music stand.

Johnny pushed between them. "You forgot it, Mommy. I brought it."

"Thank you, honey." She turned to Kaye. "So. I hear you brought me a present, too." Grinning, she held out her hand.

He felt in his pocket for the box. "Sorry it's late. Thanks for yours. Where in the world did you find it?"

Every year for the past five, Noni had sent Kaye an antique microscope, having heard from Amma that he collected them. "In New York, where else? Michelle and I found it on Madison Avenue."

When she opened the small box he'd handed her, there was a gold charm inside. It was a charm of a little sled.

"Oh, Kaye." She looked up at him, tears suddenly swelling. "I'm sorry. Look at me!"

He shrugged, embarrassed. "Well, I figured we had the charm thing going, and then, well, I happened to see this one—" He stopped, shrugged again. "Anyhow, happy birthday, Noni. I hope everything's been okay. I hear they call you the Angel of Music at Moors Elementary. That's what Dionne's kids teacher told Shani."

"And where were *you* at Debby's preschool recital? Amma was there. Tatlock was there. Shani was there. Didn't you want to hear your daughter sing the theme from *Beauty and the Beast?*"

He grinned at her. "Believe me, I've heard my daughter sing the theme from *Beauty and the Beast.*" Kaye shaded his eyes in the bright sun to see her. " I told you you'd be a great teacher."

She smiled. "Did you?"

As they talked, Johnny was stretching up to look at the charm. "How come you gave my mom this little sled?"

Noni said, "Because we used to go sledding when we were your age."

Holding out both arms dramatically, Johnny said, "On *what?*"

"On snow," Kaye told him. "Snow on Heaven's Hill that was higher than you are."

Johnny made a scoffing noise. "I bet."

"It's the truth."

Noni shaded her eyes. "Looks like it's going to snow again any minute." She looked at her watch. "Oh my gosh, I'm sorry. We've got to go, Johnny, we're late. Right now. Go go go." Hurriedly she thanked Kaye for the gift. "Great to see you." And she ran, her arm around her son, along the brick cemetery path.

Kaye watched them until they'd disappeared inside the church. Why, he wondered, would Noni think it was going to snow any minute when the sky above the winter trees was everywhere a brilliant cloudless blue?

The Tenth Day of Christmas

❄

December 25, 1995
"Noni Plays Her Piano for Me"
by Tatlock Fairley

Noni Tilden had restored the tradition of the Christmas Day Open House at Heaven's Hill that had been hosted for so many years by her parents. It struck Kaye, as he stepped into the foyer and heard the soft hum of Southern voices and the bright laughter, how everything was both the same and completely different. In the wide front hall, willow baskets of pink poinsettias lined the parquet floor and holly wreaths hung on doors from gold ribbons. Christmas cards rested in swags of white pine on the banisters. But at the end of the hall, behind the scalloped Revere punch bowl on the Italian table with the curved legs, Lucas Miller now stood, the lawyer whom Kaye and Noni had known at Moors High. He was ladling into little silver cups holiday drinks for Dr. Jack Hurd and Becky Van Buehling. Kaye had heard they were engaged now. He stood watching for a moment, missing Bud Tilden's light pleasant voice greeting his guests. "God rest you merry, gentlemen!" "Peace on Earth, ladies!"

Then Lucas Miller waved at him, his narrow earnest face kind behind the round gold-rimmed glasses. Just last night

Amma had been telling Kaye that Lucas was a good friend to Noni, but not the man Noni loved. Just last night she had made Kaye promise to come to the Open House at Heaven's Hill today because she was worried about Noni.

* * * * *

Kaye was sitting after dinner with his grandmother in the kitchen at Clayhome, where she was patiently allowing him to take her blood pressure. Since Tatlock Fairley's death the previous spring, Kaye always came over to make soup for her on the weekends. Soup was, she said, one of the few things she still took pleasure in eating. To eat it, she didn't have to wear her teeth, and it settled her stomach.

After dinner, just as he did every Sunday night throughout the year, Kaye gave Amma as much of a physical check-up as she'd allow. And, just as he did every week, he made his plea that she should leave Clayhome and move in with him and his family. As always, she refused. But when he put away his stethoscope to go, she stopped him. "Kaye, let's us talk for a minute."

He smiled, expecting the blessings lecture. "Yes, I'm a lucky man. Yes, I ought to appreciate it more."

Amma took off her apron, settled into her kitchen chair with its worn pillows, with old bleached sunflowers on their covers. "That's true, son. You got a good smart wife doing good in the world, and y'all love each other. And you got two sweet little girls."

"Sweet?"

"But I'm not talking about the gifts the Lord's given you."

"You're not?"

"I got two things I need you to do for me."

Kaye took his grandmother's gnarled hand, examined the arthritic fingers. "Why should I do something for you, when you won't listen to me? Here you sit stubborn as an old mule, with all these stairs, ninety-five years old, blind as a bat, high blood pressure, and nobody but Dionne living with you."

She pulled away her hand. "Dionne's a nurse."

"She's not an R.N. A nurse is trained. Dionne's a niece. A very competent and sensible niece but she's not a R.N." Shaking a pill from a capsule, he handed it to her with a glass of water. "That'll help the stiffness in your hands. Every six hours. Now if you moved in with Shani and me, you'd have two doctors around you all the time."

"What're y'all gonna do, keep me alive forever?" She swallowed the pill. "Now you stop nagging at me, go on upstairs and see if you can find that old leg box of Tat's."

At first Kaye was at a loss. "Leg box? You talking that amputated tibia and fibula that he and I wired together?"

She nodded. "If they mean leg bones, that's what I'm talking about. Go get it while I do these dishes."

"Don't do those dishes."

She swatted his hands away. "Kaye, if you don't stop fussing at me, I'm gonna lose what's left of my mind."

How long had it been since he had even been upstairs at Clayhome? His old room surprised him by its dwarfish size. He could reach from bed to windowsill. The dormer ceiling was so low that he had to bend his head in the corners. On the near wall, fifty or more yellowed pieces of newsprint dangled and curled, with the captions he'd added in black marker now faded to gray: "Angela Davis, ACQUITTED. George Jackson, KILLED. ATTICA."

He couldn't find the leg box. He looked under the bed and in the closet and behind crowded bookshelves (planks held up by cinder blocks painted white) of paperbacks, thinking he ought to go through them some day. He opened a nearly demolished Moors High spiral notebook, the wire binding half unraveled, the pages pressed so hard with penciled calculus formulae that they felt like pages of braille. A Valentine card fell out, a silhouette of a little fifties-looking couple fast-dancing on top of a record player. It was a silly mushy card about two hearts and one soul and always being there and always understanding. It was signed, "Thanks for helping, I love you, Noni." He couldn't remember what the help had been.

Finally in a small tin trunk shoved between the low wall and the single bed with its painted iron headboard, Kaye found the box containing the bones of Tatlock's wired-together lower leg and foot. The bones were nearly brown now. Beneath this box he saw another one: an old shoebox tied with string.

Sitting on the thin musty mattress, Kaye opened the box that his young mother Deborah, back in the projects in West Philadelphia, on a gray day, in their two-room concrete home that had looked out on a horizon of other cramped concrete homes, had first christened The Promised Land. Inside the box, Kaye saw his past lying jumbled among the little crosses that his mother had made of Popsicle sticks tied with rubber bands.

Under the dog Philly's collar with its metal name tag was one of those strips of cheap photos taken in a booth, four shots in a row of Parker and him at the bus station, clowning for the camera, back when they were in junior high. Kaye put the stained, faded picture in his wallet.

He pulled out Bud Tilden's thin, gold, old-fashioned watch and fastened the pigskin band on his wrist.

He found the red Swiss Army knife with all its little blades and tools that Noni had given him the first Christmas they met.

He found the snapshot of his father Joe Wesley at the Montgomery march that had been returned to him by the private investigator. He slid the discolored picture down in the pocket of his soft black cashmere jacket. He found the small alabaster case of his mother's ashes, engraved "Deborah King, 1938–1979."

Now there was nothing in the box but his mother's little wooden crosses, the reminders of her passionate anger, the "beau ideas." Some of the yellow sticks were broken now, their rubber bands brittle; on some, his mother's handwriting was no longer legible.

Kaye picked up one of the crosses at random and held it under the plastic lamp beside the bed. It said, "Denise McNair, 11 yrs old, bombed, Sept 15, 1963."

In four more years, Kaye's daughter Debby would be eleven years old. He'd take the crosses home and show them to her. He'd tell her that what had happened in Birmingham could not happen in Moors forty years later.

You could kill the past and bury it too deep for it to climb out of its grave. Couldn't you?

Kaye was closing the box when a glint of tarnished silver caught his eye. Twisted and tangled in the wooden crosses was the thin broken chain with the heart made of a dime that Noni had ripped from her neck in the hospital corridor, after he'd asked for it back, after she'd said she had to take care of her mother, had to take her mother out to ask Jack Hurd for help in California, couldn't tell her mother about them now, after she'd asked Kaye to wait, just wait, after she'd asked him for patience he didn't have, after the fire, after they'd made love that one time. "Reach out for me. Just call my name."

Kaye heard his grandmother shouting for him from the foot of the stairs. He put the shoebox under his arm and carried down to her the box of bones.

"Couldn't you find it?"

"I found it. What do you want me to do with these bones?"

Amma peered carefully into the mildewed box. "Take them to Holy Redeemer and give them to Deacon Hawser. Tell him I want these leg bones buried in Tat's coffin and if he can't open the coffin up, then right beside it. I wish to the Lord I'd thought about it at the time but my mind was a mess."

Kaye was surprised. "Bury the bones, what for?"

The old woman closed the box and gave it back to him. "'Cause when that last trumpet sounds, and it's time for Tatlock Fairley to go walking, he's gonna need both his legs, all the weight on that man, to carry him over Jordan. I got to be with Bill King and I won't be able to help him."

Kaye stared at the woman, thought of a half-dozen comments, some of them genuinely curious, but finally he left them all unspoken and just nodded at her. "I'll ask Deacon Hawser if it's okay."

Impatiently, she waved him away. "Don't ask him, tell him. Deacon Hawser's most comfortable when you don't raise his doubts."

Kaye laughed. "Grandma, you should have gone into politics. You should have been mayor of Moors."

She snorted at him. "I got better things to do with my time. Now, Kaye, there's something else." He sat back down, rolled his eyes comically. "And it's not funny. It's Noni."

Amma was getting worried about her. About her health. She'd been watching Noni carefully the last few weeks and now she wanted Kaye to start doing the same. She thought there might be something wrong with her, and if there was something wrong, she wanted Kaye to do something about it.

Kaye was listening intently to his grandmother. "What do you mean 'wrong,' her health? Does she go to a doctor? Does she have a doctor?"

Amma shook her head. "I don't know 'bout that. She says she's just fine, but, Kaye, I know her, I've known that child since the day she was born, and she's not herself."

Sometimes, she said, Noni seemed to lose her footing coming down the stairs or even just walking on the flat pebbled driveway. Or she'd be talking to you and she'd misplace her train of thought. It was like her sentences had jangled up inside her and she couldn't get them to come out in the right order.

And then the last few weeks she'd been saying things that weren't like her at all—snappish things to Johnny or Amma, when Noni had never had a bad-tempered bone in her body.

Kaye asked if Noni had complained of headaches.

"This past week one got so bad when it came on, she couldn't see any better 'n I can. She hides it but I can tell."

Walking across the kitchen, Kaye looked out the casement window across the dark lawn to Heaven's Hill as if he could see Noni right now beyond the brightly lit porch with its garlanded boughs and large ribboned wreaths. "Is she under a lot of stress? Sounds like migraines."

"About what?"

"I don't know. Last time I saw her, she said things were great. She loves her school, Johnny fine's….What's going on with her and Lucas Miller?"

"Lucas Miller's a good man. Mighty good. And been a good friend to her."

"She ought to marry him," Kaye said. "Marry Lucas, give that kid of hers a dad. That kid's going to be a handful."

Amma Fairley peered for a long time at her grandson through the thick glasses that magnified her old bleared eyes. Then she sighed.

"What's the matter?"

She shook her head softly. "You're the smartest fool I know, Kaye King."

"What's that supposed to mean?"

"She don't love Lucas Miller!" Amma's thin voice sharpened and her hand slapped his as it rested on the table. Shocked, he pulled away, staring at her as she kept shaking her head. Her neck was now so frail, it looked incapable of supporting the heavy weight of white hair and dark folds of flesh. "Who you think that girl's loved her whole life long since she was a child? You so smart, you know everything, who you think, Kaye King? Who you think, fool?"

✳ ✳ ✳ ✳ ✳

"Kaye King!" Someone was calling to him in the crowded foyer of Heaven's Hill. Finally he saw Bunny Breckenridge, in another of her perennial black caftans, squeezing her way toward him through the guests, holding over her head a little silver cup of punch. "It's like the Tildens' old Open House, isn't it?"

"Sort of."

She glanced into the living room with him. "I know what you mean. It's different."

"Yeah. Nobody's smoking. It used to look like a rain forest in here."

"No, here's what it is. Everything's…easy now. I hated those stuffy parties of Judy's. Except for the eclairs." She squeezed Kaye's arm. "So hi, gorgeous. Are you cast in amber, or what?"

"You're looking good yourself, Bunny."

"Seven pounds. How 'bout cutting a foot or so off my intestine, Dr. King? I hear that works. I could come in any time this spring. I'm on leave all year."

He kissed the plump cheek haloed by wild frizzy hair that was now cut shorter and turning an early gray. "How 'bout exercising? I run five miles every evening."

She swung her broad hip sharply into his side. "I bet you hang your laptop from your neck and write articles while you do it."

Kaye laughed, dropping his cashmere coat down on the other wraps that had been thrown onto the green leather bench in the hallway. Under the bench, he saw a skateboard and a dog's toy. On the console, beside the malachite pear tree with its jeweled partridge, he set the gold wrapped present that he'd brought for Noni. It was another charm, this one a tiny gold state of North Carolina. Every year he gave her a charm now.

The blue Chinese jar was filled with camellias. He ran his fingers over the cracks in the porcelain that he'd glued back together that night so long ago in the kitchen. "We can fix this good as new," he had boasted, not knowing how much more valuable the jar's oldness made it. He smiled. Early Ming Dynasty. Now he knew. Thank god, the young had no idea how ignorant they were, or they could never risk so much, never be so brave.

A chaos of incredibly loud barks and shrieks was quickly followed by a stampede into the foyer of two large dogs and ten little boys, among them the curly-haired Johnny Tilden. He was the smallest, Kaye noticed, but the fastest of the group. Guests frantically backed away, protecting their drinks, as the boys chased each other out the door and down the steps onto the lawn where they ran off skimming Frisbees in air and leaping after them.

"Holy shit," gasped Bunny. "Is that what ten-year-olds are like? No wonder they call Noni the Angel of Moors Elementary. In college, the students just sit there and sleep." She was looking around the hall. "Where's Shani? She keeps promising she's going to find me a husband. I don't necessarily mean somebody else's. But straight, single, and self-supporting is my wish list. Maybe I'm being too picky. I could let a couple of those go. What do you think?"

Kaye explained that his wife and daughters were in New York with Shani's family. Kaye would have gone too but this morning he'd had to perform an emergency triple-bypass surgery on a long-time patient. "So, what you up to on your leave, Bunny? Rabble-rousing? Or are you resting on your laurels? Give it a rest. We've got a Democrat in there, got eternal peace and prosperity, right?"

Bunny shook the little silver cup at him. "I'm not the one who needs to exit the Garden, Kaye. You're a babe in Eden if you don't think those creeps aren't still out there, figuring out how to buy and bully their way back in. But what do you care, you'll get the tax breaks."

"Whoaa, babe." Kaye held out both hands in surrender. "I pay my dues."

She spluttered her lips at him. "I sure didn't see you out hustling on election day. I saw Shani. I saw Noni. I saw me. I didn't see you."

"Is this going to be *Crossfire*, or where is Noni?"

Bunny pointed through the doorway into the living room. Kaye saw Noni standing near the piano in the center of a circle of elderly couples, some of whom he recognized from the parties long ago. They looked amazingly small and fragile to him now, when once they'd seemed so formidable in their loud laughter.

Noni wore a plain silk dress that was as black as the enamel of the grand piano beside her; the black made her luminous skin even whiter by contrast. Her silver blonde hair was loosely gathered atop her head and her neck and shoulders were bare. A shaft of afternoon light slanted through the tall windows on the pale yellow wall. Frowning, Noni closed her eyes and pressed her fingers against her temple. Then she turned back, smiling to her guests. Kaye could see the gold charm bracelet on her wrist as she reached to include in the group an old stooped woman whom he suddenly recognized as Miss Clooney, the Moors High music teacher from all those decades ago. Looking past Miss Clooney, Noni suddenly saw him and smiled widely, waving. He crossed his eyes at her and she burst out laughing.

As soon as Kaye joined them, Miss Clooney wagged a crooked finger at him. "John Montgomery King. You wouldn't join the orchestra. No patience."

"No talent. How are you, Miss Clooney?"

She gestured at herself as if nothing more needed to be said. Kaye excused them both and led Noni over to the Christmas tree, where the lights were once again red, green, amber, blue. "Amma sends her regrets. She just isn't feeling up to walking over here for the Open House this year."

"Oh bull. Zaki and Johnny told her they'd bring her over in Uncle Tat's space-age van and then wheel her up the ramp in his wheelchair. She just didn't want to come. She's stubborn. I guess that's where you get it."

"I'm not stubborn."

Noni just smiled.

"Thanks for the microscope," he told her. "It's as good as old." She grinned at the familiar joke. "Your charm's out by the blue bowl."

"Don't tell me it's a charm, it's supposed to be a surprise!"

"How can it be a surprise when I give you the same thing every year?"

"Oh, Kaye. I give up on you."

"No, you don't." Then, feeling awkward, he looked past her through the tall windows to the rose dusk falling outside. He sighed. "Anyhow, I wanted to give you something else. I found this over at Clayhome last night." He felt in his pocket for the necklace. "I asked for it back by mistake a long time ago." He opened his hand. In his palm she saw the silver heart on its broken chain. "I shouldn't have. And I apologize."

Slowly, by the heart, she lifted the chain from his hand. "Thank you." She looked up at him. "I've been wondering what had happened to my heart."

He smiled at her. Then she turned away and hung the necklace on a bough of the tree.

Abruptly, Kaye added, "Amma says you're not well."

Noni turned back to him. "Ah. *That's* why you're here today. She sent you to check me out." When he kept studying her face earnestly, she held out her hand, palm up. All the tiny gold charms slid below her wrist. "Want to take my pulse?"

"Don't think I won't." He held his fingers to her wrist. Her pulse was fast but it was strong and steady.

"Mom!" Tousled and grass-stained, a leaf in dark bronze curls, Johnny rushed over to Noni and pulled her hand away from Kaye. "Mom, it's time! Come on!"

"Can you say hi to Kaye?"

The boy muttered a preoccupied "Hi," as he thrust his slender tan arm up at his mother, showing her his large wrist-watch. "If we don't play now, everybody'll start leaving."

Noni gestured at her dress, then at his disheveled clothes. "Hey, guy, I'm ready whenever you are. You want to play right this second, that's fine with me." But Johnny scowled and spun away through the crowd. "That kid's a total clothes horse," Noni explained to Kaye. "Excuse me."

Her niece Michelle had passed near them with her shy young husband, both serving pastries on trays. Noni intro-duced Kaye and Kaye congratulated them on their marriage. "You mean," scowled Michelle, "you don't think we ruined our lives and damned ourselves to the lower middle class forever?"

"What are you, fourteen?" Kaye asked.

She scoffed. "We're, like, twenty-three, excuse me. In the Middle Ages, we'd be middle-aged."

Kaye laughed and her husband quietly smiled and they passed on, serving the guests.

Before the performance, Bunny wanted Kaye to see the large painting of Noni that was hanging over the dining room mantel. It was the final portrait in a series of paintings of Noni that Tatlock had done since her return to Moors. This one showed her alone in the yellow living room. She was seated at the black grand piano on whose top sat a vase of sunflowers. The old man had tried to capture Noni's smile by surrounding her face with rays of gold that led to the sun-flowers and by placing at the tip of each ray the tiny gold word LOVE.

Bunny said it was not only the last picture that Tatlock had completed before his death, it was unique—the only painting, out of the more than a thousand that he'd done, in which he himself did not appear. As Kaye and Bunny looked up at it, she speculated about whether Tatlock had abruptly excised his own image from his artistic vision or if he had simply passed away before having the chance to paint his self-portrait into the scene.

The title of the painting, "Noni Plays Her Piano for Me," written in gold across the bottom of the canvas, suggested to Kaye that the latter was more probable.

"Yes, I see him," said Bunny, "leaning against the piano, dressed like Count Basie maybe."

Back in April, Tatlock had died peacefully, painlessly, and in great splendor, like a French king, propped up in bed on big soft pillows, surrounded by dozens of loved ones, calling them to him to make bequests of his innumerable gadgets and to offer final words of wisdom. According to Austin Fairley, Tat's last words before drifting off to sleep and so to death were to advise his sons to sue his New York rep, who had proved to be a savage but careless embezzler of his client's profits—understating by thousands of dollars the prices he was getting for the fashionable folk art.

The Fairley sons had in fact sued this agent. And they had actually won; Tatlock's only real lawsuit had been posthumous, and successful. But, as Kaye told Bunny, they were lucky that they did win, considering what Tatlock's estate owed the IRS, after it became evident that the old man had never bothered paying any income tax on the sale of his paintings, being of the opinion that the government would just waste the money on foolishness.

"I couldn't agree with him more," Bunny said. "But I'm telling you, Kaye, two guys from Atlanta offered me five thousand each for my Tatlocks! Great-looking guys. Just my luck they were gay. Oh, shit, there's Wade."

Kaye looked into the foyer and saw Wade Tilden angrily stopping his wife Trisha from embracing her daughter Michelle. Still red-haired and freckled, Wade was now bald and had a potbelly that hung strangely on his skinny frame.

Bunny grabbed two chocolates from a silver bowl, then threw them back. "God, I can't stand that man. Noni said he's the reason why Michelle ran off and married Corey. Just to get out of that McMansion. Gordon's Landing, Jesus, I bet Wade's got "Gordon's Landing" monogrammed on his balls, just like on his towels and sheets. I mean, of course, his golf balls, but who knows? I can't stand him."

They watched Wade rapidly making the rounds, glad-handing guests as if he were running for reelection and didn't have much time at this stop.

Bunny asked Kaye if he'd heard how, right after Judy died, Wade had tried to get R.W. Gordon's will overturned in court, although Judy's own will had reproduced her father's bequests word for word. Kaye said he'd never heard anything about any of the Gordon inheritance and could care less.

"Well, this will was very specific." It left Heaven's Hill to Noni if and only if she married and had a child. She had the use of the place in her lifetime and after her death the entire property would go to the oldest male child of her body. "Married and of her body." Bunny made a face. "Guess the old Repub didn't think much of single moms or adoption. On the other hand, he had the brains to pick Noni over Wade to leave the old family jewels to."

However, were there no such male heir, then Heaven's Hill would go to Wade and his children. Or at least to his son, for Wade had "disowned" Michelle for marrying Corey. "Right, who'd want to be 'owned' by him anyhow?"

On what basis, Kaye asked, did Wade think he could break such a will? "We all know Noni got married, we all know she had a male heir."

With a disgusted glance at Wade, Bunny lowered her voice. "According to Bible Boy over there, right before Judy died, she confided in him that she wanted to change her will to negate R.W.'s—"

"And leave everything to Wade?"

"You got it."

"And why would she do such a thing? Just for love of Wade?"

Bunny moved Kaye away from the couple next to them so that she couldn't be overheard. "It's a doozy. Wade claims that Judy told him that when Noni's marriage to Roland was breaking up, Noni'd had an affair. Wade had this lawyer arguing that the clear intent of R.W.'s will was that only a male heir of Noni's marriage could inherit and that Johnny wasn't legitimate."

Kaye stared at her. "You're kidding?"

"Right! That's our Noni, the whore of Houston, recognize her? Lucas Miller told me that old Judge Hilliardson scorched Wade into ashes and blew them on the floor. Said he couldn't believe a gentleman would come into his courtroom and insult his own sister. So the will stands, and Johnny inherits."

"Do you think Mrs. Tilden actually believed that? According to Grandma, she got pretty delusional the last couple of years."

Bunny shrugged. "I didn't like Judy when she wasn't delusional. But, hey, I guess it was pretty rough, a woman like that, not able to walk."

Kaye confessed that there'd been a time when he'd suspected that Noni's mother's prolonged paralysis might have been psychosomatic.

Startled, Bunny walked him over to the dining room mantel, further away from other guests. "Psychosomatic? I thought she kept having some weird kind of strokes that they couldn't get a fix on? I thought that's why Noni had to keep taking her to new doctors?"

Slowly, Kaye shrugged. "Oh, Bunny, who knows? I sure don't. She's dead. It's over." Opening the glass face of the old French clock that sat in the middle of the white mantel, gently he moved the longer filigreed iron hand a few minutes ahead so that the clock would strike the hour. It began chiming its lovely bell sounds, six of them. He looked down at the antique Persian rug in front of the hearth. He had lain here with Noni that night. He had heard the chiming of the twelve bells just before her mother had come rushing along the upstairs hall, screaming "Fire."

Bunny was looking at him oddly. "What's the matter with you?"

Kaye pulled himself back. "Nothing."

"What's 'over'?"

"Nothing." He walked Bunny back into the room. "Listen, Amma told me she's worried about Noni. You notice anything odd about her lately, like maybe she's sick?"

"I should be so sick." Bunny shrugged dismissively. "I was here all day yesterday helping her get this thing ready and she looked fine to me."

"Does she see a doctor?"

"I don't know, but if you're worried, talk to Jack Hurd."

Exasperated, Kaye flung up his arms. "Why does everybody think that old man is God?" He looked across into the living room to where Hurd, stooped like a great heron over Johnny Tilden, was helping him move the carved music stand into place beside the grand piano. Guests were gathering around it.

The ten-year-old now wore a small blue blazer over a fresh white polo shirt. He solemnly opened his sheet music on the stand, then picked up his violin and bow. Lucas Miller walked around ringing a large bell until everyone was quiet. Then Noni joined her son at the piano. She leaned down and whispered something to him, then she kissed him.

"Johnny tells me," she said to the gathered guests, "that you very sweet and very kind and very patient friends want us to play something for you again this year."

"They do, Mom, stop worrying!" The boy tugged her by her hand over to the piano bench as adults laughed fondly.

She sat on the bench and opened the keyboard. "Okay." She nodded at him. "Take it away, Maestro."

The boy announced to the small crowd that he and his mother would now play a special arrangement that they had written—"Well, mostly my mom did it"—for piano and violin. It was in memory of Bud Tilden and it was one of his favorite pieces of music. "Bud Tilden's my grandfather," Johnny stopped to explain. "It's the *Warsaw Concerto* and it's nine minutes long and then you can go home." Again people laughed with affection.

Then the boy tucked the violin under his chin, bit down on his full soft lip, and nodded at his mother. She began to play the grand opening chords.

Kaye moved to the side of the piano and studied Noni watching Johnny as she played, accompanying the sweet sad line of his violin, her notes under and around his, following him, smiling at him with that wonderful smile that Tatlock had known to paint as gold sunlight.

Then all of a sudden Noni's hands stumbled and came off the keys. Johnny kept playing. Kaye saw that she had tightly squeezed her eyes shut and that her fingers were moving erratically above the keys like a blind person searching for something that was unexpectedly not where it was supposed to be. Kaye moved closer as Johnny abruptly turned toward his mother, puzzled, alarmed, but still playing on alone, his small bow sawing back and forth.

Just as Kaye reached her, Noni's eyes fought open; she leaned out from the piano and smiled at her son, nodding reassurances at him, and gesturing with her hand a backward circle. He seemed to understand what she meant, for finishing a phrase, he started back at the beginning of the section of music that he'd just played alone.

Noni's fingers found their place on the keys; the piano joined the violin and together they played to the dramatic end of the piece. Enthusiastic applause burst through the room. Kaye had the feeling that people might not even have noticed the pause and then the repetition. Standing, Noni took Johnny's small hand and together they bowed again and again to the warm applause. With her other hand, she held tightly to the side of the piano.

As the applause ended, Kaye was close enough to hear Johnny questioning her. "What happened, Mommy, why did you stop? Did you forget?"

She looked down at him confused. "I'm sorry, honey. I'm just a stupid old mommy. I've got to go upstairs now and get some aspirin, okay? You were just wonderful!"

Noni thanked everyone for listening and urged them now to join Lucas Miller around the piano to sing a last few Christmas carols before they left. At the motion of her hand, the lawyer came quickly forward. She said something hurriedly to him as he took his seat at the piano, pushing carefully at the sides of his glasses, watching her until she'd passed through the doorway into the hall.

In the hall Kaye took a penlight and his cell phone from his coat pockets before he made his way upstairs and along the corridor to Noni's room. He found her kneeling on the floor of her bathroom, beside the toilet. "I'm sorry," she said.

"How bad is that headache?"

"Bad."

"So bad it made you throw up?"

"Maybe I've got the flu."

He helped her to the tall four-poster bed and lifted her onto it, propped her against all the white lace and linen.

"Noni, can you see me?"

"Of course I can see you."

He told her to follow his finger with her eyes. She couldn't do it. He checked her eyes with the penlight. He asked her questions about dates and facts. They confused her.

"Okay." He looked at his watch, Bud Tilden's watch that he'd found again the night before. "Okay, Noni, I want you to pack a robe and a nightgown."

Pulling herself up on the pillows, she tried to joke. "Why? Are we eloping? I thought you were married."

His face frozen, he opened her closet door, pulled an overnight bag down from the shelf, and tossed it onto the pink couch at the foot of her bed. Then, yanking out her dresser drawers, he began throwing lingerie onto the bag.

"Are you crazy? What are you doing!" Noni twisted herself off her bed and staggered toward him.

Grabbing her arms, he held her in front of him, stared at her. "Listen to me. We're going to University Hospital. I'm checking you in tonight. I'm going to get somebody to do a CAT scan and an MRI on you as soon as they can schedule it."

"Kaye, you're crazy. I've got a headache! I'm going downstairs to my guests."

"Fine, you go downstairs and tell your guests good-bye while I make these phone calls. Then you tell Bunny you're going with me to the hospital and that you want her to stay here with Johnny."

She struggled with him. "I'm not going to do any such goddamn thing!"

"You want to cause a scene, you want to ruin everybody's good time, you want to scare Johnny?" He knew that would stop her.

"You're scaring *me!*" She fought loose, staring at him. "What do you think's wrong with me? Look at me, Kaye, *look at me.*"

He spoke to her fiercely, his hands tight on her arms. "There's nothing wrong with you. We're just going to do these tests. There's nothing wrong. If anything's wrong, I'll fix it. I'll fix it."

❋ ❋ ❋ ❋ ❋

Amma was sitting in the dark by the kitchen window at Clayhome, sitting in the quiet, listening. She wasn't playing the radio, which she rarely had on anymore. Her own thoughts were enough to keep her occupied. Thinking through the past, getting ready to leave it in order, that's what her time needed to go to now. For instance, she had to get her mind right about what she'd done that early morning at the swimming pool the day Judy died. Four years ago or more, and it was still troubling her. If you knew what was good, why wouldn't you do it? Isn't that what Amma had said so long ago to that poor man Bud Tilden? But what if, in a particular case, you lost your certainty about what was good? There was nothing worse in the world.

To Amma, the hard question was whether she'd have acted differently that morning when she'd found Judy swimming out in the pool if she hadn't heard her talking to Wade about Johnny just the day before. If Judy hadn't said what she'd said then, and what she'd said in that pool.

It had been a warm afternoon, the middle of June, and Amma'd told Dionne to take the Tildens some iced tea out to the side porch where they were sitting, the two of them looking so alike with their milky skin and pale red hair, Judy in her wheelchair and Wade on the steps, talking on and on about how they were going to redo Judy's will so Johnny would never inherit Heaven's Hill.

They hadn't known Amma could hear them from the kitchen window. Or they hadn't cared. Ever since Amma was a little girl, owners of Heaven's Hill had been talking in front of her like she was a piece of furniture. The things she'd heard in that house would freeze your blood. Or boil it.

Wade was red in the face, just steaming, telling his mother how R.W. Gordon never in a million years would have wanted Johnny to inherit his ancestral home if he'd known that Johnny wasn't Roland's baby. The very idea would have torn the old man out of his grave like robbers had dug him up.

Judy was in a state, asking Wade what could they do about it?

"Get your lawyer over here, Mom, that's what we can do about it. We can change your will."

"But it's Daddy's will that controls everything!"

"Then we'll go to court. Grandpa's clear intent, clear intent, that's what we're dealing with here!" Wade kept slapping one of his hands down on the other, as loud as a horse-whip. "You think Grandpa *intended* for some nigger bastard of Noni's to get his hands on Heaven's Hill? Come on!"

Judy had burst into tears. "I shouldn't have told you! Wade, don't say anything to Noni, please. You know what? I think she was lying to me, just to upset me. I don't think Johnny is…Kaye's."

"Oh bullshit!" Wade had thrown his tea glass right off the porch onto the brick walkway where it smashed into broken bits that somebody was going to have to clean up.

The next morning, earlier than usual, five o'clock and already light—what did Shani call it, summer solstice?— Amma had walked over from Clayhome and made her way around to the back of Heaven's Hill. She had to take her time nowadays, especially on that flagstone path. Her balance wasn't so good, and the last thing she wanted was to break her hip and have Kaye use it as an excuse to move her out of Clayhome. And there sat Judy's wheelchair, all the way at the top of that path, up on the patio. There was Judy down swimming in that swimming pool, swimming back and forth, back and forth, like somebody had wound her up too tight, like she used to swim when she was a school girl, trying to win those races that her daddy R.W. Gordon was always yelling at her to win. Leaning over the side of the pool, yelling at her: "Gordons win gold, Gordons don't win silver, they win gold!"

There Judy was, seventy-two years old, naked as the day she was born, swimming in a straight line like the hounds of hell were chasing after her.

And Amma knew it wasn't the first time Judy'd been in that pool; she'd seen the wet nightgowns hanging in the bathroom. Poor Dionne had showed them to her, wondering how they'd gotten that way, scared to ask Mrs. Tilden. Well, now they knew.

Not until she'd made her way down to the edge of the pool had Judy seen her there. Amma'd clapped her hands. "Judy! You get out of that pool before something happens to you. At your age! And weak as you are, too."

Judy spat water out like a mean child. "You can't tell me what to do." And she'd kicked her feet faster.

"Judy! You're having one of your spells and you don't even know what you're doing. You come over here to the side of this pool right now and let me help you out. You hear me, come on!"

"Get away from me, you stupid old nigger. Stop spying on me. This is my house."

Judy had never called her that before, never used the word as far as Amma knew. It showed what Wade was doing to her, showed how she'd come under his influence. Amma watched Judy swim faster and faster, churning the water, but not in a straight line anymore, and she knew something wasn't right, but all she said was, "Yes, ma'am."

"Get away from me!"

Amma had walked on back up the flagstone path, hearing the sound of the water slopping against the sides of the pool.

And the question, the question Amma still couldn't settle in her mind, was, when she'd reached the patio, hadn't she heard, "Aunt Ma! Aunt Ma!" called up to her? Or had it only been in her mind, or had it been the splashing water?

She hadn't come back out to cut her flowers until after seven. She'd just sat at the green pine table in the kitchen at Heaven's Hill, just sat listening to the house sleeping.

Judy was dead when she came back, floating face down in the pool. That's when Amma had taken the wheelchair from the patio and rolled it down the path and thrown it into the pool and thrown in the nightgown, too.

Then she'd tried to yell for help but her voice was too old and weak. So she'd rung the big iron triangle hanging from the side of the summer kitchen, that Judy said was an antique, that had once called workers up from the terraced fields below.

✻ ✻ ✻ ✻ ✻

Sitting in the dark by the window at Clayhome, Amma told herself that if she couldn't settle her mind about Judy before she died, she'd leave it up to Jesus. Maybe up in heaven she and Judy both could say they were sorry.

Across the lawn, the holiday lights at Heaven's Hill were a blur of blinking colors. Noni's party was over; Amma could hear people shouting "Merry Christmas," and the cars driving off.

Afterwards it was quiet for awhile. Out of the quiet she could suddenly hear Johnny running across her gravel path and up her steps—she could tell it was him—and then he burst through the door into the kitchen. "Aunt Ma!"

"I'm over here, honey, what's the matter?"

"Kaye took Mom to the hospital in his car! And he told me to stay here."

Amma held out her arms and, breathless, the boy ran into them. His curls were damp, the curls people probably thought he'd gotten from Roland Hurd's black curly hair, like his tanned skin. Johnny had a sweet spicy smell like cookies. She patted his back. "What's wrong with her? Just wait. Catch your breath."

Johnny huddled next to the old woman, taking in air in deep gulps. "Nothing. Kaye says nothing's the matter with Mom. It's just some tests he's got to do and it's better to do them at Christmas because it's not busy. But why couldn't I go if it's not busy?"

Amma kissed the boy's head. "Well, I guess where they do these tests is someplace children can't go. But, listen to me, honey, listen to me. Kaye knows what to do. If he says we don't have to worry, then we don't. He's the head of that whole place over there. So we can put our minds to rest, all right? It's just some tests your mama needs for those headaches she's been having."

"Maybe they can find some pills for her?"

"I'm sure they can. You want to stay the night with me?"

He nestled against her, shook his head beneath her hand. "I got to stay with Aunt Bunny. She's counting on me. Are you all alone?"

"No honey. Dionne's upstairs watching Tat's videos. You go on back home."

"Okay. Bye." And he was gone.

Amma sat there in the dark, worrying about Johnny. Something was wrong with Noni and Amma knew it, whether Kaye did or not. You can't keep your eye on a child from the day she was born and not know when there was something the matter with her.

Well, if the cup wouldn't pass from Noni, then the Lord give that little boy the strength the Lord gave Kaye when he wasn't much older. Kaye had come through, like gold in the fire, like Daniel.

And so would Johnny. He was a good boy, with his daddy's brave soul and his mama's loving heart. But deepest down he was like Amma herself. He had her love of family and of home, too. That boy loved Heaven's Hill. And it would be his.

The Eleventh Day of Christmas

❄

December 24, 1996
The Four-Poster Bed

A year later, late at night on Christmas Eve, Kaye leaned against the white wall of the hospital corridor and read the chart for Noelle Tilden. He had been in New York, flown in to perform surgery on a famous man, when his wife Shani had reached him by phone. He took the first plane he could back to North Carolina.

Pressing hard at the corners of his eyes, Kaye gathered himself into the stillness that had always saved him in the past and he opened her door. He heard the soft, sad, beautiful piano music playing on the small CD player by her bed.

"Come look at this snow," she told him. From her raised pillow she could see out the large window of her room in University Hospital. "It's our old snow, Kaye."

"Yes." There was snow in Kaye's dark hair and on the shoulders of his dark coat. There was, he told her, half a foot of snow on the ground and it was still falling. His plane had just made it down before they closed the airport.

She asked him to open her window, and when the cold sharp air and the fresh wet smell of snow filled the room she breathed it deeply in.

"I came as soon as I could." He showed her that he had seen her chart. "I'm sorry, I'm so sorry."

She gestured for him to come closer and then to lean down to her. "I know," she smiled at him. "You fixed me so beautifully and now I'm broken again."

The tumor was back, and worse, growing more aggressively, as if it had learned from the last battle new and more deadly strategies. After they had waged so long and so hard a war, it was back. Kaye had fought with every weapon he could find, could cajole or compel into being. And he thought that he had won. He thought they had routed their enemy, had so forced it into retreat that it couldn't even be seen on an X ray.

But the enemy was not defeated, was not dead. The one cell not killed, lying in hiding, seen in his dreams, searched for with bright lights and polished machines, that great enemy Death had now come crawling over the hill at him, snatching at their victory.

"Kaye," she said, "I want you to take me home to Heaven's Hill."

"I can't do that."

"Yes, you can."

"You're under treatment."

She smiled slowly up at him. "What for?"

He stared at her a long time. She was thinner and gray-white, her eyes deep and shadowed. But she was Noni.

After they'd stopped the chemotherapy in the fall, her short hair had grown back the same silvery blonde. It had made him think of the pixie haircut that she'd had when she was a teenager. Now strangely her hair was the length it had been the night he'd met her, when they were seven years old. In fact, so thin and pale was she, raised on the large white pillows in her white nightgown, lost in the white sheets and blankets, that she looked like the little girl who'd sat up in the high four-poster bed and called out to him when he'd leaned over her windowsill. "How did you get all the way up here?" she'd asked him.

"Climbed," he'd told her.

Climbed, he thought, until now he was head of the hospital, the youngest chief of staff Haver had ever had. And what good did it do?

He fought stubbornly. "You can't leave. You've got more tests tomorrow."

She reached out for his hand and he moved closer to the bed so she could hold it. "There's nothing more to do. You know that." She waited until finally he nodded at her. "I did try, Kaye."

"I know you did."

He thought for a moment that she'd drifted back into sleep, but after a while she said, "You know who came to see me today?" He shook his head. "My first-graders. Johnny and Zaki brought them." She told him that Zaki Fairley, who was now an intern at the hospital, had sneaked in Johnny with the ten younger children. They had come with their recorders and had stood around her bed and played Christmas carols from the Christmas concert that she'd had to miss. They'd played "Silent Night" and "Jingle Bells" before the nurses had discovered them and made them leave. They'd given her the Chopin CD she was playing. "They know what a hopeless romantic I am. They said there were two encores at the concert."

He smiled at her. "The Angel of Moors Elementary."

She tried to raise herself in the bed but gave up and so he lifted her onto the pillows. "Johnny didn't want to kiss me."

"He's eleven."

"I told him, sometimes you just have to kiss girls when they ask you to. You just can't get out of it." She frowned, tightening her hand on Kaye's. "If it gets bad, don't let him see me again. All right?" He nodded at her. "I looked pretty good this morning."

"You look pretty good now."

"Sure sure sure." She looked up at him. He could feel her gathering her strength. "I want to talk to you about Johnny."

"Where is he now?"

"He's over at Clayhome. He said he felt safer there with Amma. I think it really hurt Bunny's feelings." She squeezed at his hand.

"Is there something you want me to do?"

"Yes, don't ever let Wade get hold of Johnny. Don't ever let him get hold of Heaven's Hill."

"I won't."

"Lucas did all the papers." Kaye kept nodding. "I'm giving Johnny to you." He nodded again. "Will you take him?"

"Of course I will."

"Look at me, Kaye."

They looked at each other for a long time. "Johnny's ours."

"…I know that."

"Do you know what I'm saying? Johnny's yours."

"…I know that."

"Did Shani tell you?"

"No."

"Did she tell you we'd talked yesterday, that I'd asked her to come see me?"

"No, she just told me to get down here."

"Thank her."

She asked him when he'd first known Johnny was his.

Kaye wasn't certain when he'd first realized it. Maybe it had been the day when he'd met the boy in the woods by the church. He said he hadn't known for sure until last Christmas when his grandmother had called him a fool.

Noni pulled at his hand. "Do you think I was wrong? When I came home to tell you, you were getting married. And she's wonderful, Shani's wonderful. It was too late. Please tell me I did right."

Kaye heard Bud Tilden's gentle voice in the dark on the porch that night. "The thing about Noni, you can count on what she'll do. She'll do the good."

He raised her hand to her face and kissed it.

"What?"

"Yes, you did right. Always. Do you want me to tell Johnny?"

"You tell Johnny, when you want to."

"All right."

"I told Shani he's a very sweet boy…sometimes he has bad dreams….He's…" Tears fell down the line of her face, the curve of her slender neck. She let them fall.

Time went slowly by. Then she said quietly, "I'm tired, Kaye. No more tests. No more machines and shots and pills and long words that all mean the same thing. Please let me go."

But he shook his head and eased away his hand. On her wrist was the plastic bracelet identifying her as Noelle Tilden. Between two of her fingers a needle ran under her skin. The tubing lifted as she gestured at the sterile room. "Ever since I was in that hospital, remember when Mom put me in the boarding school?… I've hated these places. This is no place for life and death."

He smiled. "You were born here. Doctor Jack delivered you. He was your Deliverer, he used to say."

"Well, I've turned into an old-timey girl. I want to die at home." She closed her eyes again. "I'm asking you."

Kaye leaned against the window, looking out. The night was filled with the soft whirling light of snow in the moonlight. Whiteness everywhere floated flying in all directions.

A year ago, at her Christmas party, when she and Johnny had played their music, when Kaye had forced her to come with him to the hospital, he had already suspected the source of her symptoms—the weakness and confusion, the hesitation while she searched for words, the volatile emotions, the loss of vision. He had accepted that the tests would discover some kind of inter-cranial mass pressing on her frontal lobes; he had feared that surgery might be necessary. But he had told himself and everyone else that there were benign tumors in the brain, too, and that was what this one would be.

He hadn't believed it when the Haver neurologists had told him what they'd found. As soon as they gave him the first results, Kaye angrily accused his colleagues of misreading the MRI and the CAT scan. They'd made a mistake, he insisted.

When they gave him the results to examine on his own, he told them the data was wrong and that they had to do the tests again. They did them again. The results were the same. The words on the report were the same. Malignant. Astrocytoma. Likely highly undifferentiated. Stage III at best. Inoperable.

His colleagues said she'd be dead in three months, in six at the most.

No, she wouldn't, he told them.

They started whole-brain radiation to reduce the pressure in the cranium as quickly as possible. Then the gamma knife. Directly at the tumor. They began giving her very high doses of steroids. They gave them to her four times a day, even when she began hallucinating.

Kaye told Johnny that his mother would have to stay in the hospital for a while; they had to take care of her headaches. He told Amma and Bunny that Noni had a malignant brain tumor that they were going to treat aggressively, but that surgery wasn't necessary. He told Shani he was scared.

Inoperable. Inoperable. Inoperable. The word stayed under Kaye's eyelids like the grit of sand. He was famous because he *could* operate. He pried open human chests and fixed the hearts inside them. He repaired and replaced and enlarged and grafted new to old, plastic to living tissue, metal to breathing flesh, he made hearts beat again and go on beating.

What good were his skillful careful hands to Noni, if he couldn't operate?

He called doctors at other hospitals. He studied through the nights. The latest papers. The Internet. Calls to the best in their fields. He took her to New York and Houston. He asked doctors in Switzerland and New Zealand for advice. He hounded and bullied the neurology and neurosurgery teams at Haver until finally a young oncologist complained to Shani that she needed to back her husband off.

Shani told the man, "Kaye's best friend is dying. Maybe you don't have one."

To attack the tumor, they intensified the chemotherapy. New drugs, new protocols, experimental treatments. Anti-angiogenics, antibody-tagged chemotherapy molecules, on and on. Often, sleepless, drenched in sweat, Noni broke down into senselessness. Often, she was unable to stop crying. Often, she shouted and cursed. Often, nausea doubled her over in her bed, poisons trying to save her. Long words.

It was an unmerciful time.

"Fight for us," Kaye had told her, day after day. "Johnny needs you."

"How low can you go, Dr. King?" she had weakly smiled.

"Oh, so low," he'd told her. "Low as I need to."

Noni had fought as hard as she could.

And for a while, they had won. The tests said the tumor was gone. By summer, they could send her home. By the autumn, she was teaching again.

But now, Kaye saw how the enemy had hidden in waiting and then, in a surprise attack, had come screaming over the hilltop. Ten days ago, after Noni had searched for a word and couldn't find it, after she'd felt for a stair but fallen, they had brought her back into the hospital. They'd done new tests and found the tumor was back. Once again they had radiated her skull, once again they had put her on the powerful steroids. But then they had talked together and frowned and written on her chart. They'd told Shani, and Shani had phoned Kaye in New York. The tumor was now pressing on Noni's brain stem and her brain stem was coning down very quickly, herniating into the spinal column, compressing the respiratory and cardiac centers. There was nothing they could do.

Snowlight through the window was bright enough for him to read the words on the chart. Astrocytoma. Stage IV. Glioblastoma multiforme. Inoperable.

Kaye turned to watch Noni lying quietly in the white bed, her eyes closed, her breath soft. On the white table beside the bed, there was a small photograph of Johnny in a gold frame. Beside it was a small black velvet bag. Kaye opened the bag and poured into his hand Noni's sapphire bracelet and earrings from her father, her mother's pearls, the broken silver chain with the heart, and the gold bracelet heavy with years of charms from Kaye.

She spoke without opening her eyes, "Put those back. Those are mine."

He held up the chain. "We ought to fix this."

"Stop trying to fix everything. For once, why don't you do what I tell you? Accept it. You can't fix me. Don't you know I'm older than you are?"

"Just for tonight you are, that's all."

"If I died tonight, wouldn't I always be older than you are?"

He walked back to her bedside. "No, if you die tonight, you'll always be younger."

"That's true, you'll be a grouchy old old man like Uncle Tat and I'll be young." She opened her eyes, smiling. "Aren't I forty today?"

"Yes. You're forty and I'm thirty-nine."

"Good. I didn't want to die in my thirties. It's just too goddamn sad." She held out her arm to him. "Be my best friend."

They looked at each other. Then slowly, gently, he removed the IV from her hand and cleaned her hand and bandaged it. Then he wrapped her carefully in his long warm coat and lifted her into his arms. She was so light and yet so heavy against his heart. When they reached the door, she gestured urgently back at the bed. He brought her back there so she could pick up the little picture of Johnny and the velvet bag of jewelry and slip them into the pocket of his jacket.

In the corridor, a nurse ran after them calling, "Sir! Sir!" until she saw who he was. Then she said, "Dr. King? Are you going to ICU? Should I call down?" He shook his head at her. "We'll get her on a gurney, Dr. King."

Kaye kept walking. The nurse was shocked by the tears she saw falling down his face. She'd cried often on this hospital floor. She'd never seen Dr. King cry. She stopped following him.

Carrying Noni in his arms, Kaye walked out of the hospital and across the snowy lot to his car.

The storm was ending. The snowflakes fell unhurried, straight downward onto Noni's face. She tilted back her head, lifting her face to the snow and smiled at him. "Thank you," she said, "for taking me home."

❋ ❋ ❋ ❋ ❋

It was dawn on Christmas Day, rose in the sky and deepest blue. The soft snow was settled on the lawn and fields and woods of Heaven's Hill. Everything familiar to Noni—shrubbery, urns and fences, cars, brick garden walls and rows of outbuildings— all had been changed by the snow into a beautiful strangeness.

She heard Kaye walking back to where he had brought her at dawn. She waited, wrapped in his coat, on the garden bench that overlooked the hill beside Clayhome, the hill that swept widely down through a meadow where in summer wildflowers grew. It was the highest hill for miles and it fell steeply away through the knolls and gullies left by the earthen terraces, fell to the edge of the dark woods that guarded Heaven's Hill.

❁ ❁ ❁ ❁ ❁

She would miss the seasons moving over the fields and the woods here. Sharp new greens after April rain, late summer's deep languid shade, the red and gold and orange of autumn trees, the quiet of snow. She would miss her first sight of white crocus in winter frost and the May morning when her early roses bloomed.

Everything returns, Noni thought. There is no loss, only change. In years to come, Johnny would be here, and Johnny's children, and the seasons would move for him over Heaven's Hill, as they had for her and for those before her, as the seasons would move with the turning earth over these fields and woods for Johnny's children and for generation after generation.

Had she said the right things in her letter to Johnny? All she could be sure of was that she had said the true things. Her hope, her faith, was that true things, told in love, would do more good than harm.

She hadn't planned to ask Shani to give Johnny the letter. She'd planned to leave the letter for Bunny to give him. But Shani had come into the hospital room the night they'd rushed her to the ICU. She'd come in, holding a folder, and she'd read the papers in it, and then she'd said, "I'm calling Kaye. Kaye needs to be here."

When Noni had protested, Shani had come to the side of her bed and held Noni's hands and told her, "There's nobody in this world he's ever loved more than you. Of course he needs to be here."

Everything had been in Shani's eyes, everything Noni had never said to her or to Kaye, had never asked, fearing to cause them pain. And Noni had felt so safe, so sure, looking up into

Shani's eyes, that she had spoken without waiting for any doubt to stop her. "I'm not going to survive this, am I?"

Shani looked at her, then slowly shook her head. "No."

Noni nodded. "I want you and Kaye to take Johnny. Will you talk about it with Kaye?"

Shani looked a long while out the window, then she turned and nodded and said, "Yes."

"Thank you." Noni gestured to the bed table. "Will you give Johnny this letter when you think it's right?"

Shani took the letter, slipped it into the pocket of her white doctor's jacket.

Noni touched her hand. "You already knew."

Shani brushed back the dampened hair from Noni's forehead. "Of course I knew. You think I don't know that man's ear, or his eyebrow, or his little finger when I see it?"

Tears fell along Noni's cheek and onto the pillow. "I didn't think it would be right to tell him."

Shani placed Noni's hand on the cover. "I don't know whether he's thought about it or not. And neither does Amma. You know how she says, 'Kaye King's the smartest fool alive.'"

Noni tried to smile. "I guess you better get him here."

"I guess I better."

❋ ❋ ❋ ❋ ❋

She heard him before she could make out his shadow against the snow. And then he was standing beside her. The red childhood sled looked small in his arms.

"Stop frowning," she told him. "It's the last thing I'm going to ask you."

"You said taking you out of the hospital was the last thing you were going to ask me."

"Ho ho. Why did I always think you were so funny?" Or she thought she said that. She couldn't tell now if the words were coming out loudly enough for him to hear if she was even saying them or just thinking them. Perhaps, after all these years, he could hear her without her having to speak at all.

He lifted her carefully onto the sled at the steepest edge of the hill. "Hang on," he told her and then he was at her back gently pushing, his shoulder leaning into hers, snow flurrying around them, and then he was jumping on behind, holding her to him.

Down the hill they glided, so much more slowly, more softly, more quietly than that first time, now, like a sled ride in a dream. She could feel him warm against her back, his arms around her, all the way down the long slope to the edge of the woods. They stopped against the snowy bank. Above the white trees, the darkening sky was luminous to her. They sat on the sled, not moving, his arms around her.

"Kiss me," she said. But she didn't know if she said it aloud. She couldn't hear her words. But she felt his lips, chilled and soft, brush against her burning face, and then against her lips. "I love you," she thought she told him. "I've loved you all my life." His eyes looked down at her, dark gold, darker, and then lost in light.

He carried her into the room where they had first met and he placed her on the laced pillows and soft linens in the high tulipwood four-poster bed. Taking the quilt from her hope chest, he covered her with it and then he lay down beside her in the bed, holding her in his arms.

At noon on Christmas Day, his birthday, when Kaye awakened, her face was cold against him, her hand was cold in his.

Coming through Noni's window, where the sycamore tree bowed in its cape of snow, rays of gold light fell on him, like sunshine, like the angels his mother had promised would watch over him in heaven, the beau ideas who had taken their places with golden swords in the great army of the good.

The Twelfth Day of Christmas

❄

December 25, 2003
The Sled

He was dreaming. Once again he was at her funeral in St. John's Church, the way it had really been on that day seven years ago. The sharpest winter light came slanting through the old glass. In front of the gold-filigreed altar rail, her casket rested on a black velvet cloth, the gleaming coffin banked high with white camellias and dark red roses.

Everyone said the church had never been so crowded, not since her wedding, that everyone she loved was there, everyone who loved her. Hundreds of white candles cast a glow on their faces and on the stained glass window of the blue angel welcoming Noni's great-grandmother into heaven, and the stained glass window given by her mother, Judy, showing Christ touching the head of a small boy, one of the little children suffered to come unto Him.

Evergreens lay heaped upon window ledges and along the sides of the church. On either side of the choir stall stood four small Christmas trees, bare of any decoration.

His son Johnny stepped forward and took his place beside the casket; it happened in the dream just as it had at the funeral; his son Johnny in his newly purchased black suit, and his eleven-year-old eyes newly old. Johnny raised the violin and began to play. But in the dream, the music wasn't the sad melody that the boy had really played at the funeral, the melody Noni had loved, Bach's "Air on a G String," the music Johnny had played that day without ever faltering, in tears but not crying.

In the dream, although Johnny moved the bow across the violin, the music that came out of it was drums. Beating drums that filled the church and shook it. On and on the drums beat, a mournful death song steady and slow, relentless, monotonous, great drums marching closer, louder and louder.

Kaye awakened with a cry, and, as always in the dream, the deep drum he heard was his own heart beating.

"Honey, you okay?" Shani flung back a warm arm, touched his warm back.

"I'm going to get up."

"You get up, they'll get up." She yawned. "It's Christmas. Avery'll be tearing through stuff like a bear at a picnic." She turned back toward sleep. "Okay, I warned you."

Kaye walked quietly in his robe past all the gifts that lay arranged around the vast open living room of the new house into which they'd just moved, his third house, the largest, since he'd married Shani. It was nearly as large as Heaven's Hill. Shani and Johnny had teasingly referred to it as "Kaye's Tara."

He'd told them both, "Johnny shouldn't make jokes about Tara. He's the owner of the biggest house in Moors. He's the one Wade keeps trying to trick into selling the place off, so Wade can turn it into luxury homes and a country club."

"You can't sell history," Johnny had replied with the solemnity of his eighteen years. "I'm living at Heaven's Hill when I get back from Juilliard."

Kaye had raised his parodic eyebrows. "I'll tell you what Grandpa Tat used to tell me. 'Son, you don't know what life's going to do to you.'"

"I know what *I'm* going to do. Move back home to Heaven's Hill."

And Kaye had thrown out his arms in his old dramatic way. "How you going to have a music career in Moors, North Carolina?"

"Kaye." Shani had taken her husband's arms and hugged them around her. "Would you please leave him alone? Johnny, your dad thinks he knows everything. Have you ever noticed that?"

He grinned at her. "No, I never noticed that."

Despite Shani's prediction, their younger daughter hadn't awakened as Kaye made his coffee. He took the cup out to the flagstone verandah and sat in a deck chair watching the mist lift out of Glade Lake into the indigo sky.

Far across the lake, in the old part of town, rose the small hills of Moors; the tallest of them the one called Heaven's Hill, the one where they had sledded.

Noni had been dead for seven years. Seven years, thought Kaye. The whole body completely changed its composition in seven years; the brain grew new cells and nerves. Then why, every Christmas, did he awaken with the same deep familiar pain in those new muscles and blood?

❊ ❊ ❊ ❊ ❊

"I don't need nothing from that house to remind me of your mama," said Amma Fairley to her great-grandson Johnny. "She's in my thoughts every day of my life."

"I just wanted you to get first choice on her Gift Day, Aunt Ma." The teenager kissed the old blind woman as she sat in the cushioned wheelchair in the kitchen of Clayhome.

Amma fought the tremor in her hand as she raised it to touch his face, feeling for where he leaned over her, tall and thin—like Noni at his age. "Honey, you're my Christmas gift from Noni, that's a fact. It was Christmas she came home with you from across the sea. Did you know that?"

"Yes, Grandma, you told me. And told me."

"Are you rolling your eyes at me?"

"No, ma'am."

"Don't you mock the old. I'm going to be seeing your mama real soon on the other side. She's gonna be waiting there for me. She's got gathered up all the ones I love at the riverside. I'm going to tell her you're a sweet boy and you're a smart boy, going off to college in New York City, but you're a mocker. You want me to tell your Mama you're a mocker, when I see her up in Heaven? 'Cause Noni couldn't abide meanness, never could."

"You aren't going to tell her that. You'll tell her we've been missing her but we're doing fine."

"That's the truth, honey. We been doing fine."

"Noni's Gift Day" had been Johnny's idea. Those whom Noni had especially loved he had asked to come over on Christmas Day this year to choose something to take from Heaven's Hill; they could take anything they wanted, furniture, art, personal effects; whatever they wanted to keep as a reminder of her.

For the previous seven years, Johnny had been glad to have his older cousin Michelle and her husband Corey live in the house. Wade's daughter had loved the place and was always warning Johnny against her father's efforts to get the place away from him, for Wade had finally given up his legal pursuit of Heaven's Hill and now periodically tried to buy it through intermediaries.

During Michelle's stay there, everything had been left pretty much the way it had been at Noni's death. But now that the young couple had finished their graduate training and had moved to Baltimore, new arrangements had to be made. While Johnny refused to sell Heaven's Hill (to Wade or anyone else), finally he had agreed with Bunny—Bunny and Kaye were his trustees—that while he was away in college, it made sense to rent it out. If they picked good people, it would be better for the house, Amma told him, to have them in it than letting it sit empty. A house hated to be left alone.

So they were going to auction off the furnishings and appliances that Johnny didn't want himself. Those he did want, they would store until he could decide what to do with them. There was no rush, Aunt Ma told him. Heaven's Hill was in no hurry. It would wait for him to come home.

"You'll be waiting too," he said to her, stroking the heavy white hair.

"Hush." Toothless and bent and shriveled, Amma lifted her blind face, her laugh surprisingly rich. "I got to go. No telling who that fool Tatlock's suing now. Could be he's suing God Almighty. I got to get up there and take care of things. Put on my gold shoes and go see all the love in your sweet mama's face. You know that's what they named her for? That's when she was born, the birthday of the King of Love. Noel. That's what her name means. It means Love."

❀ ❀ ❀ ❀ ❀

There were no ivy kissing balls, no evergreen garlands, no strings of lights on the porch of Heaven's Hill. Just a large green unadorned wreath on the door with a black bow. Johnny hung the wreath there every Christmas, the anniversary of his mother's birth and death.

On the porch, Kaye sat in one of the green wood rockers until he felt ready to go inside the house. He hadn't been in it for years. "Too many memories," he told Bunny.

"What's wrong with memories," she replied.

"They hurt."

"What's wrong with that?"

The swing was still there, hanging from the oak bough. He could see the twelve-year-old Noni sitting in the swing, in that silly lime green miniskirt and white vinyl boots, laughing with him about Wade, how Wade was driving off with no idea that his Mustang now called for the impeachment of a bad president and the end of a bad war.

In the green rocker beside him, Kaye could see Bud Tilden sitting with his Sazerac and his hapless sweet smile, the night when they'd sat together after Noni had driven away with Roland, the night Kaye had heard his news about the Roanoke Scholarship. "I want someone to love her who knows who she is."

And Kaye had said nothing.

All those talks he'd had with Tilden, so many, and he could see now not only the weakness that he'd always pitied in the man, but also the goodness so quietly offered, the fatherliness.

"How's it going, Mr. T?"

Behind him Johnny had opened the door, barefoot, tall and thin, in wrinkled khaki pants and wrinkled cotton shirt. "Did you say something to me, Kaye?"

Kaye stood up. "I was just talking to Bud Tilden. I liked your mom's dad. He was good to me."

Johnny gave him a strange look. "Why didn't you come in? Door's not locked."

"You look like your Uncle Gordon." Kaye pointed at the teenager's bare feet. "It's Christmas. Aren't your feet cold? It's freezing out here."

"It's not freezing. You're old. Come on in."

Kaye walked slowly through the closed-up house where boxes and cartons stood stacked around the floors and everything had the faint smell of emptiness. In the pale yellow living room, the tall windows were shuttered and the black grand piano was covered in white cloth. The carved music stand still stood beside it.

In the dining room on the long varnished table, high heaps of china and silver were arranged in radiant rows. Kaye moved slowly along the side of the table. He felt he could touch the past now, in a way he hadn't been able to feel it before. He could reclaim memories with his careful meticulous hands.

There was the scalloped silver punch bowl and the small cups.

There was the silver loving cup engraved with the words *John "Bud" Tilden Player of the Year*. Kaye picked it up, ran a finger along the incised letters.

There was the set of white wedding-band china, the plates and bowls and cups he and Noni had served their dinner for two on, that night when the only lighting was the red and gold flames of candles in these silver candelabra and these alabaster sconces and this fireplace. That night when this French clock had chimed midnight.

"Are you all right?"

"I'm all right."

Hurriedly, Kaye walked out of the dining room and into the foyer. He was leaning against the wall and beside him on the floor were stacked framed pictures, fifty or more, collected over the last two hundred years by owners of Heaven's Hill: there was every kind of art work, from eighteenth-century British oil paintings of horses and dogs to nineteenth-century Asian watercolors of birds in trees to awful pastels of scenic vacation views to the folk portraits of Tatlock Fairley. Kaye tilted through the large stack of his grandfather's canvases, stopping at Tatlock's last painting, "Noni Plays Her Piano for Me" with the gold rays around her head that had the tiny word, "Love," at each gold tip.

Johnny followed him into the hall and stood next to Kaye, studying the picture. "Mom had a great smile, didn't she?"

"Yes, she did." Kaye took the portrait out of the stack and set it on the console. Beside the picture sat the old blue Chinese jar.

"It's early Ming Dynasty," Johnny said.

"Yes, I know." Kaye touched the cracks, followed the mending, all those pieces so laboriously put back together at the green pine table in the kitchen of Heaven's Hill. What had happened that night? The Christmas dance that Noni had gone to with Roland. Kaye had brought her home. Bud Tilden had broken the bowl and cut his feet. Kaye had bought the chain for the little silver heart. That had been the night he'd said, Reach out for me.

What if he had reached out for her then?

What if he had kissed Noni that night, leaning across the bowl, as he had wanted to do? Would it have made any difference?

"Mom loved that jar. She told me how you fixed it. 'Kaye can fix anything,' she said."

"Well, she was wrong." Kaye turned to the teenager. "If I could fix anything, if I could fix one thing ever only in my life, she would be here right now. She would be standing here right now." Kaye traced Noni's face on the canvas with his hand.

Johnny was frowning at him. Finally he said, "Actually this picture is sort of what Bunny asked for."

Kaye put it back on the floor.

Johnny held it out to him. "No listen, Bunny already said, if you wanted it, that was okay with her. She said, give it to you."

Kaye shook his head. "Let Bunny have it."

The boy looked unhappy. "You don't want anything?"

Walking to the end of the foyer, Kaye opened the hall closet and pushed aside the coats. There against the back wall, behind some summer screens, he found the red wooden sled where he had left it the day Noni had died. He pulled it out and brushed off a cobweb.

"I'd like this sled," he told Johnny. "Is that all right?"

Johnny came over and ran his hand along the rusted runner. "This is the one you took the sled ride on?"

Kaye sat down on the foot of the stairs, resting the child's sled on his knees. "It was your mother's first gift to me." Kaye's head, close-cropped and graying, bent over the sled. "And she gave me so many."

In the quiet hall, his hand on the carved round ball of the newel post, Johnny stood waiting for the man who sat on the old curving stairs of Heaven's Hill, holding the wooden sled, to retreat to that calm stillness he always had when something upset him. But instead Johnny saw tears of Kaye's fall upon the faint gold letters that curved like a wing over the sled's red bow.

Johnny wiped with his fist at his own tears. "I miss her so much. Don't you?"

"All my life, son."

Kaye's tears fell on his name. And on her name, Noelle. And on the gift that had joined the names forever.

The End

ABOUT THE AUTHOR

Michael Malone is the author of nine novels and two works of nonfiction. Educated at Carolina and at Harvard, he has taught at Yale, the University of Pennsylvania, and Swarthmore. Among his prizes are the Edgar, the O. Henry, the Writers Guild Award, and the Emmy. He lives in Hillsborough, North Carolina, with his wife, chair of the English department at Duke University.